The Magog Gambit

A Southern Magic Novel

Steven F. Warnock

ISBN-13:978-0692460207
ISBN-10: 0692460209

Wordsmith Publishing
P.O. Box 1942
McDonough, GA 30253
wordsmithpublishing@gmail.com

IN MEMORIAM

Chuck Thacker

and

Denzil Pugh

ACKNOWLEDGEMENTS

I'd like to thank the proof-reading, play-testing, ego-stroking crew: Jason & Olivia Smith, Tony & Jodi Stubbs, Jeff & Beth Passmore, Pat & Anna Young, and Tom Gillon. You guys have inspired me, uplifted me, and you just plain rock!

PROLOGUE

Mumbai, Maharashtra, India
Sanjay Gandhi National Park
Kanheri Caves
August 24, 1972

An angry sorcerer certainly could make a mess of things, Gabriel Shepherd thought to himself as he surveyed the damage that Bernard Freeman had wrought. Fires burned out of control here and there, bodies and parts of bodies were scattered about elsewhere.

"You don't do things by half measures do you?" Shepherd said with a chuckle.

The short, pudgy sorcerer glanced up at his taller, more athletic companion. "No, I don't. They stole my daughter," Freeman replied in the cultured accent he'd acquired at Eaton. "I intend to have her back."

"Me, too," Shepherd growled as he slammed a fresh clip into an old Colt 1911A1.

Freeman smiled at his companion. "I know, Gabriel. You may be a mediocre apprentice, but you've been a fine son-in-law. Now, let us sally on and save Aggie from these heathens."

"You Brits shoulda tried harder to wipe the Thuggee out back in the 1830s," Shepherd said as he holstered the Colt. He was dressed in what looked like Roman lorica armor painted black and olive drab fatigue trousers, but he was barefoot. A web belt carried the holster for the Colt as well as pouches of ammunition, grenades, and a sheathed Bowie knife.

Freeman was dressed in a muslin suit and carried a wand in one hand and a staff in the other. "Well, let's finish up what those chaps started, what?"

Shepherd rolled his neck, vertebrae popped, and he nodded. His physical form blurred as he changed from human to something more lupine. His form was still mostly humanoid, but he'd become taller, heavier, and covered in fur with a wolf's head, and claws sprouted from the ends of his fingers. The armor and the trousers had shifted to match the change of his body.

"Do you have Aggie's scent?" Freeman asked.

Shepherd nodded.

"Right-o, then. I'll just pop in and get their attention while you get our girl back," Freeman said.

A clawed hand gently caught Freeman's shoulder. "Be careful," Shepherd ground out of his inhuman mouth. "Dad."

"You, too," Freeman said.

Shepherd winked.

Then, the werewolf bounded off. He was sure that Freeman would make as much of a distraction as he could. Shepherd only hoped the old man wouldn't try too hard. He'd already burned a lot of energy to get the two of them this far into the Thugs' lair. Shepherd ran into a few guards, but dispatched them quickly with tooth and claw. His nose led him through a back tunnel that came out in a wide stone room that had been carved into a temple. Shepherd found himself behind a giant statue of Kali, Goddess of Destruction. The figure portrayed in the idol had eight arms -- seven carrying weapons, the eighth holding a decapitated head by its hair. In front of the idol was a stone slab, and atop the slab was Agamdeep Freeman, Shepherd's wife.

She'd been dressed in a red sari, which flattered her curvy figure. A crown like the one adorning the statue of Kali was fitted atop her head. Her eyes were closed, but her chest was slowing rising and falling with every breath. Shepherd padded over. He glanced down toward the front of the room.

Bernard Freeman had cleared most of the room of Thugs. All that was left was the high priest. Freeman had his staff raised in his left hand, the sigils carved in the wood glowing with eldritch power. The high priest held a dagger in one hand, pointed at Freeman. The air between them crackled with the energies of the universe. Freeman raised his wand, thrust it at his foe, and shouted something that sounded like Latin. Fire streamed from the wand, but the priest literally caught the flames in his free hand.

Aggie groaned. Shepherd reverted to his human shape.

"Hey, Aggie, you okay?" he asked softly.

Aggie's eyes fluttered open. Shepherd had always loved those eyes, dark hazel, sometimes blue, sometimes green depending on her mood. The eyes he was looking into were black.

"I am quite well," Aggie replied. "I know you. You're the husband, aren't you? What is your name? Gideon! Yes, that's it."

"I go by Gabriel, actually," Shepherd replied.

Aggie sat up. "It's not your true name, the one your parents gave you," she declared, swinging her feet around and hopping off the stone slab. "Your mother named you Gideon."

Shepherd nodded. "Yes, ma'am. And who might you be, 'cause you ain't my Aggie."

Aggie laughed. "Don't you already know? Say it."

Shepherd sighed. "Kali."

"As good a name as any, I suppose," Aggie said.

"Is my wife in there?" Shepherd asked.

Aggie glanced over her shoulder at the magical duel taking place. "Ah, the host body's father, and my soon-to-be mate," she said before turning back to Shepherd. "He desperately wants to be a god again. I'm just happy to have a real body." Aggie ran her hands over her breasts, down her stomach, and over her hips. "This is a nice body, by human standards, and powerful!"

"Daughter of a Myrddin Council wizard and a Brahman mystic," Shepherd said.

"And you! I can see you in her memories," Aggie said. "A werewolf, a maker of devices, and... ancient."

"You didn't answer my question, demoness. Is my wife still in there?" Shepherd growled.

Aggie contemplated him for a moment. "Her memories, yes, but her spirit fled when I consumed her soul. You have a choice, Gideon: join her in the afterlife or join with me in this life and become the god you were meant to be."

Shepherd shook his head, tears glistening in his eyes. "I'm sorry, Aggie."

The Bowie knife was in his hand, the blade buried to the hilt in Aggie's chest, all in the blink of an eye.

Aggie gasped in shock. "Do you really think this will stop me?"

"Bright Fang is a demonbane blade, and in the name of the One True God, I banish you back to the hell you crawled out of. Forever!"

A cry caught Shepherd's attention. The high priest was still standing, but his clothing had been burned off, flames still licked at his skin. Behind him, Bernard Freeman lay on the ground, blood welling from his nose and ears. The priest took a step toward Shepherd.

"What have you done?" the man demanded. He was European, his accent sounded vaguely Irish.

Shepherd slid the knife out of Aggie's chest. The weapon glowed brightly, the metal melting, flowing, extending into a sword. He pointed the weapon at the still-burning man. "I'm going to kill you now," he growled.

A man burst into the room from behind the ersatz Thug priest. "My Lord!"

"I don't think you're powerful enough to stop me. You're just the wizard's apprentice," the priest said.

Shepherd noted that the other man wasn't a Thug either. Something was familiar about the man, though. "Dark Word?"

"My Lord, we must flee!" the second man insisted grabbing the priest's arm. "Indian Army units are approaching."

The priest shrugged off the arm. As he did so, his form shimmered. He didn't look entirely human in that flash. His legs were like a cow's, and long horns sprouted from the sides of his head.

"Chemosh Magog," Shepherd said.

"You know me?" the priest said.

Shepherd nodded.

"Then, you know you cannot beat me," Magog said.

"Maybe not, but I will put a hurting on you," Shepherd said. "Because I'm the Big Bad Wolf."

"My Lord," the Dark Word servant shouted.

Shepherd launched himself, assuming his bigger, stronger hybrid form in mid-flight. He had Bright Fang raised in both hands. Then, the two Dark Word agents disappeared in a flash of light. Bright Fang smashed the rock floor. Shepherd threw back his head and howled in rage and anguish.

CHAPTER ONE

Atlanta, Georgia, USA
Mercy University Main Campus
Covington, GA
October 22, 2010

The day was too beautiful to waste sitting inside, Jordana Quinlan decided as she carried her tray from the cafeteria out to the patio. She sighed to herself. Apparently, everybody else at Mercy University had decided the same thing. Every table on the patio had somebody sitting at it. Most of the tables were full, but a couple had only one or two people. College is about meeting new people, Jordana decided as she picked a table with one person sitting at it, a young man looking intently into the screen of a laptop computer.

He was dressed in what Jordana had come to think of as the college uniform: Dr. Martens boots, cargo pants, and a t-shirt advertising a band she'd never heard of. On the back of his chair hung a dark brown bomber jacket decorated with patches that were so faded Jordana couldn't make out what some of them were. His computer was a current model Panasonic Toughbook, the lid of which was festooned with stickers advertising bands, computer games, and some businesses that she wasn't sure what products they sold.

"Excuse me? Are you saving these for anybody?" she asked.

He glanced up from his laptop at her, smiled, and motioned to the chair across from him. "No, ma'am. You're surely welcome to have a seat," he said in a thick Southern drawl.

Jordana decided two things. The first was that this was the most attractive man she'd ever met. The second was that he wasn't quite as young as she had first assumed. Tiny sparkles of silver threaded through his otherwise black hair, which had been cut shorter than was currently fashionable among college-age men. His strong-jawed features had a certain maturity to them, but he didn't have the first wrinkle beyond a few laugh lines around his brown eyes. Stubble covered his cheeks, and a mustache and goatee framed his mouth.

"Thank you," Jordana replied as she set her tray down and dropped her backpack by the chair. "Hi, I'm Jordana, by the way. Jordana Quinlan."

"Pleased to meet you, Jordana," he said extending his hand. "Gideon Shaw."

Jordana shook his hand, which was surprisingly rough and calloused. "Seems like everybody thought eating outside was the thing to do," she quipped.

Gideon glanced around. "Would seem that way, but why waste a perfectly good sunny day, right?"

"Just what I was thinking," Jordana said with a smile as she pulled her long brown hair back and tied it into a ponytail with a rubber band she kept around her wrist for that purpose. "Working on some homework or a paper?" she asked with a nod at the Toughbook.

Gideon smiled as he turned the laptop toward her. "No, I'm catching up on reruns of 'So You Think You Can Dance' online."

Jordana snorted a laugh and quickly covered her mouth.

"What can I say? I'm a sucker for a paso doble performed by a hip-hop dancer," Gideon grinned.

"I would not have guessed you were a classical dance fan," Jordana said.

Gideon shrugged. "Looks can be deceiving, which is why the old folks say that you shouldn't judge a book by its cover, even though we do."

Jordana nodded in agreement as she unwrapped the sub sandwich she'd purchased in the cafe. It was thick with ham, salami, bologna, pepperoni, and bacon. She opened a bag of kettle-style potato chips, took the top off her sandwich, and started placing chips on top of the other condiments. She glanced up to see Gideon watching her go through her sandwich routine. A slight flush crept into her cheeks as she said, "I like the crunch."

"No judgment here," Gideon said with a smile. "Just surprised that you're as tiny as you are."

Jordana took a big bite of her sandwich to give herself a moment to consider his comment. At a little under five and a half feet tall, she was just of average height with a slender, long-legged build. She admitted to herself that she was a little embarrassed by how much she ate, but she didn't mind how little of it seemed to attach to her butt and thighs.

"High metabolism, I guess," she said after swallowing. "Run a lot, too."

"Well, whatever you do, don't go breathing toward the vegans two tables behind me," Gideon said.

Jordana glanced over his shoulder at a group of hippie-looking girls with salads and reusable water bottles who were surreptitiously glaring at Gideon behind his back.

"They've been giving me and my leather jacket the hairy eyeball ever since they sat down," Gideon said with a small grin. "It's not like *I'm* the one who killed the cow to make the jacket."

"No, but you *are* the one who's encouraging the pillaging of Mother Earth by *wearing* leather," Jordana said with mock severity. "How dare you?"

"Simple: I'm an evil, misogynistic, meat-eating, animal hide-wearing, gun-owning, running-dog capitalist... *man*," Gideon said dropping his voice to a stage whisper on the final word.

"Wow, you and my dad would get along so well," Jordana said. "He's evil, too. And a..." she glanced around before dropping her voice to a whisper and saying, "...*man*."

"How utterly middle class of him," Gideon snickered.

Jordana laughed. "So, are you from around here?"

"Sorta. I'm from down Savannah-way originally, but my family's lived here for some time," Gideon replied.

Jordana pictured a map of Georgia in her mind. Mercy University was located on the eastern outskirts of Atlanta, in a little town called Covington. Savannah was to the southeast of there, on the Atlantic coast, about three hours away.

"And you?" Gideon prompted.

"Oh, I'm from Orlando," Jordana said.

"Disney Town," Gideon said with a smile.

"More of a Universal Studios girl, really," Jordana replied.

"Lot of kids from Florida come to school here for some reason I can't fathom," Gideon observed.

"Get away from home without getting *too* far from home," Jordana suggested. "MU actually has one of the best anthropological research programs in the Southeast, if not the whole country."

"Anthropology major, then?" Gideon guessed. At Jordana's nod, he said, "Cultural, forensic, or archaeology?"

"Everything?" Jordana giggled. She bit into her sandwich to cover the embarrassment from giggling.

"Do you always hide behind your sandwich when you're embarrassed?" Gideon asked.

"It's big and convenient," Jordana replied around a mouthful of meat and potato chips.

Gideon chuckled. "Who's your faculty advisor?"

"Dr. Conners."

"Ruth or Samuel?"

"Well, she's a woman, so I'm assuming Ruth?" Jordana said.

"Husband and wife duo. They're usually assigned to freshmen. Oddly enough, though, Sam tends to get the girls, and Ruth gets the boys," Gideon said. "Anyway, you're in good hands, and when you have to choose your major advisor, go with whoever she recommends."

"So what year are you?" Jordana asked.

"That's not a question that a lady asks a gentleman," Gideon replied laying on the southern accent extra thick.

"I'm getting the impression that you, sir, are a smart ass," Jordana said.

"Genius ass, thank you," Gideon said. He shrugged. "I... just got out of the Navy a little while ago." He brushed a hand through his hair. "Kinda enjoying the freedom of infrequent haircuts."

"Well, that explains why you look a little older than average," Jordana said. "Not that there's anything wrong with that, of course."

"I'm not a decrepit old man, ya know," Gideon pointed out.

"Yeah, maybe you kinda are," Jordana teased.

"Somebody else at this table is a genius ass," Gideon said.

The clock in the old chapel at the center of the campus chose that moment to strike one o'clock. Jordana glanced at her watch. "Shoot! I've got a class in ten minutes on the other side of campus."

"Where?" Gideon asked as he stood up and snagged his jacket.

Jordana hadn't realized how tall he was until then. He was right at six feet tall and solidly built. She liked guys that were taller than her, but not so tall that she had to crane her neck to look into their faces.

"Uh, Baxter Hall," she said.

"I'm heading that way," Gideon explained as he closed up his Toughbook. "Want some company for the walk?"

Jordana smiled. "Sure."

"Excellent," Gideon said with a return smile as reached down and picked up her backpack. He slid it onto his shoulder. "Ladies first."

Jordana tossed her trash into a nearby can, leaving the tray in the rack on top for one of the housekeeping staff to retrieve. She set off for Baxter Hall on the north side of the campus. The shortest path to the building where her class was meeting went past the old chapel. Something occurred to Jordana as they headed toward the chapel.

"Wait a minute. Isn't the old church there called 'Shaw Chapel'?" she said.

"Yep," Gideon nodded.

"Any relation?" Jordana prodded.

"The chapel is named for Gilchrist Shaw," Gideon said. "He's a direct ancestor of mine."

"Like great-great-bunch-of-times-great grandfather or something?"

"Something like that, yes," Gideon said. He looked up at the old chapel. "Old Gil was a soldier and a sailor, a preacher and a scholar. Family legend has it that he split Red Coats like ordinary men split logs of firewood, but he was one of the founders of Mercy College, which he hoped would produce ministers, doctors, and scientists."

"Sounds like a complex guy," Jordana said.

"I'm sure he was," Gideon replied. "Terrible fashion sense, though. I mean, powdered wigs and tricorn hats? So two centuries ago."

"Are you ever serious?" Jordana asked with a laugh.

"Rarely," Gideon replied. "And I fight it like hell whenever it's called for, too."

"Well, this is my stop," Jordana said. "Can I have my bag back now?"

Gideon flushed slightly as he handed over the backpack. "Oh, uh, sure. Here ya go." He paused as if he wanted to say something. "Er, it was nice meeting you, Jordana."

"You, too," Jordana replied.

"Right, well, I'd better get going myself," Gideon said.

"See you around?" Jordana said.

Gideon smiled. "Yes, ma'am. Absolutely."

"Good," Jordana grinned as she reluctantly turned and went into Baxter Hall for her class.

CHAPTER TWO

Atlanta, Georgia, USA
Magee House, Bell Arbor Plantation
Covington, GA
October 22, 2010

Led Zeppelin's "Immigrant Song" started playing on Gideon's phone. With a sigh he set aside his leather bound first edition of *The Hound of the Baskervilles* and picked up his Android smartphone. He grinned when he saw the caller ID.

"County Morgue. You stab 'em, we slab 'em. Bubba speaking. How can I help you?"

The other end of the line was silent for a moment. "That was funny when I did it to you. Not the other way around, and it's 'Junior' not 'Bubba' speaking."

"But I'm not 'Junior.' I'm Bubba," Gideon grinned.

Heavy sigh. "Sometimes, talking to you is like arguing with a four-year-old."

"Kettle."

"Fair enough. You busy?"

"Not particularly."

"You hungry?"

"I could nosh."

"Skinner's Steakhouse in twenty?"

"I'll see you there."

Fifteen minutes later Gideon parked his Jeep Wrangler Unlimited behind the restaurant next to a 1965 Pontiac GTO convertible. A big man sat behind the wheel of the classic muscle car moving his hands as though he were directing the orchestra that was performing "The Flight of the Valkyries" on his stereo. He grinned over at Gideon.

"Wagner. Gotta love that guy, you know?" Matt Einarsson declared.

"Junior, I got to do no such thing," Gideon laughed. "Did you call me while you were sitting here?"

Matt just grinned.

"I thought you were hungry," Gideon said.

"I also said twenty minutes. You're five minutes early," Matt declared.

"Sometimes, talking to you is like arguing with a toddler," Gideon quipped.

"So I've been told... pot," Matt chuckled.

The song ended, and Matt sighed.

"Can we go eat now?" Gideon insisted.

"Sure," Matt said climbing out of the car.

He was a mountain of a man, standing around six and a half feet tall and weighing in somewhere north of two hundred pounds. A very colorful Hawaiian shirt did little to hide the heavy muscles that were straining against his t-shirt. Carpenter jeans and Blackhawk Light Assault boots rounded out his ensemble. His dark blond hair was grown out long and tied into a ponytail, and he kept his beard and mustache trimmed into a devilish-looking cut that framed his heavy Scandinavian features.

"I bet you're just grouchy 'cause I called while you were reading a book," Matt teased. "What was it?"

Gideon sighed. *"The Hound of the Baskervilles."*

"The one Doyle signed?" Matt guessed.

"No, the one Watson signed," Gideon retorted.

The two of them continued their good-natured ribbing as they walked around to the front of the building. Skinner's Steakhouse was something of a local legend. It had been family owned and operated for more than four generations. It was located in a refurbished antebellum mansion just off the main square in downtown Covington.

"Table for two," Matt said to the young woman at the door.

"Gonna be a twenty-minute wait," the girl replied.

Gideon slapped the back of Matt's head. "You coulda gone ahead and got us a table, but you had to have your Wagner minute."

"I will lay you out in front of the lovely young lady if you don't start to behave," Matt growled. He returned his attention to the hostess. "That will be fine. We'll wait at the bar. Name's Matthias."

She handed him a pager with a smile. Matt accepted the pager with a wink and a smile as he pocketed it.

As they headed into the bar area, Gideon whispered, "You're too old for her."

"I'm too old for all of them, but I don't let that stop me," Matt chuckled. "I need two Glen Moray speyside single malts on the rocks."

"Did you get paid today or something?" Gideon laughed.

"Look, I have a stressful occupation, and every once in a while, I need a good carouse to blow off some steam," Matt replied.

The bartender set down two shot glasses with the requested Scotch and ice. Matt paid with cash, downed his drink in a gulp while handing the other over to Gideon.

"Wow, that'll clear your sinuses," Matt declared.

Gideon savored the first sip of the Glen Moray. Speyside was his favorite style of Scotch. "You shouldn't just toss it back like a Philistine, Matt."

"One more," Matt told the bartender. He glanced at Gideon. "I'll 'savor' this one. Promise."

"So, how's tricks over at Magna Tech Solutions?" Gideon asked.

"I so wish I was still a soldier," Matt groaned.

"You're the one who went to MIT to get a good degree in computer science," Gideon reminded his friend. "You didn't think it would be endless days of World of Warcraft, did you?"

Matt sighed. "I was kinda hoping."

"Well, with the way the world is today, you could sign up with an outfit like Black River, head to Iraq or Afghanistan, and make loads of dough as a contractor," Gideon said.

Matt snorted. "I make loads of dough fixing computers for various idiots in the metropolitan Atlanta area, and nobody shoots at me." Matt paused. "Okay, there's the client who I play Call of Duty with, but I don't think video game bullets count."

"No, I don't think virtual bullets count," Gideon agreed clinking his glass against Matt's.

"And how are the halls of academia treating you?"

Gideon shrugged. "You know I love teaching and learning, and it's always nice to be around young people, but I tell you, they get weirder and weirder every year."

Matt shook his head. "And you say that year after year. You know as well as I do that people stay the same no matter how much the world changes around them."

Before Gideon could reply, the pager buzzed.

"Looks like we got a table sooner than expected," Gideon said.

The hostess showed them to their table in a room that had once been a ballroom. Their table was in a corner where several tables were starting to empty out, mostly families who wanted to get in and out before their children's bedtimes.

"Your server will be with you shortly. Would you gentlemen like another drink?" the hostess asked.

"I think we've had enough," Gideon said before Matt could reply. "Two iced teas, please."

"Aw, c'mon," Matt whined. "I'm a big boy, and I'm in a drinking mood."

"I'm not driving your oversized carcass home tonight," Gideon retorted.

"But your backseat is sooo comfortable!" Matt said. "And you've got that nice bucket back there for me."

"That wasn't a bucket. That was a pre-Colombian urn, a priceless artifact of a lost civilization," Gideon sighed.

"Then, why was it in your backseat?" Matt retorted.

"Because I'm an assistant professor of Anthropology, and I was bringing it to the school for a class," Gideon said.

"Oh." Matt blinked a couple of times. "Sorry."

"You're forgiven," Gideon said. "You're also buying dinner."

"I was gonna buy dinner anyway," Matt chuckled. "*I'm* not the one on a teacher's salary."

The server showed up with their teas.

"Here you go, guys," she said. "I'll be your server tonight, my name's..."

"Jordana?" Gideon said.

Jordana grinned. "Small world, Gideon!" she exclaimed.

"Small town more likely," Gideon replied.

He had to admit that Jordana looked really fetching in her low-rise jeans and Skinner's Steakhouse t-shirt. Her long brown hair was pulled back in a ponytail, and her dark brown eyes were sparkling.

"So, uh, you work here at Skinner's, huh?" Gideon stammered.

"That I do," Jordana replied. "My dad pays for my tuition, my books, and my housing, but it's my responsibility to feed and clothe myself. Hence, the job."

"How terribly old-fashioned of him," Gideon chuckled.

Matt cleared his throat. "Uh, thought you were hungry, old buddy."

"Oh, right, I am," Gideon exclaimed. "Whole reason for letting you con me out of the house tonight."

Matt gave Gideon a look and nodded once at the girl.

"Oh! Sorry, uh, Jordana Quinlan, my new friend, meet Matt Einarsson, my oldest friend," Gideon said.

The two shook hands.

"You should know, I eat here a lot," Matt said. "So, the key to getting a big tip from me is being cute and keeping my drink filled, and you're already halfway there."

Gideon sighed. "Please excuse him. He's an idiot. A good-hearted idiot, but still an idiot."

"I have friends like that, too," Jordana assured him. She turned to Matt. "And, don't you worry, I'll keep your glass full, make sure that you've got what you need, and I might even manage to keep the kitchen staff from garnishing your food with dandruff... or worse. No guarantees, though."

"Fair enough," Matt laughed.

"Okay, do you guys need a minute with the menu or do you know what you want?" Jordana asked.

"I want the Big Bull," Matt declared.

"Are you sure? That's two *pounds* of porterhouse steak," Jordana cautioned.

Gideon and Matt looked at one another and laughed.

"What's so funny?" Jordana asked.

"Ever hear of the Big Texan Steak Ranch?" Gideon asked. "They have a 72-ounce sirloin on the menu that's free if you can eat it and all the sides in an hour."

"We've both beaten the challenge," Matt added. "Twice."

"So, the Big Bull isn't much of a challenge," Gideon said.

"No wonder the vegan girls hate you," Jordana laughed.

"That, and I've flunked a couple of them," Gideon said.

"Flunked?" Jordana repeated. "Wait, you're a professor?"

Gideon nodded. "Uh, yeah. Anthropology."

"Oh my goodness! I just assumed you were a student," Jordan said flushing.

"He is kinda baby-faced," Matt teased.

"Don't worry about it, Jordana. I'm not your professor, if you're worried about being seen having lunch with me today," Gideon said.

Jordana took a breath. "No, just kinda... surprised. So, uh, Big Bulls for the table? How do you want them?"

"Medium rare," Gideon replied.

"Put it on a hot plate and walk it through a warm room for me," Matt said.

"So, medium rare for both, then, since we can't serve raw meat," Jordana said. "Let me guess, you want some kind of potato for your sides?"

"Fries, house salad, Italian dressing," Matt said.

"I'd rather have onion rings, and ranch on the salad," Gideon said.

"Okay, well, I'll go put this order in, and I'll be back to check on your drinks in a minute," Jordana said.

Matt watched her leave. "My god. Can I be a college professor, too?"

"Shut up," Gideon sighed.

Matt's head snapped back around. "Jesus H. Christ! You're into her, aren't you?"

"Don't blaspheme," Gideon said.

"Don't avoid the question. Are you or are you not into that girl?" Matt insisted.

Gideon sighed. "I feel... a connection."

Matt's ham-like fist thumped the table. "Yes! About time!"

"Would you stop it? I'm not a monk," Gideon sighed.

"But you've been living like one for the last thirty or forty years," Matt said.

Gideon rolled his eyes.

"Well, you kind of have," Matt said.

"I want to enjoy my dinner," Gideon said.

"Look, if you don't ask that girl out, I will," Matt said.

"They'll never find your remains if you do," Gideon said with a sweet smile.

Matt looked up. "Thank you, Lord, for this miracle, for reminding my friend that he's a man."

"Would you keep it down?" Gideon sighed.

"Gideon, seriously? What would you be doing if you were me?" Matt asked.

Gideon snorted. "The exact same thing. Only louder and funnier."

"That wounds me," Matt gasped. "You really think you're funnier than me?"

"Funnier *and* better looking," Gideon said.

"She seems to think so," Matt said pointing a thumb over his shoulder toward where Jordana was returning toward their table with a pitcher in either hand.

"Sweet or unsweet?" she asked.

"Okay, you just don't ask a southern gentleman a question like that," Matt gasped.

Jordana winked as she topped off each of their glasses with the pitchers in either hand. "Kidding. Sweet tea it is."

"Do you have a sister?" Matt asked.

"Yes, but she's fourteen, and that's a bit creepy," Jordana said. "But you're a computer geek, so it's understandable."

Gideon nearly spit tea out of his nose. "Don't say things like that while I'm trying to drink," he guffawed.

"Back with your salads in a minute," Jordana said.

"I think I need to talk to Skinner and find out when this girl is working," Matt said. "I do believe I've just found my new favorite waitress."

"First, they're called 'servers' now, and, second, Peaches will be disappointed," Gideon chuckled.

"Peaches got engaged and quit working here last week," Matt said.

"Ah, so *you're* the disappointed one," Gideon said.

"Not exactly. I introduced them," Matt replied.

"Sometimes, I forget what a yenta you can be," Gideon said.

"Well, to keep me from nagging you from now until the end of time, and you know I'll do it, I want you to promise me that you'll ask that girl out," Matt said.

"I don't know if that's such a good..." Gideon stammered.

"Your word, brother," Matt insisted.

Gideon sighed. "Alright, alright, you've got my word. I'll ask her out."

"When?" Matt said.

"I'm sorry?"

"I want a timetable, mate," Matt said.

Gideon growled. "Okay, tonight, after she gets off work."

"Your word?"

"My word."

Matt leaned back and grinned. "Good."

"I will get you for this," Gideon promised.

CHAPTER THREE

Atlanta, Georgia, USA
Skinners Steak House
Covington, GA
October 22, 2010

Gideon had excused himself from the table to talk to Jordana.

"Oh, hey, did you need something?" she asked.

"Uh, yeah, um, I, uh, well, I wanted to know, uh, what time you, er, got off work tonight," Gideon stammered. "I mean, I'd like a chance to talk. Uh, about today..."

"About the fact that you let me think you were just another student?" Jordana said.

Gideon sighed. "Yes. And... other... stuff."

Jordana pursed her lips and tapped her chin as she looked up in thought. "Well, I suppose, since you're all stammery..."

Gideon smiled. "How about coffee?"

"Coffee sounds non-threatening," Jordana chuckled. "My shift ends at ten. Meet me at the SBC in the plaza."

So, at 10:30 Gideon was sitting in the Seattle's Best Coffee shop in the Newton Plaza Shopping center waiting for Jordana to come in. He was afraid he might have been stood up or worse, and had just decided to go looking for Jordana when she walked in the door. She'd changed out of her Skinner's Steakhouse "uniform," opting for a flannel shirt and an Army surplus field jacket.

She hadn't arrived alone, either. A good-looking young man of either Indian or Latin heritage walked in with her. They were laughing and talking to one another in the easy manner which identified them as longtime acquaintances. Jordana said something to her companion before heading over to Gideon's table. The young man went up to the counter.

"Your, uh, boyfriend?" Gideon asked as he stood to greet her.

Jordana frowned slightly. "Evan?" Then, she smiled. "No, he's just my best friend."

Gideon glanced at the strikingly handsome young man who was placing his order at the counter. "Is there something wrong with him? He gay? Not that there's anything wrong with that," he added with a stammer.

Jordana laughed as she sat down. "No, there's nothing wrong with him. No, he's not gay... not that there's anything wrong with that."

"You are an unusually self-possessed young woman," Gideon said. "While I am quickly becoming a stammering, stuttering idiot."

"Yeah, but it works for you," Jordana said.

Best friend Evan walked over and set a cup down in front of Jordana. "Does Her Highness need anything else?"

"No, that will be all," Jordana replied with an imperious little wave. "Peasant."

"You know, we won't treat you very well when the Revolution comes," Evan teased. He turned his attention to Gideon. "Hi, I'm Evan Khanderia."

"Gideon Shaw."

The two men shook hands.

"Okay, I'm gonna leave you two alone while I go clock in," Evan said. "You guys behave. See, the night shift cops *love* stopping in here while they're on patrol. Just remember that. Especially you, Your Highness."

"You don't have any brothers, do you?" Gideon said.

Jordana raised an eyebrow. "What would make you guess that?"

"Well, you mentioned to Matt that you've got a fourteen-year-old sister, so you've got a sibling, at least one, but the way that you and Evan there interact, it's sibling-like. If I had to guess, I'd say that your sister is your only sibling, and other than your dad, you don't have any close male relatives to bond with. Ergo, Johnny Handsome there gets to be your bubba of choice,"

"Interesting observation from an assistant professor of anthropology," Jordana said with a little smirk as she sipped at her coffee.

"Well, it's like detective work, and I've got a degree in psychology, too. I'm a keen observer of the human condition," Gideon chuckled.

"Okay, *Professor*, explain to me why you let me think you were another student?" Jordana said.

Gideon sighed and shrugged. "Because a pretty girl entered into my orbit, and I liked being treated like I was just another guy, not because she was currying favor with her teacher."

"Fair enough," Jordana replied.

"Besides, I don't know about you, but I felt a definite... connection," Gideon said. "I'd... I'd like to see where that connection might lead... If you're interested, that is."

"Am I correct, Professor, in inferring that you are asking me out on a date?" Jordana said.

Gideon nodded. "Yes, ma'am, I suppose I am."

"Doesn't this violate some university policy or something?" Jordana said.

"You're not my student. We're both consenting adults. No policy against two consenting adults engaging in a social activity of their choosing," Gideon said.

"Alright, good point. I'll make a deal with you: I'll go on a date with you, if you'll answer one question for me," Jordana proposed.

"If it's within my ability to answer," Gideon said with a nod.

"I looked you up in the class catalogue. You're, and I quote, 'G.D. Shaw, MS, Assistant Professor/Instructor in Anthropology', correct?" Jordana said.

"Is that your one question?" Gideon asked.

Jordana just frowned at him.

"Okay, not *the* question," Gideon surrendered. "Yes, I'm that Shaw."

"Here's my question, then," Jordana said, growing quite serious in her demeanor. "What is your middle name?"

Gideon snorted. He grabbed a napkin, pulled a pen from his pocket and printed a word on the napkin: Dyrnwch.

"Oh my god, *that's* your middle name? Where are the vowels?" Jordana laughed.

"Okay, it's Welsh. Welsh apparently doesn't utilize traditional vowels," Gideon chuckled.

"Durn-witch?" Jordana guessed.

"Uh, no," Gideon chuckled. "The 'w' is just that: a double 'u,' and the 'y' is used like an 'I.' Plus, there's a hidden syllable, too. It's pronounced 'dew-er-nooch' or 'dwer-nooch' if you say it fast enough."

"Did your mother hate you or something?" Jordana laughed.

"No, I was named for her father," Gideon said.

"Was he bullied as a child?" Jordana said.

Gideon shrugged. "Never really knew him. The name, though, is from Irish mythology. One of the kings of Ireland was served by a Welsh giant who had a magic pot that wouldn't cook the food of a coward."

"So, you had to be brave or you didn't eat," Jordana said.

"I guess so," Gideon replied. "Personal bravery was highly valued among the ancient Celtic peoples."

"Well, you answered my question, Dyrnwch. I guess I have to go out with you now, stupid name notwithstanding," Jordana sighed.

"Why, thank you for your pity," Gideon said. "Bless your heart."

Jordana laughed. "I've heard it said that a Southern woman can say that with a perfectly straight and sincere face and still make it sound like she's just invited you to do something anatomically impossible."

"It's true," Gideon said. "Got aunts, cousins, who'll skin your hide a layer at a time, and never once raise their voices or speak in anything other than the sweetest tones."

"Any other family?" Jordana asked.

"It's just me and a sister these days," Gideon replied. "Pretty much everybody else in my immediate family has passed away."

"I'm sorry to hear that," Jordana said. She reached out and placed her hand on top of Gideon's.

Gideon shrugged. Then, he smiled. "So, do you have a cuisine preference or am I expected to surprise you?"

Jordana nodded and patted his hand. "Nice non sequitur, Dyrnwch."

"You know, it's not entirely fair that you know my middle name, and I don't know yours," Gideon pointed out.

"Roxanne. My middle name is Roxanne."

Gideon snorted a laugh. "And you're giving me a hard time about Dyrnwch?"

"What? I was named after the character from the play *Cyrano de Bergerac*!" Jordana insisted.

"No, you were named after a Police song," Gideon laughed. Then, he started singing in a high falsetto, "Roxanne! Don't put on the red light!"

"Stop it," Jordana insisted though she was laughing.

"I could sing something else. Little Sinatra? Some Elvis? Something more modern?" Gideon offered.

"I like Italian," Jordana said.

"Uh, okay, but I'll have to brush up first. My Italian's kinda rusty, and opera's really not my thing," Gideon said.

"No, dummy, I like Italian *food*," Jordana clarified.

"I happen to know of a couple of good restaurants in the metro area," Gideon said. "Tomorrow good for you?"

Jordana nodded. "Let me see your phone," she said.

Gideon raised an eyebrow, but turned his phone over anyway. Jordana tapped the screen a few times. Then, she typed something very rapidly with just her thumbs.

"I always find that impressive," Gideon said. "I'm the slowest texter in the world, even with a qwerty keyboard on the phone."

"It's a skill that requires young, limber fingers," Jordana said. "Here, my phone number and address are programmed into your contacts list, and I've put the time for our date in your calendar with an alarm every few hours."

Gideon looked at the screen of his phone. "You are a remarkably self-possessed young woman."

"You've said that already," Jordana said.

"You keep giving me reasons *to* say it," Gideon said. He glanced at his Luminox EVO watch. The hour was definitely getting late. "Uh, I hate to say it, but I need to get going. I have stuff to do, papers to grade, hopes to dash..."

"I understand," Jordana said. "No carefree collegiate lifestyle for you."

"What about you?" Gideon asked.

"I'll hang here until Evan's shift is over and give him a ride home. My laptop's in the car, and I've got this huge World History paper to work on," Jordana said. "Good thing that I don't sleep too much."

Gideon's ears perked. "Really?"

"I don't know what it is, but all I really need is about four hours of solid sleep, and I'm good," Jordana said. "My dad says it's youth and too much caffeine in my diet, that I'll start having to sleep longer once I'm out of college, but I don't know. I mean, I used to sleep a full eight hours every day all through middle school and most of high school, but about junior year, I just started sleeping less."

Gideon rubbed his chin. "Interesting," he muttered. Then, he shook himself. "Okay, enough dallying. I have to get to those papers tonight if I wanna have anything to do this weekend." He glanced at his phone's calendar. "And you've scheduled an early evening."

"I'm expecting more than just dinner, you know," Jordana said.

Gideon smiled. "I'll come up with something, but it's been a while. I hear they've invented these things called 'motion pictures' that are just a hoot."

CHAPTER FOUR

Atlanta, Georgia, USA
Mercy University "BOH Row"
Garden Manor
Covington, GA
October 23, 2010

Jordana glanced at the clock on her desk and moaned. Her roommate, Tammy Gilbert, looked up from the book of Emily Dickinson she was reading and smirked. Tammy's smirk was a thing of legend, combining disdain, sarcasm, and arrogant apathy all in one little half-smile. The girls had been friends since middle school when Tammy had discovered that Evan wasn't Jordana's boyfriend and had begged the other girl to introduce them.

"Don't sit there," Jordana whined. "Help me!"

Tammy laughed and got off her bed. "Would you like some cheese to go with that whine?"

"Less funny, more helpful," Jordana growled.

Tammy shook her head. "Look, you were cool enough to snag a date with your older man, why are you panicking now?"

"I don't know!" Jordana exclaimed with a heavy sigh.

Tammy just chuckled. "First question: do you want to borrow any of my clothes?"

The girls were roughly the same size. Jordana was the more slender of the two, but they could fit into one another's clothes. Tammy's style, though, tended toward lots of black, semi-Goth, semi-Emo, all scary, and despite growing up in Orlando, Tammy had managed to maintain pale, alabaster skin that contrasted sharply with her clothes and dark hair.

"Under normal circumstances, no," Jordana admitted, "but these are hardly normal circumstances. I mean, I'm turning to *you* for fashion advice."

"Yeah, the first Addams Family joke you crack, and you're on your own, sister," Tammy snarked.

Jordana giggled. "Fair enough, but if you call me 'Puggsley,' I will hurt you."

"Okay, seriously, do you trust me?" Tammy asked, her blue eyes twinkling with mischief.

"Y-yes," Jordana said hesitantly.

"Good," Tammy murmured.

She stepped into the walk-in closet they shared and came out with several articles of clothing, which she handed to Jordana.

"Leather pants? Really?" Jordana said.

"Sweetie, you may like to hide it, but for a skinny girl, you've got some junk in the trunk, and you need to show it off," Tammy said.

"And this top?" Jordana demanded holding up a short, shimmering gold tank top.

"Jeez, Jordy, you have an *amazing* figure. Why you insist on hiding it, I will never understand," Tammy grumbled as she ducked into the closet again. When she stepped out, she handed Jordana a somewhat longer tank top. "Layer it with this."

"Why do you have this stuff?" Jordana asked. "This isn't your style."

"No, I bought it for you," Tammy answered. "In the hopes that I could get you to dress up someday, and praise the lawd, that day has a-come!"

"You are an exceptionally strange person," Jordana chuckled.

"Less talky, more dressy," Tammy said with a shooing gesture as she disappeared back into the closet.

Jordana stripped out of the baggy sweats she'd been wearing and was about to step into the leather pants Tammy had picked, when her friend stepped out of the closet and said, "No! You are not wearing the granny panties and K-Mart bra."

"Okay, first, these are not 'granny panties,' and I got the bra at Wal-Mart," Jordana retorted. "Besides, nobody but you is gonna see my underwear."

Tammy growled. "Whether *anybody* else sees it or not, *you* need to know that you're dressed to impress from the skin out. Do you think Evan has seen any of my stuff yet?"

"Yes," Jordana said.

Tammy paused. "Okay, so, he has, but before that I'd still wear my good lacy undies because they made me feel sexy. Get it?"

"Yeah?" Jordana hesitated.

"Look, confidence is sexy. This guy's confidence got you to agree to a date with him," Tammy explained.

"Actually, it was kind of his goofy lack of confidence," Jordana chuckled.

"No, he worked up the confidence, and *that's* what attracted you to him, and vice versa," Tammy said. "Trust me on this."

"How do you know? The only guy you've ever dated is Evan," Jordana scoffed.

"I watch Oprah," Tammy said as she stepped over to her dresser. "Pay attention. Feel sexy equals feel confident. Feel confident, and you won't be nervous." She fished out a silky red bra and panties. "My lucky undies."

"I really don't want to know that," Jordana said.

"Put 'em on. Dress to kill, sweetie," Tammy said. Then, she grinned. "Maybe they'll be lucky for you."

Jordana flushed scarlet. "You're terrible."

"You're the one with the dirty mind," Tammy retorted. "Oh, and wear the boots. The heels will make your legs and ass look fantastic. I'll be downstairs with Evan. I want to meet your older man."

"Don't scare him away," Jordana shouted as Tammy left the room.

Jordana looked at the red underwear in her hands. With a sigh, she changed into the clothes Tammy had picked.

CHAPTER FIVE

Atlanta, Georgia, USA

Mercy University "BOH Row"

Garden Manor

Covington, GA

October 23, 2010

Gideon parked his Jeep on the street. The neighborhood was called "BOH Row" by the students of Mercy University. "BOH" was shorthand for "Big Old House," and the neighborhood on the edge of the campus was full of just that. Since the fifties, the university had been buying up the old houses in the neighborhood and converting them into housing for the faculty at first, and later for students.

Some of the BOH's were used exclusively by certain fraternities or sororities or similar organizations, like the ROTC, but several of the houses had organically "grown" into Greek-like associations of their own, many even being co-ed. Gideon had always liked the neighborhood, the sense of camaraderie the housemates often shared, the sense of youthful exuberance that seemed to waft through the air.

He got out of the Jeep and looked up at the house. It was a two-story country home-style townhouse, probably built in the late fifties, attached garage, four bedrooms, big front porch. If it was anything like the other BOH's, the garage had been converted into an apartment, and the main house had been divided into smaller apartments as well. On the other hand, if it was one of the houses that had formed into a quasi-fraternal group, it might still have the original floor plan, but he kind of doubted that. Gideon climbed up the steps onto the porch.

The original door was the only one he saw. A few of the BOH's had become studded with doors leading to the various apartments that the big houses had been cut into. He rang the doorbell and waited. A few seconds later, Evan stepped out of a doorway on the left. The young man opened the front door with a grin.

"Welcome to Garden Manor," Evan declared.

"Family called the Jardines used to live here," Gideon said with a chuckle.

"Probably where the name came from," Evan agreed. "Come on in."

He motioned for Gideon to follow him. Gideon followed the younger man down the hall to the back of the house into a large kitchen-come-lounge area.

"The downstairs shares the kitchen. The apartment upstairs has a kitchen of its own, but they all share one bathroom," Evan said. He pointed to a young black man with short dreads who was cooking something on the stove. "That's Zeb, my roommate."

"Yo, dude, you Jordy's date?" Zeb called out.

"Yes, sir," Gideon replied.

"Hear you teach over at MU," Zeb said.

"That I do," Gideon confirmed.

"Cool. You a good teach?" Zeb asked.

Gideon shrugged. "Pass more than I fail. So, I'm not that good."

Zeb laughed. "Ah'ight. Might have to look into taking a class from you, then. For the challenge."

"Your funeral," Gideon said with a grin.

Evan pointed over to the lounge area where two equally scrawny young men were furiously engaged in some first person shooter on an X-Box 360. "Those are Iceberg and Kill-Billy, otherwise known as Ron and Willie."

"Halo?" Gideon asked.

"Call of Duty," the dark-haired Ron, aka "Iceberg," replied absently.

"Modern Warfare," the blond Willie, aka "Kill-Billy," added. "Pwned!"

"Dude!" Ron groaned.

"They're such... scintillating conversationalists," Evan snorted.

"Hello," purred a female voice behind Gideon.

He turned and nodded to the young woman who'd just come down from upstairs. "And hello to you, too."

"My girlfriend, Tammy," Evan announced.

"Jordy is getting dressed," Tammy said as she openly appraised Gideon. "She wasn't kidding when she said you're a hottie."

"Uh, thank you?" Gideon said as a slight flush crept into his cheeks. He turned back to Zeb. "So, uh, what're you cooking there, uh, Zeb?"

"Jambalaya," Zeb replied. "Spicy jambalaya."

Tammy rolled her eyes and growled.

"Don't let her hard exterior fool you," Evan said. "Tammy here has a soft, chewy center."

"I don't like all the spices you two seem to insist on trying to kill one another with," Tammy groused.

Evan shrugged. "I'm Indian. I grew up with curries. Zeb's from New Orleans. So, we try to see who can cook the hottest dish. It's how we bond."

"That and a mutual love for Miles Davis," Zeb said.

"Do you mind?" Gideon asked motioning toward Zeb's pot.

"Knock yourself out, Professor," Zeb replied offering Gideon a spoon.

Gideon dipped some of the jambalaya out, sniffed it, and then downed a mouthful. "Damn, son, but that's good!"

"Not too hot for ya?" Zeb asked.

"Well, a lesser mortal might not be able to handle it, but I lived in Mumbai for a few years, and spicy foods don't bother me near as bad as they once did," Gideon said.

"That's where my Dad's family is originally from," Evan said.

"And your mom?" Gideon asked.

"Toronto," Evan said.

"Nice city," Gideon said. "Very clean. Fantastic natural history museum."

"So Mom tells me," Evan laughed.

Tammy had wrapped herself possessively around Evan's waist, but she was still staring at Gideon like she was a snake contemplating whether or not to eat the mouse that had been dropped into its cage. "You don't look old enough to be a college professor," she said.

"I've aged well," Gideon said.

"How old are you?" Tammy asked.

"Old enough to know better, but too old to care," Gideon replied.

Tammy snorted, but before she could ask another question Evan covered her mouth with his hand. "Be nice," he said. "Gideon is our guest."

Tammy raised an eyebrow and glanced pointedly at his hand.

"Bite me," he dared her.

She pulled his hand away. "There are better, nicer ways to shut me up," she purred.

Gideon cocked his head to one side and looked at the two of them. "It's like the lady and the tiger rolled into one."

Evan snickered, and Zeb bellowed a laugh.

"I smell food!"

The shout was followed by a tiny red-haired girl who bounced down the stairs and bounded into the kitchen.

"Zeb's cooking! Yay!" she exclaimed. Then, she saw Gideon. "Oh! Hi! You must be Jordy's man-man!"

"Ariel, sweetie, have you been drinking Red Bulls all day?" Tammy demanded.

"Maybe? Yes! No?" Ariel said.

"That's Ariel," Evan said. "She lives upstairs with the rest of the girls, and she's... excitable."

"I think I might need a scorecard to keep you all straight," Gideon chuckled.

"Next time, we'll all wear those 'Hello, my name is' tags," Zeb suggested.

"No more caffeine for you, young lady," Tammy said.

"Aw," Ariel groaned.

"Hey, why don't you go set the table for me," Zeb suggested. "We're gonna eat out on the deck while it's still nice."

"Goody!" Ariel exclaimed and bounded off to do as she'd been bidden.

"Are there any more of you?" Gideon asked.

"Just Micky who is at the library, and Darman, the guy who lives in the garage apartment, but he doesn't bother us, and we don't bother him," Tammy said. Then, she shrugged. "Well, much."

"You don't mean George Darman, do you?" Gideon asked.

"Yeah, why?" Evan said.

"I own a couple of his paintings. He's kind of brilliant," Gideon said.

"He's kind of insane," Tammy smirked.

"Well, honey, he is an artist," Evan said, chucking her under the chin.

Tammy was about to say something when she noticed something past Gideon's shoulder. "Well! Look who's here!"

Gideon turned around. He actually felt himself stop breathing for several heartbeats. "Wow," he managed to say once he took a breath.

Jordana smiled at him self-consciously, which only made the incredibly sexy vision in front of him that much more attractive. "Thank you."

"Uh, ready to go?" Gideon asked.

Jordana nodded. "Yes. Please."

"Um, okay," Gideon stammered.

"Wow, Jordy, you knocked the cool clean out the man," Zeb chortled. "That's how fine you lookin'."

Jordana blushed. "Aw, guys, you're sweet, but stop it. No, really, stop it."

Tammy hugged Jordana and whispered in her ear, "You should let him get lucky. He's hot."

Ariel came dancing back into the kitchen. "Oh, Jordy! You're so shiny!"

"Thank you, Ariel," Jordana said. She glanced over at Willie and Ron who were still deeply engaged in their game. "Bye, guys."

"Yeah, whatever," Willie said with an absent wave.

"Pwnage!" Ron shouted. "Burn in hell, newb!"

"And to think, neither of them has a girlfriend," Jordana said. "Such fine gentlemen."

"I should call Matt, and introduce them to one another," Gideon said.

"No, I wouldn't do that to Matt," Jordana said. "He's likeable."

"He'll be so happy to hear that somebody other than me likes him," Gideon chuckled. He turned his attention to Jordana's housemates. "It was a pleasure meeting you all."

"Have her home before her first class Monday," Tammy said with her signature smirk.

"No promises," Gideon said with a wink.

He walked Jordana out to his car, opened the door for her, and made sure she was safely in the seat before closing the door.

"So, where are we going?" she asked once he was in the driver's seat.

"Well, I gave it some thought, and I figured a movie would be fun, but not really a good way for us to get to know one another, and you mentioned Italian, but I figure that's more of a second date kind of cuisine, since I can cook pasta," Gideon rambled as he pulled the Jeep away from the curb.

"You're already planning the second date?" Jordana teased.

"Yes, ma'am. Never accept less than total victory," Gideon replied with a chuckle. "Anyway, I was thinking that you might like to go someplace where you might get a little insight into me... Gee, that sounds a little conceited, doesn't it?"

Jordana laughed. "Maybe. Just a tiny little bit, but I understand what you mean. So, what is this special place?"

"It's called the Red Lion. It's a kind of pub. Good food, good music, interesting... ambiance," Gideon said.

"Sounds... interesting," Jordana said.

"It's a bit of a drive, though," Gideon admitted. He gestured to the iPod docked in the Jeep's stereo. "You can browse my playlists, if you want."

"Oh, I intend to," Jordana said, "but I was kind of hoping we could, you know, talk."

"Ah, in other words, you have questions," Gideon chuckled. "Tell you what: I'll trade you a question for a question."

"Alright, I'll see your question for a question, and I'll raise you the truth," Jordana countered.

Gideon sighed. "I'll tell you the truth to any question you ask, but I reserve the right to refuse to answer any questions that might... violate confidences."

"Confidences?" Jordana said with a raised eyebrow.

"I have a lot of secrets, and not all of them are mine to share," Gideon said. "Can you accept that?"

"Okay, that's fair, and I'll make the same reservation. Agreed?"

"Yes, ma'am," Gideon said. "Ladies first."

"Why, thank you, sir," Jordana said in a rather over-the-top Southern accent that made Gideon groan. "First thing I want to know is: are you now or have you ever been married?"

"No, I am not currently married. Yes, I have been married before," Gideon answered. "My turn."

"What?" Jordana exclaimed.

"Question for a question," Gideon reminded her.

"That was hardly an answer," Jordana said.

Gideon shrugged. "You'll get another question," he said. "Now, what's your favorite color?"

"Purple," Jordana said. "Tell me about this ex-wife of yours."

"Not properly phrased as a question, but I'll let it slide," Gideon said. He glanced over at Jordana. "Her name was Aggie, and she... passed away, and this is the first date I've been on since."

"How long..." Jordana stammered.

"My turn," Gideon said. He glanced over at Jordana with a smile. "Besides, I'd rather not talk about that particular subject."

"Okay," Jordana said.

"Right, then, favorite flavor of ice cream?"

"This is silly," Jordana said. "Mint chocolate chip."

"Yes, it is silly, and now it's your turn," Gideon said.

"Alright, why are you asking me silly questions?"

"Because I want to know the silly little trivia of what you like and dislike, for when it comes time to buy you birthday presents and such," Gideon replied.

"Wow, that's... practical," Jordana snorted.

"Least favorite color?"

"Pink. How old are you?"

"Same age as my tongue and a little older than my teeth," Gideon said.

Jordana paused mid-reply and stared at him. Then, a smile slowly spread across her face. "What a coincidence! That's exactly how old I am."

"Nifty how that works out, ain't it?" Gideon chuckled. "Dogs or cats?"

"Dogs. Do you have pets?"

"If you count Matt, yes."

"That's not funny," Jordana laughed.

"Okay, you're right. Uh, I have a tank of tropical fish, but they're more like... a living decoration than pets, and I have a parrot named Bruce that Matt gave me after teaching it to swear," Gideon said.

"You're serious?" Jordana said.

"Oh, yeah, Bruce knows and uses all the good four-letter words," Gideon chuckled. "My turn. Same question: pets?"

"I have a little mixed breed dog, Princess, and if you're counting it, my little sister, Kitty," Jordana answered.

Gideon laughed. "If I can count Matt, you can count, uh, 'Kitty'?"

"Short for Katherine," Jordana explained.

"Does she have a rock-song middle name, too?" Gideon teased.

"Hey, it's my turn to ask a question," Jordana pointed out.

"Sorry," Gideon said. "Please continue."

"What are the names of your family members?" Jordana said.

"Uh, immediate family?"

"Sure."

"My dad is Gil; my mom is Arianrhod; my stepmom is Amaranth; my older brothers are Dylan and Llew, and my baby sister is Rebecca, but she goes by 'Becca' these days," Gideon replied. "Same question to you."

"Dad is Tom. Mom is Lucinda, and you already know my sister's name," Jordana replied. She paused for a moment. "Gideon, would talking about your family bother you?"

Gideon took a deep breath. "A little. Mom, Amaranth, and my brothers have all passed on. It's just me, Dad, and Becca now."

"I can't imagine what that would be like," Jordana said.

Gideon was quite for a moment. "I won't lie. Losing people... it still hurts, but that old saw about time healing wounds? It's mostly true." He smiled sadly. "Sometimes, though, just forgetting for a while is the balm you need."

"So, what is your favorite flavor of ice cream?" Jordana asked.

"Wait. I thought it was my turn to ask a question," Gideon said.

"No," Jordana said with a straight face.

"Liar," Gideon chuckled. "Rocky road."

"Favorite music?"

"Okay, I'm pretty sure it's my turn now," Gideon said.

"I am exercising my woman's prerogative to change the rules of the game," Jordana explained.

"Really?"

"Yes, really. Now, quit stalling and tell me what your favorite music is," Jordana ordered with an imperious wave.

"I see why Evan calls you 'Your Highness'," Gideon said. "Uh, I don't really have a favorite. Currently, I'm kind of fond of what the kids call the, uh, 'rock and/or roll'."

Jordana picked up the iPod and opened the playlist directory. Then, her jaw dropped. "Holy cow! You've got ten gigs of just classic rock! You've got Mozart and Beethoven, Jay-Z, Run DMC, and Tupac, Breaking Benjamin, Say Anything, Coldplay, and Buckcherry. Good grief, you've even got Hank Williams, Sr., and SHeDAISY! Is there anything you won't listen to?"

"Just crap," Gideon replied. "I may not like an entire genre, but I can enjoy examples from the genre. I don't care for most hip hop, but, as you pointed out, I've got it on there." He snorted. "Wait 'til you see my music room."

"You have a whole room just for music? What, like a room with your stereo?" Jordana said.

"No, a room where I keep my stereo and my instruments," Gideon said. "I, uh, kind of come from a musical family."

"You may not realize this, but I am a total music geek," Jordana said. She pointed emphatically at the iPod. "This is... This is better than using candy to get me into your creepy van."

"It's a Jeep," Gideon said.

"Smart ass," Jordana snorted. "I mean, genius ass."

"Thank you."

"Now, let's see what's your most-played song on here," Jordana said. "What is 'Ye Jacobites By Name' and who are Seven Nations?"

"It's a great song about a bad period in history performed by a self-made band of men in kilts," Gideon said.

"Kilts? Really?" Jordana laughed.

"Just listen to the song."

"Okay," Jordana said, and pressed play.

The song started with what sounded like a chant and went into an up-tempo melody with acoustic guitars and a tin whistle. Jordana found herself tapping a foot and nodding her head to the beat.

"I like the whistle solo," she said.

"Yeah, too bad he left the group," Gideon said. "Really talented piper, but he wanted to have time with his family and start a solo career."

"You sound almost like one of those hipsters. You know those guys that go on about this really cool group that nobody's ever heard of, and then when they become famous, accuse them of selling out and start hating them," Jordana teased.

"God, I hate those guys. They're as bad as the metal heads who started hating Metallica when they cut their hair and started crossing over to Top 40 radio. Like success makes them less talented or less committed to their art," Gideon said. "You wanna know who I respect in the music industry? Gene Simmons. He's honest about wanting to make money. Of course, he'll slap the Kiss name on, literally, anything to make a buck."

"How do you really feel?" Jordana laughed.

"Here, try this guy," Gideon said, reaching over and changing the setting on the iPod. "Marc Broussard. This boy's got soul."

"You know, even if the rest of tonight is a bust, this is officially the best date I've ever been on, ever," Jordana said.

"Because of my obsessive-compulsive need to collect every song imaginable?"

"Yeah, pretty much," Jordana said.

"Finally, the OCD pays off!"

Jordana laughed, and they spent the rest of the drive talking about music.

CHAPTER SIX

Atlanta, Georgia, USA
Red Lion Pub
Sandy Springs, GA
October 23, 2010

The Red Lion was located just off Roswell Road, in Atlanta, in an old shopping center. The location had once been a small grocery store that had been driven out of business by the Kroger down the road. The storefront had been extensively remodeled, as had the interior. From the outside, it still looked like an old grocery store that had been partially boarded up. Inside, it looked like a wood-paneled British pub complete with booths and a bar backed by a big mirror.

"Wow, this place is amazing," Jordana exclaimed as they walked in.

The hostess was a pretty young girl whose face lit up when she saw them walk in the door. "Gideon!" she exclaimed and threw her arms around him.

"Hey, Kim," Gideon laughed. "Can't breathe."

The girl released him with a laugh and a slight blush. "Charlie is gonna be so stoked to see you."

"Good, because he owes me a good dinner," Gideon said.

Kim scoffed. "You know your money's no good here," she said. She glanced at Jordana. "Hi, welcome to the Red Lion! I'm Kim Dewar, and Gideon here is a real American hero. You're a lucky girl, honey."

"So far, so good," Jordana said. "Oh, look, you made him blush!"

Gideon cleared his throat. "Uh, how 'bout that booth, huh, Kim?"

Kim just smiled at him and wiggled a finger for them to follow her. The booth she led them to was in a corner near the small stage. "Okay, today's special is Shepherd's Pie, made with ground mutton," Kim said as she seated them. "Charlie is really thrilled with the recipe, by the way. Oh, and, unfortunately, no live music tonight."

"What happened?" Gideon asked.

"Stew's wife went into labor," Kim explained. "The whole band is at the hospital. You'd think they were all the father the way they're acting."

"Good for Stew," Gideon said. "And the band. That kid'll be spoiled."

"For sure," Kim agreed. "You guys want something to drink?"

Gideon stopped before he could order his usual Guinness. He'd suddenly realized that Jordana was most likely underage -- not a minor, but also not old enough to drink. Kim and Charlie were his friends. He couldn't knowingly allow them to serve alcohol to an underage drinker.

"Uh, sweet tea," he said.

Then, he waited while Jordana seemed to consider what she wanted.

"The same," she said.

Gideon let go of the breath he was holding.

"Alrighty. Be back in a few, then," Kim said before turning to go fill their drink order.

Jordana grinned at him. "My Granny once told me that a proper young lady shouldn't drink alcohol on the first date. Especially if she wants to *stay* a proper young lady."

"Not to mention that it's still illegal for you to drink until your twenty-first birthday," Gideon said.

"I really don't get that, you know," Jordana said. "I mean, when I turned eighteen, I was deemed old enough, or 'mature' enough, to vote, to choose the people who'll run the government for me. I'm mature enough to manage my own finances, to join the military and die for my country, to already be an experienced and licensed driver, but I'm not old enough to walk into a grocery store and buy myself a beer."

"Well, technically, the human brain doesn't really 'mature' until you're about twenty-five, but I understand your concern," Gideon said. "Here's the thing: voting, managing your finances, stuff like that, doesn't immediately endanger people. Drinking to excess, which is something that you do when you're young, *does* pose an immediate danger, especially when you factor in automobiles."

"But if I'm mature enough to choose whether or not to drink, aren't I old enough to know better than to drink and drive?" Jordana retorted.

"Granted, but alcohol makes everybody stupid at some point in the evening, which is why you should never drink to excess anyway, no matter how old you are, but you'll never know what you can handle if you don't test your limits," Gideon chuckled. "So, the first time I tied one on, my father was with me. I was under the supervision of an adult, and my mother used to give us watered-down wine with meals as kids. We were taught to handle alcohol from an early age so that it wouldn't handle us."

"Your mother gave you wine?" Jordana said with a raised eyebrow.

"I told you, she's Welsh. She grew up in Wales, and that was part of their culture. She brought it here to America with us," Gideon said. He shrugged. "You've got to remember, though, that most of America was founded by Protestant intellectuals, men who saw indulging as not only a sin against God, but a sin against Reason. The result today is a culture where alcohol is a common social lubricant, but it's still something of a taboo in many places."

Jordana started to say something when she suddenly winced and groaned.

"Jordana? Are you alright?" Gideon asked. He was kneeling beside her in an instant.

Jordana nodded. "Yeah." She took a deep breath and relaxed. "I'm okay now. That was just... sort of... sudden."

"Are you sure you're okay?" Gideon asked, his eyes searching Jordana's.

She smiled. "Yes, I'm fine. I've been... I don't know how to put it."

Gideon resumed his seat. "Tell me."

Jordana rolled her head, the joints in her neck audibly popping. "It's just this weird... not 'pain,' but I guess that's what you'd call it. My joints have felt... I don't know, uh, 'stuffed' for the last several weeks. Then, all of a sudden, they'll all flare into this sharp... It's not quite a pain. I mean, it's unpleasant, but it doesn't hurt so much as it surprises me, and it feels like my bones want to... burst from my skin."

Gideon had cocked his head to one side. "Have you been taking painkillers, like aspirin, or an anti-inflammatory like ibuprofen?"

"Yeah, but they don't really work," Jordana said, "but you know what does? Eating. Usually something with meat in it. Protein, I guess. Weird, huh?"

"Yes," Gideon said. He saw Kim coming with their drinks. "Hey, forget the menus, Kim, we're gonna have two of my usual."

"Really?" Kim said.

Gideon nodded. "Yes, please, just as quick as Charlie can get 'em out to us."

Kim smiled. "Okay."

"What's your usual?" Jordana asked.

"Angus steak, nearly bloody. Unlike your employer, Charlie will serve undercooked meat," Gideon said with a grin.

"Uh, okay," Jordana replied.

"Feeling better?" Gideon asked.

"Yeah, back to normal. It comes and goes pretty quick," she admitted.

"Gideon Shaw!" bellowed a deep voice.

"Charlie Dewar," Gideon bellowed back.

The deep voice belonged to a very dark-skinned black man who was barely taller than Jordana herself. His dark, tightly curled hair was cropped close to his head, and he was clean-shaven. A scar bisected his face from above his left eye, across the bridge of his nose, and ended half-way down his right cheek. Otherwise, he was a handsome man. Jordana was a little surprised by his outfit, though. He wore a brown tee-shirt decorated with a red heraldic lion and the name and address of the restaurant and a kilt. In all the pictures that Jordana had ever seen of men in kilts, they were pale, white guys.

Gideon had stood up and was embracing the smaller man in a back-slapping bear hug. "How the hell are ya, Charlie?"

"I'm good, baby," Charlie declared. "Got my pub, got my blushing bride, and I've got two good legs under me, thanks to you."

Gideon snorted. "That's because you had good doctors."

"That *you* carried me to," Charlie said. "*On your back*." Charlie glanced into the booth at Jordana. Then, he whistled to himself. "Kim wasn't kidding. She's hot."

"Uh, thank you," Jordana chuckled.

"Sweetheart, if I wasn't already deliriously in love with my little Kim," Charlie cooed. Then, he shrugged. "Well, if you like my boy here, you one alright young lady."

"Thanks. I think," Jordana chuckled. "How do you know one another?"

"We were swim buddies in BUDS," Charlie replied.

"What's buds?" Jordana asked.

"Basic Underwater Demolitions and SEALS training," Charlie responded.

"He never mentioned he was a SEAL," Jordana said.

"He wouldn't. Dumb cracker never did understand how the trident was a golden ticket to a world of..." Charlie glanced at Jordana. "Let's just say 'worldly delights' and leave it at that."

"I think the sight of your scrawny black legs have boggled her," Gideon joked with his friend.

"Yeah, a brother in a kilt is usually a shock to people. Most of 'em think I'm a crossdresser," Charlie laughed. "I'm adopted. Mom couldn't have kids. So, she and Dad decided to give kids from poor countries a chance at a better life, but Dad insisted that we all be... steeped in his Scottish-American heritage. I came from Somalia. My brother, Bill, came from Korea, and my sister, Mary, is from Romania."

"We think Angelina stole the idea to adopt around the world from Charlie's mom," Gideon said. "Hey, if you're here jawing with me, who's making my steak?"

"Juan Garcia, my apprentice chef," Charlie replied.

"Wait, Mary's Juan?" Gideon chuckled. "You conned your brother-in-law into working in your kitchen?"

"Who conned?" Charlie said looking wounded. "He begged me, *begged* me, to take him on."

"You and Bill guilted him somehow," Gideon laughed.

"No, Mom guilted him," Charlie laughed. "Told him it was safer in my kitchen than on the Atlanta P.D."

"Wait, you and Bill both went into the SEALS, and your mom is worried about a son-in-law who's a cop?" Gideon said.

Charlie shrugged. "Bill and I both got medical discharges, bro. Mom doesn't want another shot-up son. Or son-in-law for that matter."

"Well, how does Juan like it back there?" Gideon asked.

"Oh, he *hates* it," Charlie laughed.

"And you're reveling in it, aren't you?" Gideon guessed.

"Of course, I am. He stole my sister," Charlie replied with a wink. "Ah, I better get back there and make sure he's doing it right."

"It's good seeing you, Charlie," Gideon said.

"You, too, and if you try paying, again, I will personally shove the money back in your wallet," Charlie said.

"Do I at least get to tip the server?" Gideon chuckled.

"No, 'cause that's gonna be me or Kim," Charlie said.

"Alright, I'm tired of arguing with you about it, but you're making me look bad in front of the girl," Gideon said.

"Bullshit," Charlie laughed. He looked at Jordana. "This man carried my shot-up ass out of the Hindu Kush on his back."

"I didn't want to face your mother and Kim if I didn't," Gideon said. "They scare me."

Charlie just laughed and shook his head. "Whatever, bro. Whatever. Back in a flash with those steaks."

Jordana gave Gideon a look when he sat back down.

"What?" Gideon said.

"You're a war hero," Jordana said.

Gideon blushed slightly. "No, not really. I just did what anybody would do for his buddy. Charlie's kinda blown it out of proportion."

"He said you carried him out the Hindu Kush, which I know are really tall mountains, on your back," Jordana said. "That's more than just helping out your buddy."

"Well, like I said, his mother and wife scare me," Gideon replied.

"Really?" Jordana challenged.

"No, not really, but I did promise Kim that I'd make sure Charlie made it home in one piece," Gideon said.

"And Gideon Shaw keeps his promises," Kim said as she arrived with a pitcher to top off their mostly untouched drinks. She patted Gideon's arm fondly.

Gideon blushed again. "Not all my promises, but I do try."

"That's good to know," Jordana said.

"And he's smart, too," Kim said. "Good-looking, nice to small children and animals. Why, he's like a male Mary Poppins, practically perfect in every way."

"Uh, please stop, uh, 'helping' me," Gideon groaned.

"Honestly, I was half convinced that he was gay, he's so darn near perfect," Kim continued.

"Thank you, Kim," Gideon said. "Mind checking on those steaks for me?"

"I think he comes from money, too," Kim added.

Jordana was trying, unsuccessfully, not to giggle at Kim's antics.

"See what she does? Professes her love and devotion, and then torpedoes me," Gideon sighed.

"Only because I genuinely love you, doll face," Kim said with a grin. "You're like the little brother I never wanted." She winked to Jordana as she left.

"I think I've got some hemlock for my tea," Gideon chuckled softly.

"I think it's adorable how they treat you like family," Jordana said.

Gideon shrugged. "Well, they are family, but it's family I chose, not family an accident of birth stuck me with. I'm glad you like them, because you'll be next on their list to tease."

"Bring it on," Jordana said. "I'm tougher than you."

"We'll see," Gideon chuckled. "We'll see."

Chapter Seven

Atlanta, Georgia, USA

Turner Lake Park

Covington, GA

October 23, 2010

"That was really good," Jordana said. "Best steak I think I've ever had."

"It's just too bad the band wasn't on tonight," Gideon said as he held open the car door for her. "They do a cover of the Police's 'Roxanne' that's actually pretty good."

"Funny," Jordana smirked as she slid into the Jeep. She winced.

"What's wrong?" Gideon asked.

"Just a twinge. It's nothing," Jordana said.

"Well, let's get you home, then," Gideon suggested.

"Way to screw up the date, Jordy," she scolded herself.

"Don't be silly," Gideon said as he climbed in the other side.

"What else did you have planned?" Jordana asked.

Gideon shrugged. "Beyond dinner, I didn't have a plan. I was just gonna play it by ear. A moonlight stroll was on the agenda."

"Let's do that, then," Jordana said. "I'm feeling better."

"Are you sure?" Gideon asked.

"Yes, I'm sure," Jordana insisted. "It was just a passing twinge."

"Alright," Gideon said.

He put the Jeep into gear and pulled out of the parking lot. They arrived back in Covington forty-five minutes later. Gideon pulled the Jeep into the parking lot at the Turner Lake recreational facility.

Jordana glanced around. They were alone in the parking lot. "Isn't this place closed?"

"Yep, but I have... an acquaintance who left the gate open for us," Gideon replied.

"Acquaintance?" Jordana repeated with a raised eyebrow.

"Night guard who's easily bribable," Gideon admitted.

"Ah," Jordana chuckled as she got out of the car. "I'm not exactly wearing hiking boots, you know."

"No, I noticed," Gideon said, "and they're very fetching, by the way. Not that I have a shoe fetish or anything..."

Jordana laughed as Gideon blushed. "You are such a dork."

"Part of my charm," Gideon laughed. He offered Jordana his arm. "Shall we?"

"We shall," Jordana said taking the offered arm and tucking herself up against Gideon's side.

Gideon swallowed a lump in his throat. He hadn't been this close to a woman in... a very, very long time, he realized. Jordana was close enough that he could smell the shampoo in her hair, jasmine and apples. No perfume to dilute the scent either, just her natural aroma, which he was finding quite heady.

They walked down to the shelter on the shore of the tiny "lake" that gave the area its name. The full moon was halfway up in the sky, shining over the lake, reflected in its surface. The only flaw to the setting was the sodium security lights set up around the recreation building.

"It's pretty," Jordana said. Then, she winced in pain again.

"Okay, that's it," Gideon said. "I'm taking you home and see what we can do about this."

"It's... okay," Jordana gasped. "It'll pass."

She groaned again and doubled over.

"Step away from the girl," said a deep, accented voice.

"Bugger off," Gideon snarled as he wrapped a protective arm around Jordana's shoulder.

The speaker stepped out of the shadows that had been concealing him. "I am afraid, *señor*, that I cannot do that."

Gideon glanced at the man. He was taller than Gideon and heavily muscled. His eyes were unusually dark, the white almost completely obscured by black iris. Most disturbing of all, though, was the glint of steel in the man's hand.

"Look, pal, I'll give you the hundred bucks in my wallet, but you really don't want to pick a fight with me," Gideon growled.

"*Señor* Shaw, it is noble that you want to protect the girl, but *she* is our objective, not your money," the big man said in a rather reasonable tone.

Gideon didn't like the sound of that "we" or the fact that they knew his name. He heard a scuff to his left. The second man was larger than the first, and he was lazily swinging a *macuahuitl*, of all things, in one hand. The weapon was of Aztec origin, a sword-like wooden club edged with sharpened obsidian blades. Anecdotal evidence suggested that the weapon could behead a man.

"Last chance, fellas. If you know who I am, then, you know I'm not somebody you want to mess with," Gideon said.

A snicker to the right alerted him to the presence of a third man, this one just as dark as the other two, but smaller. He was balancing a throwing knife on the tip of one of his fingers.

"You are a college professor, recently discharged from the American Navy, one of their vaunted commandos, yes?" the leader chuckled. "We are not impressed, of course."

"Because you three are so badass?" Gideon chuckled.

He watched the leader's eyes. Color flashed through the irises, going from black to amber and back again. He nodded to himself and took a deep breath. Scents flooded his nostrils.

"Gideon, I feel weird," Jordana moaned.

"That is your power coming into its own, *señorita*," the leader declared. *"¡Para la gloria de la Palabra Oscura!"*

Gideon laughed. "Are you serious?"

The leader smiled. "Deadly serious."

"No, I mean, are you serious that you really don't know who I am?" Gideon laughed. "You're Dark Word assassins, and you don't know who *I* am?"

"Gideon!" Jordana screeched as she bent double. Then, she straightened up, her eyes glowed blue, her teeth had elongated, and new hair was sprouting rapidly from her skin.

"The change!" the Dark Word leader snapped. "Jorge!"

The knife thrower raised a tube to his lips and blew. The dart never connected with Jordana. Gideon plucked it out of the air, spun, and threw it back at Jorge. The dart impacted Jorge's left eye. The small man cried out in pain and spun away.

"Leave the girl be," Gideon growled. "Your fight is with me!"

The leader snarled, his face taking on a feline cast. "Kill him!"

The big man with the *macuahuitl* came in swinging. Gideon stepped into the man's attack, blocking the blow with his left arm, and pounding his right fist into the big man's face. He followed up with a series of elbow strikes, and finished up by throwing the big man into his leader even as that man was trying to grab Jordana.

Jordana had fallen to the ground, her body rippling unnaturally. Clothing ripped as her body stretched and compacted. Nails became hardened claws, teeth sharpened and elongated. Her jaws stretched out into a muzzle. Hair was becoming fur. Her form was still roughly humanoid, but becoming less human by the moment.

Gideon scooped up the *macuahuitl* that he'd forced from the big man's hands, casually slinging it out into the lake. His arms were rippling, too. Hair sprouting, teeth sharpening, claws growing.

The leader shoved his man off him. "Get the girl," he spat in Spanish. "I will deal with this one."

Gideon rolled his neck, joints popping as he did so. "You just don't get it, do you? *Soy el lobo malo grande.*" He chuckled. "*The* big, bad wolf."

The leader's eyes narrowed. He pulled another knife from a sheath on his belt. Both blades glinted silver in the moonlight. "If that is true, *Señor Lobo*, I will gain great honor within the order for killing you."

"Bring it," Gideon snarled. He was no longer entirely human. He'd grown several inches taller and bulkier, his clothing torn to rags around his changing form, and his head and face had become more wolflike than human.

The Dark Word leader attacked. He feinted at Gideon's muzzle. Then, he drove the blade in his other hand straight at Gideon's heart. Gideon took the blow to his snout. The cut was shallow and closed up on its own in seconds. His clawed hand caught the assassin's wrist, blocking the thrust to his chest. The other hand came up, claws splayed and raked the assassin's side.

With a snarl of pain, the assassin twisted with the blow. Then, he yanked himself free of Gideon's grasp. The feline cast to his face was more pronounced now. He reached down and touched his side where Gideon's claws had scored him. His fingers came away bloody. Gideon half-snarled, half-smiled and wiggled his claw-tipped fingers.

Jordana howled as the big Dark Word assassin grabbed her. She'd completely changed shape -- no longer human, mostly animal, canine. She snapped her jaws, gnashing her teeth at the big assassin. He lifted her from the ground. She squirmed, struggling for freedom, maddened with fright. Her twisting brought her around just enough to let her sink her teeth into the assassin's shoulder. This time, *he* howled, in pain, but he kept his grip.

"Tlaloc!" he screamed to his leader. "*¡Ayudame!*"

"Shoulda brought more men," Gideon ground out through his less-than-human visage.

He lunged at the leader, Tlaloc, catching each of the man's wrists in one of his own claw-hands. Gideon pulled up and apart, darted his head in, and tore out the assassin's throat. A second bite severed the head. Gideon pulled again on Tlaloc's arms, ripping them from the sockets. The assassin's knives were still grasped in the hands.

Jordana was gnawing on the remaining assassin's shoulder as he tried to get her under control, but she was too large and too strong for him. He never saw Gideon bury the two knives into his back. He dropped to the ground with a sigh. Jordana broke free of his weakened grip and danced out of the way on all fours, her form now entirely wolfen. She snarled at Gideon who was quickly reverting to his human form. He made a shushing noise.

"Jordana, it's alright. You're safe. Just relax," he cooed. "Remember who you are, Jordana. Remember!"

The wolf snorted once, like a sneeze. Then, she shivered and collapsed. Quickly, she began reverting to her human form again. "What?" she managed to mutter.

"System shock. The change burned up a lot of your energy," Gideon said as he wrapped the remnants of his jacket around her shoulders. "Fighting for your life didn't help."

"Oh," Jordana said. "Huh?"

"Just... sleep," Gideon said. He pulled a capsule from his pocket and popped it under her nose. A tiny cloud of dust burst forth. "Sleep."

Jordana's eyes glazed over. "Okay," she sighed and passed out.

CHAPTER EIGHT

Atlanta, Georgia, USA
Magee House, Belle Arbor Plantation
Covington, GA
October 24, 2010

Consciousness didn't come back to Jordana all at once. The first thing she realized was that she was in a very big, very comfortable bed with high-thread-count sheets that felt wonderful against her skin. Then, she snapped fully awake when she realized she was feeling the sheets against *all* her skin

"Oh, my god, I'm naked!" she exclaimed sitting up in bed, the sheet and comforter falling away.

With a yelp, she grabbed the sheet and pulled it up to her neck. She looked around. This room was definitely not hers. The bed she was in was a big four-poster with a canopy, an *actual* canopy! The bed's linens and comforter were all pink, as were the gauzy curtains over the windows through which sunlight was streaming. The floors were hardwood, polished to a shine, but big Persian rugs were laid out. Besides the bed, the room contained a big chest-of-drawers, a dressing table and chair, a wardrobe, and a pair of wingback chairs with a little table between them, all made from the same type of wood as the bed. The whole bedroom suite had been made to match.

Jordana looked around at the walls. They'd been painted a light shade of pink to match the bedclothes and the curtains. Framed paintings adorned the walls. Most were landscapes or still lives of flowers or bowls of fruit, but a couple were portraits. One portrait was of a young woman with dark hair and striking green eyes. Jordana judged from her clothes that the girl must have lived during Civil War times or earlier. Another portrait caught Jordana's eye. It was a family sitting, a man with the beard and sideburns typical of the Civil War period, dressed in a Confederate officer's uniform, with a woman and the girl from the other portrait, their similarity of appearance making her think mother and daughter, and a younger man, also dressed in a Confederate uniform. Except for the thick beard, he was the very image of Gideon Shaw.

"Are you sure about that?"

Jordana's head whipped toward the door on the far side of the room. The voice had been muffled, but she'd heard it clearly enough. It was masculine, but oddly high-pitched. She didn't recognize the voice.

"Yes, I'm sure." That voice belonged to Gideon. "Just... just do it, Knobs."

"As you command, Master," the other voice, Knobs, replied with a kind of chuckle-cackle.

"You're not as funny as you think you are," Gideon said.

"Yes, I am," Knobs chuckle-cackled again.

Jordana almost jumped a second later when somebody softly rapped at her door.

"May I come in?" Gideon asked.

"Uh, okay?" Jordana replied as she grabbed the comforter and wrapped it around her, too.

Gideon came into the room and smiled. "Good morning. How do you feel?" he asked as he crossed over to the wardrobe.

"Uh, slightly nauseous and very confused," Jordana replied.

"That's understandable," Gideon replied. He opened the wardrobe, extracted a thick white robe, and brought it over to Jordana. "You had a, er, rough night."

He turned away so that Jordana could pull the robe on without him seeing anything. "Mind telling me why I'm naked?"

"Your clothes got... well, they got shredded by the change," Gideon replied.

Jordana had the robe half on when he said that. She stopped and stared in shock. "So... That really happened? I really... I mean... I'm a... *werewolf?*"

"Well, technically speaking, you're a therianthrope, a shapeshifter, but considering that your instinctive alter form was canine... Yeah, you're pretty much a werewolf," Gideon said. "*Mazel tov.*"

"You think this is *funny?*" Jordana snarled as she wrapped the robe around herself and belted it tightly. She jumped out of the bed.

"No," Gideon said. "Well, maybe. A little." He turned around. "You didn't know, did you?"

"Know what?"

"That you're a thrope," Gideon said. "You're not adopted are you?"

"No!" Jordana snapped. Then, she frowned. "At least, I don't think so. I mean, I look like my mom and all..."

Gideon ran a hand through his hair. "Well, adoption or your thrope parent being... I don't know... unaware, might explain why you weren't prepared, but it doesn't explain why this didn't happen earlier."

"What do you mean?"

"You're born a thrope. That whole 'bitten by a werewolf, turning into a raving monster every full moon' schtick is pure Hollywood. One or the other of your parents is a thrope, maybe a grandparent, and then, the gene expresses itself at puberty. You hit thirteen or fourteen, and, boom, add shapeshifting to the laundry list of teenage angst inducing problems in your life," Gideon said. "The fact that you, my dear, went through your first change in your late teens, early twenties is... odd. It indicates that something else is at work in your genes."

"So, lycanthropy is genetic?" Jordana said.

"More or less, but you're not a lycanthrope. You're a therianthrope. Just because a wolf is your totemic form, doesn't mean it's your only form," Gideon said.

"What?" Jordana exclaimed.

"Let's have a seat," Gideon suggested with a wave toward the wingback chairs.

The upholstery of the chairs was a deep, plush red velvet, which was a sharp contrast to how the rest of the room was decorated.

"This is a very pink room," Jordana groused as she settled into one of the chairs. "I hate pink."

"It's my sister's old room, and I kinda hate pink, too," Gideon admitted, "but this is the closest room to mine."

"How long have I been asleep?"

Gideon looked at his chronograph. "Uh, about eight and a half hours. You were pretty tired."

"You roofied me!" Jordana exclaimed.

"No, I applied an inhaled healing draft. It has a mild sedative component, but not enough to render you unconscious. *That* resulted from the change and the fight. You burned up a lot of energy changing. Always do the first time. It'll come easier as time goes by," Gideon said.

"How do I get rid of it?" Jordana demanded.

Gideon sighed. "You don't."

"How. Do. I. Get rid of it?!"

"What color are your eyes?" Gideon asked.

"What?"

"Your eyes. What color are they?"

"Brown."

"Your hair."

"It's brown, too."

"Straight or naturally curly?"

"Straight. What's this about?"

"How tall are you?"

"Five-five and a half. Start making sense," Jordana growled.

"Okay, your parents combined their DNA to create a five-foot-five-and-a-half-inch tall young woman with brown eyes and straight brown hair. Now, you can't change any of that. You can cover it up. You can wear heels to make you look taller; you can put in contacts that change your eye color, and you can bleach your hair blond or dye it red, but underneath that, you're still the five-five-and-a-half, brown-eyed, brown-haired woman that your parents brought into this world," Gideon said. "Being a shapeshifter is like being... white or female."

"I'm half-Latina," Jordana said as she rubbed her hands over her face.

"And I'm half-Welsh," Gideon chuckled. "My mother was a werewolf. My father is... complicated, but he's a shapeshifter, too. I grew up knowing that I was different from the other boys in the village. *They* couldn't turn into a wolf and go running through the forests at night, hunting rabbits, and just reveling in the sweet poetry of *running*."

"You're a werewolf, too," Jordana said. "I remember now, you changed, but it was... different."

Gideon chuckled. "Yeah, well, I've been doing this for a long time. I'm a shapeshifter, not just a werewolf. Physical form to me is a matter of what I will it to be."

As he spoke, Gideon's face changed. First, his skin darkened and his features became somewhat broader until he looked like his friend, Charlie. Then, his skin became sallow, his eyes took on an almond shape, and he'd become an Asian version of himself. Finally, he returned to normal.

Jordana's jaw hung open. "How did you do that?"

"Same way I got to Carnegie Hall," Gideon replied. "Practice."

Jordana gasped suddenly. "Oh, my god! Those men!"

"Are not going to hurt you," Gideon said. "I promise."

"I... I think I killed one of them," Jordana groaned. "I remember... *biting* him. He was... grabbing me, and I just... I just wanted to be free... to..."

"Run?" Gideon asked softly.

"Yeah," Jordana said.

Gideon chuckled. "That's the wolf spirit in you. Wolves *love* to run, especially with their pack. Very social animals, wolves. Just like people that way, I suppose."

"Who were they, and... what happened to them?" Jordana said.

"They were Jaguar Warriors, specifically assassins for *La Palabra Oscura*," Gideon replied.

"Let's pretend I have *no* idea what you're talking about," Jordana said.

Gideon chuckled. "I don't exactly want to overwhelm you." He sobered slightly. "The Dark Word is a secret society, a sort of Al Qaeda network of demonic doomsday cults. Depending on which sect we're talking about, they worship a variety demons and/or dark gods that are intent on sundering the Veil of Shadows and ushering in an Apocalypse like something out of an episode of 'Buffy the Vampire Slayer' or just sowing chaos for chaos' own sake."

"Please tell me you're kidding," Jordana sighed.

"God, how I wish I was," Gideon snorted. "These nihilistic, chaos-loving, demon-worshiping assholes have been a pain in my ass since... Jeez, since before that painting was done," he said pointing to the family portrait on the wall.

Jordana snickered a little laugh. "Look, I get that you're older than me, but you're not *that* old."

"How old do you think I am?" Gideon asked.

"I don't know, I thought maybe you were in your early twenties, but I've kinda figured out that you're probably somewhere in your thirties," Jordana said. She smiled slyly. "You, ah, look really good for your age, by the way."

Gideon blushed slightly. "Thank you, but you're kinda way off."

"Am I?" Jordana said.

"Yeah, you see, uh, thropes don't age like our mundane human cousins," Gideon said. "Typically, a thrope's life span is anywhere from thirty-five to seventy percent longer than that of a mundane human with access to the same level of nutrition and medical care."

"Okay, so, you're what, then, eighty or a hundred years old?" Jordana said.

Gideon grinned shyly. "Uh, yeah, that'd be about right if I was a typical thrope, but I'm atypical, like my father."

"The, uh, 'complicated' shapeshifter," Jordana said.

"Yeah," Gideon said. He stood up and walked over to the portrait. He pointed to the young woman. "My sister, Rebecca," he said. He moved his finger to the woman beside her. "This is Becca's mother, my father's last wife, and, pretty much the finest woman I've ever known, Amaranth Magee." He smiled fondly at her. "As stepmothers go, she was the best." Then, he moved his finger to the older man. "This is my father, Gilchrist Shaw."

"Wait, like the Gilchrist Shaw the chapel is named after?" Jordana exclaimed.

"The very same," Gideon replied. "I didn't lie when I told you he was my ancestor. What I didn't mention was the fact that he's my ancestor by one generation."

"And that's you, isn't it?" Jordana guessed as she got up and joined him at the painting.

"Yes, ma'am," Gideon replied. "We sat for this portrait right before Daddy and I went off to join Company B of the 18th Georgia

Volunteer Infantry. He was a captain, and I was attached as medical officer."

"Medical officer?" Jordana repeated.

"I graduated from the Medical School of Harvard in 1857," Gideon said.

"Shut up! You're a doctor?" Jordana exclaimed.

"Well, technically, you could say that my license to practice medicine expired some time ago," Gideon chuckled.

"Hold on," Jordana said. She closed her eyes for a moment as she did the math in her head. "Assuming you were twenty-five when you graduated from medical school, you'd be... uh, one hundred and seventy-nine years old!"

"A logical assumption, but wrong," Gideon said. "My sister, by the way, is a hundred sixty-nine, but I only bring the exact number up on her birthdays to irritate her."

"Then, how old are you?" Jordana asked.

"When I was a teen, I was with my father to greet John Knox when he returned to Scotland from Geneva," Gideon said.

"Who's John Knox?" Jordana asked.

"Uh, he's the priest who pretty much founded Scottish Presbyterianism," Gideon said. "As a young man, I carried a pike and fought for James Stewart against his sister, Mary, at the Battle of Langside."

"Wait, you mean 'Mary, Queen of Scots' Mary?" Jordana said.

Gideon nodded.

"But she lived in the 1500's, didn't she?"

"Yes, ma'am," Gideon said. He smiled. "I'll be five hundred years old this coming Valentine's Day."

"That's... that's..." Jordana stammered.

"Impossible?" Gideon offered.

Jordana nodded.

"Yeah, it would be if I weren't my father's son, which means that I'm effectively immortal," Gideon said.

"I think I need to sit back down," Jordana replied.

"Information overload?" Gideon asked as he led her back over to her chair.

"Maybe just a little," Jordana chuckled as she settled back down in her chair. "Dude! You're older than America!"

"No, just the United States," Gideon said. "Columbus discovered America in 1492. That was just a few years before I was born."

"Is that your real accent, even?" Jordana asked.

Gideon laughed. "Yes, more or less. I've lived here so long that I've picked up the accent." He cleared his throat. "I kin still tool aboot wi' th' Highland brogue when th' mood takes me," he burred. He shifted back to his natural voice. "I'm pretty handy with other accents, too."

Someone knocked on the door. Then, the door swung open and a short man walked in. He was dressed in a black butler's suit with a tray balanced in one hand and a bundle tucked up under his other arm. He was chubby with a round head and fat cheeks, and a long, hooked nose. His skin was pale and a little blotchy, and his mousy brown hair was somewhat disheveled.

Jordana blinked. Suddenly, the little butler looked different. His blotchy, pale skin was suddenly *green*, and his hair had become black with shiny green highlight. His ears had elongated into points, and the teeth he was grinning at her with were all sharply pointed.

"Holy cow! What are you?" she shrieked.

"Knobs, I thought you'd glamoured yourself," Gideon growled.

"I *did*, Master, but the young mistress Saw through it," the butler replied. "She has the Sight, she does." He cackle-chuckled. "Oh, very interesting. *Very* interesting!"

"Dude, what are you?" Jordana demanded.

"I, Mistress Jordana, am the butler," the creature replied as he placed the tray down on the little table between the chairs. "My name is Philemon Knobs, by the by. You may call me 'Mr. Knobs' or just 'Knobs' if you like, and while you are in this house, I am at your service."

Knobs bowed deeply before Jordana. Then, straightening up, he presented her with the bundle that had been under his arm. "Master Gideon asked me to fetch you some clothing. None of Mistress Rebecca's clothing would be... appropriate, but Mistress Agamdeep's clothing is of a size with yourself, if a bit dated fashion-wise."

Jordana accepted the bundle. "Thank you, Mr. Knobs."

Knobs nodded gracefully. "Shall I pour, sir?"

Jordana glanced at the tray and realized that it was a tea service.

"Please, Knobs," Gideon said with a small smile.

"Dude, seriously, what are you?" Jordana repeated. "Besides a 'butler'?"

Knobs cackle-chuckled again as he poured tea into the two cups on the tray. "I thought a chamomile would be more appropriate, soothing to the nerves as it is, but Master Gideon prefers black tea. I compromised with a lovely rooibos, a red tea from Africa. Milk or cream?"

"Uh, milk," Jordana said.

"Lovely," Knobs replied. "One lump or two?"

"Are you gonna hit me?" Jordana asked.

Knobs laughed. "A connoisseur of cartoons, I see. No, Mistress, sugar."

"Two," Jordana said.

Knobs glanced at Gideon. "I like her. She's funny. The usual, sir?"

Gideon nodded. "Thank you, Knobs."

Knobs picked up one of the cups and handed it to Jordana. "My species, Mistress Jordana, is goblin."

"I thought goblins were... you know... uh, monsters?" Jordana said.

"Says the neophyte werewolf," Knobs snorted.

"Touché," Jordana admitted.

"Goblins are fairy creatures, what we call 'wild fae'," Gideon explained. "They usually are under the sway of Unseelie Ard Sidhe, serving them as warrior slaves, but here, on this side of the Veil, they have free will and can choose to be Seelie instead."

"Who and what?" Jordana said.

"The Ard Sidhe are the High Ones, what you'd think of as 'elves'," Knobs said. "Seelie and Unseelie are, basically, good and evil elves. In the world of Faerie, which lies parallel to this Earth, all intelligent beings, of which there are many, are ruled by the Ard Sidhe. If your lord is Seelie, you are Seelie. If Unseelie, so are you. No choice, no will."

"That's... awful," Jordana said.

"Which is why we Fae creatures try so hard to pass through the Veil to be here. Here, we can enact our free will," Knobs said. Then, he sighed. "Not always for the better, though." The goblin butler picked up the other cup and passed it to Gideon with a sad smile. "I was not always a butler, Mistress, but Master Gideon's father took pity on me, treated me with mercy, showed me a better way to live. Now, I serve his family." He drew himself up, straight, chest swelled with pride. "Now, I am Seelie because I *choose* to be Seelie." Then, he winked at Jordana. "I also choose to be Baptist because it irritates Master Gilchrist deep down in his Presbyterian soul."

Gideon chuckled. "When you get to know my dad, that will actually be kind of funny. Well, on second thought, probably not. He's gotten downright Pentecostal in his old age."

"A veritable snake handler," Knobs chuckle-cackled.

"Yeah, this is that locational humor. You know, you just had to be there," Jordana said.

"Oh, she's a sharp one, Master," Knobs giggled. He bowed to Jordana again. "I will take my leave, Mistress, but should you need me, wherever you are in the house, just speak my name, and I will come to you in seconds."

"What, like teleporting?" Jordana said.

"Teleporting, moving *really* fast, it's all the same to me," Knobs said with a shrug. He bowed again, and blurred away.

Gideon chuckled at Jordana's expression. "Uh, goblins aren't like the wussy little critters you see in popular fiction. They're actually some of the most powerful Fae around. That's why the Unseelie Lords like them."

"Wow," Jordana sighed.

"Yep, with ole Knobs watching over you, you'll be safe," Gideon said. He drained his tea cup in one long pull. "Look, there's a bathroom right through there. Why don't you enjoy a nice, long shower, use all the hot water you want, and when you've changed clothes, come find me in the music room, and we'll continue our talk."

"Uh, how do I find the music room?"

"Just ask Knobs."

"Okay."

"I've got to check on a couple of things," Gideon explained.

"Gideon, what happened to those men, those Jaguar Warriors?"

Gideon frowned. "I killed them. It's what I do to those Dark Word assholes whenever I find them. So, don't you worry about them. They can't hurt you."

"But more will come, won't they?" Jordana guessed.

"Very likely," Gideon admitted.

CHAPTER NINE

Atlanta, Georgia, USA
Magee House, Belle Arbor Plantation
Covington, GA
October 24, 2010

The bathroom was tiny. Jordana guessed that it must have been added at some point after internal plumbing became widely available. Maybe it had been a closet or a dressing room at one time. Now, it held a sink with a postage stamp-sized counter, a toilet, and a stand-up shower. The whole arrangement was very modern. A towel and washcloth were already laid out, and Jordana found shampoo, soap, and a razor in the shower. A toothbrush, toothpaste, and a roll-on deodorant were laid out on the tiny counter next to the sink. She'd stayed in hotels that were less well-equipped for guest's needs than this tiny bathroom.

Taking Gideon's suggestion to heart, Jordana stood under the hot water for a long time, her mind churning through what had happened to her in less than two days, how upside down and inside out her world had suddenly become. After a few minutes, she shook off the funk and cleaned herself up. When stepped out of the bathroom, she saw that the bed had been made, and the clothes that Knobs had given her were laid out on top of the coverlet.

"Vintage" came to mind as she looked at the outfit. The shirt was a Rolling Stones concert tee from their 1965 British Tour. The pants were bell bottom blue jeans decorated with little flower patches. A Wal-Mart bag containing underwear and socks rested atop a box with a new pair of Converse tennis shoes. The shirt was a little big on her, but the jeans fit almost perfectly.

Once again fully clothed, Jordana walked to the door and stepped into the hallway beyond. "Uh, Mr. Knobs?"

"Yes, Mistress?" the goblin butler replied from just beside her.

Jordana jumped. Knobs *had not* been there a second ago.

"Apologies, Mistress," Knobs said. "I did not mean to startle you."

"Oh, it's not just you, Knobs," she sighed. "Uh, I'm supposed to meet Gideon in the, er, music room?"

"Certainly, Mistress. I will escort you," Knobs said. "Follow, please."

"You don't have to call me that," Jordana said as she fell into step with the goblin. "Uh, 'Mistress' I mean."

"Ah, but I do, Mistress. I am, after all, a servant," Knobs replied. "If the term makes you uncomfortable, I could call you 'Miss', if you prefer."

"Or we could just be friends and you could call me 'Jordy' like all my other friends do," she suggested.

"I would happily consider you a friend, just as I do Master Gideon, but I'm afraid it is quite impossible for me to use a... nickname," Knobs said. "I am under a *geas* that prevents it."

"A, uh, 'gay ass'?" Jordana repeated.

Knobs snorted another one of his cackle-chuckles. "That's pretty close. No, more like rhyming with 'vase'. It is a... taboo? A curse, maybe? Among Fae kind, the 'gifting' of *geasa* is common. They are... constrictions against the potentially unlimited power at our command."

"So, you are prohibited from using nicknames?" Jordana said.

"Yes, quite so," Knobs replied.

"What if a person is introduced to you by their nickname?" Jordana asked.

"I would be able to use the nickname until I gained knowledge of their full name, and then, I would be unable to use the nickname again," Knobs replied. "It gets tiresome, Miss Jordana, but I don't mind. It's less odious than some *geasa* I've encountered."

"Like what?" Jordana asked.

Knobs shook his shaggy head. "A... litter mate of mine... was compulsed to consume human flesh in order to maintain his strength."

"Um, ew," Jordana said.

"Rightly so, Miss Jordana. Rightly so," Knobs nodded.

The goblin butler had led her down the hallway to a grand staircase.

"Where... I mean, what kind of house is this? And where is it?" Jordana asked.

Knobs paused at the top of the stairs. "The house is called, simply, 'Magee House', and the estate is called Belle Arbor Plantation. We are just beyond the city limits of Covington, but within the Newton County line."

"Magee House," Jordana repeated.

"Yes, named so for Mistress Amaranth, Master Gideon's stepmother. Though he was considerably older than she when his father married her, Gideon does often call her his 'second mother' and 'the mother of his heart'," Knobs explained. "We are currently on the second floor. Above, the third floor is given over to servants' quarters. That is where I live. This floor is the family's apartments. The ground floor contains the kitchen, the grand dining room, the library, the music room, the drawing room, and several other rooms I neither know the name or purpose of, and I've lived here for two hundred years!"

Jordana giggled.

Knobs offered her his hand. "Shall we continue, Miss?"

"Sure," Jordana replied taking the goblin's hand. "Say, what ever happened to your... brother?"

"Litter mate," Knobs corrected. He waggled his head back and forth as he led her down the stairs. "It is difficult to explain. I should say, the words come to me, but the concept is quite... alien to humans, even other Fae. Goblins are neither male nor female for most of their lives. When permitted to breed, some assume... female genitalia, and a smaller number are permitted to become male, to impregnate the females. Once the young are born, in litters of little neuters, the male and female goblins revert to their natural neuter state. The same goblin can be both mother and father during its lifetime."

"You don't seem... female to me," Jordana said.

"The male form is best suited for war and labor, Miss, no offense to your gender, and so the goblin neuter gender is more masculine than feminine, but surely you've noticed the lovely high octave of my voice," Knobs cackle-chuckled. "Miss, *your* voice is deeper than mine!"

"I didn't want to say anything," Jordana giggled.

"Ah, you are a kind girl, truly you are," Knobs giggled with her.

At the bottom of the stair, they came into the grand foyer of the great house.

"This is so beautiful," Jordana exclaimed as she looked around. Then, she stopped. "Hey, nice trick distracting me from my original question."

"Thank you, Miss Jordana," Knobs said with an impish grin. Then, he sighed and grew quite sad-looking. Jordana's heart melted for the monstrous creature who was quickly becoming one of her favorite people. "As I said, my litter mate was compulsed to consume human flesh. I... stopped him."

"I'm sorry, Knobs," Jordana said.

The goblin smiled, and even though his teeth were crooked, jagged, and looked quite lethal, Jordana felt the genuine warmth and kindness of the smile. "You are a good girl, Miss Jordana. I feel this in my heart," he said patting his back side.

"Your heart's in your butt?" Jordana gasped.

"Gotcha!" Knobs cackled.

"Oh, you booger," Jordana laughed.

"Are you feeling better, Miss?" Knobs asked.

"Considerably," Jordana admitted. "Must have something to do with the company."

"Oh, such a good girl," Knobs cackled.

Knobs directed their journey toward the front of the house. Jordana could hear voices coming from one of the rooms. The door they were heading toward opened suddenly. An almost perfectly round black woman came trundling out, shaking her head, a smile splitting her dark face as she came. Then, she spied Knobs and Jordana.

"Knobs! Why din you tell me the girl was unnerfed!" the woman belted out. "Laws, girl, you need some meat on dem bones! You hungry?"

"Uh," Jordana stammered.

"O' course, you hungry! You a wolf, girl! Wolves always hungry!" the woman boomed.

"Bernadette, you are frightening Miss Jordana," Knobs said. "Miss Jordana, this is Bernadette Cook, our... cook."

"Sweetie, you sure are a sight fo' sore eyes," Bernadette said taking Jordana's hands in her own warm, callused paws. "We gettin' worried-like that Gideon never get out. Well, other than to run crazy with that Matt character. Him a bad influence!"

"I heard that!" Matt shouted from the room Bernadette had just vacated.

"I know!" Bernadette shouted back. "I is LOUD!" She winked at Jordana. "Gots to keep dese boys on dey toes. I makin' a big lunch, but I'll bring you a snack, okay?"

"That would be... nice," Jordana said.

"We put some meat on you bones, girl. Get you fed up right," Bernadette promised.

Then, the big woman was gone in a hustling, bustling whirlwind of intent.

"Is she...?" Jordana asked.

"Mundane. Completely and utterly normal," Knobs said. "But her family has served the Shaws since Gilchrist bought her ancestors' entire family to keep them from being separated and then granted them their freedom."

"So, she's normal, she knows what's going on, and she's okay with it?" Jordana said.

"Yes, but Bernadette grew up knowing about the hidden world," Knobs said. He knocked on the door.

"Come in, Knobs," Gideon called out.

Jordana gasped when she entered the music room. It was bathed in sunlight from big windows on two walls. The other two walls were stacked with instruments and shelves of music books, CDs, even old fashioned vinyl records. Several guitars were set on stands along the wall by the windows, and in the very middle of the room was a grand piano. The biggest, most beautiful grand piano Jordana had ever seen. For her, the piano was love at first sight.

Matt Einarsson was standing with Gideon by one of the windows. The big man turned with a grin when he saw Knobs. "Dobby!" he shouted.

Knobs rolled his eyes. "Bernadette is right. You *are* a bad influence."

"Aw, you love me," Matt said. "Just admit it. You'll feel better if you do!"

"Kiss my verdant gluteus maximus," Knobs said with a grin.

Gideon snorted a laugh.

Matt just grinned. "Told you the little guy loves me." He then sized up Jordana. "Damn, I remember that shirt!"

"Matt," Gideon warned.

Matt rolled his eyes. "That was a frickin' awesome concert! I bought Aggie that shirt so we'd have matching clothes." The big man came over to Jordana, took her shoulders in his meaty hands, and turned her back and forth. "Aggie had bigger boobs, but you look damn good in that shirt, kiddo."

Jordana leaned around Matt. "Can I hurt him?"

"Feel free to try," Gideon said. "But I warn you, his obliviousness is like plate armor. On a battleship."

"It's true," Matt agreed. "I'm dense like dark matter."

"Wow, you're actually hard to stay mad at," Jordana giggled.

"Yeah, it's part of my charm," Matt guffawed. Then, he sobered a little. "Good to see you made it through your first change, kiddo." He nodded his head back toward Gideon. "Drives some people around the bend."

"I'll let Knobs kick your ass," Gideon growled.

"Oh, please, Master, may I?" Knobs asked bouncing from foot to foot, clapping his hands merrily.

"Is this place an asylum?" Jordana asked.

"Feels like it some days," Gideon admitted. "Matt, go bother Bernadette for a while, okay?"

"My plump love muffin? Don't have to ask me twice," Matt laughed. "Come on, Dobby. We're gonna check on lunch."

"I should never have given you those books for Christmas," Knobs grumbled.

"No, you probably shouldn't have," Matt agreed as he draped a comradely arm across the goblin's shoulder. "Do me favor and don't die like the real Dobby."

"I'm not an elf, you jackass," Knobs sighed as the door closed behind them.

"You should see them do Abbot and Costello's 'Who's on First' routine," Gideon chuckled. "Matt's right about one thing, you do look good in those clothes. I'd kind of forgotten what a flower child Aggie was."

"Your ex-wife," Jordana said.

Gideon nodded. "You're the only person outside my family that knows I was married recently. Relatively speaking."

"When did she die?" Jordana asked.

"Nineteen Seventy-two," Gideon replied. "Dark Word agents killed her."

"No wonder you hate those guys," Jordana said.

Gideon shrugged. "Just kinda refined the hate, but it was already there."

"Why are they interested in me? Were they really after you?" Jordana asked.

"No, you were their primary goal," Gideon said. He snorted. "They didn't even know who I was. About the only person higher on their 'we'd like you dead' list is my dad."

"Family business?" Jordana teased.

Gideon laughed. "Something like that." He waved her over to the piano. "You play?"

"Yes," she sighed as she sat down on the bench in front of the piano. "Oh, baby, where have you been all my life?"

Gideon laughed as he sat down next to her and lifted the cover off the keyboard. He ran his fingers over the keys and played a quick scale. Then, he started playing "Chopsticks."

Jordana laughed. "Okay, how long have you been playing?"

"Since, uh, 1745," Gideon replied. "I like these new pianos much better than the originals. Sound quality is vastly improved." He switched to "Für Elise."

"Wasn't the piano invented in, like, 1700?" Jordana said, joining him and playing along on her end of the keyboard.

"I think so, but I didn't encounter a proper piano and a proper teacher of the piano until 1745," Gideon replied.

"You're pretty good," Jordana said.

"I've been playing longer than there's been a United States. I should be good by now, or at the very least proficient," Gideon snorted. "I had to learn to entertain myself long before there was cable TV and the Internet, and I only sleep about four hours a day."

"Why do we sleep so little?" Jordana asked.

Gideon shrugged and switched to something more upbeat. Jordana recognized the tune from Marc Broussard's album.

"Well, I have a theory," he said. "It has to do with the Demon War."

"The what?" Jordana said.

"Ever heard of Atlantis?"

"Who hasn't?"

"Well, Atlantis was a colony from Faerie. The Ard Sidhe that Knobs was telling you about? They're human, or close enough as to make no practical difference. So, these Fae humans, elves if you like, come to Earth, set up a colony. Rival elves from a rival enclave do the same. The two colonies start duking it out, okay?

"In the middle of all this hostility are the native, essentially powerless humans. The Ard Sidhe get real tired, real quick of dying for their war, so they recruit mundane humans. They pose themselves as gods or angels or what have you, con the cave men into fighting for them, and send their new proxies off to die for them.

"Eventually, one side or the other escalates and starts summoning demons as weapons, but demons tend to turn on their summoners. So, demonic energies are bound into human slave warriors, the first Weapons. The Weapons are really efficient at killing, well, pretty much everything. They rarely sleep; they're ruthlessly efficient, and they're pretty much psychopathically in love with killing.

"Then, some Weapons get it into their heads that they're human. Their main target has been the populations of unaltered humans, their own kin, and that pisses them off. They mutiny. The Ard Sidhe start summoning wild Fae as well as demons to fight their former slaves. In short, they make a big freaking mess of everything. Eventually, God steps in. If you've been to Sunday school, you may know this part. He floods the planet, washes away everybody. What you don't hear is that a lot of that flooding is caused when He smites Atlantis with a meteor. Boom! The Veil of Shadows just sort of pops up, and the demons can no longer be physically summoned.

"You don't sleep too much, and you turn into a wolf or wolf-like creature because you're a Weapon, a relic of a war that ended before the world as we know it existed," Gideon said. "That's the short version."

"I'm a weapon?" Jordana stammered.

"Capitalized, but, yeah," Gideon said. He stopped playing. "You didn't turn into a dove or an alpaca. You turned into a wolf, a predator. You heal incredibly quickly, your senses are abnormally acute, and you're significantly stronger and faster than your mundane friends. You do have a choice, though."

"I do? What choice?"

"Well, are you gonna be a wild wolf, that raider of livestock and scourge of the farmer, or are you gonna be that domesticated wolf, the one that protects the sheep instead of preying upon them?" Gideon asked.

"Can't I be both?" Jordana said with a feral grin.

"The question is: are you gonna be a good dog or a bad dog?" Gideon chuckled in reply.

"I want to be a good dog, I guess," Jordana said. "Does this mean I have to be housebroken or something?"

Gideon laughed. "No, but we will have to work on teaching you to control the change and to use the wolf, not let the wolf use you."

"I'm oddly cool with that," Jordana said.

"We also need to figure out why those Dark Word morons are after you," Gideon said. "Knowing them, it involves a dark ritual for summoning one of the Ancient Elders' material form into this world."

"That would be bad?" Jordana guessed.

"Assuming a scale of one to ten, with one being finding a half-eaten cockroach in your salad and ten being the Holocaust, that would be somewhere north of nine hundred," Gideon said. "That's the goal of just about every Dark Word plot. At least the ones that we've found out about."

"You're right. They *are* a bunch of assholes," Jordana said.

Knobs stuck his head in the door with a knock. "Master, Deputy Parker is here."

Gideon jumped up and headed for the door. Jordana followed in his wake. Just inside the front door was a young white man dressed in the brown and khaki uniform of a county Sheriff's deputy. Gideon shook hands with the officer.

"What's up, Tim?" Gideon asked.

"We cleaned up your, uh, mess at the park," Deputy Parker said. He shook his head. "They really picked the wrong guy to mug."

"Is that what you're writing it up as? A mugging?" Gideon asked.

"No, we're writing it up as a bear attack. Extremely rare, but known to happen, and since it happened to some drug-running, South American cartel-types, definitely an Act of God situation. Don't worry, our department knows how to hush this kind of thing up," Parker replied.

"Did you get the tox report on that dart?" Gideon asked.

Parker nodded. "It was laced with a pretty heavy dose of belladonna."

Gideon rubbed his chin. "Thanks, Tim."

"No problem," Parker said. "Hey, it could've been a couple of mundane deputies who tangled with those guys. Last thing I need is Jaguar Warriors running loose, drawing attention to the community."

The men shook hands again, and Deputy Parker left.

"Belladonna's a poison," Jordana said.

Gideon nodded. "It also prohibits the change in thropes. Our bodies can handle toxins far better than a mundane human can. So, a poison that would kill a normal person, immobilizes us and keeps the change from happening. The change is our primary offensive capability."

"So, they were gonna dope me up with poison, carry me off to God knows where, to do God knows what," Jordana said throwing her hands in the air. "That's just... peachy!"

"Look on the bright side," Gideon said.

"What bright side?"

"At least it wasn't *my* fault our first date was a disaster," Gideon said.

"You're trying to make me laugh," Jordana frowned.

"Is it working?" Gideon asked.

"No, try harder," Jordana pouted.

Gideon grinned. "Now, *you're* trying to make me laugh?"

Jordana grinned back. "Is it working?"

"You're handling this quite well, young Miss Quinlan," Gideon said.

Jordana shrugged. "No, I'm really not. I'm hearing things that are far away like they're up close, and I'm... *smelling* stuff that I've never smelled before. Oh, yeah, and I'm a freak!"

"You're in good company," Gideon pointed out.

"Yeah, Knobs is great," Jordana said with a wink.

"Oh, that hurts," Gideon chuckled. "Let's see how Bernadette's doing on lunch."

CHAPTER TEN

Atlanta, Georgia, USA
Magee House, Belle Arbor Plantation
Covington, GA
October 24, 2010

The kitchen was at the back of the big house, and at some point had been remodeled into a modern marvel of culinary preparation. The kitchen at Skinner's wasn't nearly as well equipped as the one at Magee House. Bernadette stood at the stainless steel range stirring something in a big pot. The scents hit Jordana's nostrils and made her mouth water and her stomach growl. Matt and Knobs sat at a big kitchen table. The table space between them was littered with colorful cards. They were arguing some point of the rules in whatever game they were playing. Jordana noticed her purse sitting on one end of the table.

"Hey! I thought I'd lost that," Jordana exclaimed.

"Uh, no, actually, Matt went over your stuff with a fine-tooth comb," Gideon said.

"What? Why?" Jordana stammered.

"Well, those Jaguar Warriors had to find you guys somehow, didn't they?" Matt drawled.

"How? Did they magic my stuff?" Jordana said.

"No, they put a bug in your phone," Matt replied.

"Technology? Not magic? I'm very confused again," Jordana groaned as she sank into a chair and started going through her belongings.

"Yeah, well, magic is a kind of technology," Gideon said. "What makes it 'magic' is that you don't know how it works. Imagine how a Cro-Magnon man would react to a Bic lighter."

"Better yet, ya ever seen one of those Penn and Teller specials where they explain how the illusions work?" Matt said.

Jordana nodded.

"Well, it's always a combination of showmanship, misdirection, and clever engineering, and magic is like that. It's clever engineering with built-in showmanship," Matt said.

"The irony," Knobs added, "is that Penn and Teller are Mages."

"They're what?" Jordana exclaimed.

"Humans born with the innate talent to perform real magic," Gideon said. "They're not fireball-tossing wizards, but they *are* master artificers and enchanters. Uh, they build magical machines and objects."

"Misdirection," Matt chuckled. "They hide the fact that real magic exists by debunking stage magic. Clever wizards."

"So, it's a secret? I mean, werewolves, wizards, goblins, and... stuff," Jordana said.

"It's an 'open' secret," Gideon replied. "We can't completely hide that creatures like us exist, but there are organizations out there, as well as individuals like Penn and Teller, who... hide the secret in plain sight."

"Oh, that weren't nothin' but a skunk ape," Bernadette said in a pretty good imitation of a stereotypical southern accent. "An' Elvis done come down in his flyin' saucer an' took me to Graceland in space, hallelujah!"

"People, mundanes, don't *want* to believe that vampires and werewolves and other monsters stalk the night. They want to believe that their world is sane and safe and normal," Gideon said. "Of course, that works for us, too, because most of us creatures of the night just want to be left alone. We've got jobs and mortgages and taxes just like any of those mundanes. We *really* like the idea of our neighbors *not* coming for us with torches and pitchforks."

"Most paranormals aren't as powerful as the four of us in this room, either," Matt added. "The bulk of our community are of... diluted stock."

Jordana frowned. "What does that mean?"

"It means they're more human than not," Gideon replied. "Remember, the original Weapons, the monsters of legend, were created from humans. They had human souls and human love. Those that could mated with humans and sired generations more of humans. Every once in a while, a monster would be born to an apparently normal human family, but for the most part, even then, the child was still more human than not."

"Is that what I am, some kind of genetic freak? A throwback to an earlier generation?" Jordana asked.

"It would explain why your parents never prepared you for the change," Gideon replied. "It wouldn't explain, though, why the change happened so late. Bernadette, do you have any rosemary in your spice rack?"

"Don't you go using up all my good spice!" Bernadette warned.

"Just need a pinch," Gideon promised. "Knobs, fetch me some mistletoe, will you?"

"Of course, Master," the goblin said. He glared at Matt. "I have a photographic memory, Matthias. I'll know if you messed with my cards."

"Are you calling me a cheater?" Matt demanded.

"No, I'm implying that you're a cheater," Knobs said.

"Oh, well, in that case," Matt said with a little wave.

Knobs did his *blurring* thing again. Suddenly, he was standing next to Gideon with a sprig of mistletoe.

"Thank you, Knobs," Gideon said.

"Of course, Master," Knobs said with a smile and a nod.

Gideon went over to the kitchen's cutting table, took a knife, and started cutting the berries off the mistletoe. He placed them in a pestle, sprinkled them with rosemary, and started grinding them together.

"What's he doing?" Jordana asked.

"Something either herbal or alchemical," Matt replied. "That's his own personal brand of magic."

"Huh?" Jordana said. "I'm getting tired of saying that, but huh?"

Matt chuckled. "Gideon is one of the Wise, a wizard, but his magical talent is in potions and enchanting objects. He's probably cooking up some spell to help him figure out what's going on with you."

Bernadette set a bowl down in front of Jordana. "In da meantime, girl, you need to eat."

"Oh, my god, that smells good," Jordana said, nearly drooling. "What is it?"

"My own secret Brunswick stew recipe," Bernadette replied. "The secret be that I shred the meat instead of dicin' it."

Jordana dug into the stew with a will.

"Hey, where's mine, love muffin?" Matt whined.

"You hush up, Matt Einarsson! You almost five hundred year ole, and you whine like you still five!" Bernadette scolded.

"But... I'm hungry," Matt whined again. "And I love you and your cooking more than anything in the whole wide world."

"Don't you be flatterin' me!" Bernadette growled, but she set a bowl down in front of him anyway.

"Thank you, Bernadette!" Matt said in a childish sing-song.

Knobs just rolled his eyes.

Jordana giggled around a mouthful of the best Brunswick stew she'd ever eaten. She managed to swallow her current mouthful before declaring, "This is delicious! What's in it?"

"Pork, tomatoes, potatoes, sweet corn, few secret spices and ingredients," Bernadette replied. She leaned down and whispered in Jordana's ear. "The pork come from a wild pig Gideon hunted."

"As a wolf?" Jordana asked.

"No, he used a thirty-aught-six," Matt replied. "Not that he hasn't done the whole wolf-shape hunting thing before, but this time, it was a hunting rifle. We had Charlie along, and we couldn't really... you know."

"Charlie doesn't know?" Jordana said.

"No, why burden the guy with it?" Matt said. "He practically worships Gideon as it is. Hey, did you try his Shepherd's Pie?"

"Uh, no, we had Angus steaks," Jordana replied.

"Oh, dear lord, those are good steaks," Matt said.

"You think about food a lot, don't you?" Jordana said.

"I'm a simple guy. Good food, good fight, and I'm happy," Matt chuckled.

"Simple mind, too," Knobs teased.

"That's me, Simple Matt the Viking Moron," the big man guffawed.

Bernadette set a bowl of stew down in front of Knobs. "Un-huh. Right. Now, where did you go to college, recently?"

Matt blushed. "MIT."

"Right, right," Bernadette said. "An' where you go to school 'fore that?"

"Cal Tech," Matt sighed.

"You the best educated idiot, ain't you?" Bernadette said matter-of-factly. She shook her head at Jordana. "These boys just like playin' like they stupid, but they not. Matt tutored me in math and calculus. Gideon, there, he taught me chemistry. Knobs, here... Well, he not book smart, but he cute."

"Dobby got burned!" Matt laughed.

"She said I was cute, and you're still a jackass," Knobs replied.

"Are my cadre of jesters keeping you entertained?" Gideon asked as he joined them.

"Quite," Jordana chuckled. "What's that?"

Gideon held up a small bowl. "This is a fairy detection spell. Or it will be once the final ingredient is added."

"And what's the final ingredient?" Jordana asked.

"I need a drop of your blood," Gideon replied.

"Come again?" Jordana exclaimed.

"If you have Fae blood, it will react with the potion, and it'll answer one of our questions: why your change happened so late in life," Gideon said.

"Fae age more slowly than their mundane human counterparts," Knobs said.

Jordana sighed and held out her left arm. "Make it quick," she squeaked.

"I just need a drop, not your whole arm," Gideon chuckled. "Besides, watch what happens."

He had a small, sharp knife in his hand. He held the point against Jordana's thumb and pricked it. Jordana's eyes widened. She barely felt the cut. Gideon squeezed out a drop of blood. As Jordana watched, the tiny cut sealed up. Then, it healed as if it'd never been cut.

"Whoa!" Jordana exclaimed.

"Werewolf metabolism," Gideon said. "Same reason you're always eating. Now, don't think this means you're indestructible. You're not. Just nearly so."

"Cool! I'm a superhero," Jordana laughed.

"Check it out," Gideon said showing her the paste. It had started glowing. "Well, we now know that one of your parents is Fae, possibly even one of the Sidhe."

"So, are you gonna mix up another potion to find out?" Jordana asked.

"No, I figure we could just do a DNA test, but I don't have the equipment for that kind of testing here, and it also doesn't answer *why* the Dark Word wants a hybrid werewolf/Sidhe," Gideon said.

"The bio lab at the university would work," Matt suggested.

"It's Sunday. Lab's closed on Sunday," Gideon mused.

"You're faculty," Jordana said. "You could get in, you know."

"Yes, but it would be noticed," Gideon said. "I think we should avoid drawing attention right now. I think the answer is in your parents. I should meet them."

"Whoa, moving kinda fast there, aren't we, Professor Dog Breath? This was just our first date. I don't want to introduce my parents to my *five-hundred-year-old boyfriend*."

Gideon grinned. "So, you think I'm your boyfriend?"

Jordana blushed. "Shut up."

"I bet they need her to still be a virgin for whatever sacrifice they want to use her for," Matt said. "I mean, that would be typical, wouldn't it?"

"Matt, don't go there," Gideon growled.

"Sorry, buddy, but you're gonna have to take one for the team," Matt said.

"Oh!" Jordana exclaimed and blushed even darker than she had before when she realized what Matt was getting at.

Bernadette walked up behind Matt and swatted him in the head with a wooden spoon. "Knobs right. You a jackass."

Matt rubbed his head where Bernadette had smacked him. "Yeah, but I'm right."

"The rub of it is that he really is correct," Knobs sighed. "By, er, 'removing' Miss Jordana's, uh, virginity, you would effectively nullify her usefulness in most summoning rituals."

"Yeah, because I always dreamed that I'd lose it to protect myself from being sacrificed to Cthulu," Jordana snapped.

Gideon, Matt, and Knobs stared at her.

"I've read more than just a Harlequin novel," she groused.

"Dude, Lovecraft is kinda intense," Matt said. "Even by our standards."

"And shockingly accurate at times," Knobs agreed.

"That doesn't make me feel better," Jordana said.

"It's also irrelevant. They may not care if she's a virgin or not," Gideon said. "There may be something unique about her blood that they need or even her specific life force."

"And that makes me feel even less better," Jordana sighed.

"It gets worse: what if what they want is your body?" Gideon said. "What if you're the result of a program to breed the perfect host for whatever demon lord of the week they want to summon?"

"I think I just lost my appetite," Jordana moaned.

Bernadette's spoon cracked against the back of Gideon's head. "I just got the girl eatin' and you go and ruin it!"

Gideon glared at the cook for a moment. "Okay, first, ow. Second, I still sign your paychecks. Third, Jordy, *none* of that is gonna happen to you. I won't let it. I promise."

"And you always keep your promises, don't you?" Jordana said.

"Yes, ma'am. I certainly do try."

CHAPTER ELEVEN

Atlanta, Georgia, USA

Mercy University "BOH" Row

Garden Manor

Covington, GA

October 24, 2010

"So, is it safe for me to come back here?" Jordana asked as she stared out the Jeep's window at the big house she shared with her friends.

Gideon took a deep breath and sighed. "I don't really know, but I'm sure you'd rather have some of your own things rather than borrowed clothes from the ex-wives storage closet."

"Wait: ex-*wives*?" Jordana said giving Gideon a hard look.

"I've been married three times," Gideon said. "My first wife was an arranged marriage. Her name was Fiona, her father was an Irish baron, and she was... a very nice girl."

"In other words, she was unattractive," Jordana guessed.

"Plain, but very sweet. She wanted to make the best of a bad situation, and I was grateful for it. I even came to love her in time, to *want* to have a family with her," Gideon said. "We never had any children, though. She... died of complications during a miscarriage."

"Oh, I'm sorry," Jordana whispered.

"It was a very, very long time ago. The sort of situation that wouldn't happen nowadays with what we know about neonatal care," Gideon said. "I was barely twenty when we got married, kind of old to be a bachelor for the time."

He fell silent.

"And your second wife?" Jordana prompted.

"About a hundred years later," Gideon said. "I was in Italy at the time. Her name was Rufina. She was from a poor fishing village."

"Was she pretty?" Jordana asked.

"Very," Gideon chuckled. "And completely mundane. I was a 'wealthy' foreigner, which kind of gave me an edge over the other men in the village, and she agreed to marry me."

"What happened?" Jordana asked.

"She found out I was a werewolf, gave me an hour's head start, and then informed the village priest and the Inquisition. The marriage was annulled, and I never saw her again. I hear that she married a Venetian wine merchant, got fat, and had lots of babies," Gideon said.

"That's hardly fair," Jordana declared.

"Life rarely is," Gideon sighed.

"Yeah, I get it," Jordana sighed. "Guess we'd better get this over with."

"Remember the cover story?" Gideon asked.

Jordana nodded. "It's close to the truth: somebody tried to kidnap me last night. We were with the police for hours. You're taking me to the airport, and I'm going home for a few days while the police straighten this mess out."

"You forgot the part where I'm your hero for rescuing you," Gideon said with a grin.

"No, I didn't. I just don't want you getting a fat head," Jordana grinned back.

"Okay, let's do this," Gideon said.

Jordana noticed Gideon adjusting the handgun he'd brought with him.

"Is that really necessary?" she asked.

"It's a tool," Gideon said. "Right tool for this particular job."

"Guns are just... icky, I guess," Jordana said.

Gideon grinned. "You've never shot a gun, have you?"

"No," Jordana said.

"I think I know what our second-date activity will be," Gideon said.

"Yeah, I haven't decided if you're getting a second date yet or not," Jordana said.

"Oh, come on, I'm being all 'white knight in shiny armor' here! Doesn't that get me any consideration?" Gideon said.

"No." Jordana strode away.

"Hurtful," Gideon snickered to himself.

"What do I tell Tammy and Evan about... you know?" Jordana asked as they approached the front door.

"Whatever you want, but consider whether or not you want to turn their world inside out the way yours has," Gideon suggested.

"I don't want to lie to them, and Tammy lives with me. She's going to notice something is different," Jordana said.

"If you think she can handle the truth," Gideon shrugged.

"Okay, but not right now. We deal with this Dark Word thing first," Jordana said.

Tammy was waiting for them in the foyer. "Dude, I was kidding about having her back before classes tomorrow. Where have you been, and this had better be the best first-date story, *ever*, or I'm getting the cops involved."

"They already are," Jordana said.

"What?" Tammy exclaimed. "Hey, what happened to your clothes?"

"Uh, well, somebody tried to kidnap me while we were out. The police took my clothes, for evidence, and Gideon gave me these. He's been great, by the way. Saved my life," Jordana explained. "Look, I'm... I'm kinda... I really can't get into it right now, but I'm going to go home for a couple of days while the cops straighten this all out."

"Oh, sweetie!" Tammy exclaimed wrapping Jordana in a big hug. "Would you like me to do anything for you?"

"Just, you know, let my professors know that I won't be in classes this week. Gideon is taking me to the airport," Jordana said.

As soon as Jordana was headed upstairs, Tammy turned on Gideon. "What happened?"

"Three men attempted to grab Jordy while we were at Turner Lake Park last night," Gideon said.

"And you fought them off?" Tammy smirked.

"There were only three of them," Gideon smiled back.

"Really?" Tammy was unconvinced.

"Yes, really," Gideon replied. "I have a black belt in Kung Fu, and I was a SEAL once upon a time. Three thugs aren't much of a challenge for me."

"Oh," Tammy said.

"There's a Sheriff's Deputy, Tim Parker, he may be coming by at some point to interview you guys about whether or not you've seen anybody... unusual in the neighborhood. You might want to make sure that you and the other girls travel in groups just in case," Gideon said.

"Jeez, as if it weren't scary enough just being a girl in college," Tammy sighed.

"The world is a terrible place," Gideon agreed.

"Is Jordy okay? She gonna be okay?" Tammy asked.

"Yes, she is," Gideon said. "I'm gonna go with her, watch her back." He took a business card from his pocket. "If anything happens, this is Deputy Parker's card. Just give him a call, okay?"

"Okay," Tammy said, taking the card and staring at it.

"Right. I'm... I'm just gonna go check on Jordy," Gideon said pointing.

"Yeah, see, you claim to be a bad ass, and then you get all stammery and dorky," Tammy snarked.

"Ever see a little movie called 'Road House'?" Gideon asked.

"Patrick Swayze, doesn't dance but plays a bouncer-slash-philosopher-slash-martial artist," Tammy said.

"Yeah, he said something in that movie that I believe was a little nugget of wisdom. He tells his men to be nice until it's time to *not* be nice. I'm a dork. Until it's time to *not* be a dork," Gideon said with a wink. Before Tammy could respond, he dashed up the stairs.

The landing at the top of the stairs held a small kitchenette and a bathroom. The two bedroom suites were on either side of the landing. Jordana was in the room on the left. She was rapidly stuffing clothing into a large duffel-like fabric suitcase. A travel bag of cosmetics and toiletries followed suit. Jordana glanced up from her task to catch Gideon leaning in the doorway watching her.

"Is that how you get your jollies? Trying to get a glimpse of my delicate unmentionables?" Jordana said with a small smile.

"I've already seen your unmentionables... and everything else," Gideon replied with a grin. "But I assure you I acted in a medically professional manner to ascertain if you were injured in any way. I took no pleasure from it."

"Right," Jordana scoffed.

"Hurtful," Gideon said. Then, he chuckled. "I've never seen a woman pack as fast as you do."

"Are you saying that I'm atypical in your experience?" Jordana asked as she began to rummage in her closet.

"Entirely. Between three wives, five girlfriends, a sister, and numerous cousins and nieces, *you* are the fastest suitcase packer I've ever seen," Gideon said. "Aggie would pack for a weekend like she was preparing for a campaign across the Alps."

"Okay, the *five* girlfriends are a discussion for another time, but I'd like to know about Wife Number Three," Jordana said.

Gideon heaved a sigh. "You're like a dog with a bone. No pun intended."

"Quit stalling," Jordana said.

"Her name was Agamdeep Freeman. Her father was a British ex-pat, and her mother was Indian. Bernard, her dad, was a member of the Myrddin Council, a wizard, the 'shooting fire and lightning from his fingertips' kind, but I met Aggie while I was studying at Oxford back in 1965. Your shirt, it's from our first date. Matt was there ostensibly as my, er, 'wingman' to be her roommate's date," Gideon said with a smile as his mind drifted back. He shook himself. "Aggie and I got married in 1967. Moved to Mumbai, and I went to work for her dad. Then, one day, couple years later, Bernard discovers that the Dark Word was trying to resurrect the Thuggee Cult and summon the demoness Kali."

"You stopped them," Jordana said.

"Yes, ma'am, but doing it cost me my wife and my father-in-law," Gideon said.

"I'm sorry to hear that," Jordana said. She stepped over to Gideon and wrapped her arms around him, hugging him tightly. "I'm so very sorry."

Gideon hugged her back. "You can probably understand how motivated I am to keep you alive. I refuse to let these bastards have anyone else I care about."

Jordana pulled back and smiled at him. "I know."

Their faces were barely an inch apart. The kiss just happened naturally. It wasn't a face-chewing, tongue-dueling, trying-to-swallow-the-other-person kind of kiss, just a simple touching of lips. However, both of them felt as if they'd just been hit by a bolt of lightning. Having been struck by lightning before, Gideon knew that this was much, *much* better.

"Um, wow," Jordana sighed.

"Er, yeah, uh, I, ah, I think I gotta go remember some, ah, baseball box scores or something," Gideon stammered. "Yeah, that'll have to do until I can get a cold shower."

Jordana giggled. She started to pull Gideon toward her for a second kiss when Micky Dumont, her other housemate, came pounding up the stairs, shouting, "Jordy!"

Jordana felt Gideon stiffen up. For some reason she was reminded of how her dog acted when a stranger came to the house. "Uh, hey, Micky," she said, pulling, reluctantly, away from Gideon.

"I just heard what happened from Tammy. Are you alright?" Micky demanded.

Jordana nodded. "Yeah, I'm fine, but I, uh, think it might be best if I went home for a couple of days while the cops straighten everything out."

"Oh, sweetie," Micky cooed and wrapped Jordana in a hug. Jordana wrinkled her nose. Something smelled... off, but so much but so much that she smelled now was so different or so intense. She just ignored the smell and hugged her friend back.

Gideon, however, had barely restrained his instinctive tactical urge to pull and use the Glock in his waistband with sheer will and centuries of strategic training. He observed the other girl closely. She was a year or so older than Jordana, but she was similar in features, olive skin, high cheeks, brown eyes and hair. The two might have passed for sisters. He'd smelled the same thing Jordana had, but he recognized the scent for what it was, but he couldn't act on the knowledge. Not yet.

"Oh, uh, Micky, this is Gideon," Jordana said by way of introduction.

"Professor Shaw!" Micky exclaimed.

"Miss Dumont," Gideon replied with a nod.

"You know one another?" Jordana said with a confused frown.

"Sure, Professor Shaw was Doctor Turner's assistant when we went to South America for Anthro-Sociology 201 this past summer," Micky said.

"Yes, I remember having a bad headache for most of that trip," Gideon said with smile that he didn't feel pasted to his face.

Jordana could feel that something was off, but she didn't want to say anything in front of Micky. "Look, I'm flying out tonight, but I should be back by next weekend."

"Oh, really? You're flying?" Micky said.

"Yeah, I'm taking Jordy to Hartsfield-Jackson. She's taking AirTran Flight 860, should have her home by 10:30," Gideon supplied.

Jordana glanced at him, but just nodded agreement. "Yep. That's it."

"Why so late?" Micky asked. "It's only, what, three in the afternoon now."

"Gotta stop by the Sheriff's office, and, then, there's airport security to deal with," Gideon said. "Personally, I'm looking forward to the full-body scan, but I might decline for a pat down if the TSA guard is cute."

"Ha, you're funny." Micky turned to Jordana. "Call me as soon as you get there, okay?" she insisted.

"Sure will," Jordana said.

Micky gave Jordana another hug before going into her room and closing the door behind her.

Gideon turned and grabbed Jordana's bag in his left hand. "We're going," he said. "Now."

Jordana started to ask what was wrong, but Gideon shook his head. Downstairs, Jordana repeated the same flight information to her other friends, accepting hugs and well wishes from Evan and Zeb, even bleary acknowledgments from Willie and Ron. Ariel started to cry, but Tammy took charge of the other girl and shooed Jordana and Gideon out of the house.

The whole time Gideon kept glancing up, occasionally sniffing the air. Outside, halfway to the Jeep, Jordana demanded to know what was going on, but Gideon wouldn't answer. He just placed her bag in the back of the Jeep, told her to wave to her watching friends, and then hustled into the car.

"How long have you known Micky?" he asked as he maneuvered out of the neighborhood.

"I've known her since my freshman year when she was our rush advisor at Tri-Gamma Sorority," Jordana said. "We hit it off, even though I didn't pledge Tri-Gam."

"Okay, the girl that I met in South America, the one who took Turner's wacky, party-hearty field trip? That... *thing* that lives across the hall from you *ain't her*," Gideon said.

"What the hell?" Jordana exclaimed.

"Not entirely sure what it was, but it... *reeked* of undeath," Gideon said. "Didn't you smell her?"

"Yeah, I smelled something... I don't know... bitter? Rotten? But not," Jordana stammered trying to grasp words to describe smells she didn't know.

"Like decay caught on the verge, frozen in time," Gideon supplied.

"Yeah, I get that," Jordana said.

"That's undeath," Gideon said.

"Like a vampire?" Jordana guessed.

"Sort of, but not," Gideon replied. He shook his head. "Okay, I told you that thropes were designed to be weapons, right? Well, we were designed to fight a number of different demons that would inhabit... vessels, usually dead bodies. These demon vessels would be inhabited by a number of different kinds of demons, but what they all had in common was that they required life force to keep their bodies from rotting, and that life force could be taken through a number of mediums. Some ate flesh, some drank blood, and some just sucked it right from a victim's mouth.

"Thropes were patterned on demons called barghests that could shapeshift. The difference between them and us is that we were *alive*, and they were undead, but thropes weren't the only Weapons. Those ancient Ard Sidhe also created beings in the image of the ghouls, incubi, and succubi, the ones that fed on flesh and blood and breath."

"Vampires are Weapons like werewolves?" Jordana guessed.

"The living ones are," Gideon replied. "In Eastern Europe they coined the term 'dhamphir' for living or 'half-vampires.'" He glanced over at Jordana. "Your friend Micky has been replaced by something undead, but not a vampire."

"What?"

"Don't know, but I don't like it," Gideon said.

Instead of turning south toward the interstate, he turned north.

"I thought we were going to the airport," Jordana said.

"We are. Just not the one I told them we were going to," Gideon replied.

They passed a sign directing them to the Covington Municipal Airport. Jordana nodded. "Okay, I get it. You laid a false trail."

"Yes, ma'am."

"Just in case Undead Micky is a Dark Word agent."

"Seems likely," Gideon sighed.

"No, no, no," Jordana groaned. "Not Micky! Wait! What about the others? Are they safe?"

"For the moment, probably," Gideon said.

"I really hate 'probably'," Jordana said.

"Me, too," Gideon said. "Me, too."

They rode the rest of the way to the airport in silence. The Covington Municipal Airport was a collection of buildings and hangars and two runways. It didn't even have an air traffic control tower. Some of the buildings belonged to companies that provided maintenance services for small aircraft. One building was for a skydiving school.

"I've always wondered about that," Jordana murmured.

"About what?" Gideon asked.

"Skydiving," she replied.

"I can teach you," he offered. "If you like."

"You skydive?" she said with a raised eyebrow.

"Not recreationally," he replied. "But I was a SEAL and jumping out of perfectly good airplanes is one of the things they trained us to do."

"Is it scary?" she asked.

Gideon shrugged. "Not to me, but I can turn myself into a bird or a bat if something goes wrong and just fly down on my own."

"That's... handy," Jordana giggled.

"It's never happened, and I'm assuming that I wouldn't be too panicky to consciously reshape my body to the desired form," he said. "I've really only tried the bird thing under controlled conditions, but I'll teach you that, too, if you'd like."

"Cool," she said.

Gideon parked the Jeep next to an old Pontiac GTO beside a hangar at the far end of the airport. Jordana glanced around as she got out of the car. Most of the planes were single-engine prop jobs, little planes not much bigger than a family car. A couple of the planes were twin engine jobs and marked with the logo of the skydiving school. The incongruous plane was a small executive-style jet sitting in the hangar where they'd parked. A black Chevy Suburban was parked in front of the hangar. As she and Gideon approached, the driver's side door opened, and a tall, beautiful woman dressed in a business suit got out. Gideon handed Jordana her suitcase.

"I'll be just a minute," he assured her.

The woman in the suit smiled at Gideon, and Jordana felt a sudden stab of jealousy.

"Good to see you again, Sir," the woman said.

"Same here, Raven," Gideon replied before giving her a hug and kissing both cheeks. "Been too long."

"That it has," Raven agreed, her smile never wavering.

This new person, Raven, was taller than Jordana, almost of a height with Gideon. She was blond and curvy and just too damn good-looking in Jordana's opinion.

Raven had a folio with her that she opened up and rummaged around in for a moment. "Here are your credentials," she said as she came up with a leather wallet. "Bob went ahead and reactivated your status, fixed your background records to match your, er, current appearance."

Gideon nodded his head toward Jordana. "She knows how old I am," he said.

"Really?" Raven said. "I've known you most of my life, and you've *never* admitted your real age to me."

"Fella's got to have a few mysteries to keep the ladies interested," Gideon chuckled. "Besides, she tortured it out of me."

"Sure," Raven snorted. "Okay, your permits are in order, and we've laid down a trail of false flight plans. I have a couple of glamoured agents who'll be posing as you at the AirTran terminal just in case these guys decide to do something there. Matt is already on the plane. Your pilot is a new guy named Perkins. He's pretty competent, but he's also all the backup we can provide you."

"I've got Matt. I don't need much more backup than that," Gideon said. "You need to get an agent onto her house. They've replaced one of her roommates with some kind of undead doppelganger."

"Which roommate?" Raven asked.

"Michaela Dumont," he replied. "Don't know what kind of undead she is now, but she fairly reeks of the scent."

"Only to a thrope's nose," Raven chuckled. "I'll personally look into it." Raven snapped her fingers. "I almost forgot." She reached back into the SUV and handed Gideon a laptop. "Your new threat matrix database. It's loaded with all the latest intel we have on paranormals, abnormals, supernaturals, and various groups, organizations, and even individuals of interest."

Gideon accepted the laptop with a grin. "And what are the junior agents calling it nowadays?"

"Uh, somebody got started calling it a, uh, 'pokedex' and it kinda stuck," Raven replied.

"Dear Lord, you kids just keep getting younger and younger," Gideon laughed.

"It's not as bad as the guys from the 80's who still insist on calling it the 'Monster Manual'," Raven retorted.

"We called it the 'Monster Manual' back in the 40's, too. Probably where Gygax got the idea from," Gideon chuckled. "Thanks, Raven."

"Okay, well, look, I know this is totally unprofessional, but do me a favor and don't get yourself killed, okay?" Raven said as she suddenly hugged Gideon.

"No promises, kiddo, but I always do my best," Gideon said as he hugged her back. "You know me, I'm nigh indestructible."

"Yeah, it's that 'nigh' part that always worries me," Raven chuckled as she released him. She turned her attention to Jordana. "You do what Agent Shaw tells you, Miss, and you'll be fine, and don't worry about your friends. I'll make sure they're all safe."

"Uh, sure," Jordana growled.

Raven nodded, gave Gideon a quick peck on the cheek. Then, she got into her Suburban and drove off.

"She one of the ex-girlfriends?" Jordana demanded more hotly than she intended.

"Raven?" Gideon exclaimed. Then, he started laughing. "You're jealous of *Raven*?"

"I'm not jealous," Jordana growled.

"Yes, you are. You're jealous," Gideon teased. He took her suitcase, and still laughing, strode over to the plane.

Matt was stepping out of the passenger hatch as Gideon approached.

"What's so funny?" he asked.

Gideon nodded toward Jordana. "She's jealous of Raven," he said.

Matt threw back his head and howled a laugh.

"Somebody had better start explaining real fast, or I'm getting all wolf-bitch on both of you," Jordana said.

"Raven is..." Gideon searched for the right words for a moment. "Okay, legally, you could say that she's my daughter since I adopted her and raised her from when she was about seven years old, but she's really my..." He paused for a moment to calculate... "great-great-great-great-great-grand-niece. I told you about my brothers, Dylan and Llew, but my father has had a few more children over the years, most of them fairly mundane. Only my brothers, myself, and my sister inherited any measure of Father's immortality. Those mundane half-siblings are the source of those nieces and cousins I keep mentioning."

"So, she's... I mean, this Raven is..." Jordana stammered.

"My one and only little girl," Gideon chuckled.

"I think I need a drink," Jordana said.

"More information overload?" Matt asked.

Jordana just nodded.

"Well, let's get your luggage stowed, and then you'll have a couple of hours to rest during the flight," Gideon said.

"Okay," Jordana said.

Matt chuckled as he helped her into the plane. "You're doing fine, little bit. Handling this whole thing better than anybody else I've ever met in the same situation."

"You've been in this situation before?" Jordana scoffed.

"Darling, me and Gideon are close to five hundred years old. Ain't a whole lot we ain't seen at least once already," Matt said. "So, we've kinda got standard operating procedures in place. Of course, we also got a standard operating procedure for when we run into something really new."

"Yeah, what's that?" Jordana asked.

Matt's answering grin was feral. "When in doubt, set it on fire."

CHAPTER TWELVE

Orlando, Florida, USA
Leesburg Municipal Airport
Leesburg, FL
October 24, 2010

The cabin of the jet was more like a comfy living room with seatbelts than what Jordana had expected. Once they were in the air, she'd taken Gideon's suggestion, stretched out on the couch and gone to sleep. Just before arriving at their destination, Gideon had shaken her awake and suggested that she buckle in for the landing.

"What time is it?" she yawned.

"About a quarter to six," he replied. "Sleep alright?"

Jordana nodded. She felt surprisingly refreshed. "Am I gonna sleep even less now than I did before?"

"Yes and no," Gideon said. "It depends on how much shifting you do, whether or not you work any magic, if you can learn magic. But I know a few thropes who hardly ever shift, maybe once a month to celebrate the full moon, and they usually sleep four to six hours a day. Whenever I use a lot of energy to shapeshift or work a spell, I'll wind up needing a solid eight hours. Results may vary, as the packaging says."

Jordana stretched. She caught Gideon staring at her. She smiled.

Gideon shook his head. "Really, really gonna need a cold shower."

She just laughed and buckled herself in. Gideon smiled back.

The plane descended and touched down with little if any bounce. Ground personnel directed the small jet to a private hangar where the engines shut down. The silence was odd after the constant hum and vibrations of the flight. The pilot stepped out of the cockpit.

"Gentlemen and lady, we have arrived," he said.

The pilot, Perkins, was a short, slender man dressed in black slacks and a white uniform shirt with sky-blue tie. He wore dark aviator sunglasses, which he pulled off to reveal all black eyes. His longish blond hair had streaks of green through it. A scruffy little chin beard completed his punk-like personal appearance.

Jordana cocked her head to the side as she considered the pilot. The eyes and the hair could be explained by contacts and dye, but she just *knew* it was natural. "What are you?" Suddenly she blushed. "I'm sorry. That was rude."

"No offense, ma'am," Perkins said with a toothy grin that revealed several sharp teeth. "I'm paranormal, but only barely. My mother is part sprite, and my dad is just plain human. About all I inherited from her is my good looks. My mad skills on the control stick is all Dad."

"Who's your dad?" Gideon asked.

"Jeremiah Perkins, Sir," the pilot replied.

"I knew a Jeremiah Perkins once. Flew Spitfires for the RAF," Gideon said.

"My grandfather, Sir," Perkins said. "Been a Perkins involved in some facet of aviation since the Wright Brothers took flight at Kitty Hawk."

"Glad to see you've kept up the family tradition," Gideon said. "Now, if you'd be so good as to blend in again, see if the vehicle we arranged for has been delivered."

"Yes, Sir," Perkins said with a salute.

When he put his sunglasses back on, the green streaks disappeared from his hair, and he looked just as normal as the next person. He nodded to Jordana before exiting the plane.

"That was pretty cool, the thing with the sunglasses," she said.

"Yeah, it's actually pretty easy to build a glamour into an article of clothing," Gideon said. "I do it all the time. I've even got some clothes that I've enchanted to shapeshift with me."

"Now, that sounds like something I'd like to have," Jordana chuckled.

She noticed for the first time that Gideon was wearing a business suit. The suit was dark charcoal in color with a white shirt and a maroon tie. A tiny American flag was pinned to his lapel. A noise attracted her attention to the back of the cabin where Matt was bringing forward some luggage. He, too, was dressed in a dark suit, white shirt, and a black tie.

His long hair hung loose, but he'd carefully combed it back and behind his ears.

"How do I look?" he said with a grin and a wink as he passed by.

"Like somebody did an excellent job of stuffing a gorilla into a cheap suit," Jordana replied.

"Cool. Just the look I was going for," Matt chuckled.

"Nobody ever expects the goon to be smart and observant," Gideon said. "He stands in the background looking all kinds of menacing, and people will generally ignore him while he's observing everything."

"So, what's with the suits, and why did... er, Raven call you 'Agent' Shaw?" Jordana asked.

"Because we *are* agents," Gideon replied showing her the credentials he'd been given. The badge and ID identified him as Supervisory Special Agent Gideon Shaw of the Federal Bureau of Investigation. "Only we're not *actually* FBI agents. That's just cover."

"So what are you agents of?" she asked.

"Well, it's gone by many names over the years. Currently, the agency calls itself the Washington Program," Gideon replied.

"Like 'Washington, D.C.'?" Jordana guessed.

"Only indirectly," Matt replied as he passed between them on his way to the back of the plane.

"Did you know that George Washington, while he was still just 'General' Washington, was also America's first spymaster?" Gideon said. "He successfully ran a ring of spies during the Revolution."

"I did not know that," Jordana replied.

"Well, here's something else you didn't know: some British necromancer sent a vampire to assassinate Washington with the blessings of the Crown," Gideon replied.

"What? Really?" Jordana exclaimed. "Okay, so, obviously the vampire didn't kill him, right? Or was our first president a vampire?"

Gideon chuckled. "No, he was mundane. A great man, but mundane, perfectly normal. He was saved by a Seelie knight and a couple of thropes."

"Were you one of those thropes?" Jordana asked.

"No, but my Dad was," Gideon replied. "He's still kinda old-fashioned in a lot of ways. He pledged his fealty to Washington and the American cause, and ole George decided that people in general didn't need to know about paranormals, abnormals, or supernaturals beyond their already well-entrenched superstitions, but he also decided that *all* Americans needed to be protected from monsters like the vamp that nearly killed him. So, he started a secret agency with my dad, the Seelie knight, and any other volunteers who wanted in. The Program is the modern version of that first circle of protectors that George Washington himself commissioned."

"I thought you were just a college professor," Jordana sighed.

Gideon laughed. "I am, but I'm also several centuries old. I've been a lot of things: soldier, sailor, scholar, farmer, musician, wizard, actor, businessman, and, well, a man of leisure. For a lot of that time, I've been an agent of the Program, too, but there's rules in place that allow the really long-lived agents to take sabbaticals. I've been on a sabbatical of sorts for over thirty years, not counting my time in the Navy."

"So, you're a super-powered spy?" Jordana said.

"No, I do a spy-like job, but spying isn't my job. The job of a Program agent is to keep the world at large safe from threats like the Dark Word," Gideon replied.

"Coming through," Matt announced as he returned with another load of luggage.

"Was meeting **me** part of your job?" Jordana asked, eyes narrowing.

"No, that was... fate," Gideon replied.

"And from what I hear, *you* introduced yourself to *him*, not the other way around," Matt pointed out. "So, if you're not an agent of evil, what do you think it is if not fate?"

Jordana stared at him for a minute.

"Hey, not just another pretty face," Matt said. "Okay, we gonna play this as good cop/bad cop or are you gonna be the boyfriend and I'll be the snoopy investigator."

"Well, I'm already dressed in my 'good cop' outfit," Gideon pointed out.

"Hey, how old is Professor/Agent Shaw?" Jordana asked.

Gideon looked at his ID. "Uh, twenty-eight."

Jordana thought for a moment. "Did you go into the Navy out of college or before?"

"Out of college, why?"

Jordana chewed her lip. "Go change. Put on something that looks like older, but not too 'old boyfriend.' I think my parents might be more comfortable around the new boyfriend who rescued me from potential kidnapper/rapists than your 'Men in Black' impression."

"I totally call Will Smith," Matt said.

"Dude, you are *so* white," Jordana said, "but Gideon *is* way more Tommy Lee Jones than you."

Perkins stuck his head in the hatch. "Good news, Sirs, the rental company has delivered a Suburban as requested."

"Thanks, Perkins. Now, go get us another car, something that a guy on a budget might rent," Gideon said.

"My pay-grade budget, Sir, or yours?" Perkins asked.

"Let's see, do you know what at Navy Petty Officer First Class earns?" Gideon asked.

"Depending on time in service, a little over $2,500 per month," Perkins replied.

"Alright subtract two grand for bills, and think of a guy with five hundred bucks who just bought two tickets on a budget airline and needs a budget car and money to pay for a motel room and food," Gideon said.

"Well, Enterprise has some good deals. Would another SUV be suitable?" Perkins asked.

Gideon nodded. "Or a pickup."

"I'll get right on it, Sir," Perkins said with a smile.

"He's sure eager to please, isn't he?" Jordana said.

"Uh, that's the sprite blood showing through," Matt said. "In Faerie, you know, different critters have different... castes, I guess. Sprites are servant caste."

"The shoemaker's elves? They were sprites," Gideon said. "Not as fearsome as goblins, I suppose, but just as powerful in their own way."

"I checked his jacket, by the way," Matt said to Gideon. "Besides being a dang good pilot, our little helper is something of a logistics and supply genius. Raven may not have been able to get us a team, but little Perky is worth three agents just for what he can scrounge."

"Daddy's little girl," Gideon chuckled.

Jordana rolled her eyes. "Go get changed already, okay?"

"Yes, ma'am," Gideon said with a little salute.

A few minutes later Gideon returned from the cabin in the back dressed in jeans and a nice white shirt. He had a sports coat in hand. Jordana stood up and inspected him. "Where's the gun?" she asked.

"Ankle holster," Gideon replied.

"Where's the other stuff?" Matt asked.

"Collar, waistband at the small of the back, right front pocket, other ankle, and right wrist," Gideon replied.

"What stuff?" Jordana asked.

"Silver stiletto, garotting wire, tactical folding knife, wooden stake, and Bright Fang," Gideon said.

Jordana noticed for the first time that Gideon was wearing a leather band on his right wrist. The dark leather was worked with Celtic knots and embossed with a silver medallion of a snarling wolf. He'd replaced his expensive chronograph with a different watch with the same kind of leather band. Gideon pulled the band off his right wrist and handed it to her. Jordana took it, admiring the craftsmanship, when she felt her vision blur, just as it had when she'd seen through Knobs' glamour and when she'd known she was seeing Perkins' true face. She wasn't holding a simple piece of jewelry.

"It's a sword!" she exclaimed.

"You can see it?" Gideon asked.

Jordana nodded. "Yeah, kinda. It's like I can see its... potential."

"Bright Fang is an enchanted weapon. It can shapeshift, become a piece of jewelry, a knife, a sword, or whatever tool I need it to be," Gideon said. "You really do have the Sight."

"Sight? Gideon, the girl's got an Ard Sidhe's True Vision," Matt exclaimed.

"What?" Jordana said.

"The Ard Sidhe, you know, the High Elves, well, they can see through all kinds of glamours and disguises, especially those crafted with Fae magic. They can even see through physical transformations if they concentrate. So, fooling an Ard Sidhe is really, really tricky," Gideon explained. "Of course, by the same token, they are the masters of illusion, transformation, and disguise. Telling a disguised Ard Sidhe from the original of whatever it's copying takes another Ard Sidhe, and even then, it's iffy."

"So, are you trying to say that my dad or my mom is an Ard Sidhe?" Jordana asked.

"Not full-blooded, no," Gideon said. "My father is part-Ard Sidhe. So is Matt's mother. That's where we inherited our immortality from. Well, *near*-immortality."

"My head is starting to hurt again," Jordana sighed. "Let me see if I have this straight: you're both, what, like a quarter elf, and you think because I have this 'Sight' I might be a half- or quarter-elf, too?"

"It's a theory, and the rosemary potion did react to elven blood," Gideon pointed out.

"How do we find out, for sure? Blood tests?" Jordana asked.

"It's one way, but when I meet your parents, I can pretty quickly figure out who's a thrope and who's an elf, and then we'll have to figure out why neither of them ever prepared you for the change," Gideon said.

"How can you know?" Jordana demanded.

Gideon tapped his nose. "I'll smell it. Literally. One thing a glamour, even one created by an Art Sidhe, can't change is scent."

"That's one reason why so many elves have an animal familiar hanging around," Matt added. "An intelligent dog or cat or... ferret or whatever that can literally sniff out potential enemies."

"Excuse me, sirs and ma'am," Perkins said ducking back into the cabin. "I managed to secure a second vehicle, Agent Shaw, but they were out of SUV's. They, did, however have a Dodge Dakota pickup truck. Will that suit you?"

"Nicely," Gideon said, getting up and slipping his sports coat on. "Let's get going. Perkins, is the jet secure here?"

"Yes, sir, or it will be shortly," Perkins replied.

"Okay, you and Matt stow our gear in the Suburban and secure the plane. Once that's done, set up surveillance on the Quinlan house. Jordana and I will take the pickup and make primary contact," Gideon said.

"Got your back, brother," Matt said with a nod.

"Well, Jordy, are you ready to go?" Gideon asked.

"Let's do this," she said as she handed Bright Fang back to him.

CHAPTER THIRTEEN

Orlando, Florida, USA
Quinlan Residence
Brantley Circle, Clermont, FL
October 24, 2010

"Nice neighborhood," Gideon said, and it was.

Orlando, like most major metropolitan cities, was actually composed of several smaller cities and towns surrounding the primary center of business and commerce. The town of Clermont lay due west of Orlando proper, nestled between Lakes Minneola and Minnehaha. Instead of flying into Greater Orlando Airport, like the commercial flight they had told everyone they were on, Perkins had deposited them at Leesburg Municipal Airport, a little over a half-hour north of Clermont.

The Quinlans lived in a huge house on Brantley Circle, which was on a stubby peninsula that jutted out into Lake Minnehaha. All the houses that surrounded it were equally large and expensive. The lawns were all meticulously well kept. Palm trees were also fairly common. The Quinlan house stood out because a flower garden had been planted next to the house behind a chest-high hedge.

"It's okay, I guess," Jordana replied. She looked around and smiled. "I actually liked it better when we lived over in Kissimmee, but Dad got this promotion, and we just *had* to move to a better neighborhood."

"Where you live matters less than *who* you live with," Gideon said.

"Like a goblin butler and a cook who insists that you're too skinny," Jordana giggled.

"Or even a foul-mouthed parrot named Bruce," Gideon smiled as he pulled the pickup into the driveway.

The house had a two-bay carport which housed two expensive vehicles, a silver Lexus LS sedan and a green Range Rover. A red 2001 Chevy Cavalier was parked in the driveway. Gideon parked behind the Cavalier.

"One of these things is not like the others, and I don't mean this truck," Gideon said.

Jordana smiled. "I worked hard to earn that old piece of junk," she declared.

"Whose car are you driving at school?" Gideon asked.

"Tammy's. We drove it all the way up there from here," Jordana said. "Next semester, we're supposed to take my car back with us."

"You ready?" Gideon asked. "Here come the parents."

Jordana nodded and opened her door to hop out of the truck.

Gideon climbed out and grabbed Jordana's suitcase. He watched as the first of her family ran up to her. The woman was middle-aged, but well preserved, olive skin, raven hair, and the same cheekbones as Jordana. The mother. Close behind the woman was a teenage girl, like Jordana in miniature, but enough different not to be mistaken for her older sister. The man who brought up the rear had to be the father. He and the younger daughter bore as much resemblance to one another as Jordana and her mother did to one another. The family engaged in a group hug, but Jordana made a point to give each of her family members a specific hug and kiss on the cheek.

"Jordy, are you okay?" the mother asked. She had the barest trace of a Latin accent.

"Who's your friend?" the father asked, suspicion written all over his face.

Gideon didn't need any special training in reading micro-expressions to see the ferocious parental desire to protect his offspring. "I'm Gideon Shaw, sir." He extended his hand to the other man.

"He's the one who rescued me, Daddy," Jordana said.

The father stared at Gideon's hand for a heartbeat. Then, he grabbed the offered hand in a surprisingly rough grip. "I owe you a debt of thanks, young man. I'm Tom Quinlan."

Gideon shook his head. "You don't owe me anything, Mr. Quinlan."

"Let's go inside. I'm sure you two have had a long trip," Tom said. "We weren't expecting you until this evening."

"We were able to finish with the police sooner than expected, and a friend expedited our way onto an earlier flight," Gideon replied.

The inside of the Quinlan house was well appointed, but at the same time had a homey, lived-in feeling. The front living room was something of a showpiece, but the rooms beyond had the nicks and dings of an active family. Tom led the way into the showpiece living room. He was gracious, but he still hadn't thawed toward Gideon.

Lucinda, Jordana's mother, on the other hand, had latched onto Gideon's free arm with one hand while keeping the other wrapped around Jordana. "Thank you so much for what you've done for my daughter, Mr. Shaw."

"It's 'Gideon', ma'am."

"Careful, Mom," Jordana said. "He blushes."

Gideon was directed into a stuffed chair while Jordana's parents took the couch flanking their daughter. The sister, Kitty, was directed to deposit Jordana's suitcase in her sister's room.

"So, uh, Gideon..." Tom said. "Uh, how do you and Jordy know one another?"

"From MU, sir," Gideon replied.

"Gideon's a grad student," Jordana said.

Tom considered the young man sitting across from him. "You seem a little... old for college."

"I just got out of the Navy last year, sir, and I'm working on my doctoral degree in Forensic Anthropology," Gideon said.

"Much of a future in that?" Tom asked.

Gideon shrugged. "Well, it's more about the past, really," he said with a smile.

Tom frowned slightly.

"Okay, *that* joke fell flat," Gideon sighed. His phone started buzzing. He reached into his pocket and pulled it out. "I do apologize, but I need to take this. I'll just step outside so that I don't bother anyone."

"He seems very polite," Lucinda said once Gideon had stepped out.

"Something seems a little... off about him," Tom groused.

Lucinda laughed. "He's in love with Jordy," she said.

"Mom!" Jordana exclaimed, flushing red.

"Well, he is, and your father is... well, your father," Lucinda explained with a chuckle.

Tom didn't say anything, just glared at his wife, but he knew she was right. His suspicions were founded entirely in his dislike of any man who showed an interest in one of his daughters.

"How old is he?" Tom asked.

"Twenty-eight," Jordana replied promptly.

"He's too old for you," Tom declared.

"Dad, you're twelve years older than Mom," Jordana said. "And to be fair, I hit on him first."

Tom closed his eyes and covered his ears. "I do not need to hear this!" Then, he glanced at Jordy and winked.

"Oh, Daddy," she giggled.

Lucinda stood up. "I think I should start cooking dinner. Jordy, let Gideon know that I fully expect him at table."

Tom frowned again.

"Tom, we at least owe the man a meal," Lucinda scolded.

Tom sighed. "Yes, you're right."

"I'll go get Gideon," Jordana said.

Jordana found Gideon in the garden. He was squatting down looking at the flowers arranged in one of the beds. His phone was still against his ear as he listened to the person on the other end. The frown he gave Jordana made her smile. Maybe her mother was right. Maybe he *was* in love with her.

"That's not good news, Raven," he said into the phone with a sigh.

"What?" Jordana asked softly as she crouched down next to him.

"Hold on, Raven, I'm putting you on speaker," Gideon said. He hit a button on the phone. "Okay, Jordy is here with me. Repeat what you just said."

On the other end of the call, Raven sighed heavily. "Michaela Dumont slipped surveillance. We lost her, but that's not the worst thing. The bodies of the men you killed. They're gone."

"What do you mean by 'gone'?" Jordana demanded.

"I don't mean somebody stole their remains. Well, not entirely. The one that Uncle Gideon decapitated is pretty much permanently dead, but the other two were intact enough that somebody, some*thing*, managed to reanimate them," Raven replied. "They killed a deputy and a morgue attendant and took their bodies along with their buddy's with them."

"Uh, why? Are they gonna eat them?" Jordana gasped.

Gideon chuckled. "No, real zombies are nothing like Romero's ghouls. Reanimated bodies don't need food, water, or air. They continue to decompose, and it gets to a point where they fall apart. So, the other two bodies are probably for minion fodder."

"That's what I figure, too," Raven said. "Oh, I did catch a glimpse of Dumont, and she's not dead, Uncle Gideon."

"I *smelled* her," Gideon growled, almost bristling.

"So did I, not that I knew that was what I was smelling," Jordana replied.

"Maybe so, but I scoped her with a thermograph, and she was giving off body heat," Raven replied. "Then, she just... popped away."

"Like, teleported?" Jordana said.

"What is with you and teleporting?" Gideon snorted.

"I think it would be cool, that's all," Jordana said.

"My boyfriend is a teleporter, and it is cool," Raven replied. "And, yeah, what she did was very much like teleporting. Probably some kind of space-warping through the spirit realms would be my guess."

"Okay, first, I have not authorized you to have a boyfriend, young lady," Gideon said. "Second, how hot was she running?"

"Uh, first, I'm a grown woman, and you actually *like* my boyfriend. Second, she was giving off a little over normal body heat, uh, like a hundred point one, I think," Raven replied.

Gideon slapped himself in the face. "I am such an idiot!"

"How so?" Raven and Jordana said at the same time.

Gideon looked from the phone to Jordana.

"You really should see his face right now," Jordana giggled.

"Oh, take a picture for me," Raven chuckled.

"As I was saying, I'm an idiot. The girl's been mounted by a loa," Gideon explained.

"Wait, I actually *know* this one. Loa are like the 'gods' of voodoo, right?" Jordana said.

"They're demons, and I'm not saying that as a Christian, but as a statement of fact. The loa are demons, spiritual beings from an infernal dimension, but they're not necessarily evil, just amoral," Gideon said.

"They possess a willing host, hang out, enjoy corporeal existence, pay for the ride with some magic or some advice, and they go back to the spirit realms until summoned again. A few loa, though, *are* evil."

"And you're guessing that Micky is possessed by an evil loa," Jordana said.

"Makes sense with the reanimation of the henchmen," Raven added.

"Pass this info on to Matt for me," Gideon said. "I've got something to deal with here at Casa de Quinlan."

"Roger that, Uncle Gideon," Raven said. She disconnected from her end.

"I thought she was your daughter," Jordana said.

"Legally, she is, but she's always called me 'uncle'," Gideon replied. He pointed at the flowers. "Do you know what these are?"

"These are nightshade," Jordana said indicating some bluish-purple flowers.

Gideon pointed to a plant next to the nightshade.

"That's monkshood," Jordana said. "Both are pretty, but they're also poisonous. That's why we don't let the dog into the garden."

"Who taught you about them? Mom or Dad?" Gideon asked.

"The garden is all Mom," Jordana said.

Gideon nodded. "I thought so." He pointed to a couple of herbs nearby. "That's fennel."

"Yeah, Mom grows her own herbs and spices, too," Jordana said.

Gideon shook his head. "No, not what I'm talking about. Nightshade is another name for belladonna."

"Which paralyzes thropes and keeps us from shapeshifting," Jordana said.

"Another name for monkshood is wolfsbane," Gideon said. "And wolfsbane is a component in spells to transform oneself into a wolf, but not if you add fennel to the potion. Fennel twists other herbs' magical function. Add it to wolfsbane and the potion is no longer one of transformation, but one of blocking it. Throw in a little belladonna, and you've got a fine recipe for preventing the change."

"My mother is a werewolf," Jordana said, jaw dropping in shock.

Gideon nodded. "Caught her scent as soon as she came out the door. It's different from yours, though. Does your mom, er, suffer from really bad menstrual cycles?"

"As a matter of fact, yes," Jordana said. "She'll lock herself away in her room for three or four days sometimes because of the cramps."

"The cramps are because of the anti-transformation potion she's been taking for years. Have you ever noticed that your mom's periods always occur on the full moon?" Gideon said. "Is your mom diabetic, by any chance?"

"Yeah."

"She use insulin?"

"Rarely. Wait. That's how she shoots up her anti-werewolf serum, isn't it?"

"That would be my guess, and it's why she gets such gnarly cramps during her full-moon periods. She's shooting up toxins that should be killing her, but her werewolf metabolism is burning them out too quickly," Gideon said as he stood up and stretched.

"I guess this means my dad is the elf, then," Jordana mused as she straightened up from her crouch.

"No, your dad is perfectly mundane, and he's not your dad," Gideon said with a heavy sigh.

"What do you mean, 'he's not your dad'?" Jordana growled.

"Take a deep breath and look at your hands," Gideon said.

Hair and claws were sprouting from Jordana's fingers.

"Just concentrate real hard on being human," Gideon said. "You can't afford to lose control right now."

Jordana took several deep breaths, imagining her hands back to normal. The changes began to fade.

"Very good," Gideon said. "Now, keep doing that while I explain."

"Okay," Jordana ground out.

"In the ways that count, legally, emotionally, and financially, Tom Quinlan is your father, but biologically-speaking, he's not your father," Gideon said. "If he had even the merest hint of an Ard Sidhe about him, I'd smell it. He's definitely your sister's biological father, but, honey, he's not yours."

"But he's my daddy," Jordana insisted.

"Yes, he is. He's the man who raised you, nurtured you, and taught you to be the woman you are today. He's standing in the window over there watching us right now because he's your father and he loves you more than his own life, but he's not the one who sired you," Gideon said. "I doubt he even knows."

"Hold on," Jordana said. "My mother would *never* cheat on my father."

"Doesn't have to be a willing union to sire a child," Gideon said. "She could have been raped by force or..." He frowned. Then, he face palmed himself again. "God, I'm just... retarded!"

"What?"

"Think about our conversation earlier, about the Ard Sidhe being masters of disguise?" Gideon said.

"Yeah, so?"

"Do you know the story of how King Arthur's father sired him?" Gideon asked.

"Uh, didn't Merlin turn Uther into the spitting image of some lady's husband? I think that's what I remember from that movie 'Camelot,'" Jordana said.

"Yeah, that's pretty much how it happened, and that's also how Zeus got his get-off on so many little Greek girls, but he was something different than an Ard Sidhe, and that's irrelevant to the conversation at hand," Gideon said. "Some High Elf prick turned himself into your dad, knocked up your mom, and twenty years later, the Dark Word shows up looking for the product of that union."

"Well, this is certainly gonna make dinner awkward," Jordana sighed.

"I think it's about time I break cover... about time *we* break cover," Gideon said. "Your mom knows what she is, but not why. Otherwise, she wouldn't be shooting up belladonna and wolfsbane. She wasn't an orphan by any chance, was she?"

"Yeah, she grew up in Costa Rica in an orphanage," Jordana said.

"That would explain why she's not part of the local paranormal community," Gideon said. "Your dad is blissfully ignorant."

"And Kitty?"

"Will probably start feeling the change soon if she hasn't already," Gideon said. "We need to sit everybody down and explain to them all what's really going on."

"Yay. Sounds like... What do you call the precise opposite of fun?"

CHAPTER FOURTEEN

Orlando, Florida, USA
Quinlan Residence
Brantley Circle, Clermont, FL
October 24, 2010

Lucinda kept the meal simple. She chopped up fresh vegetables for a stir fry, tossing in chunks of chicken for a little protein. Rice was a staple of almost every meal she cooked. So, a pot of that was ready in a bit. She had Kitty set the table in the good dining room.

"They're just standing in your garden," Tom grumbled when came into the kitchen. "Thought I might've caught them making out, but they were just poking at some of your flowers."

"Really?" Lucinda replied. She paused in the middle of stirring the vegetables in the big wok. Then, she went back to work. Jordy knew which plants not to play with. Lucinda had made sure that both of her girls knew which plants were safe and which weren't.

"They headed for the backyard," Tom said as he reached into the refrigerator for a beer. He grinned as he popped the cap off the bottle. "He's about to meet Princess."

Kitty came in from the dining room gaping at her father. "Daddy! That's just mean what you're thinking."

The family dog, a Briard-Poodle mix called "Princess," was a large, shaggy beast with a nasty temperament toward strangers. Tom had often made a point of meeting Jordy's dates at the door with Princess. The dog would immediately become aggressive with most boys. Those that she didn't flip out over, Tom would reluctantly agree to allow his daughter to date. That Khanderia boy was about the only man, other than Tom himself, who she seemed to actually like.

Kitty rushed to the back door and looked out. "Uh, Daddy, you need to see this."

Tom ambled over, the beer halfway to his mouth for another pull. The bottle stopped mid-motion. He just stared. Princess was bouncing around, playing catch like a puppy.

"I'll be damned," Tom muttered.

"Language, Daddy," Kitty chided. "You need to put a dollar in the swears jar."

Out in the yard, Jordana glanced toward the back door of the house, spotted her father and sister watching them. She smiled as she distinctly heard her sister chiding their father for his language.

"I take it your father is... displeased that your dog likes me?" Gideon asked.

"More like shocked that Princess didn't try to take a chunk out of your hide," Jordana replied.

Princess dropped her tennis ball in front of Gideon and looked up at him expectantly, tail swishing back and forth rapidly.

"Very good girl, Princess," Gideon said to the dog, rubbing her ears. "One more toss, and then we have to go inside and make the rest of the family very unhappy."

The dog just cocked her head to one side and regarded the human who smelled like a dog. She yipped her impatience to play again. Then, she averted her gaze and assumed a submissive posture. The human was an Alpha, in charge, like unto a god, to her little doggy mind. The ball was picked up and a good throw was tossed. Princess chased the ball, which bounced several times, making the chase even more fun. Tennis ball once again secured, Princess trotted over to the new Alpha and her human, Jordana, who was also an Alpha now. Princess basked in the attention her two gods granted her and loved them back for it. The male human Alpha produced a piece of dried meat from his pocket and gave it to her.

"You certainly know the way to my dog's heart," Jordana laughed as Princess pounced on the little piece of jerky that Gideon offered her.

"We've always kept dogs. My sister has the current generation living with her," Gideon replied. "Gabriel Ratchets, uh, kinda like magical cross between a German Shepherd, an Irish Wolfhound, and a bear. Rebecca has very little magic beyond her long life, and Dad and I decided that she should have the protection."

"From what?" Jordana asked.

"The enemies that Dad and I collect like baseball cards," Gideon chuckled. He turned and waved to Tom and Kitty.

Kitty waved back, and Tom glowered.

"Your dad hates me," Gideon said still smiling.

"No, he doesn't," Jordana assured him. "He's just being... Daddy. Like you were when you told Raven she couldn't have a boyfriend."

Gideon smiled. "I *do* understand the psychology, but your dad just doesn't like me, and what we have to tell them isn't gonna make him like me any better."

"Well, everything should be more or less okay as long as you don't tell him about Matt's plan that you should just de-virginize me just to be safe," Jordana said.

"Did you say 'de-virginize'?" Gideon said.

"I did."

"That's what I thought. I have very good hearing, you know."

"Let's head in. I can smell Mom's cooking," Jordana said. "We should hold off on the big reveal until after we've eaten."

"I'd also like to have Matt and Perkins in place in case I need a hostile extraction," Gideon said.

They walked into the kitchen laughing.

"Dude, that was awesome! Princess hates *everybody*," Kitty exclaimed. "How'd you do that?"

Gideon pulled a package of beef jerky out of his coat pocket. "I was, uh, lucky that she liked my favorite airplane snack."

Tom snorted from the counter where he was counting out a dollar in change into a big mason jar that had an index card with the caption "Swears Fund" taped to it.

"Oh, Daddy," Jordana sighed. "Anytime we use bad words, we put a dollar into the jar. Whoever puts the least money in gets to keep the money at the end of the year."

"Nice way to teach the girls to watch their language," Tom said.

"Much better than the homemade soap my mother used on me that one time," Gideon said.

"Come into the dining room," Lucinda directed. "Let's all sit down and enjoy a nice meal together. Gideon, would you care for a glass of wine with your dinner?"

"Uh, no, thank you, ma'am. I'm driving," Gideon replied. "But don't let me stop you from enjoying."

"Hadn't planned on it," Lucinda said with a wink.

"Mom, could I have wine?" Kitty asked.

Lucinda smiled at her daughter and said, "No."

The teen looked crestfallen for all of a few seconds.

"Maybe for your birthday," Lucinda sighed.

Kitty beamed a bright smile. "Yes!"

"You're growing up much too fast, *mija*," Lucinda laughed.

The family settled around the table in the formal dining room. Tom sat at the head of the table, and Lucinda sat opposite him. Kitty and Jordana sat opposite one another, Jordana taking the place with an extra plate set next to it. That spot placed Gideon next to Tom. Lucinda had already plated the meal and placed them on the table. She poured herself a glass of white wine. Tom still had a beer. Gideon and the sisters had water.

"Tom, perhaps we should ask Gideon to return grace?" Lucinda suggested.

Tom shrugged. "Sure. You mind, Gideon?"

"Not at all," Gideon replied. He bowed his head and intoned, "Lord, some people have food and no friends/Some people have friends and no food/We thank you that on this night we have both. Amen."

He glanced around at the other people at the table. "Uh, it's what my father taught me when I was a little kid," Gideon explained. "Except he taught it to me in Gaelic."

"Gaelic?" Kitty exclaimed even as she picked up her fork and tore into her food.

"Yeah, he's Scottish," Gideon said.

"Immigrant family?" Tom said.

Gideon shrugged. "I suppose, but we're all immigrants in America. My family came over with Sir James Oglethorpe when he founded the colony of Georgia. We've had Shaws living in and around Savannah ever since." He took a bite of food. "But we've also always remembered that we came from somewhere else. So, somebody in the family always preserves that history and culture."

"And in your family that was your father?" Lucinda guessed.

Gideon nodded. "Yes, ma'am. In a manner of speaking. Usually, though, it's the Shaw women who do the remembering."

"Uh-huh, hand that rocks the cradle," Kitty said.

Gideon raised an eyebrow at the girl.

"What? I read," she declared.

Jordana snorted a laugh. "You mean something other than fashion magazines?"

"Sometimes," Kitty replied. "When the teacher assigns it."

Gideon chuckled. "This is delicious, Mrs. Quinlan."

"It's Lucinda."

"Yes, ma'am."

Tom cleared his throat. "So, Gideon, you were a sailor?"

"Yes, sir, I was," Gideon replied.

"He's being modest, Daddy," Jordana said. "Gideon was a SEAL."

"Is that so?" Tom mused.

Gideon nodded. "Yes, sir, it is."

"You're not going to elaborate on that, are you?" Tom said.

"No, sir," Gideon replied. "I'm proud of my service, but a lot of what I did was of a classified nature. So, I figure it's best not to talk about any of it."

"You kill anybody?" Kitty asked.

"Kitty!" Jordana hissed at her sister.

Gideon smiled and shook his head. "It's a natural question. I was a combat soldier. I did what was necessary to survive and to complete my missions."

"Oh," Kitty said.

"Let's move on to another topic, shall we? I think this discussion is making Gideon uncomfortable," Lucinda said.

"Uh," Gideon stammered, glancing at Jordana.

She shrugged. "Now is as good a time as any," she decided. "Mom, Dad, I have to tell you guys something."

"Oh, god, you're pregnant!" Tom groaned.

"Daddy! No!" Jordana exclaimed. "I'm still a virgin. Jeez!"

"Oh, that's a relief," Tom sighed.

"Tom!" Lucinda exclaimed.

"Are you two getting married?" Kitty shouted next.

Jordana rolled her eyes. "No! No, I'm not getting married, and I'm not pregnant. I'm a freaking werewolf!"

Gideon was watching Lucinda for her reaction, but quickly glanced around the table at the others. Kitty was grinning like she'd just heard the best joke ever. Tom was staring blankly at Lucinda. Lucinda was in gape-jawed shock, which quickly turned to a look of pure horror.

"No," she said in a bare whisper.

"Mom," Kitty said in that voice that only a teenager can achieve, the one that conveys equal parts scorn and affection. "Jordy's kidding."

"No, Kitty, I'm not," Jordana said. "I changed for the first time last night when those men tried to kidnap me."

"And your mother, to her horror, does believe Jordy because she's a werewolf, too," Gideon said. "When did you start using the anti-transformation serum?"

Lucinda's shocked stare turned to him now. "What? How?"

"Your garden. You have the ingredients for the serum growing together. Do you harvest them and process the serum under the new moon? Is that how you were taught to prepare the potion?" Gideon asked.

"Mom?" Kitty said, confusion etched on her young face.

"But, how?" Lucinda said.

"It's hereditary, Mom," Jordana said.

"No, it's a curse! I was cursed by God for the sins of my family," Lucinda exclaimed.

"It's not a curse," Gideon said. "It's a natural part of who *we* are."

Tom got up from the table, went into the kitchen, and came back with the Swears Jar. He calmly pulled a twenty-dollar bill from his wallet and stuffed it into the jar. "Son, you'd better goddamn start making some goddamn sense right goddamn now!" he shouted, "before I fucking boot your ass out of my house!"

"*Palabra Oscura*," Gideon said.

"*¡Madre de dios, no!*" Lucinda wailed.

"Mom, what do you know about them?" Jordana demanded.

"They... they... I am an orphan because of them," Lucinda wept. "My *papa*, your grandfather, he was one of them. It is why God cursed me."

"What the hell is going on here?" Tom demanded, his temper rising. "I need an explanation, right fucking now!"

Gideon turned on him, suddenly not human, but some amalgam of man and wolf. "What's 'going on' is that a cult of demon-worshiping neo-nihilists have plans for world destruction and/or domination and your daughter is integral to that plan, but we don't know how. So, for the moment, Tom, sit down, shut up, and quit interrupting!"

Tom's rump thumped into his chair.

Gideon's form returned to normal.

"Okay, I was wondering why your clothes were so baggy," Jordana said.

Gideon rolled his neck, joints popped and cracked. "Yeah. Now, Lucinda, you were saying that your father was a member of the Dark Word? Your mother, too?"

Lucinda nodded, staring in shock at Gideon. "How did you do that? Are you in league with the devil?"

Gideon rolled his eyes. "Lady, somebody sure sold you a bill of goods. No, I am definitely *not* in league with the devil. Quite the opposite in fact."

"Mom, Gideon's a good man. Please trust him," Jordana said.

Lucinda nodded at her daughter.

"Now, who taught you about your 'curse' and how to make that serum?" Gideon asked.

"It was a nun at the orphanage where I grew up, Sister Teresa. She said she was with the Inquisition, that it still existed to protect good people from monsters like my parents... and me," Lucinda said.

"Wait, Mom, you don't mean old Tia Teresa, do you?" Jordana asked.

Lucinda nodded again. "She came to America just to keep an eye on me and our family. To ensure that I was not a threat, that I made the serum and took it as she had taught me."

Jordana turned to Gideon. "Tia Teresa is, like, this natural health guru that Mom gets her best herbs for the garden from. She's a nutritionist. We've known her, literally, all my life."

"It kind of makes sense. Somebody within the Dark Word wanted to keep tabs on your mom, and I can really only think of one reason why somebody would get a thrope hooked on an anti-transformation serum," Gideon said.

"What do you mean?" Lucinda asked.

"The change is mostly voluntary. Your first change isn't, but most thropes quickly learn to control it before the next full moon, especially if they have a knowledgeable teacher, like a parent or mentor. Even on your own, just wanting *not* to change would have prevented it. Lunar phases are more about symbolism than any actual influence on shapeshifting abilities," Gideon said. "No, this Teresa person wanted you scared, and more importantly, ashamed, guilty."

"What do you mean?" Lucinda asked.

"That potion, while it does block the change, isn't about making you not a werewolf. It's about poisoning the wolf in your soul. Even in your human form, you should have heightened senses, smell and hearing mainly, and rapid healing, slower aging. That crap you've been shooting up is robbing you of years off your life, dulling your senses, and making you vulnerable," Gideon said. "Teresa wanted you weakened so that you'd never notice that she was feeding off your negative emotions, the guilt and the shame. Not to mention the fact that you never noticed that Tom, here, isn't Jordy's biological father."

"Now, see here!" Tom bellowed, but Gideon's clawed hand on his shoulder shoved him back down in his seat.

"Tom, I know you've had a series of emotional and psychic shocks this evening, but all I'm telling you is the truth," Gideon growled through wolfish teeth. His features returned to normal. "Somebody, other than you, is Jordana's biological father. *You* are her 'Daddy' where it counts, though: in her heart, and I really don't think that the other thought running around in your head is healthy either. Your wife didn't cheat on you. I figure she was the next best thing to raped."

"I've never been with a man other than Tom!" Lucinda insisted.

"Mom, think back to when you and Daddy were first trying to get pregnant," Jordana said, soothingly. "Do you remember being with Daddy at some point, and it was, I don't know, different?"

"Was he a little rougher than usual or just clumsy compared to his usual style of lovemaking?" Gideon added. "And afterwards, did he act like he didn't remember?"

Lucinda's eyes grew wide in shock. "Yes."

"What?" Tom exclaimed.

"When you were working on the Splash Mountain project, you came home in the middle of the day, said you wanted to try a 'nooner', but that night when you came back home you complained about the long, difficult day that you'd had," Lucinda said. "I... I thought maybe it had been a dream, that I'd dozed off and had a..."

"Sex dream, Mom?" Kitty said with a giggle that had a hysterical edge to it.

"Wasn't a dream. My theory is that it was... someone in disguise," Gideon said.

"It was *my husband*!" Lucinda declared with an absolute certainty that crumbled a second later when she added, "I think."

"There are... people, *things*, out there that can make themselves appear to be just about anybody," Gideon said.

Princess began barking at that instant.

Gideon's head whipped around in the direction of the dog's excited fury. He rushed from the table to look out the back window, to see what had Princess's hackles up. The dog was facing the lake, barking and snarling at something Gideon couldn't see.

"We've got trouble," he announced as he returned to the dining room and pulled his phone from his pocket.

"What are you doing now?" Tom demanded.

"Calling in the cavalry. I think you all might be in danger," Gideon said.

"Who the hell are you?" Tom demanded.

"Well, Tom, I'm the monster that all the other monsters are afraid of."

CHAPTER FIFTEEN

Orlando, Florida, USA
Quinlan Residence
Brantley Circle, Clermont, FL
October 24, 2010

"Where are you?" Gideon demanded as soon as Matt answered on the other end.

"Right outside, brother," Matt said. "Neighborhood dogs just started up..." Matt had stepped out of the Suburban while he was talking. The scent hit him like a club across the face. "Crap. Smells like undead."

"Well, this day just keeps getting better and better," Gideon growled. "Put Perkins on and get in here. I think the Quinlans are going into info overload."

Matt handed the phone to Perkins and grabbed a duffel out of the back of the SUV that the smaller agent had just parked in front of the

Quinlans' door. Perkins stared at the phone for half a second. He put it to his ear. "Yes, sir?"

The door was unlocked when Matt burst through. He slammed it shut and threw the deadbolt just to be safe. A thought occurred to him. He pulled his credentials out of his pocket and hung the badge around his neck by a chain. Hopefully seeing the badge would slow the family down before they started wondering too hard what a man as big and scary as himself was doing showing up in their midst.

Gideon came striding out of the dining room going into the kitchen, his phone to his ear, Jordana on his six. He pointed toward the dining room and said, "Keep an eye on them."

"Got it. Which cover did we go with?" Matt asked, but Gideon was already in the kitchen. Matt shrugged and walked into the dining room. "Wow, that smells really good."

"Jesus Christ! Who the hell are you?" Tom Quinlan demanded.

"Name's Einarsson. Matthias Einarsson, but you folks can call me 'Matt'. I'm Gideon's partner, and, Mr. Quinlan, if I were you, I'd think real hard about not taking the Lord's name in vain around a guy who's practically a real-life paladin. Gideon gets touchy when *I* do it, and he likes me."

Matt had shoved the plates and dinnerware aside and dropped his duffel bag onto the table while he was talking. He started pulling out items and stacking them on the table.

"Are you FBI?" asked Kitty.

"Indirectly," Matt replied. "I actually work for a secret government agency that polices paranormal threats to national security, but to any local law-enforcement types, I'm a Feeb."

"The Inquisition?" Lucinda gasped.

Matt snorted. "Oh, hell, no. The Inquisition, at least the organization you're thinking of, doesn't exist anymore. The Church's paranormal investigation branch is the Sacred Order of St. Hubert."

"But I know a woman, a nun, who is an Inquisitor," Lucinda insisted.

Matt snorted again. "Not likely. The Inquisitors who survived, they're all men, they're hardcore, and they're no longer affiliated with the Church." He held up a kevlar vest. "Who's first to get fitted? Let's start with the smart-mouthed little sister."

Matt quickly, efficiently, wrapped each member of Jordana's family in body armor.

"Why are we wearing bulletproof vests?" Tom demanded even as he let Matt secured the kevlar around his chest.

"Well, just in case you ask another stupid question, and I want to shoot you, I won't have to worry about killing you," Matt replied with a big grin. "Not everything we fight is old-fashioned. Some of the bad guys we deal with use guns, too."

Gideon and Jordana returned with a large, mixed-breed dog. The dog kept looking back the way they had come from. She was straining to attack whatever was threatening her territory.

Matt nodded to the dog. "Kinda reminds me of your mom," he said to Gideon.

"Naw, Ma wouldn't have been so restrained," Gideon replied. He looked around at the Quinlans. "Somebody's been a busy beaver."

"I do like to keep busy," Matt chuckled as he tossed Gideon a tac vest. "I'll let you strap Jordy into her vest. Okay, family and friends, listen up!" Matt boomed with a big, loud hand clap. "We are going to get you folks to a safe location. That would be somewhere that is not here. So, when Gideon or I tell you to do something, you do it. No arguments, no questions. Am I clear, *Tom*?"

Tom nodded. "Yeah, clear."

"Splendid!" Matt exclaimed with another huge grin.

"Here's the plan," Gideon said. "We're gonna run, now. There's a Suburban parked in the driveway. Pile into it. Back seats. Jordy, you're driving."

"I am? Cool!" Jordana said with a feral grin. Her eyes were glowing blue.

Matt shrugged into a heavy tac vest loaded with equipment and ammo. "What'll we be doing? As if I didn't know?"

"Positive security," Gideon said. "Did you bring the good toys?"

"Please," Matt scoffed. He waved a hand at the table.

A pair of Atchisson AA-12 automatic shotguns rested on the table. The stubby weapons looked lethal even without the magazines inserted. Matt picked up one of the magazines he'd set out. It had a blue band around the bottom. "Got two mags each of deer slugs." He picked up another magazine, this one with a green band. "Two each of Jack-of-All-Trades." Finally, he picked up a magazine with a red band around the bottom. "And we have one each of these. They're impact detonating, high-explosive grenades."

"Good grief, Matt," Gideon exclaimed. "I'm glad you've over-prepared."

A wail sounded from outside, mixing equal parts rage and pain. The dog started snarling and barking again.

"What the hell was that?" Tom demanded.

"Revenants," Gideon replied. "Got a good whiff of them when we went out to get Princess. Alright, everybody, we're gonna go out the front door. First, me and Matt. We'll cover you guys. Then, Jordy, Lucinda, Kitty, and Tom. Remember: get in the back seats. Once you're in, get down. Matt and I will pile in after, and Jordy will hit the gas."

"What about Perkins?" Matt asked.

"Already sent him on an errand," Gideon replied.

"Okay, but he's got my phone," Matt said.

Gideon rolled his eyes as he stuffed magazines into his pockets and slammed one home in the well of the gun. "Then, let's get going." He looked at the dog. "Princess!"

The dog looked at him.

"Let's go for a ride, girl," Gideon said to the dog, who wagged her tail at the idea.

Gideon went out the door first, sweeping to his left. Matt, who was left-handed, followed and swept right. The revenants wailed again, closer this time. "Jordy, go!"

Jordana dashed to the Suburban, opening the passenger side door, and slid across into the driver's seat. Princess was right behind her. The dog jumped into the vacated passenger seat. Lucinda and Tom were right behind her with Kitty between them. Tom fumbled at the latch on the door, but he managed to tug it open. Kitty was scrambling over the back of the middle seat into the back seat when the first revenants rounded the corner.

They were corpses that had been reanimated with a necromantic ritual. Some were still more or less human, but most were in various states of decay. They turned as one, like a flock of birds, wailed their eerie battle cry and charged. Gideon methodically cycled through his first clip. He'd chosen the impact detonated grenades.

His first target was a dead man who might have been a football player in life just by his size alone. The grenade hit him center mass and sent pieces flying in all directions. The shockwave from the detonation knocked down the corpse people on either side of him. Gideon moved the barrel to point at a woman who'd been massively fat in life, but in death moved with preternatural grace and speed. Her face was screwed into a rictus of rage, her mouth bared, fingers curved into grasping claws. The grenade sent her head high into the air, while the gore that had been her torso splattered everything in a fifteen-foot radius.

Gideon's third target was the next largest revenant. Then, the fourth largest, the fifth largest. Then, he targeted the closest three, and the bolt of his gun locked open on an empty chamber. "Move!" he snapped at Matt as he let the AA-12 swing from its sling and he pulled the Glock from his waist band. The .45 caliber handgun wouldn't be nearly as effective as the grenades had been, but it would still do the job. Matt dashed to the SUV and jumped into the passenger seat. Even as he did so, he was slamming another magazine into the shotgun. Jordana grabbed Princess and pulled the dog close to her to avoid Matt crushing the animal.

The revenants had been severely reduced in numbers, but more were coming. A couple staggered to their feet from where the detonations had thrown them. Gideon double-tapped the first five in the head. Then, the slide on the Glock clicked back.

"Gideon!" Matt bellowed. He threw his freshly loaded shotgun to Gideon, and Gideon threw his empty to Matt.

Gideon shot down three more revenants while he calmly walked to the back of the SUV. He jumped into the cargo bay in the back, leaving the rear screen up. "Go!" he shouted.

Jordana threw the heavy SUV into gear and stomped on the gas.

"Try not to hit 'em," Matt suggested. "Don't want to bust the radiator or spider-web the windshield."

"Gotcha," Jordana growled she slung the wheel hard to one side and clipped a revenant with the passenger side headlight.

Matt laughed as he pumped a deer slug into the undead creature's chest.

Gideon dropped the shotgun and grabbed one of the cases Matt had loaded into the cargo area. Inside was an FN F2000 assault rifle. He grabbed a 30-round clip and slammed it home in the well behind the pistol grip. The F2000 looked like some kind of sci-fi show weapon, but it was a fine product of Belgian firearms tradition. He flipped the selector to semi-auto and began to methodically place head shots using the integral scope to line up his shots, but the revenants weren't what he was searching for as the SUV careened down the street and out of the neighborhood.

Then, he saw her, an older Latina woman. She was dressed in black, her face painted like a skull. A small burlap bag was clutched to her chest. A cadre of four undead linebackers surrounded her, acting as her bodyguard. She chanted to herself and moved her free hand to direct her minions.

Gideon inhaled deeply. Then, he released half a breath and between heartbeats, sent four rounds downrange toward the necromancer. The head of each of her four guards exploded. The necromancer screamed as the four re-dead bodies toppled on top of her. Gideon grinned.

"Would you look at that!" Tom exclaimed. "The zombies just started attacking one another."

"Revenants," Gideon corrected. "Corpses animated with spirits of anger and hatred bound to the will of the necromancer who summoned them."

"Why are they attacking each other?" Kitty asked.

"I just disrupted the necromancer's concentration. Managing a horde of ravening undead requires concentration. Having four dead bodies as big as Matt fall on you tends to disrupt that concentration," Gideon said.

"Slow down," Matt said to Jordana as he rolled his window up and tucked the AA-12 out of sight.

Jordana took her foot off the gas, and the SUV slowed down to the speed limit. Around a curve in the road came a swarm of police cars and a SWAT van followed by fire trucks and an ambulance.

"Right on time," Gideon said. "That Perkins is good."

"Shouldn't we warn the police about the zombies, er, revenants?" Tom said.

Gideon shook his head. "They wouldn't believe us anyway. No, the necromancer will hear the racket, get her horde back under control, and she'll hightail it for the nearest escape route. This will all get written up as some kind of drug-gang riot or something equally stupid but plausible."

"Where are we going?" Jordana called from up front.

"Back to the plane," Gideon replied. He looked at Lucinda. "We still have a lot to talk about, ma'am."

Matt leaned across the dog to Jordana and whispered, "I don't think your dad likes Gideon."

Princess sniffed the big man, and he scratched her ears. The dog's tongue lolled out. She loved having her ears scratched.

"Yeah, well, Gideon did just tell him that his wife was raped by his doppelganger and that I'm not his daughter. Not to mention that whole 'Night of the Living Dead' incident just now," Jordana scoffed. Then, she grinned. "On the other hand, saving everybody's lives will go a long ways toward making Dad like him better, and if you keep being you, Gideon will look so much better in comparison."

Matt snorted. "I think the safe house we're gonna take you guys to will do that trick."

"Magee House?" Jordana guessed.

Matt nodded. "That place is pretty much a fortress. Be kind of nice to have the estate crowded with people again. Dogs, too." He glanced toward the back of the SUV where Gideon was explaining the difference between revenants, zombies, and ghouls to Tom. "He's been alone for far too long. He's been in a funk ever since Aggie died. I thought maybe taking care of Raven or even when he joined the Navy, that might snap him out of it, but he was still kinda depressed." Matt studied Jordana's profile. "That changed Friday."

CHAPTER SIXTEEN

Orlando, Florida, USA

Leesburg Municipal Airport

Leesburg, FL

October 24, 2010

Perkins was waiting when Gideon jumped out of the Suburban. "Really hope you got the insurance when you rented this thing, Perky."

The small agent blinked at his superior. "I'm not stupid, sir." He glanced around Gideon at the Suburban. "To be honest, from the way Director Gold spoke of the two of you, I was expecting one or the other vehicle to wind up totaled."

Gideon laughed. "That's why we let Jordy drive." He slapped a friendly hand on Perkins' shoulder. "Did you get the other things I requested?"

"Yes, sir," Perkins beamed.

"Right, then, while I'm taking care of this, you get the plane warmed up," Gideon said.

"Our destination, sir?" Perkins asked.

"Back where we started," Gideon replied, "but don't file any flight plans to that effect."

"No, sir, of course not. This plane is going back to Quantico, where it started out from," Perkins replied with a wink. "Uh, sir, might I make a request?"

"Shoot."

"I really hate the nickname 'Perky'."

Gideon shook his head. "You should never have admitted that, Perky, 'cause now that's all me or Matt will ever call you."

Perkins sighed. "Figures."

"Look on the bright side, Perky: if we didn't like you, we wouldn't even have bothered with thinking up that much of a nickname," Gideon said with chuckle. "Get going, kid. I wanna be wheels up as quick as possible."

"Roger that, sir," Perkins replied and bustled off to get to work.

Gideon turned to the gathered Quinlans. "We've only got a few minutes before we can get airborne, but we need to do a couple of things first."

"Airborne? I've got a job, and Kitty's got school tomorrow," Tom exclaimed.

"Tom, you need to get a grip on the fact that your world has just turned inside out," Gideon said. He clapped a reassuring hand on Tom's shoulder. "I'm trying my level best to keep you and your family safe, okay?"

Tom Quinlan took a deep breath and nodded. "Okay."

"Good man," Gideon said with a smile. "Now, I'm gonna ask you guys to do a couple of potentially uncomfortable things because the bad guys kinda zeroed in right on you guys."

"Okay," Tom agreed.

"First, I need you to give your phones, wireless devices, Bluetooth, all that kind of electronic communications stuff to Matt. He's gonna make sure that nobody is using electronic means to follow us," Gideon said.

The Quinlans handed over their phones, and Kitty reluctantly parted with her iPod Touch.

"Don't worry, kid," Matt assured her. "I'll get it back to you. Eventually."

"Okay, second thing: you guys are now incommunicado. No email, no Facebook, no Twitter. Hell, no Friendster or Live Journal either. We've got tech nerds who're gonna go through all your accounts to make sure they're safe and set up new ones for you in the future. Clear?"

"Oh, man," Kitty whined. "Jordy, your new boyfriend is starting to suck."

"Yeah, well, get ready to hate me a little more," Gideon sighed. "We're gonna need the clothes that you're all wearing right now."

"What?" Tom exclaimed.

"There could be tracking devices sewn into the linings or even bits of lint that are part of a tracking spell, and speaking of tracking spells, I'm gonna have to ritually cleanse you guys before we get on the plane. I had Perkins get you guys some fresh clothes," Gideon said. He gestured toward the hangar. "Right this way. Let's get this over with."

"Is this really necessary?" Jordana whispered.

Gideon shrugged. "Being in the air will disrupt most tracking spells, you know, being out of contact with mother earth, that sort of thing, but once we touch back down, the spell will reconnect, and here come the walking dead. We break the link now, get in a plane, fly around for an hour or two, and when we set back down, whatever magic they're using to track you and your family will be thoroughly confused."

"Well, I'd better get the treatment, too, then. Maybe it'll make Dad feel better," Jordana suggested.

"I really kind of doubt that," Gideon chuckled.

A few minutes later the Quinlan family, Jordana included, were dressed in cheap sweats and knock-off Disney World t-shirts. Gideon had drawn out a large circle on the floor of the hangar with sidewalk chalk. Then, he'd drawn a pentacle inside the circle.

"Are you sure this isn't... black magic?" Lucinda asked with a quiver in her voice.

"No, ma'am, it is not," Gideon said firmly. "The star, the pentacle, represents the five elements of magic: Earth, Air, Fire, Water, and Spirit. The circle that encloses the star represents the universe, God's Creation, if you will."

As he spoke, Gideon set a lump of playdough down at one point of the star, a burning incense stick at another, a lit candle at the next, a bowl of water at the one after that, and a Raggedy Ann doll at the final point. He tilted his head to one side to look at what he'd done. Then, he nodded.

"Okay, all of you into the center of the star, and don't knock anything over," Gideon said.

The center of the star was a tight fit for all of them. The family huddled together, and Tom wrapped his arms protectively around his wife and daughters. Gideon nodded. He raised his right arm, summoned his will and released it into the artifact on his wrist. With a bright flash the bracelet on his wrist flowed into his hand growing into the form of a sword. The pommel and the tips of the crossguard were worked into snarling wolf's heads. The hilt was wrapped in black leather overwire. Runes descended the length of the blade, and images of a wolf pack on the hunt cavorted among the runes.

"Holy crap!" Tom exclaimed.

"Cool!" Kitty and Jordana said in unison.

"This is gonna be a quick and dirty cleansing ritual," Gideon said. "I'll need you guys to be quiet while I do this, okay?"

The Quinlans all nodded.

"Matt?"

"Ready," the big man intoned. He was holding a bundle of sage to the tip of a blowtorch. The plant bundle had caught fire, and he smothered it enough that it would smoke.

Gideon stepped up to the circle. He passed his left palm over the edge of the sword, Bright Fang. Blood welled from the cut. He dribbled a few drops at each point of the pentacle, and then he willed the circle closed.

"I think my ears just popped," Tom said.

"Shh," Gideon shushed.

Tom blushed but was quiet.

Gideon began whispering quietly to himself. Then, he took the smoking sage from Matt and started walking around the circle counter-clockwise. As he went, he waved the burning sage through the air and dribbled the ashes on the ground. Gideon made the circuit seven times.

At the end of the final circuit, he raised the sword into the air, and then slashed it down hard toward the ground.

"Alright, I want you guys to follow me, single file, tucked right up behind me. Jordy, Kitty, Lucinda, and Tom. Matt brings up the rear," Gideon said. "Let's go."

He walked straight from the circle to the plane, boarded, and then turned to help the others aboard.

"Okay, settle in, get comfortable, but don't leave this cabin, got it?" Gideon said.

The Quinlans all nodded.

Gideon smiled. "This is almost over for now," he assured them. "I just gotta clean up the mess I left."

He left the Quinlans and quickly gathered up his ritual materials. The blood he'd sacrificed for the cleansing had been consumed by the spell. So, nobody would be able to use it to track him or cast a hostile spell at him. However, a part of himself had been invested in the icons and the ritual circle. Matt had dragged an empty fifty-gallon drum into the hangar area. Gideon grabbed each of his icons and dropped them into the drum. Matt doused the lot with lighter fluid, and dropped a burning rag in on top of them. Gideon struck the circle in four places, corresponding to the cardinal points of the compass, with Bright Fang. Then, with an effort of will, the sword flashed and flowed into his hand and then around his wrist once more looking like a wrist band. Finally, Gideon dumped a bucket of soapy water onto the circle and mopped it away.

"Quick and dirty thaumaturgy," Matt chuckled.

"Yep," Gideon agreed. "Thanks for playing my lovely assistant."

"Gosh, I'm glad you thought I was lovely," Matt chuckled.

"Let's roll," Gideon said.

"Happy to. I'm about done with the Sunshine State for one day," Matt said. "Nothing like zombies to ruin a visit to the Happiest Place on Earth."

CHAPTER SEVENTEEN

En route to Atlanta, Georgia, USA
Somewhere over the Gulf of Mexico
October 24, 2010

"So, why're we just flying in a big circle?" Jordana said as she stared out the window at the water passing beneath them.

Gideon looked up from the Dagwood sandwich he was inhaling. He'd already cleaned out most of what was in the plane's tiny galley. He swallowed the current mouthful and set aside his sandwich.

"More like a big square, a parallelogram, just a box with four sides," Gideon replied. He sipped from a can of Coca-Cola and smiled. "You know, I remember when this stuff had actual cocaine in it. I prefer this formula."

Jordana turned a smile on him. "And what does that have to do with the conversation at hand?"

He shook his head. "Sorry. I start woolgathering when I'm tired. Uh, so, what was your question?"

"Why are we flying around in a big, er, parallelogram?" Jordana said.

Gideon nodded. "Right, we're not. I mean, we *are*, but it's just a byproduct. You see, magic is like technology, but it's a technology based on strength of will and a natural ability to interact with, well, magic itself, and magic is all about symbolism."

"Symbolism?" Jordana repeated.

"The circle, the pentacle, the icons of the Elements, the ritualism," Gideon said. "In order for the magic to work, you've got to *believe* it will work, especially with something you have little talent for, the way I do with thaumaturgy, er, ritual magic."

"You don't normally do things like that, do you?" Jordana said.

Gideon touched the Bright Fang bracelet. "No, my talent is for artifacts, like my sword, like some of my battle gear. I craft items, artifacts, and I imbue them with magic, with a part of my will, and then, they do things. That's how I create most of my spells. That and potion crafting.

"See, anybody can do magic, really. They just need to learn the skill, the symbolism, and they have to have the will to believe, and whatever spell they're doing, should work," Gideon said. "*Should.*"

"Let me guess, because if they don't have sufficient talent, and they have *any* doubts, the spell won't work," Jordana said.

Gideon nodded. "Something like that. Magic also demands payment. You could think of it as... 'fuel' for the technology. Most of that fuel comes from the bounty of the universe itself, but a significant bit *must* come from the practitioner."

"Your blood," Jordana said.

"Merely a symbol of my life force, but, yes, and now, I'm having to replenish the energy I used in creating the cleansing spell that I worked on you and your family," Gideon said.

"That still doesn't explain why we're flying around in circles or parallelograms," Jordana said.

"Symbolism. Most tracking spells are channeled through the earth, mostly because everybody is in contact with the planet, except, of course, when we're not," Gideon replied.

"We're in the air!" Jordana said. "No contact with the ground, so no way for the tracking spell to follow us."

"Oh, there's more than that going on," Gideon said. "First, we're flying south. Then, we fly west, which takes us out over the Gulf of Mexico, the ocean for our intents and purposes."

"Ah, the separation of the dry land from the wet sea from the air above, like in Genesis," Jordana said. She grinned at Gideon. "I went to Sunday School."

Gideon chuckled and nodded. "Yes, we're passing over a demarcation between one of those three symbolic terrains. We're also marking the cardinal points of the compass."

"South, west, and I suppose we'll turn north soon?" Jordana said.

"Into Texas. Then, we'll turn east and back to Atlanta." Gideon ran his finger in a mostly square pattern in the air in front of his face. "Thus, parallelogram."

"Interesting. Complicated, but interesting," Jordana said.

"Well, we had the resources for complicated. Most folks don't, but there's other ways to protect yourself," Gideon replied.

"Such as?" Jordana prompted.

"Running water," Gideon said.

"Like a creek or a river?"

"Yeah, but a shower would work, too. Good hygiene and good way to, literally, wash away whatever whammy somebody else has put on you," Gideon said. "Another trick is making a circle."

"A circle?"

"A ritual circle, and it doesn't have to be complicated. Those circles you see on TV with all the symbols and stuff written in faux Latin and/or Greek are... Well, they're fluff, but that goes back to the whole 'need to believe in order for it to work' thing. Really, all you actually need is a circle. You can draw it on the ground with chalk, dig one in the dirt with a stick or your finger, paint it on the floor with house paint." Gideon snorted a chuckle. "One time I used a Sharpie marker on a floor made of imported Italian tiles. God, the guy who owned the house was more pissed about that than the fact that I'd just killed a basilisk in his kitchen."

Gideon rolled his neck. "Anyway, you empower the circle with your will, but you have to spill some blood to seal the deal. The downside to a circle is that while you're in it, you're in it. You move outside of it, you break it. Scuff it with your foot, it's broken, and when the circle is broken, it's useless. However, while it's unbroken, nothing spiritual or magical is getting in."

"They could still shoot you, though, couldn't they?" Jordana said.

"If they have opposable thumbs and trigger fingers, yes," Gideon chuckled. "The best way to protect yourself, though, is just to shoot the other guy before he can lay his mojo on you."

"Your preferred method, I take it?" Jordana teased.

"There are very few problems in the universe which cannot be solved by a vigorous application of firepower," Gideon said. "Shoot it enough, and it'll die."

"Okay, speaking of that, here's something that's been bugging me for a few hours: what about silver bullets?" Jordana asked.

"Will kill just about anybody, really," Gideon chuckled. "Are you especially vulnerable to silver as a therianthrope? Sort of. You can wear silver jewelry, you can even eat using real silverware, but if somebody sticks a piece of silver in you? It's toxic, not immediately lethal, but it will slow a thrope's metabolism down to a crawl. We actually fill steel hollow-point bullets with silver nitrate. The silver nitrate causes the wounds to keep from sealing, and steel is proof against Fae."

"What?" Jordana frowned.

"Fae are vulnerable to iron. It's toxic to them the way silver is toxic to us," Gideon said. He smiled. "It's one reason why Fae creatures hide from humans. We have lots of weapons made from steel, which is just refined iron. Of course, high-velocity lead is just as toxic to them as it is to any mundane human."

"Good to know," Jordana said.

"So, I'm still thinking that maybe going shooting would be a good second-date activity," Gideon said.

Jordana nodded. "Yeah, but I don't know if I'd call playing with guns an appropriate second-date activity. It's more of a... third or fourth date kind of thing."

"Is that so?" Gideon smiled.

"Uh-huh, but I think we could do that the next time we go out," Jordana said.

"Second date," Gideon said.

"No, not if we count lunch today as our second date, and having a meal with the family is a definite third date kind of thing. So, we're up to date number four by default," Jordana said.

"At this rate, we'll be picking out china patterns by the end of the week," Gideon said.

"Not yet, buster," Jordana teased. "It'll be at least two weeks. I plan to have a career, you know."

"Good for you! Feminists of the world, rejoice!" Gideon snarked.

Kitty came over and flopped down on the couch next to Jordana. "So, what are you guys talking about?"

"We were just trying to figure out which color would be the least flattering for your skin tone. You know, for when we ask you to be the flower girl," Gideon said.

Kitty's eyes bulged.

"He's kidding!" Jordana exclaimed, but she smiled at Gideon. "He's something of a smart ass."

"Genius ass," Gideon chuckled.

"Eww, you guys are having a moment," Kitty gagged. "Gross!"

"You're just jealous," Jordana teased as she wrapped an arm around his sister.

"Am not," Kitty insisted.

"So, are you here to spy on us for your dad or did you want something?" Gideon asked.

Kitty bit her lower lip as she considered her answer. "A-am I... you know, am I like Mom and Jordy? Am I a werewolf?"

Gideon gazed steadily at her for a moment before taking a deep breath and saying, "The best answer I can give you right now is... maybe."

"Not... helpful," Kitty said.

Gideon shrugged. "You've got about a fifty/fifty chance of expressing the therianthrope gene sequence. You're the right age for the first change to happen normally, but Jordy here was a late bloomer. Now, that might be because of the elven gene sequences in her DNA or it might be due to your mom's long-term use of an anti-transformation serum. The same could be true of you, too. On the other hand, you could wolf out two minutes from now."

"Why two minutes from now?" Kitty asked.

"Ask Jordy," Gideon said with a nod.

"Holy cow, Jordy! Your eyes!" Kitty exclaimed.

"Did they change?" Jordana asked.

Kitty nodded. Jordana's eyes had turned blue-white.

"My, what big teeth you have," Gideon said.

"He's right, your teeth are all pointy-like," Kitty said staring up into her sister's mouth.

"The moon is up," Gideon said, "and while werewolves aren't necessarily locked into the phases of the moon, it does exert an influence. Mostly because young werewolves *believe* it should exert an influence."

"So, I don't have to change unless I want to," Jordana said. She closed her eyes in concentration. When she opened her eyes they had returned to their normal, warm brown.

"That is so cool," Kitty declared.

"The only change that is entirely involuntary is the first," Gideon said. "Jordy is actually a pretty quick study. I've mentored other young thropes and nobody's caught on quite as fast as she has."

Gideon sniffed. "Your dad's coming."

"Girls, can I have a moment alone with Gideon?" Tom asked.

"It's a small plane, Daddy," Kitty said. "Don't know how private it can get."

Tom rolled his eyes and jerked a thumb over his shoulder. Gideon chuckled. The girls got up and joined Matt and their mother at the rear of the main cabin.

"Something on your mind, Tom?" Gideon asked. He wrapped the remains of his sandwich in a napkin on the hunch that he wouldn't get to finish eating.

Tom sat down with a heavy sigh. "I, uh, just wanted to say, er, thank you for what you've done for Jordy and for saving our family. I'm not... ungrateful, just..."

"Overwhelmed? Confused? Frustrated? All of the above?" Gideon supplied with a small smile. "Believe it or not, I understand. I've seen this happen countless times."

"Countless, huh?" Tom chuckled. "What are you, twenty, thirty years old?"

"Older," Gideon said. "I fought in the American Revolution.'

Tom's eyes bulged. "How- how is that possible?"

"I am, more or less, immortal, and it's because my paternal grandparents and my father were born immortals. My grandmother is one of the Ard Sidhe, the High Elves, the same race as the man who raped your wife while wearing your face," Gideon said.

"Wait... does that mean...?" Tom said glancing toward his older daughter.

"It's very likely. She's inherited other High Elf traits. I don't see why she wouldn't be immortal," Gideon said. "And, by the way, 'immortal' just means you don't age. It doesn't mean you're indestructible or invulnerable. The werewolf side grants a certain amount of indestructibility, but that doesn't mean she's not in danger. We have to keep her safe until we figure out what's going on."

"Do you have any idea about that?" Tom asked, leaning forward.

Gideon shook his head. "The Dark Word is... obtuse. Some of their plots are completely random, senseless, just about causing as much chaos as possible in the world. Other plans of theirs were initiated before the dawn of recorded history and won't see fruition until long after the end of time." Gideon looked Tom in the eye. "I *really* hate these guys. I am *very* motivated to thwart them however possible. Right now, keeping Jordana away from them is doing that."

"Why are you so motivated?" Tom asked.

Gideon's jaw tightened, flexed, and relaxed. "I was married once, back in the late 60's, early 70's. These Dark Word jackasses decided that she was the perfect host for one of their demon goddesses, Kali. They kidnapped her while I was out of the house. Her father and I went after her. He was an old-school, fireball-tossing wizard," Gideon chuckled. "Ole Bernard was like having close artillery support. We killed a bunch of Thuggee cultists that day, but not before they managed to complete the ritual and bind the demon into my wife."

"What happened?" Tom asked, his voice barely a whisper.

Gideon's hands tightened into fists until his knuckles went white. His eyes started to glow amber as he remembered the scene, the demon taunting and tempting him with Aggie's voice. "I... I killed her."

"What?" Tom hissed.

"Had to," Gideon growled. "The only way to stop the demon was to kill the host. Aggie was gone. Kali had eaten her soul in the process of joining with her. I stabbed my wife through the heart with my magic sword, Tom. I *never* want *anyone* to have to go through something like that again. I will *die* before I let the Dark Word do anything like that to Jordy."

Tom reached out and placed a hand on Gideon's shoulder. "I know you will. Whatever you need us to do to help, we'll do."

Gideon nodded his thanks. "And I'll do my level best to protect your family."

"Don't worry about me or Lucinda. Our daughters are far more important than ourselves," Tom said. "Do you have children?"

"None of my body, but I have an adopted daughter. She's one of the agents who'll be meeting us when we land," Gideon said.

"You've never fathered children? Is that because you're immortal?" Tom asked.

Gideon laughed. "No, it's not like the 'Highlander' movies. Immortals can sire children. That's how the immortal gene sequence is passed on. My father is immortal because his parents were immortal, but his children... Well, he's only had four children in a thousand years who have inherited the gene. Only two of us are alive. I have had numerous mortal siblings, but they all grew old and died."

"Is that why you've never had children? You don't want to watch them grow old and die like your father has had to?" Tom asked.

Gideon shook his head. "No, I'm one-quarter Fae. All Fae are born with a *geas*, a taboo or curse. Mine is that I can't have a child of my body until I am with my destined true love. I've only been married three times, and every one of my marriages ended in tragedy of one kind or another."

Tom didn't know what to say. He just patted Gideon's shoulder again. The two men sat together in companionable silence for the rest of the flight.

CHAPTER EIGHTEEN

Atlanta, Georgia, USA
Covington Municipal Airport
Covington, GA
October 24, 2010

"Home again, home again, jiggedy-jig," Gideon muttered as he glanced out the window.

The plane was just passing over Atlanta and descending toward Covington. They'd be touching down in another ten minutes. Gideon stepped up to the cockpit. Perkins was speaking to someone at Traffic Control. Gideon tapped the pilot's shoulder to get his attention. Perkins glanced up, then back down and switched off the radio.

"Yes, sir?" he said.

"Perky, I'm gonna need a few more minutes in the air. Something I gotta do before we touch down on earth again," Gideon said.

"Magic stuff, right," Perkins nodded. "I'll get that cleared right up, sir."

"Yeah, uh, thanks," Gideon snickered.

He stepped back into the main cabin. The gear that he needed was in the aft cabin. Gideon quickly went and retrieved the objects that he needed. Then, he returned to the main cabin. From the tiny fridge he grabbed four small bottles of water.

"Right," he said getting everyone's attention. "I've got one last thing I need you guys to do before we touch down," he explained as he handed each of the Quinlans a bottle of water.

"More magic stuff?" Kitty sighed.

"Sort of," Gideon said. He pulled a small plastic baggy from a pocket. Inside were four black capsules, each slightly larger than a vitamin pill. "I want each of you to take one of these."

"What's it for?" Tom asked as he eyed the capsule Gideon gave him suspiciously.

"Think of it as the final step in my anti-tracking spell," Gideon replied.

"Why are they black?" Kitty asked.

"Well, I wanted blue pills and red pills, but I figure only half of you would take the pills if I did that, and the other half would be trapped in the Matrix forever," Gideon replied.

Kitty stared at him. "Jordy is right: you *are* a smart ass."

"That'll be a dollar for my swear jar," Gideon said with a wink. "Don't worry, mostly, it's a multi-vitamin."

Jordana popped the pill into her mouth and washed it down with a swig of water. "There. Done and it didn't even taste bad."

The rest of the Quinlan family quickly followed suit. Gideon nodded approval. "Okay, let's all get buckled in and ready for landing."

Twenty minutes later, they were exiting the plane. A pair of black Suburbans sat on the tarmac waiting for them. The tall, blond agent, Raven, stood beside the first truck. She smiled when she saw Gideon step out of the plane and look around.

"I've got the area secured," she said stepping forward to greet him.

"Doesn't stop me from double-checking," Gideon grunted. "Where's my Jeep?"

"Took the liberty of returning it and Uncle Matt's car to your house," Raven replied. "Wasn't expecting you to return the same day."

"Unpredictability is one of my better features," Gideon said.

He noticed the other agent standing by the second SUV. Gideon raised an eyebrow at Raven.

"What?" Raven demanded with a perfectly straight face.

Gideon crooked a finger to beckon the other agent over. "Carmichael," he said.

Agent Levi Carmichael smiled a goofy grin as he trotted over. He was well over six feet tall, somewhat gangly, dark-haired and blue eyed, and handsome in an earnest, well-meaning way.

"Mr. Shaw, good to see you again, sir," Levi said, offering his hand.

Gideon just looked at the hand, but he didn't bother to take it. "Carmichael," he repeated.

Levi swallowed the lump that suddenly formed in his throat. He glanced at Raven who was trying very hard not to smile.

"Uncle Gideon," Raven chided.

"My prerogative as your father to not like your boyfriend," Gideon growled. Then, he sighed and grabbed Levi's hand. "I'm actually glad you're here, Levi."

Levi grinned in relief.

"How far can you teleport with passengers?" Gideon asked.

"Uh, depending on the extra mass, uh, much less than I can unencumbered," Levi replied.

"Give me some numbers, kid," Gideon said.

Levi sighed. "Uh, well, I could teleport one of these SUV's about ten, maybe twenty, feet. I could take you or Matt and your personal combat load about a mile or two..."

"What about two teenage girls, combined mass under two hundred fifty pounds?" Gideon asked.

Levi frowned in thought. "Two passengers? Yeah, mile and a half, two miles maybe..."

Gideon frowned, then sighed heavily. "Okay, that'll have to do. So, you couldn't jump from here to Belle Arbor with two passengers, right?"

"I could make it there by myself easy, but not with additional mass," Levi confirmed. "I could skip the whole way."

"Skip?" Gideon repeated.

"Series of short jumps, line of sight. Exhausting as hell, but doable," Levi explained. "Not to mention the last time I tried it with a passenger, she got really, really nauseous."

"Better puking my guts out than dead," Raven said.

"Okay, Levi, you're gonna be my plan B, the ejector seat. Your top priority is gonna be the safety of Jordana and Katherine Quinlan. We get into any kind of ambush, you teleport them out. Skip them *into* Magee House if you have to. Raven's right. Puking beats dead or captured," Gideon said. "Come with me, you two."

Gideon led them to the plane and the disembarking passengers. He nodded to Tom who had one arm around his wife's shoulder, and the other gripping Kitty to his side. Jordana was on her mother's other side. They all looked terrified, but were keeping it in check. For a moment, Gideon allowed himself to admire the bravery of their family.

"Alright, here's the plan: we're gonna go to a safe house, but we've got about an eight-mile drive to get there. Because I'm a professional paranoid, we're gonna assume that the bad guys will try to ambush us at some point between here and there," Gideon said.

"I thought all that mumbo-jumbo you did was to throw them off our trail," Tom said.

"Like I said," Gideon replied pointing to himself, "professional paranoid. Plan for the worst, hope for the best."

Tom nodded. "Gotcha."

"Okay, we're gonna take two SUV's. Perkins and Matt will be in one truck with Tom and Lucinda. Jordy and Kitty will be in the other truck with me and Raven. Ladies, this is Agent Carmichael. You'll be sitting on either side of him. He's a teleporter. Should we get hit, his job is to get you two to safety. There might be... unpleasant side effects, but you'll be alive, and that's our highest priority," Gideon said.

"Define 'unpleasant'," Kitty challenged.

"Do you like roller coasters?" Levi asked.

Kitty nodded.

"The kind that turn you inside out and make you swallow your own stomach?"

"Uh," Kitty hedged.

"Yeah, like that," Levi said. "Only with more puking."

"Okay, that does sound unpleasant," Kitty agreed.

"Better puking than dead," Raven added.

"What about Princess?" Jordana asked.

"She rides with us, in the back of the SUV," Gideon replied.

"Okay," Jordana nodded.

"Let's not stand around here talking all day. Let's get loaded into the trucks and rolling," Gideon said.

"Which route do you want to take?" Raven asked once she was seated behind the wheel of the lead SUV.

Gideon shrugged. "Doesn't really matter 'cause there's at least two choke points we'll have to cross through, and then only one road leading into Belle Arbor."

"Might as well take the shortest route, then," Raven said.

"Good plan," Gideon agreed as he checked the action on the M4 carbine that was nestled in a mount in front of the passenger seat. The Suburban was a fully equipped law-enforcement vehicle down to the police band radio, laptop computer, and lights and sirens.

"What's 'Belle Arbor'?" Kitty whispered across Levi to Jordana.

"Uh, it's the, uh, estate where Gideon lives," Jordana replied.

"I'm sorry, did you say 'estate'?" Kitty gasped.

"Yeah, it an old antebellum plantation," Levi explained. "It's pretty cool. There's a mansion called Magee House and an old coach house that's been converted into a guest house, old slave quarters, a barn, a really pretty flower garden with a gazebo. It's like a little oasis of Old South charm right in the middle of a bunch of subdivisions."

"And Gideon lives there?" Kitty repeated.

Levi glanced over at Jordana who seemed to be embarrassed. "Yeah, he does with a bunch of other folks, mostly people who work for the estate."

Gideon leaned around. "Kitty, my family is, technically speaking, rich."

"Define 'rich'," Kitty said.

"Uh, I can't buy and sell nations, but I can afford to buy Apple products without worrying about the cost," Gideon said.

"Okay, Jordy, now I understand why you like older men," Kitty said with a wicked grin.

"Shut up," Jordana sighed at her sister.

Gideon turned around with a smile. He listened to the sisters as they teased and bickered with one another, but with only half an ear. The bulk of his attention was focused outside the Suburban. Raven drove quickly, but no more quickly than anybody else on the road. Gideon glanced back and noted that Perkins was keeping the other Suburban close enough to provide support, but not so close that both vehicles could be taken out with the same bomb or grenade if that happened.

He felt himself tense at the passing of every van, SUV, and pickup truck. Once or twice, he almost placed his finger on the trigger of the M4, but restrained himself when he realized that he'd almost considered opening fire on an actual church van. Their route took them down Emory Street, over the railroad tracks, past the restaurant built into the old Depot building. Emory crossed over U.S. 278, the main commercial strip through town, and Gideon had pegged the intersection as the best place for an ambush. The interstate was fairly close by, and attackers had their choice of a QuikTrip, a bank, and a Papa John's Pizza from which to launch an ambush.

A dump truck was idling at the intersection. Gideon's attention focused on the vehicle. Quite a lot of road construction was being carried out just up the road, but this was Sunday night. What legitimate reason would a driver have for being out and about in a dump truck on a Sunday night?

"I see it," Raven said.

Gideon's finger slid onto the trigger. He picked up the microphone on the radio.

"Viking, one o'clock, the dump truck. Be alert, over."

"Roger that, Highlander," Matt's voice replied from the speaker. "I don't see anything else, though. Over."

"Could be veiled. Over," Gideon replied.

The Suburban passed through the intersection without incident. The dump truck continued to sit at the light. The following SUV then passed through the intersection behind them. Gideon remained on high alert for several more moments, but nothing happened. He slipped his finger out of the trigger guard. Their route then carried them through a tight little warren of back streets through Covington's historical district.

"I've never seen this part of town," Jordana commented as they passed cheap clapboard houses.

"The university kind of frowns on students coming out this way," Gideon replied. "Bit of a drug problem in this area."

"A town this small has drug problems?" Kitty scoffed.

"*Every* town has drug problems, big or small," Levi said.

Kitty frowned up at him. "Really?"

Levi blushed slightly. "I, uh, sometimes work for the DEA."

"The Program hides its agents within other agencies: FBI, CIA, NSA, DEA, and so forth," Gideon explained. "Choke point coming up."

"Got my eyes peeled," Raven said.

They turned off Ga. Highway 36 onto Piper Rd. The two black SUV's rolled quickly down the road and turned onto Magee Road at the end of Piper. Gideon let out the breath he hadn't realized he was holding.

"We can relax a little," Gideon declared.

"Why?" Kitty demanded.

"Magee Road marks the beginning of Belle Arbor," Raven said.

"And Belle Arbor is warded," Gideon added.

"What's that mean?" Kitty asked.

"A ward is like a magical security system, a mystical barrier that protects an area from certain kinds of danger," Gideon said. "The wards here block spells mostly, but if anybody comes onto the land with hostile intent, they get directed away. If they muscle their way in, the wards become more... actively hostile."

"And there's a really tight technological security net, too," Raven said. "Video cameras, face recognition software, infrared sensors, motion detectors, seismic vibration sensors, electric fences, land mines..."

"*Land mines*?" Kitty and Jordana said in unison.

"She's kidding," Levi declared. "You *are* kidding, aren't you?"

Raven grinned. "You do know my family, don't you?"

"Well, suddenly, I'm less comfortable with our little walks in the woods," Levi said.

Gideon snorted. "There aren't any land mines, but we do have the option of placing claymores and automated weapons if we need to." He turned around in his seat. "Ladies, when I called this a 'safe house' I wasn't kidding. It'd take an army to get at you in Magee House."

"So, you basically live in a fortress," Jordana said.

"Yeah, but so does Superman," Gideon replied. "My fortress, though, is much more comfortable and a lot prettier."

CHAPTER NINETEEN

Atlanta, Georgia, USA
Magee House, Belle Arbor Plantation
Covington, GA
October 25, 2010

Gideon ran the brush along the horse's flank in long, steady strokes. The horse snorted contentedly at the attention. Keith Urban's latest single was coming from the speakers mounted in the barn's corners. Princess was sniffing at one of the speakers.

"Get away from there, dog," Gideon warned.

Princess pranced over to him, tail wagging. She sat down next to him, waiting.

Gideon smiled. "When I'm through with the big one, you can have a turn."

"Give the bitch a scratch," squawked a large blue and yellow macaw perched on the door to the horse's stall. The bird repeated himself twice and then cackled like the mad scientist from an old movie.

"Behave, Bruce," Gideon said, but the admonition was pro forma. Bruce the Foul-Mouthed Parrot was a creature of habit.

Princess eyed the bird, not sure whether this was a fellow animal or a strangely disguised person, since it could talk.

"Pretty bitch," Bruce declared. Then, he wolf-whistled and started singing to himself something that sounded suspiciously like the song playing on the speakers.

Gideon chuckled and continued grooming the horse.

"Knobs said I'd find you out here," Jordana said as she walked into the barn.

Princess came bounding over to her, and Jordana knelt down to give the dog a hug.

"Did you sleep alright?" Gideon asked.

Jordana nodded.

"Your family?"

She shrugged. "I don't think Mom and Dad got much sleep. I think they must've stayed up all night talking. Kitty slept, though. I could hear her snoring from my room. Thanks, by the way, for moving me out of your sister's old room. It's more Kitty's style anyway."

Gideon chuckled. "If you want, we can move you into the coach house or the old slave quarters. Just so, you know, you can get away from your family."

"No, I like the new room just fine, thank you," Jordana said. She stepped up to the horse and gently touched his snout. The horse snorted and whinnied at her. "You never mentioned horses when I asked you about pets."

"I don't consider horses as pets," Gideon replied.

"What do you consider them?"

After a moment's thought, he said, "Transportation."

Jordana laughed. "Are you serious?"

"The automobile is a relatively recent invention, dear. Until I bought my first Model T from Henry Ford, my primary mode of transport, after my own feet, was a horse, like Patches here," Gideon said.

"Patches?" Jordana raised a single eyebrow.

"He's a Paint Mustang. Kinda looks like a patchwork quilt," Gideon said.

"I can see that," Jordana said. "Okay, but if you think of horses as transportation, not pets, why do you have a horse at all? I mean, I know you own a Jeep."

"Actually, I still have that old Model T," Gideon chuckled. "As well as several of the cars that I've owned over the years. Patches here is a direct descendant of my favorite horse that I rode when I lived in Texas."

"Let me guess: you were a cowboy," Jordana said. She grabbed a brush and started working on the horse's other side.

"In point of fact, before the War for Southern Independence, I did, indeed, raise beef cattle in Texas. Wasn't able to stay, though. Had a... disagreement with one of my neighbors over water rights. It... ended badly," Gideon said.

"What happened?" Jordana asked.

"We fought a duel. Pistols at twenty paces," Gideon replied. He touched a spot on his chest just below his heart. "He put a ball through me. As you may be aware, I'm kind of... indestructible, or at least really, really close to it. However, in a normal human being, it was a death blow. So, I faked my death."

"What happened to the other guy?" Jordana asked.

"Well, my aim was better, and he wasn't as... sturdy as I am," Gideon replied. "He died instantly. It was all an exercise in pointless futility. We both lost." Gideon shook his head. "It was one of the reasons that I decided to go to medical school and become a doctor. I'd gotten sick of killing." He smiled sadly. "That didn't last too long, though. Fate always seems to stick me in a situation where something needs killing, and I'm the one that has to kill it."

"'We sleep safe in our beds because rough men stand ready in the night to visit violence on those who would do us harm'," Jordana quoted.

"George Orwell," Gideon said. "I'm impressed."

"I read. It's a terrible habit, I know, but I just can't seem to break myself of it," she replied with a mischievous grin.

"Are you calling me one of Orwell's 'rough men'?" Gideon asked.

"I slept safe in my bed because I knew you were out here, ready to shoot the crap out of anything that dared go bump in the night," Jordana said.

"Shoot the shit!" Bruce shrilled.

"Nice timing, dumb bird," Gideon growled.

"Uh-oh, Bruce fucked up the moment," the macaw moaned and hid his face behind a wing.

"Um, is that your parrot?" Jordana asked.

"Did the profanity give him away?" Gideon asked.

"Oh, definitely," Jordana laughed.

"Come here, Bruce," Gideon ordered holding up his arm.

The bird flew from his perch and landed on the offered limb. He fluttered his wings, ruffled his feathers, and then settled down.

"Bruce the Foul-Mouthed Parrot, this is Jordana," Gideon said.

"Well, helloooo, Angel Tits!" Bruce declared with an accompanying wolf whistle.

Jordana glanced down at her chest. "Uh, thank you?"

"Put her there, hot stuff," the bird squawked and held out one of his feet.

"He wants to shake your hand," Gideon explained.

"With his foot?" Jordana chuckled, but she took hold of Bruce's offered appendage. "Uh, pleasure to meet you?"

The bird whistled and said, "Pleasure the girl, Giddy!"

"He has trouble with my name," Gideon sighed.

"Pretty Bruce!" the bird declared. "Pretty Angel Tits!"

"It's like he has Tourette's and can't help himself," Jordana laughed.

Gideon smiled. "Something like that. Would you like to hold him? Foul language aside, he's really a very loving animal."

"Hold me, hug me, fuck me, love me!" Bruce chortled.

Jordana laughed. "Well, he has an impressive vocabulary."

"And he makes most of it up as he goes," Gideon sighed.

"Giddy loves Bruce," the parrot said as he stepped from Gideon's arm to Jordana's. "Bruce loves Angel Tits."

"Looks like I got a new nickname," Jordana said as she stroked the feathers on the top of the parrot's head. Bruce made contented noises and declared his love several more times.

"Bruce, you behave for Jordy, okay?" Gideon told the parrot.

Bruce bobbed his head and whistled.

Gideon returned Patches to his stall. "I promised Princess that I'd brush her, too, if she behaved."

"She probably could use it," Jordana agreed. She sat down on a convenient hay bale while Gideon ran a brush through the dog's fur. "I think my dog is starting to like you more than she does me."

"I wouldn't say that," Gideon replied. "She's had her eyes on you the whole time."

"So, why would Matt give you a cussing parrot?" Jordana asked.

"He thought it would be funny, and he knew I needed a familiar," Gideon replied.

"Wait, what? Like a witch's familiar?" Jordana said.

"Not exactly. Typically, a familiar is a helper spirit that takes physical form, usually humanoid or animal. At least, that's the folklore. The reality is that people with the talent to do real magic can... enchant an animal, make it more than it was. It's still the same animal it was before, but it's been enhanced with the infusion of magic into its physical being," Gideon explained.

"And what did you do to Bruce here?"

"Well, Bruce is sort of like a biological recorder. He remembers all my alchemical recipes for me. He's also part of the security system," Gideon replied. "I've tied a couple of the wards to the bird. Anybody trying to spy on you with magic while Bruce is around... Well, they get a lot of confusing, foul language spoken in a loud, shrill voice."

"Like a magical white noise generator?"

"You get a gold star!"

Jordana grinned. "Well, speaking of gold stars, I've been thinking..."

"There you go again."

"Like I was saying, I've been thinking that since I can't exactly go to school right now, I might as well learn more about this shapeshifting stuff. That is, if you still want to teach me," Jordana said.

"Of course," Gideon exclaimed. "But, uh, we might want to *not* tell your Dad what we're up to."

"Why not?"

"I really don't want to explain to him why training you to shapeshift will involve nudity," Gideon said.

"And why would this involve nudity?"

"You do remember what happened to your clothes the last time, right?"

Jordana blushed. "Oh, yeah, right. Shapeshifting is hard on the wardrobe."

"Exactly," Gideon said. He ruffled the dog's ears. "You're good to go, Princess."

"Pretty bitch," Bruce declared.

"He's right. Were you a dog groomer in a previous life?" Jordana teased.

Gideon shrugged. "Something like that. I like taking care of animals."

"And people have been caring for animals a lot longer than they've had cars to look after, right?" Jordana said.

"Right."

Bruce squawked. "Giddy loves Angel Tits!"

Gideon was about to reply when Knobs blurred into the barn. "Master Gideon, sorry to interrupt, but Mistress Morrigan requests your presence in the study. She said it was important, but not overly urgent."

"Thanks, Knobs. Tell her I'll be there momentarily," Gideon replied.

Knobs nodded. "Of course, sir, and good morning to you, Miss Jordana."

"And good morning to you, too, Knobs," Jordana replied.

"Would you like breakfast?" Knobs asked.

"Silly question," Jordana said with a wink.

"Of course. What would you like?" Knobs asked.

"Surprise me," Jordana suggested.

"And you, sir?" Knobs said turning back to Gideon.

"Breakfast surprise sounds good... as long as Bernadette is cooking," Gideon replied.

Knobs snorted. "Like I'd let Master Matthias near the appliances. I'll take my leave then." Knobs nodded and blurred away.

"Who's 'Morrigan'?" Jordana asked once Knobs was gone.

"Oh, that's Raven's real name," Gideon replied.

"Okay, I was wondering why a tall blonde got a name like 'Raven'. I mean, I look more like a Raven than she does," Jordana said. "Now, you're gonna have to tell me how she got the nickname."

"When she was a tiny little girl, before her parents died, I gave her a stuffed black bird, told her it was 'Morrigan's Raven'. Well, in her little-girl mind, she kind of inverted it one day and insisted that the bird was Morrigan, and *she* was the raven. Ever since then, that's what we called her. Makes for a pretty good code name now that she's grown up," Gideon said.

"That makes a twisted sort of sense now," Jordana chuckled. "So, does everybody get a nickname around here?"

"Pretty much," Gideon said.

As they walked out of the barn, Jordana slipped her hand into his. Gideon glanced down at her small hand clasped to his large, rough hand, but Jordana continued on as though holding hands was something that they did every day.

"What's your nickname?" she was asking.

"Uh, 'Highlander'," Gideon replied.

"Because you're from Scotland?"

"And mostly immortal."

"Right. And Matt?"

"Viking. Mostly because, well, he's a Viking," Gideon said.

"And you're calling poor Perkins 'Perky', which I'm guessing he hates," Jordana said.

"Pretty much why we call him that," Gideon agreed.

"So, what's my nickname?"

Gideon snorted. "I'm kinda partial to Angel Tits."

Jordana replied with a swift kick to Gideon's back side.

CHAPTER TWENTY

Atlanta, Georgia, USA

Magee House, Belle Arbor Plantation

Covington, GA

October 25, 2010

"Two hearty breakfasts to go," Bernadette declared when Gideon and Jordana entered the kitchen. She handed each of them a large bowl filled with grits, cheese, chunks of ham, and scrambled eggs. "They's already coffee in the study."

"Portable," Jordana observed as she accepted the bowl and lifted out a spoonful of the mixture. "Tasty, too," she added after eating a mouthful. "Thank you, Bernadette!"

"I likes me a girl what likes to eat, honey," Bernadette laughed. "You wants more, let Knobs know, an' I'll bring you another bowl full."

"Deal," Jordana said.

"Why the rush?" Gideon asked.

"Raven say it important, but she too nice to rush y'all," Bernadette replied.

"But not you, right?" Gideon chuckled.

"Oh, Lawd, no! Now, get yo' selves along. Get!" Bernadette urged. "Now, little doggy, where you think you goin'?"

Princess tilted her head at this new human and was on the urge of growling at her when a bowl of tasty-smelling food hit the floor in front of her. The dog ignored everybody and everything except what was in her bowl.

"I'll look after the dog, don't worry," Bernadette assured them.

"Take her out to the kennel when she's done. Let her loose in the dog run, maybe," Gideon suggested.

Bernadette rolled her eyes. "Like I don't know how to take care of a dog. You taught me! Now, get!"

"You have a kennel?" Jordana chuckled.

"Like I told you: my family's raised dogs for... well, for longer than *I've* been alive. Even though my sister has the dogs with her down in Savannah, we still have facilities for them here. In a few years, she and I will probably switch houses, and she'll bring the dogs with her," Gideon said.

He led her to a room she hadn't seen before, across the hall from the music room. The study was another tall ceiling room, the walls lined with bookcases. The centerpiece of the room was a large table with cubbyholes built into it, filled with rolled-up maps and scrolls. In one corner was a small desk and modern office chair. The desk held a small, but powerful, computer and a telephone. The only other furnishings in the room, other than the chart table and bookcases, were several wingback chairs with small side tables, and a bird perch that Bruce flew to as soon as they entered the room.

Matt and Raven stood at the chart table, which held stacks of files and musty-looking books. A silver coffee service sat on the table, too, and Matt and Raven both had coffee cups in front of themselves. Levi sat in the office chair, staring intently at the screen of the computer. Perkins stood at one of the tall windows, staring out and taking occasional sips from his coffee cup. Matt, Raven, and Perkins were dressed in the cheap business suits that seemed to be the uniform of federal agents. Levi, on the other hand, was wearing blue jeans and a Star Wars t-shirt.

"Alright, what's up?" Gideon asked.

"We finally got a line on Michaela Dumont," Raven said.

"Really?" Gideon said.

"She showed up at the airport to check on her minions, and one of our agents, a Seer, got a good look at her," Raven explained. "You were half-right about the loa thing. She's definitely possessed by a spirit with loa-like features, but it's not a loa. It's definitely a soul-feeder."

Gideon sighed and shook his head. "Damn."

"What's a 'soul-feeder'?" Jordana asked.

"It's kind of a catch-all term for any spirit entities that require the life force of corporeal beings in order to exist within our reality," Matt said. "Basically, your living dead."

"In most cases, the invading spirit rapidly depletes the life energy, the *anima*, of the host. Then, it spends the rest of its 'life' in the host feeding on the anima of other creatures to sustain its current form," Raven added.

"Vampires, wendigo, ghouls, and such," Gideon said. "They need a medium to take the life force of their victims, something like their blood, or their flesh, or even their breath. Succubi and incubi actually absorb life force through, uh, sexual contact..."

"So, what's this have to do with Micky?" Jordana demanded.

"Loa don't hurt their hosts. They ride them, and when they're done, they return to wherever they came from, and the host carries on with life like normal. It's actually a mutually beneficial relationship in most cases," Gideon said.

"What *this* thing has done is it's entered your friend, and it's taken its time to eat her soul," Raven said. "Even if we manage to exorcize the demon, Micky is damaged beyond repair."

"The only thing keeping her 'alive' is the thing living inside her," Gideon said. "We'd kinda been hoping we could save your friend, but it doesn't look like that's possible anymore."

"So, in addition to trying to kidnap me for... God knows what, these... assholes have tried to kidnap and/or kill my family, *and* they've slowly killed one of my best friends while using her body to *spy* on me?" Jordana snarled. Her eyes had changed color to an icy blue, hairs had begun sprouting on her face, and her teeth and nails were elongating.

"Temper," Gideon warned softly.

"I really hate these guys," Jordana hissed. She closed her eyes and concentrated on calming down. When she opened her eyes, they were still icy blue, but otherwise she looked like a normal human again.

"What else have you learned?" Gideon asked.

"Well, once we figured out that Micky had been possessed by a soul-feeder that acted like a loa, we started by searching *De Jonker's Compendium Demonicum*, looking for a catalogued demon that matched what we know of the thing that stole Micky," Raven said patting a large, dusty-looking, and very old book.

"What she means is that since your copy of the *Compendium Demonicum* is in the original Dutch, I searched it," Matt said.

"Well, I don't speak Dutch, and it's, like, your native tongue," Raven said.

"Swedish. My first language is Swedish. I was born in Sweden where they speak Swedish," Matt grumbled.

"Focus," Gideon growled.

"Okay, so, after spending half the night going blind reading through this thing," Matt said tapping the book, "I came up with about half a dozen possible suspects. Ole De Jonker may've been batshit insane by the time he finished the book, but he was pretty thorough in his research and field work."

"Once we had Matt's list, I had Levi run them through the Program's database," Raven added.

"And I got nothing," Levi said.

"Until he widened his search to some of our allies' databases," Raven continued.

"Still got nothing," Levi clarified.

"Let me guess: you started hacking?" Gideon chuckled.

"Yes, sir," Levi said with a grin as he spun around to face the room. "The Unseelie Committee should look into better security for their servers in St. Petersburg."

"The who-where?" Jordana said.

"Dark fae who joined the Communist Party back a hundred years ago," Gideon said. "They're more or less the old USSR's version of the

Program, closely allied with the KGB, and like their KGB buddies, they've become gangsters since the collapse of communism in Russia."

"They're evil, but in a 'let's abuse our power to make a lot of money' way, not in a 'let's kill everybody on the planet and eat their souls' way," Matt added.

"I take it that you're making sure the Program is getting evidence of the Committee's latest plots and schemes?" Gideon said to Levi.

"Of course," Levi said and hit a button on the keyboard. "Now."

"What did you get that's useful to us?" Gideon asked.

"A name and a profile," Levi replied.

Raven slid one of the file folders toward Gideon. "We put this together for you," she said.

Gideon flipped open the file. "Nahasheron."

"De Jonker classifies her as a sub-species of succubus that he called an 'Interloper'," Matt said. "Basically, the Interloper is a spy/infiltrator. It enters the host, and just watches and waits while it nibbles away at the host's life force."

"Like a sleeper agent?" Gideon mused.

"Pretty much. The demon builds up its strength to take control of the host body, and when it does, that's when it starts to reek of undeath," Matt said.

"After that, the host's body starts to run hot, like a loa's mount. It's still alive, but the original owner is no longer in residence," Raven said.

"How does it feed to maintain the host?" Gideon asked.

"It doesn't," Matt replied. "It burns the current host out within a matter of weeks. Then, it starts looking like a ghoul for a while, and pretty soon it has to transfer either to a new host or a phylactery until a new host can be found for it."

"That's awful," Jordana said.

"The Committee used Nahasheron a few times as a sleeper agent, but she was never one of theirs. Their file refers to her as a 'mercenary'," Raven said.

Gideon flipped through the pages of the file, looking for the "known associates" page that all these files had. When he found it, he scanned through the names. The file fell from his suddenly numb hands. He glared across the table at Matt.

"Yeah, I noticed that, too," the big man sighed.

"What?" Jordana asked.

"Nahasheron is, basically, a slave," Matt explained. "Her ability to remain in our reality is tied to a physical object, a vessel for her spirit essence called a phylactery, kinda like a genie's lamp, but it can be anything -- a ring, a jewel, a stick --- and whoever controls that object, pretty much owns the demon tied to it."

"And I know the dink who owns Nahasheron," Gideon growled. "He calls himself Chemosh Magog, and he's the Dark Word overlord who destroyed my family." Gideon snarled and smashed his fist into the table cracking the surface.

"Uh, why don't you go get some air, buddy," Matt suggested.

"He up to his old tricks?" Gideon snarled.

"That's the going theory," Matt confirmed.

Gideon nodded. "Yeah, I need... air..."

He stalked out of the room, slamming the door behind him.

"Is he okay?" Jordana asked.

"No, but he'll be functional once he's blown off some steam," Raven replied. "Have you heard the story about what happened to his last wife, Aggie?"

"Not entirely," Jordana said. "I, uh, overheard him and my dad talking on the plane, though."

"So, you know that Aggie was kidnapped by the Dark Word to serve as the human host for one of their demon gods, and that Gideon was too late to save her," Matt said.

"Yeah, and that he, uh, had to kill her," Jordana said softly.

Matt nodded. "And even though Aggie was long gone, it was still her face that he was seeing even as he stabbed her with Bright Fang. Chemosh Magog was the Dark Word overlord who created the ritual and chose Aggie as Kali's mortal host."

"Wait a minute, do you think he's trying again? Is this asshole trying to turn me into Kali's mount?" Jordana snarled.

Raven and Matt looked at one another. Then, they turned to Jordana and nodded.

"Pretty much," Raven said.

"But not with Kali. Bright Fang is a demonbane blade. It kills demons... permanently. So, we figure Chemosh is courting a different demoness or goddess this time, and we figure his little run-in with Gideon convinced him that he's gonna need a sturdier host than a wizard this time," Matt said.

"Me?" Jordana gasped.

"You're half-werewolf and half-Ard Sidhe. Nigh-indestructible and pretty much immortal. I'd say you'd probably fit the bill pretty good," Raven said. "Throw in hot co-ed, and you've got yourself a pretty irresistible morsel for a super-villain type."

Matt blushed slightly and cleared his throat. "Here's another disturbing thought: Magog is an Ard Sidhe, an Unseelie High Lord who *willingly* bonded with a powerful old Canaanite god, Chemosh. So, we're talking a high elf with superior shapeshifting ability..."

"Jesus, Matt! Do you think this... Chemosh Magog person is..." The words choked in Jordana's throat.

Matt nodded. "I think he's your biological father."

CHAPTER TWENTY-ONE

Atlanta, Georgia, USA
Belle Arbor Plantation
Covington, GA
October 27, 2010

Jordana didn't see Gideon for a couple of days. She had no idea what had happened to him, and Matt assured her that Gideon would return when he "calmed down." She tried not to think about Matt and Raven's theory that Chemosh Magog was her biological father *and* that he wanted to use her body to house his... mate. Her stomach turned at that particular thought every time, which is why she shied away from that line of thinking.

She distracted herself by taking care of her family. The irony of that task made her smile a little. Her father, in particular, was having the hardest time adapting to the sudden change in their circumstances. Tom Quinlan was an engineer. Engineers dealt in mathematical absolutes. In a world where magic was actually real, he wasn't quite sure what was absolute and what wasn't anymore. Of all the people in the house, Knobs turned out to be the one who was best suited for explaining the change in Tom's reality. The goblin even used PowerPoint and had a full-color brochure.

Kitty had adapted the best to the change in situation. At first, she thought she was getting a vacation, but then, a tutor had shown up with a full list of assignments from her school. Only the fact that the tutor was a very attractive young man had salved the wound of homeschooling. The one-on-one approach was working, though. After a couple of days, Kitty's grades were already improving.

Jordana worried the most about her mother. Lucinda had become depressed, spending most of her time in the flower garden behind Magee House. Jordana had talked to Knobs and Bernadette, and between the three of them, they'd come up with several ways to keep Lucinda busy between caring for the garden and helping in the kitchen. Still, Lucinda's depression continued.

Toward sunset on Wednesday, Jordana decided that she was the one in need of air. Taking Princess with her, she walked out of Magee House and went in search of some seclusion. She'd been warned not to go into the woods surrounding the main house, but anything within the confines of the outbuildings was open to her. Jordana went as close to the edge of the woods as she dared and just sat down on a decorative log. Princess went exploring, sniffing around, looking for something interesting.

"Don't stray, Princess," Jordana ordered the dog.

Princess's head came up and looked at her person. Then, she trotted over and placed her muzzle in Jordana's lap.

Jordana chuckled and ruffled the dog's ears.

Suddenly, Princess went rigid and turned toward the woods. A strange new scent wafted into Jordana's nostrils, musky and somewhat masculine. She strained her ears, listening with all her enhanced ability. Princess growled. Then, she whined. Then, the dog relaxed.

A big, black dog -- no, a *wolf* -- came trotting out of the tree line. It stopped and stared with brilliant amber eyes at Jordana and Princess. Then, it shook its huge head and trotted toward them. Part of Jordana wanted to be afraid, but she wasn't. She just *knew* that she had the power to protect herself if it came down to it. She could feel the change starting. The wolf stopped several feet away and sat on its haunches. Even as it sat back, the wolf's form started flowing into something else.

Gideon was squatting in front of her and Princess. The dog yipped a greeting and rushed over. Gideon smiled as he patted the animal. He looked up at Jordana.

"You really shouldn't be out here by yourself," he said.

"I'm not by myself. Princess is here," Jordana said. She shook her head. "Okay, let's not fall into the witty banter thing. Where the hell have you been?"

"Nearby," Gideon said. "Running. Hunting. Thinking."

"I'm sorry? Running, hunting, and thinking?" Jordana snapped, standing up. She'd clenched her fists, but instantly released them when the claws in her fingertips dug into her palms. "You abandoned me!"

"I was angry, but I *never* abandoned you," Gideon snapped back, standing up, bringing his greater height to bear in the argument.

Princess whined and cowered away from her people.

"I've been in these woods for the last two days, and I've been watching over you, but I needed time to think!" Gideon continued.

Jordana's retort died on her lips. Suddenly, she was blushing and grinning.

"What?" Gideon demanded.

"You're naked," Jordana laughed.

Gideon rolled his eyes. "Oh, lord. I thought we were having an argument?"

"Dude, do you seriously think I can argue with you while your..." Jordana pointed in the general direction of Gideon's nether region, "while your junk is all hanging out? Now, go put some clothes on so I can finish yelling at you."

"Not really an incentive for me to get dressed, is it? Not if it's just to get yelled at," Gideon said.

Princess whined again.

Gideon squatted down and rubbed the dog's ears. "It's okay, Princess," he soothed as he stroked the dog along her spine. "Mommy is just taking her frustrations out on me. She's not really mad at me, just the situation," he told the animal. Then, he glanced up at Jordana. "Well, mostly she's not mad at me, but she is some."

"I can't stay mad at a naked man petting a dog. It's too ridiculous," Jordana said with a chuckle.

"I really am sorry, though, Jordy. We don't really know one another, but something that I wanted to keep from you is... Well, it's my temper," Gideon said. "I don't lose it often, but when I do..." He sighed. "Random, destructive things happen around me when I get like that, and I didn't want you to see it or be a victim of it.

"Sitting around in a defensive posture is contrary to my nature. I prefer to be on the attack, but until we can find out where Chemosh

Magog is hiding this time, I have to sit tight. So, I went into the woods here and took my frustrations out on two hapless deer and a pukwudgie."

"A what?" Jordana exclaimed.

"Pukwudgie," Gideon repeated. "Fae creature, shapeshifter, kinda half-porcupine, half-troll, poison arrows... I'm not making this up."

"I can't exactly take you seriously right now. Will you *please* put some clothes on?" Jordana said.

Gideon sighed. "Knobs, could you bring me a change of clothes?"

The goblin butler *blurred* into their presence. "I had a feeling this would happen when you ran out of the house all hell-bent and..." He saw Jordana standing there. He looked at Gideon. "Well... Isn't this just... awkward, sir?"

Gideon snorted a laugh and took the Navy sweats that Knobs had brought. "My, aren't you just so funny?"

"Yes, sir, I am," Knobs agreed with a perfectly straight face. Then, a crooked grin split his green face. He whistled to the dog. "Come along, little Princess. Old Knobs has a nice soup bone for you. It even has some meat left on it."

Princess wagged her tail and barked happily. Knobs picked the dog up gingerly and blurred away with a nod for both of the humans.

"He's a useful person," Jordana observed. She turned back to Gideon. "Now, where was I?"

"You were wanting to yell at me some more," Gideon said.

Jordana waved that idea off. "No, I'm kinda yelled out. You kind of had me distracted."

"Was it the rock hard abs? The bulging pecs? The super-cut definition in my delts?"

"It was that tiny little thing between your legs," Jordana snarked.

"Tiny? You wound me, madam. Verily," Gideon said affecting a melodramatic pose.

Jordana laughed. "Thanks. I think I needed a laugh as much as I needed to yell at somebody. Sorry I took it out on you."

"Don't be. That's what I'm here for," Gideon said.

"Are you hungry? Mom and Bernadette have been really tearing it up in the kitchen today," Jordana said.

Gideon shook his head. "No, two deer and a pukwudgie, and I'm pretty much full."

"Pukwudgie? Is that for real? I mean, it's a funny word: pukwudgie," Jordana said.

"No, they're real. In their natural form, they're like trolls with these porcupine quills covering their back. They're incredibly strong and tough. They make arrows from their quills, poison them, and use 'em to catch their prey, which they eat paralyzed and still alive," Gideon said. "Nasty buggers."

"Sounds like it," Jordana asked. "Are they really big?"

"Just about three feet tall," Gideon snickered.

"What?" Jordana scoffed.

"Terrible things come in small packages," Gideon replied. "Take Knobs, for example. He's barely five-foot-two, but I've seen him go toe-to-toe with a stink ape three times his size, and Knobs barely broke a sweat. Just played with the critter like a cat with a mouse."

"Good point," Jordana said. Then, she giggled. "Pukwudgie."

Gideon snorted. "Yeah, it really *is* a fun word to say."

"I just realized something," Jordana said. "We're kind of even now."

"Even, how?"

"You've seen me naked, and now I've seen you naked."

"Are we actually keeping score on that count?"

"Maybe."

"So, what else are you keeping track of?"

"Our dating schedule. You're behind, mister."

"Sorry. Been kinda busy."

"Sure. You've been hanging out with your little friend, Mr. Pukwudgie, drinking, playing video games, probably doing drugs..."

"Uh, yeah, typical guy stuff," Gideon frowned.

Jordana smiled and touched his cheek. "Aw, I've hurt your feelings."

"Maybe."

Jordana stretched up and kissed Gideon lightly on the lips. "Does that make it better?"

"No, but it helps," Gideon smiled.

Jordana smiled at him. Then, she turned toward the house and started walking away.

"What? You're just gonna leave me hanging?" Gideon moaned.

Jordana looked back over her shoulder. "Pretty much."

"I'm surrounded by comedians," Gideon sighed.

Jordana held out her hand to him. "Are you coming?"

"I'm so glad Bruce isn't here right now," Gideon muttered as he took hold of Jordana's hand and pulled her to him.

"Hey," Jordana protested, but she was smiling.

"We still have unfinished business," Gideon said, and he kissed her.

"Wow," Jordana sighed. "We need to argue more often."

"Let's skip the arguing and just stick with the making up," Gideon chuckled.

CHAPTER TWENTY-TWO

Atlanta, Georgia, USA

Coach House, Belle Arbor Plantation

Covington, GA

October 27, 2010

"Pukwudgie," Jordana said and started giggling again. "I'm sorry, but that's just a funny word."

Gideon chuckled as they walked toward the coach house. He had an arm draped around Jordana's shoulder, and she had one of her arms wrapped around his waist. Their heights were complementary enough to make it comfortable, natural.

"Where are we going?" Jordana asked.

"Coach house," Gideon replied.

"What *is* a coach house, anyway?"

"Well, its original role was a place to store one's coaches and/or carriages, and oftentimes included an apartment above the... I guess you'd call it a garage. Anyway, the coachman usually got a small apartment in the loft," Gideon explained. "Later on, folks took to converting the whole thing into a house, usually a guest house on an estate, kinda like a pool house."

Jordana scoffed. "Rich people and your spare houses."

"I'm not rich. My family is rich, but I'm not," Gideon said.

"Really?" Jordana scoffed.

"No, not really," Gideon chuckled. "I married into my first fortune."

"Fiona, right?" Jordana said.

Gideon nodded. "Got a title and a small fortune, mostly real estate, and back in those days, estates produced an income. I invested that income. Some of my investments paid off. Most didn't, but if you live long enough the losses don't really matter, and I made pretty good money as a mercenary."

"Mercenary?" Jordana said giving him a look.

"I wasn't always the paragon of virtue that I am nowadays," Gideon admitted.

They'd arrived at the coach house and went inside. The lower floor where the carriages had originally been stored was now used as a garage for Gideon's Jeep, a pair of motorcycles, and a classic car from the '40s or '50s.

"I was kinda hoping to see that Model T," Jordana teased.

"It's in storage," Gideon replied. "I've just got a couple of cars here. The Jeep you know." He pointed to the two motorcycles. "That bike is a Honda CBR 600RR, and *that one* is a BMW S1000RR. Hello, darling, have you missed Daddy?"

"I take it you like racing bikes," Jordana giggled.

"Just a little," Gideon admitted with a grin.

"And what kind of car is this?" Jordana asked running a hand along the gently curved flank of the fire-engine red car.

"That, my dear, is a 1957 Chevy Bel Air convertible," Gideon replied.

"It's kind of... beautiful," Jordana said.

"That's kinda what I thought when I bought her," Gideon said, "and if you're living in California, you gotta have a convertible. Don't drive her much anymore, though."

"Why not?" Jordana asked.

"Well, when I bought the car, gas was five cents a gallon. She's not what you might call 'fuel efficient'," Gideon said. "Besides, she predates seatbelts and air bags."

"I'd still like to take a ride in it sometime," Jordana said.

"We will certainly do that, come warm weather," Gideon said. He moved over to the stairway leading up. "Coming?"

"Sure," Jordana replied as she joined him on the stairs. "So, you didn't bring me in here to show off your favorite modes of transportation?"

"No, I came to use the shower," Gideon chuckled.

"Yeah, you do kinda stink," Jordana teased.

"Two days in the woods and a murthering great battle with a pukwudgie does not leave one smelling of roses and fresh soap," Gideon said.

"Pukwudgie," Jordana repeated with a giggle. "C'mon, how terrifying can you be with a name like 'pukwudgie'?"

"Ask a little girl named Alice about a critter called a jabberwocky," Gideon retorted. "Or ask the Salish tribes of the Pacific Northwest about the sisiutl."

"The sissy-what?" Jordana frowned.

"Sisiutl. Uh, it's a sea serpent with heads at either end of its body and a human face in the middle," Gideon said. "The actual creature is a manifest form demon with a taste for human flesh."

"That sounds... like it would be hard to sneak up on," Jordana said.

"First time I encountered one, I was with a group of Salish Indians. I was the only survivor, and that's because I ran away," Gideon said. "Came back twenty years later with twice as many guys, armed with Tommy guns, a Browning .30 cal, and as many hand grenades as we could carry. Still lost about half the team, but we killed the sucker."

"Ever fought a jabberwocky, then?" Jordana asked.

They came out on the second floor, which was an open studio-style apartment. The apartment was long and wide, a single room taking up the entire second floor with a few partitions. At the far end of the apartment, behind a low wall, was a kitchen with a tiled floor. The refrigerator and stove looked positively ancient, but the microwave on the counter was brand-new. Just in front of the kitchen was a dining area with an old, blue linoleum-topped table and six matching blue chairs.

Just to their right as they came up the stairs was an old couch against the wall and a couple of easy chairs arranged in a conversation nook around a coffee table. Just ahead of the entrance to the apartment was an entertainment center with a stereo, a TV, a DVD player, and an impressive collection of CDs and DVDs. Across from the entertainment center, just beyond the conversation nook, was what appeared to be an ornate wardrobe. The rest of the apartment between the living space and the dining area was open space.

"No, I've never fought a jabberwocky, but that's because it was something that Lewis Carroll made up, not a mythic beastie based upon something left over from the ancient Demon War," Gideon said. He swept off the sweatshirt and tossed it onto the couch as he strode toward the far end of the apartment.

"Aw, I was hoping they were real," Jordana said.

Gideon laughed as he pulled aside a partition next to the kitchen that exposed the bathroom area. Like the one in her room in the big house, this bathroom was tiny, but well appointed.

"Sorry to disappoint you," he said as he shucked his sweatpants.

"Are you completely lacking in modesty?" Jordana gasped.

"It's not like you haven't already seen me naked," Gideon said with a wink. "Uh, there's food and beverages in the fridge. That thing that looks like a wardrobe is a Murphy bed, and feel free to put on whatever music or movie takes your fancy."

Jordana rolled her eyes. She grabbed the sweatshirt and walked over and snatched up the sweatpants. "I'm sure your mother raised you better than this."

Gideon was still standing there when she stood up with the pants. Jordana gasped. Then, she punched him in the stomach.

"Tough chick. I like that," Gideon chuckled. "Look, this is where we'll do our shapeshifter training. You're gonna have to get used to being naked until I can make you some kind of clothing that'll shift with you."

"You stink. Go. Wash," Jordana commanded.

Gideon leaned in and kissed her quickly on the lips.

"Pukwudgie," he whispered.

Jordana cracked up.

CHAPTER TWENTY-THREE

Atlanta, Georgia, USA

Coach House, Belle Arbor Plantation

Covington, GA

October 27, 2010

Jordana decided that the Beatles suited her mood. Gideon had the Beatles Box Set, and she chose *Rubber Soul*. "Drive My Car" started playing, and the sound was incredible. The stereo system's speakers were strategically placed around the room for maximum effect. Whoever had wired it up knew what he was doing. Jordana settled onto the couch with a deep sigh. She closed her eyes and just enjoyed the music.

"Would you believe the first time I heard the Lads from Liverpool was in a German strip club?" Gideon said.

Jordana sat upright with a start. She'd dozed off.

Gideon smiled at her. "'Norwegian Wood' does the same thing to me, too."

Jordana blushed. "No, I'm just... tired. I haven't slept in thirty-six hours."

"Sorry," Gideon said with blush.

Jordana waved the apology off. "Not your fault. Well, not entirely."

"Gee, thanks," Gideon snorted. He held a hand out to her.

Jordana was half-pleased, half-disappointed that he was dressed. Instead of the sweats, he'd put on jeans and a plain black t-shirt. He was still barefoot.

"Do you have something against shoes now?" she asked as she took his hand.

Gideon pulled her up off the couch. "No, but shoes don't stand up well to shapeshifting. So, if I know I might be doing a lot of changing, I go barefoot. Tonight, though, I'm barefoot because I don't have any shoes here in this apartment. Other than combat boots. Besides, I like going barefoot."

"Wow, something smells good," Jordana said, noticing for the first time that the table was set.

"I cooked us some supper while you were asleep," Gideon said.

"How long was I out?"

"Hour, hour and a half," Gideon replied.

"Guess I was tired," Jordana chuckled. "A normal person would've slept through the following day, but, no, we thropes take quick power naps and we're ready to go again."

Gideon chuckled as he held a chair out for her to sit down. "It's actually worse for vampires," he said. "They don't sleep at all. Well, they still need rest, but they don't actually sleep, and they have waking dreams, which tend to come at odd, random times."

"I take it you mean the living kind of vampires, right?" Jordana guessed.

Gideon nodded. "The undead kind don't sleep either, but they go dormant, usually during the day, so that the demon inside the host body can... digest whatever life force it fed on during the night."

"That's just disturbing," Jordana sighed.

"So, let's not talk about it," Gideon suggested. "Well, this evening's meal is gonna be... eclectic. We'll start off with a nice cock-a-leekie soup."

"What?"

"It's a Scottish chicken soup made with leeks and prunes," Gideon said. "I generally leave out the prunes. Never have liked 'em."

"Okay," Jordana said, mentally preparing herself while Gideon fetched the first course from the kitchen. When he set the bowl in front of her, Jordana dipped into it with her spoon, lifted a bit to her mouth, and, with hopes for the best, tasted it. "Hey, that's pretty good!"

"Thank you," Gideon said. "You go ahead and be finishing your soup while I get the rest of it ready."

"Okay," Jordana said with a smile.

Gideon came back moments later and placed a dinner plate on the table in front of her. "Okay, we have here a *Wiener Schnitzel vom Schwein*, also known as a pork schnitzel, Southern-style potato salad, and steamed Asian green beans."

"How very international," Jordana giggled.

"Mostly these are re-heated leftovers, to be honest," Gideon said. "I spend a lot of time out here, and I keep the fridge stocked."

"Working on your cars and bikes?" Jordana asked as she set the soup aside to cut a bite off the pork schnitzel.

"Grading papers, contemplating my navel and its place in the universe, things like that," Gideon chuckled. "Whenever my dad and sister are in residence, I pretty much live out of here."

"Your Fortress of Solitude? I mean the Fortress of Solitude within the Fortress of Solitude," Jordana teased.

"Pretty much," Gideon agreed. "Would you like tea or Coke? Something stronger?"

"Define 'stronger'," Jordana challenged.

"Well, since I don't have a liquor license, and we're in a private home, I will allow you a beer if you would like," Gideon said.

"Hmm, tell me more of this 'beer' that you speak of," Jordana said. "Being an innocent and naive college coed, I have no knowledge of this... What did you call it? *Beer*?"

"You're having too much fun with me," Gideon snorted.

"Yes, I am," Jordana admitted. "What's on tap?"

"No tap, but I've got bottles of Moosehead lager, some Guinness extra stout, and for some odd reason, Corona, and by 'some odd reason' I mean that Matt likes Mexican beers, and I keep a couple of bottles for him, just in case, but I don't think he'll mind if we raid his stash," Gideon chuckled.

"Actually, the stout sounds good," Jordana said. "Daddy's been a Guinness man forever... I guess that's different for you, huh?"

"I predate their brewery, yeah," Gideon said, "but I grew up drinking ales that had been brewed 'just down the lane.'" He fetched the beers from a cabinet above the stove.

"They're not cold?" Jordana said.

Gideon raised an eyebrow. "Ale is served at room temperature." Then, he winked. "I stuck a couple of glasses in the freezer when I got out of the shower and saw you sleeping."

"You're not as funny as you think you are," Jordana said. "Genius ass."

"Warm is most often how beer was drank, you know, before refrigeration. Not that I don't like it cold, but sometimes, just for old times' sake, I drink it warm," Gideon said as he brought Jordana a chilled glass of dark ale. "Savor it because that's all you're getting, young lady."

"And here I thought you wanted to get me drunk and have your way with me," Jordana said with a wink.

"I don't need alcohol to have my way with you," Gideon said.

"My, aren't you confident?" Jordana teased.

"Yes, ma'am, I am," Gideon said. "Am I wrong?"

Jordana blushed. "No, you're not."

Gideon smiled. "Which is why we're both staying sober and not doing anything... fun, but wrong..." Gideon cleared his throat. "So, you want some dessert?"

Jordana raised an eyebrow. "What do you have in mind?"

"Fruit. Just fruit," Gideon said, suddenly flustered. "You need to stop that right now."

"Stop what?" Jordana asked with a frown.

"You're doing... that thing..." Gideon got up and went into the kitchen. He came back with a bowl of strawberries. "It's a... thing that some thropes can do, part mystical, part pheromonal," Gideon explained, "and you're kind of doing it right now."

"I am?" Jordana said. "Hey, have you been doing that to me?"

"No, but that's because I don't have that ability," Gideon said. He smiled. "I've had to get by on good looks and charm."

"So, I can make men attracted to me, right?" Jordana said.

"Yeah," Gideon said. "I think it's something that you need to learn to control because not all men have my self-control. Oh, and those pheromones work on both genders."

"Well, that might explain some of the looks I've been getting from Tammy over the last couple of months," Jordana chuckled.

"I knew a thrope, a male selkie, about thirty years ago, who had that ability," Gideon said. "He was very popular. *Very* popular."

"That sounds... uh, fun?" Jordana said.

"Was until he was killed by a guy who overreacted to his attraction to another man," Gideon said. "Shot him three times in the head with a .44, doused the body in gasoline, and set him on fire."

"Oh my god, that's awful!" Jordana exclaimed. "What happened to the killer?"

"He was dealt with by the Program," Gideon replied. "We can't have regular people going around killing paranormals, and then threatening to expose us to the world during his trial."

"Were you the one who...?" Jordana asked.

Gideon nodded. "He had a perfectly legitimate 'insanity' defense. So, I couldn't just, you know, kill the guy. I shot him up with a potion that rendered him catatonic and burned out most of his memories. He's been in an asylum ever since, re-learning how to talk and walk."

"Killing him would have been kinder," Jordana said.

Gideon smiled sadly. "I agree, but those weren't my orders."

"Well, as stories go, that one was a definite mood killer," Jordana said.

"Yeah, but mood killing is about the only way to curb back that... thing you were doing," Gideon said. "Besides, you don't need it with me."

"I don't?" Jordana said.

Gideon shook his head. "Those brown eyes are all you really need."

Jordana blushed. "Are you trying to get by on your charm?"

"Only if it's working," Gideon chuckled.

"It might be," Jordana smiled.

"So, how do you feel about doing something utterly mundane for tonight's entertainment?" Gideon asked.

"Like what?" Jordana asked.

"Watch some TV, maybe a movie?" Gideon suggested.

"Sounds very domestic," Jordana agreed. "Let's take the strawberries. How did you know this is my favorite fruit?"

"I didn't. It's mine," Gideon said with a smile. "What are you in the mood for, then: movie or TV?"

"Movie," Jordana replied as she got up from the table and snagged the bowl of strawberries. She frowned at the couch arrangement. "How do you see the TV from the couch?"

"Usually, I don't. I watch from the Murphy bed," Gideon replied.

He walked over to the wardrobe-like cabinet across from the entertainment center and pulled. The front folded out into a bed.

"Inviting me into your fold-away bed isn't conducive to good behavior," Jordana said.

"I'm willing to trust that you have no designs on my honor," Gideon said. "You pick a movie while I get this thing set up."

From the cabinets to the sides of the bed, Gideon started pulling pillows and a comforter. While he was doing that, Jordana glanced at the DVDs stacked on the entertainment center.

"So, don't you have any movies from *this* century?" Jordana teased.

"I do, but they're mostly in the media room in the big house," Gideon replied. "I've got digital cable. We can watch something from the on-demand menu."

Jordana gasped. "Oh... my... gosh! You have the *Road* movies!"

"Ah, Bob, Bing, and the lovely Dorothy Lamour! Thoughts of that woman in a sarong got me through some pretty rough nights during World War II," Gideon said.

"Okay, first let me say, ew! I don't need to know who's in your spank bank," Jordana said. "Second, let's start with *Road to Morocco* and just see where we can go from there."

"My 'spank bank'?" Gideon snickered. "Such language, young lady."

"Look, it's one thing to hear about the women you were married to before, but I don't want to know about your sexual fantasies," Jordana said as she loaded the first movie into the DVD player.

"Oh, but don't you?" Gideon teased.

Jordana paused in mid-retort. "Yeah, okay, I'll give you that, but I don't want to hear about dead old women. That's what's creepy."

"She wasn't old or dead. She was about your age at the time," Gideon pointed out.

"Maybe so, but she's an old dead lady now, and that's where my mind went," Jordana replied.

She joined him on the surprisingly comfortable Murphy bed. Gideon had piled several pillows at the head of the bed for them to recline against. Jordana kicked her shoes off and cuddled up next to Gideon.

"Does old age scare you?" Gideon asked softly.

"I don't know. I'm nineteen. I'm not old enough yet to know if aging scares me," Jordana said.

"Wise answer, but you're likely immortal considering your... heritages. The physical aspects of aging won't be a problem. On the other hand, you'll still feel the psychological effects of getting older, maturity, I guess," Gideon said. "Sometimes, I don't feel old, and then, I'll remember an adventure I had when I was younger and realize that was a decade ago or two centuries ago, and there's really not anybody around, other than Matt and my Dad, who'll get it."

"That brings up a question: did you ever get to meet any famous historical figures?" Jordana asked.

"Uh, well, how far back do we go? I mean, I used to work for Gustav Adolph, the King of Sweden during the Thirty Years War. That's more than four hundred years ago," Gideon replied. "I kinda knew George Washington. I was Ben Franklin's bodyguard for a few weeks."

"How 'bout Bob and Bing there?" Jordana asked.

"I saw several of Bob's USO shows, and I got to meet him a couple of times, but we were never friends," Gideon replied.

"Do you think you would have been friends with him?" Jordana asked.

Gideon shrugged. "I don't know. He was a funny man, and braver than most of the characters he played. The man tempted death to bring a little taste of home to soldiers on the front lines, and he did it until he was too old to do it anymore. I admire that about him. Meant a lot to me when I was there."

The movie started playing, and Gideon and Jordana enjoyed the adventures of Bob, Bing, and Dorothy.

CHAPTER TWENTY-FOUR

Atlanta, Georgia, USA
Mercy University
Department of Anthropology, Watson Hall
Covington, GA
October 28, 2010

Gideon parked the S1000RR in the same spot where he usually parked his Jeep. He hadn't taken the bike out for several months, and he made a mental note to take the Honda out for a quick run in the near future. The older bike probably felt neglected since he'd purchased the BMW. Gideon shook his head with a chuckle. He knew better than most that machines didn't have feelings. The anthropomorphizing of one's tools was a common thing among human cultures. Another chuckle escaped Gideon's lips. He had slipped back into "professor" mode without even thinking about it.

He'd hated leaving Belle Arbor, but he had a cover to maintain. His teaching assistant couldn't be expected to keep running the class. Not anymore than he could have expected Perkins to continue on with them. The useful young agent had been summoned back to his home office. Matt had driven Perkins out to the airport, where the junior agent would retrieve his plane and fly it back to Virginia. Gideon hated losing Perkins. He was resourceful, efficient, and, best of all, obedient. He could follow an order.

Gideon's office was on the second floor of Watson Hall, which faced directly across the quad from Newton Hall, where the administration offices were located. Shaw Chapel and Baxter Hall rounded out the other two sides of the roughly square lawn. Smaller buildings were clustered around each of those buildings, but those four main buildings marked the heart of Mercy University's campus.

The offices of the Anthropology Department instructors were a warren of interconnected closets and cubbyholes. Only years of experience and conveniently placed signs allowed the academic staff to find their way through the maze to their various offices. The cubbyhole Gideon called "home" was somewhere along the wall facing into the quad, which granted him a single window with a view of the lawn. The office was by no means spacious or well organized. He had bookshelves and filing cabinets stuffed in every possible bit of space. A little open area in the middle of the office contained the heavy, wooden table that he used as a desk.

Terry O'Dell, Gideon's teaching assistant, stood at the table organizing stacks of research papers that she had collected from the students in Gideon's three classes. As the junior professor in the department, he was expected to teach the introductory-level sections --

classes which could be handled, easily, by a graduate student. Terry was just such a grad student. She was a cute, curvy blond with curly hair, bright green eyes, and a cute little button nose. She was also ferociously intelligent, tough-minded, and more than willing to establish her authority whenever Gideon wasn't around.

"Over the cold, boss?" Terry teased when Gideon came into the room.

"Cold? Is that the excuse I used?" Gideon replied as he plopped his laptop onto the table. "What've you got for me?"

"The research papers that you assigned last week. Surprisingly, everybody turned one in on time," Terry said. "Will marvels never cease?"

"Yeah, bet it was the horny guys who got theirs in first," Gideon snickered as he picked up the packet off the top of the nearest stack and started speed-reading his way through it.

"No, they're too busy with other things on their tiny little minds. It was straight girls, lesbians, gay guys, and then straight guys," Terry surmised.

"Did you actually track the order by sexual orientation?" Gideon asked with a raised eyebrow.

"No, of course not," Terry snickered. "Although it might make for an interesting study..."

"It would never make it past the PC patrol," Gideon pointed out as he grabbed a red pen from the cup on the table. He made a note, wrote a letter grade on the cover sheet, and grabbed another paper.

"I'm always amazed at your ability to multi-task," Terry said.

Gideon shrugged. "It's a skill like any other," he replied as he flipped through the pages of the paper. "Life is too short to waste time on trivial things." The red pen came out; he wrote another note and a grade, and moved on to the next paper. "Of course, being able to assign short papers helps."

Terry chuckled. "Whatever, man. It took me an hour to read what you've done in, like, five minutes."

Gideon laughed. "Okay. Did you figure out grades for the ones you read?"

Terry nodded. "Yep. This stack here. My grade and notes are on a Post-it note on the front."

"Alright, I'll endorse your grading, and that'll save me time," Gideon said.

"I appreciate the vote of confidence," Terry said.

"What's a TA for if I can't take advantage of you?" Gideon said. "Besides, this job'll be yours someday. Might as well get in some practice."

Gideon graded four more papers. Terry took the stack of growing graded papers and began entering the grades into the ancient computer tied to the university's network. The equally old phone by the computer started ringing. Terry picked up the handset.

"Professor Shaw's office. Terry speaking." She listened for a moment. "Yes, he's here. I'll tell him, then."

Gideon looked up from the paper he was grading. "What's up?"

"Dean Anderson wants you," Terry replied. "Now, according to his secretary."

"How odd," Gideon said. "Alright then, Terry, you finish grading these papers. Then, get the stuff together for the next lecture."

"Want me to take the class for you?" Terry asked with a grin.

"Don't know, but I'll call your cell if I need you to," Gideon said.

"I was kidding," Terry said.

"I know, but things are going on right now that might affect my ability to keep up with my work schedule," Gideon replied.

"What's up?" Terry asked.

"Stuff I can't really talk about," Gideon replied as he slipped on his leather jacket. He patted the inside pocket where he'd put his FBI credentials. "I'll be back when you see me coming."

"Okay, boss," Terry said. "Take care."

Gideon grinned. "Don't I always?"

He walked across the quad to Newton Hall and climbed the stairs to the third floor where Dean Anderson's office was located. Jonathan "Jack" Anderson was the Provost of Academic Affairs, the university's equivalent of head of Human Resources. He was the reason that Gideon had a cushy teaching position without first gaining that doctorate that other instructors needed to get ranked within their departments. Of course, he didn't know that Gideon already had several doctorate-level degrees, but explaining those degrees would have necessitated Gideon filling Jack in on the real nature of the world and the fact that Gideon, himself, was nearly five hundred years old.

In the lobby of Newton Hall, on his way to the left-hand staircase, Gideon spotted a couple of men loitering by the glass-enclosed directory of the various offices in the building. They wore cheap suits, the kind that came off a rack from a Men's Wearhouse store, patent leather shoes -- the kind that he'd sworn off when the tennis shoe was invented -- and concealed weapons, which caused unsightly bulges that altered the hang of the suit coats. They even both sported cheap haircuts, slightly longer than regulation buzz cuts.

Gideon hit the door to the stairwell, ran up to the next landing, and paused. Sure enough, the door opened again, and one man entered the stairwell behind him. Gideon took a deep breath and gathered in the man's scent. The other man smelled of cheap aftershave, gun oil, and expensive foreign cigarettes. Gideon shook his head to himself. Like most men of previous ages, he'd been a smoker, mostly pipes and cigars, but he'd given up the habit, mostly because it had dulled his sense of smell. Cancer wasn't really a concern to him, but that had also influenced his decision to give up tobacco. On the other hand, his body remembered the nicotine high and would long for it when reminded.

Quickly, Gideon ascended to the third floor. Outside the stairwell door he listened. The man who had followed him was speaking, probably on a cell phone, letting his partner know that Gideon was on the third floor. Gideon almost smiled to himself as he strode down the hall to Jack's office. A tall, thin, rather severe-looking woman named Sheila was Jack's gatekeeper. Her place was in a small anteroom that held her desk, a couch, and a pair of chairs for anyone waiting to get in to see the Provost. His habit was to flirt shamelessly with Sheila, but Gideon noticed her demeanor was reserved, worried, when he arrived.

"Go on in, Professor Shaw," Sheila said. She always used everyone's title and last name. "They're waiting for you."

"They?" Gideon repeated. "What's up, Sheila?"

Sheila sighed. "Can't say." She glanced behind Gideon.

He sniffed the air, catching the scent of gun oil and expensive tobacco. "Okay."

Gideon knocked on the door and walked into the office. Only the office of the university's president was larger and better appointed than the provost's office. The mahogany desk by the window looked large enough to land aircraft on, and a couch, coffee table, and easy chairs in one corner created an informal meeting area within the office. The walls were paneled in dark wood, matching the desk, and decorated with framed degrees, certificates, commendations, and photos of Jack and people that he'd known around the world. Before entering the halls of academia, Jack Anderson had been an officer in the U.S. Air Force -- not a pilot but an intelligence officer. Several of the pictures showed Jack in uniform with some foreign local he'd befriended.

The man hadn't changed much from the sandy-haired young officer to the graying man in the nice suit who rose up from behind the big desk to greet Gideon. Jack was tall, still trim, and had a sparkle in his eyes that hinted at both intelligence and mischief. Gideon happily shook the other man's hand, but he glanced over at the other man in the room.

"Gideon, this is Marcus Bloom, one of the university's lawyers," Jack said by way of introduction.

Bloom was a dark-skinned African-American man of average height, build, and looks. He was so bland that except for the darkness of his skin, people would be hard-pressed to describe him within even a few minutes of meeting him. However, he exuded an aura of confidence, even competence. Gideon felt strangely reassured by the presence of the lawyer. Part of him wondered if Bloom might not be a paranormal with a psionic gift for projecting positive emotions. Mentally he shrugged and decided not to worry about it unless the legal shark morphed into a real shark and tried to eat them.

"What's going on, Jack?" Gideon asked, skipping the niceties.

Jack took a deep break and sighed heavily before answering. "Gideon, first, there's something that has come up. A student has made an accusation that you are... uh, well, that you're having an affair with one of your students."

Gideon frowned. "What 'student' am I supposed to be, uh, having this affair with?"

Jack consulted a document on his desk. "Uh, Jordan... no, Jordana Quinlan."

"Well, Jack, firstly, Miss Quinlan *isn't* one of *my* students. Secondly, I just met her this past weekend, and we have gone out on a date. Nothing has happened beyond that," Gideon said.

"Okay," Jack hedged, glancing at Bloom. "Well, there are a couple of agents here from the FBI, and it seems that Ms. Quinlan has been abducted, and they want to talk to you."

"Really?" Gideon asked, thinking of the two men he'd seen. "Did you see their credentials?"

"Uh, yeah," Jack said. "Look, they wanted to go directly to your office, but I told them they couldn't question you on school grounds unless I and a lawyer were present."

"Which is where I come in," Bloom added in a surprisingly deep, melodic voice.

"Wow, dude, did you swallow James Earl Jones?" Gideon blurted. "Sorry."

Bloom laughed. "It's okay. I get that. One kid asked me if I was Darth Vader once."

"I bet you're really great in a courtroom," Gideon chuckled.

"Gideon, I know you like chasing rabbits, but can we focus on the problem at hand?" Jack said.

"Where are we meeting these very special agents?" Gideon asked.

"The conference room down the hall," Jack replied.

"Let's go," Gideon said. "No point in keeping them waiting. I mean, they already know I'm here."

With that, Gideon turned on his heel and strode out of the room, heading straight for the conference room. The man who like cheap aftershave and expensive tobacco was startled by Gideon's sudden appearance.

"Don't strain yourself, partner. We're just going to meet your buddy in the conference room," Gideon told him.

Gideon hit the conference room door hard enough to make it bounce. The other man from the lobby was waiting in the room with a woman in a pantsuit that was only slightly more expensive than what he and the tobacco lover were wearing. Gideon took a deep breath, gathering in the scents in the room.

The other man on the team smelled of mint with traces of gun oil. The woman smelled of a floral perfume, not a high-end scent, but something that one might get at Macy's, a scent touted as an expensive luxury, but not really. The perfume barely covered the smell of gun oil on the woman. Gideon smiled inwardly. Gun oil was the common scent on these people, a clue as to who and what they really were.

"So," Gideon boomed, "who the hell are you?"

The man and woman looked at one another and presented leather folders with FBI badges and ID cards.

"I'm Special Agent Veronica Durham. This is my partner, Special Agent Rey MacKeon, and that's Special Agent Vance Pugh," the woman said as the tobacco-lover filed into the conference room behind Jack and Bloom.

Gideon smiled. "Well, it's certainly nice to meet you, Very Special Agent Durham." He motioned to the chairs around the table. "Why don't we have us a seat and talk a spell, as the old folks used to say."

Durham consulted a notebook she took from her pocket. "Are you Gideon Shaw, place of residence 2169 Washington St, Apartment 1B?"

Gideon cocked his head to one side. As a part of his current cover legend he maintained a small apartment near downtown Covington. The only time he ever actually used the apartment was when he was entertaining his colleagues from the university. He made a note to himself to send some kind of thank-you gift to the gang at Langley who backstopped all the cover legends that he'd used in recent years. These idiots really didn't know who he was.

"That would, indeed, be me, Very Special Agent, ma'am," Gideon said.

Jack glared at Gideon from across the table.

"Are you acquainted with a young woman named Jordana Quinlan?" Durham asked.

"Yes, ma'am," Gideon replied. "Lovely young woman. Bright, intelligent, digs older men..."

Durham frowned at him. "Miss Quinlan was reported missing Monday evening. Her parents were contacted, and they reported that she has not been in touch with them since Friday. Miss Quinlan's roommates were questioned and reported that she had departed with you Saturday evening. Do you know where Miss Quinlan is?"

Gideon smiled. "As a matter of fact, I do."

"Well? Where is she?" Durham demanded.

"Can't say," Gideon replied.

"Can't or won't?" Durham growled.

"Amounts to the same," Gideon said, still grinning.

Bloom cleared his throat. "Uh, Gideon, maybe you should tell the agents what you know so that we can clear this mess up."

Gideon shook his head. "I don't think so." He turned his attention to Durham. "Very Special Agent Durham, may I see your credentials, please?"

"What?" Durham growled.

"Your badge and ID," Gideon repeated. "May I see them? Please?"

"You don't believe I'm an FBI agent?" Durham snorted.

"No, I don't," Gideon said with the same lopsided grin he'd been wearing the whole time.

Durham snorted, but tossed her folder down the table to Gideon. "Knock yourself out," she said. "You can even call the Atlanta Field Office and confirm my identity."

Gideon flipped open the folder. He ignored the badge and studied the ID. Then, he handed it to Jack. "Tell me, Very Special Agent Durham, what color is your hair?"

"I'm getting tired of your flip attitude, Mr. Shaw," Durham snapped.

"Marcus, what color would you say Very Special Agent Durham's hair is?" Gideon said.

"Uh, brown?" Bloom replied.

Gideon nodded. "Jack, what color does that ID say her hair is?"

"Red," Jack said glancing from the ID to Durham to Gideon and back again.

"Yep," Gideon said.

"I changed the color," Durham snapped.

"No, you didn't," Gideon chuckled. He looked back at Bloom and Jack. "You see, fellas, this ID and badge are fake, and these folks are impersonating federal agents."

"How dare you?" MacKeon roared standing to his feet.

"Oh, shut up," Gideon snapped. "Dude, Rey MacKeon, the *real* Rey MacKeon, is a *WOMAN*!"

The faux MacKeon stopped mid-rant and stared at Gideon. "Uh, what?"

Gideon nodded. "Yep. I've known her all her life, in fact. She's my niece." He looked at faux-Durham. "Ronnie Durham is a friend of mine, like a sister to me, in fact." He reached into his inside jacket pocket and pulled out his folder and dropped it onto the table so that it fell open to reveal the badge and ID. "We were in the same training class at Quantico."

Everyone in the room stared at the badge on the table.

"Oh, did I forget to mention that I'm a deep-cover FBI agent?" Gideon said, his grin becoming feral.

He stood quickly, knocking his chair back, and turned toward the man calling himself Vance Pugh, the tobacco lover. Faux-Pugh hadn't sat down, but had remained by the door. He had his hand wrapped around the butt of a silenced semi-automatic, which he was bringing into line with where Gideon's head had been. The handgun made a coughing noise, and Gideon felt a pinch and tug on his left side. He ignored it. Instead, he'd pulled the tactical folding knife from his pocket, flicked open the blade, and drove it into faux-Pugh's throat. With his other hand, he caught the would-be assassin's shirt front, and spun around, shielding himself with faux-Pugh's body.

Durham and MacKeon had also drawn handguns. The two weapons barked, unsuppressed and incredibly loud in the confines of the conference room. Gideon noted in a detached part of his mind that Jack had grabbed Bloom and dived under the table. Gideon bodily hoisted Pugh's carcass toward his partners even as they tried to shoot *through* him to get at Gideon. One round pegged Gideon through his left biceps, and another caught him in the right thigh, but both wounds rapidly sealed and began healing. Durham and MacKeon dodged out of the way of Pugh's body. Gideon had enough time to focus his will into the leather band on his right wrist. Durham and MacKeon were both shocked when a sword appeared out of thin air in Gideon's hand.

Bright Fang flashed out, the tip piercing MacKeon's sternum and the heart behind it. Gideon didn't bother reversing the blade. He pulled straight out and rammed the pommel in Durham's face. The blow sent the woman sprawling. He focused his will again, and Bright Fang disappeared back around his wrist. He dropped a knee into Durham's solar plexus, forcing the air out of her lungs, and causing her not a little bit of pain. He snatched the gun from her hand, a Russian-made MP-443 "Grach."

"Well, now *this* is certainly *not* federal issue, Very Special Agent not-Durham," Gideon said as he pointed the pistol into the woman's face. "Who hired you?"

"Go fuck yourself," Durham snarled, spitting blood and teeth at Gideon.

Gideon made a buzzing noise. "Wrong answer!" He placed the barrel of the weapon against her right knee and squeezed the trigger.

Durham screamed in pain.

"Gideon!" Jack shouted. "What are you doing?"

"I'm going Jack Bauer on this piece of terrorist wanna-be trash," Gideon said. "No trials, no Gitmo, bitch. Tell me what I want to know, or I'll take you apart one joint at a time." He let his eyes shift amber and his teeth grow out.

Durham's eyes widened. "It was a woman, a girl. Didn't catch a name. She provided us with the cover and a file on you. Bad file."

Gideon relaxed his features back to normal. "Describe her."

"Uh, five-six, black hair, brown eyes, pretty, looked kinda Hispanic," Durham jabbered.

"Thank you," Gideon said and slammed the butt of the pistol into her temple. He stood up. "Jack, Marcus, I'm sorry. I'll explain one of these days, but I've gotta book. If somebody hasn't already, call the police. Get Deputy Parker. He knows the score."

"Uh, okay," a clearly shaken Jack muttered. He looked at Gideon. "You're bleeding."

"This?" Gideon said pointing to the bloody wound on his left side. "Just a flesh wound. Hardly feel it at all." He was already walking out of the room, hitting the speed dial on his phone.

CHAPTER TWENTY-FIVE

Atlanta, Georgia, USA
Belle Arbor Plantation
Covington, GA
October 28, 2010

"Matt! Where are you?" Gideon demanded as he roared down the road toward Belle Arbor.

"Uh, I'm about ten minutes from the house," Matt replied.

"I just got jumped by mercs pretending to be FBI agents, *Program* FBI agents," Gideon said, "and I can't get an answer from any of the lines at the house."

"I don't think I'm gonna get there any faster, not with the construction going on between the interstate and the house," Matt growled.

"Quick as you can, brother," Gideon said and hung up. "Dial Raven," he barked at the phone's voice-activated dialing program. No answer. Gideon swore. Vehemently. In several languages. He'd tried the main house line, Raven's cell, the coach house's direct line, the extension in the barn, even Levi's cell, and he'd gotten no answer from any of them. The cells had gone to voice mail, and the land lines were dead. A knot of dread had built up in his stomach. Gideon was certain he was about to throw up.

The gate to the main drive leading up to Magee House came into view. Not only was it wide open, but the left-hand gate was hanging, twisted, from one hinge, and the hedges on either side were singed. Gideon slowed to a stop. He turned the bike off and parked it to one side of the driveway. As he got off the bike, he reached behind himself into a special pocket on his backpack.

The first call he'd made when he'd exited from the conference room had been to Terry to tell her to meet him at his bike with his helmet and the pack that he normally carried his laptop in. To the mundane eye, it was just a hard-shell biker's backpack, but Gideon had modified it with an extra, magical, pocket. The extra pocket didn't take up any space in the actual pack, but it did open into its own small dimension. Gideon used the pocket as a holster for a weapon, a P90 submachine gun. He liked the little SMG. It was compact, well balanced, and the 5.7mm round packed a wallop. With the spent casing ejector located on the bottom of the weapon, it was truly ambidextrous. He could even fire it one-handed with a fair amount of accuracy. Besides, it looked like some kind of futuristic space gun.

That thought had always amused him before, but today he didn't even think about that. He just wanted to find his loved ones and assure himself that everybody was alive and well and that the lack of communication was just a coincidence. Gideon prowled up the driveway in a crouch, the P90 up in front of him. He found the first biker just where the driveway split into the loop in front of Magee House. A heavy-duty Harley-Davidson cruiser was crashed to one side of the drive, wrapped around a skinny oak tree. Gideon was pretty sure the biker was dead. Besides dozens of bloody gashes all over his body, the biker's throat had been sliced open, right down to the spine. Gideon also noted that the biker wasn't human, not entirely at any rate.

The heavy jowl, the sloping forehead, the gray skin, the protruding tusk-like lower canines, and the horns curling back from his forehead marked the biker as an ogre. Gideon flipped the corpse over so he could get a look at the biker's colors. The emblem on the back was a human skull with ram's horns growing from the forehead. A stylized M16 and AK47 were crossed over one another under the skull. The rocker above the patch carried the name: "OUTCASTS M.C." The rocker under the patch identified this biker as belonging to the Georgia chapter. Gideon also noted how well-armed the biker was, too. In addition to a 12 gauge pump shotgun still clutched in one hand, the ogre biker had been carrying a Smith & Wesson .44 Magnum -- the gun from the "Dirty Harry" movies -- a couple of M67 frag grenades, and a pair of hatchets stuffed into his belt.

He moved forward. More bikers fairly littered the driveway, all of them dead, all of them cut to ribbons. In addition to another couple of ogres, Gideon identified a trio of orcs, like ogres without the horns; an oni, a Japanese ogre with bulging eyes and blue skin; two satyrs and a Sasquatch rounded out the Outcasts. All of them were armed with a variety of heavy-caliber weapons. One of the satyrs even had a Vietnam-era M79 grenade launcher. Significant damage had been done to the front of the house. Something vaguely humanoid-shaped was still burning fiercely on the front steps of the house. Gideon wasn't going to be getting in that way.

He circled around the house. The side he went down seemed intact. The back of the house looked worse than the front, though. The back door and the wall around it were gone, the yard littered with debris, as though the back of the house had exploded or been ripped open by a giant's hand. A body laid across the threshold. Gideon recognized him as one of the Jaguar Warriors who'd attacked him and Jordana almost a week ago, the little one he'd darted in the eye with atropine. He looked pretty good for a reanimated corpse that had since been blown nearly in half. The undead Jaguar Warrior had been shot in the chest and the face with what appeared to be deer slugs.

A keening wail drew Gideon's attention to the remains of his kitchen. The tableau before him nearly ripped his heart from his chest. Knobs, his clothes in blood-spattered tatters, sat in the middle of the floor, a pair of wickedly curved and jagged knives dropped carelessly to the floor on either side of him. Cradled in his arms was Bernadette Cook, her head and neck twisted at an unnatural angle. Knobs' face was streaked with tears as the goblin wailed and moaned, tenderly stroking Bernadette's face with one hand while cradling her with the other.

"Bernadette," Gideon whispered, grief catching at his voice.

"Oh, master!" Knobs wailed. "Master, oh, master, I have failed you!"

Gideon stepped into the ruined kitchen and dropped to his knees in front of the grief-stricken goblin. "Knobs, what...? What happened?"

"Oh, master! I have failed you! I have failed in my duty to ward your home," Knobs cried. "My poor Bernadette, my poor child! She's dead, master! Murdered."

A hacking cough interrupted Knobs and drew Gideon's attention to a corner of the kitchen. Behind an overturned table he found Tom Quinlan. The big engineer had a horrible wound in his stomach and bones had broken through the flesh of both his legs. Gideon dropped the P90 and immediately reached into another extra-dimensional pocket on his pack to retrieve a medical kit.

"Hang in there, Tom," Gideon said as he popped the kit open and started working on Tom's wound.

The big man shook his head and coughed again. Bloody foam speckled his lips. "I'm done for," he declared.

"Don't talk like that," Gideon snapped.

Tom grabbed one of Gideon's hands in both of his. "I. Am. Done. For.," he enunciated. "That... bitch... Teresa, she... sucked the life outta me... like she tore out part of my soul..."

Tom was breathing heavy, and Gideon nodded in understanding. "Necromancer," he said. "She's the one that raised the revenants that attacked your house. She do this, too?" Gideon gestured at the stomach wound.

Tom shook his head. "No, that was her boss. Figured out he was the one who... raped Lucinda." He pointed toward the body of the Jaguar Warrior. "Got that one when he stepped in front of his boss. Got one off at the boss, but it... stopped. In midair. Like in that "X-Men" movie, you know?"

Gideon nodded.

"Got shot with my own bullet," Tom cough/laughed. "That sucks." He stared into Gideon's eyes. "He took my girls. *Our* girls. You gonna get 'em back, right?"

"Yeah, I am," Gideon said.

"How? You did that whammy thing, make us untrackable... didn't it work?" Tom said. At Gideon's nod, Tom coughed more blood and said, "How you gonna find 'em?"

"Remember that pill I made you guys take?" Gideon said.

Tom nodded. "Multivitamin magic..."

"No, it wasn't magic. The Program has access to some technology so cutting-edge that it's almost like magic. The pill contained a nano-transmitter. It attached itself to the intestinal lining. I can follow the signal anywhere in the world," Gideon said.

Tom grinned. "Score one for us mundanes, right?"

"Yeah," Gideon replied with a smile that he didn't feel.

Tom squeezed Gideon's hand. "Save our girls," he commanded.

"I will," Gideon promised, but Tom Quinlan no longer lived.

Gideon stood up and turned his attention back to Knobs. The goblin had laid Bernadette out on the floor, arranging her in a state of slumber-like repose, and covered her sightless eyes with his coat. Knobs gathered his knives and came to stand before Gideon, presenting the hilts of the weapons.

"I have failed as your warden, master. Only my death will balance this dishonor," Knobs declared.

"Philemon Knobs, who am I?" Gideon demanded.

"You are Gideon Dyrnwch Shaw, my liege lord," the goblin replied.

"How long have you served me, Knobs?"

"Since the day you were born, my lord. Your father, my first master, commanded that I should be your guardian and serve you however you saw fit."

"Do you still accept me as your liege lord, Philemon Knobs?"

"Absolutely, my lord!"

Gideon nodded. "Then, I tell you this, I forbid you to die, Knobs. I forbid you to take your own life or to ask me to take it for you. You *will not* die until after we have recovered our loved ones and paid blood justice to those who have wronged us. Will you stand by me on this quest, Philemon Knobs?"

A glint appeared in the goblin's eyes, a hard, frightening gleam. "Aye, my lord," he growled. "Hunt the enemy, steal back what was stolen from us, and avenge the wrongs dealt us. Yes!" He twirled the knives and slammed the blades back home in the sheaths on his belt. Then, he took Gideon's hands in his own, very much like Tom had done. "Master, you are too generous with your mercy to me."

Gideon shook his head. "No, Knobs, I'm not. You're family, not a slave, and you've been wronged today, too. I saw the bikers. I know your work when I see it."

"Yes," the goblin hissed. "They were a distraction. I felt the wards weaken; they had an oni shaman with them. They charged the gate directly. I went to do battle so that Mistress Morrigan and Master Levi could get Miss Jordana and her sister to safety."

"I take it that didn't work out too well?" Gideon said.

Knobs shook his head. "The real attack came from the rear. Chemosh Magog, Nahasheron, and a necromancer of considerable power came out of the woods with undead warriors and a cadre of Dark Word soldiers. They had an EM field generator."

Gideon winced. Teleporters could be affected by strong electromagnetic fields. A strong enough field, attuned to the right frequency, could effectively trap the teleporter in one location. If he tried to fold space/time within the effect of the field, bad things could happen to him physically. Worse, the teleporter had no way of knowing that an EM field was being projected in his area.

"What happened?" Gideon asked.

"Master Levi was... 'bounced' back into the kitchen with both Miss Jordana and Miss Katherine," Knobs reported. "The girls were both suffering from what Miss Morrigan calls 'jump shock', and Master Levi had blood running from his eyes and nose." Knobs wiped a tear from his eye. "I was fully engaged with the bikers about that time." He looked up at Gideon. "They brought a troll."

If one creature in the multiverse could prove a physical match for a bad-ass goblin like Knobs, it was a troll.

"That explains the bonfire on the steps," Gideon said. Fire was one of the few things that could permanently stop a troll. Of course, said troll usually had to be chopped into hamburger first.

Knobs nodded. "Aye, master. I was too late to stop Chemosh Magog from making off with the girls." He gestured at the kitchen. "Mistress Morrigan had brought the family here to make a run out the back while I dealt with the bikers. The plan was to make for the barn and take the SUV Master Levi had parked there."

Gideon nodded. He knew about the Suburban parked in the barn. It had been the backup if Levi was unable to teleport the girls away and the primary for getting Tom and Lucinda out.

"Mistress Morrigan fought bravely, master," Knobs said, his gaze becoming distant. As the warden of the house, he knew everything that went on within his domain, like a living closed-circuit surveillance system.

Gideon swallowed a lump that suddenly formed in his throat. "Is she..."

"No, master, Miss Morrigan yet lives!" Knobs cried out. "Oh, foolish, foolish goblin!" He thumped himself in the head. "When the villains absconded with Miss Jordana and Miss Katherine, they deactivated their EM field. Nahasheron ported them away. Master Levi awoke. He ported Miss Morrigan to the hospital."

"What happened to Bernadette?" Gideon asked looking down at the body of his cook, a woman he had actually helped to raise.

"Brave, brave Bernadette," Knobs moaned, grief threatening to overcome the goblin again. He took a deep breath. "She shielded the girls with her own body. Nahasheron killed her, twisted her head when she pulled Bernadette away." Knobs snarled suddenly, rage replacing grief. "Foul murderer!"

"What about their mother?" Gideon asked.

"Taken with the daughters," Knobs said. Then, the goblin grinned. "The villain did not get away unscathed, though."

"What do you mean?" Gideon asked.

Knobs pointed to another corner of the room. For the first time Gideon noticed a shaggy form lying in the floor. Princess. He rushed over to the dog.

"The brave dog attacked Chemosh Magog when he laid hands upon Miss Jordana," Knobs declared. He grinned a sadistic, evil-looking goblin grin. "Made the bastard *bleed*! Good dog! Brave dog!"

Gideon felt his own rage boiling up. The dog was dead, its body broken in half internally.

"Vile villain kicked noble Princess dog," Knobs snarled, "but she'd taken his measure, made him *bleed*!"

Gideon stroked the animals' blood-stained fur. Then, he frowned. He leaned in and examined Princess's teeth. He opened his medical kit, retrieved some tools, and picked something out from between the dog's teeth: a tiny scrap of skin and muscle. He smiled. "You did good, Princess. Earned your way into doggy Valhalla, for sure."

"For Princess, for my sweet Bernadette, for my family's pain and suffering, I will make you *bleed*, villains!" Knobs screeched at the ceiling.

Gideon didn't bother to rein in Knobs' ranting. An angry Knobs would serve his purposes better than a sad, suicidal Knobs. He knew that Knobs was working himself into a state of near-frenzy, just to keep the grief at bay.

"Knobs, I'm going to my lab," Gideon said. "I need to get some gear. Then, we're hunting these bastards down."

"Yes, master," Knobs said. "And then we make them *bleed*!"

"Bleed them dry," Gideon agreed.

CHAPTER TWENTY-SIX

Miami, Florida, USA
Ochoa Estate
Star Island, Miami Beach, FL
October 28, 2010

Jordana's eyes snapped open. Then, she groaned in pain. Her whole body ached.

"That's just a side effect of the anti-transformation serum," said a smooth, deep male voice with a trace of a foreign accent, possibly Irish. "It'll wear off. Just not before we give you another shot of it." He chuckled. "Can't have you going all hairy and toothy and possibly killing one of my people. Not before I'm done with you, at any rate."

Jordana forced herself to look up and into the eyes of the man who was speaking. She remembered him. He was the one who'd waved a hand and torn the back off the house. The same man who'd so casually stopped a bullet in mid-air and then sent it flying back into her father's stomach; who'd ordered his minions to kill Bernadette when she tried to protect Jordana and Kitty with her own body. The man who'd killed her dog.

"Who are you?" she demanded, rage burning in her chest like she'd never felt before in her life.

"Haven't you figured it out?" the man said with a grin. He was boyishly handsome, with golden blond hair, perfect white teeth, and brown eyes that were rimmed with gold.

"I'm guessing you're Chemosh Magog," Jordana said.

"Good, and what else?" Magog prompted.

"A murdering bastard," Jordana snarled.

Magog laughed. "You've got what the kids call 'spunk', don't you? I like that in my women."

Jordana looked around, taking in her surroundings. She was actually tied to a chair, an ordinary office chair, with *rope*! The rope was rather strange looking, though. It was silvery and very thin, about the thickness of an ordinary shoelace. The rope coiled around her chest, under her arms, wrapped her forearms to the chair's arms, looped around her thighs, then her calves. She couldn't see where it was knotted, assuming that it was behind her back.

Jordana was not alone with Chemosh Magog. Two other girls were trussed to office chairs the same as herself. They were about the same age as Jordana, maybe a year or two older, maybe younger. The girl closest to her was blond, pale-skinned, and blue-eyed. She had a ball gag in her mouth, which looked uncomfortable as well as humiliating. The other girl looked to be of mixed heritage, mostly Asian. She had long dark hair, bronze skin, and dark eyes, and like the blonde, she, too, had a ball gag in her mouth.

The room itself was some kind of unfinished, cinder-block basement. Tiny windows up near the ceiling let in a little sunlight, which let Jordana know it was still daytime. The other light source in the room came from tiki torches and candles. Besides the office chairs the three girls were tied to, the only piece of furniture in the room was a table covered with a black cloth. Candles burned at the four corners of the table, but Magog's body blocked her view of whatever else was on the table.

"What? No snappy comeback?" Magog teased.

"Just deciding which of these walls I want to see your hide nailed to," Jordana snapped.

"Oh? And who would be doing the, er, nailing? You?" Magog said.

Jordana flexed against the rope holding her in the chair. "Why don't you untie me, and we'll find out."

"No, no, no," Magog said, wagging his finger in warning. "That rope is braided from strands of kevlar, spider silk, and steel wire, *and* it's been enchanted for to be unbreakable."

"What about the chair?" Jordana said as she stretched and twisted her body.

Magog chortled. "Oh, ho! We hadn't thought about that! I know you're very strong, but that strength is dependent on food to fuel it."

Jordana's stomach rumbled, as if in response.

"See? You'll use up your strength to break the chair, but barely have enough to run away," Magog said. "And what about these poor flowers, hmm? Surely, a well-bred, correctly raised child such as yourself wouldn't abandon these helpless strangers to someone as, quote/unquote, 'evil' as me, would you?" Magog had even made air quotes with his fingers when he said the word "evil."

Jordana's eyes bored into Magog's. She felt the "shift" as her perceptions changed from the mundane to the supernatural. For the first time, she was seeing past the glamour and the shapeshifting to what Chemosh Magog really looked like, and she was both fascinated and repulsed. The real Magog was about the same size as the image he projected, and the face was pretty much the same. The differences were obvious, though. Horns, like a bull's, sprouted from the sides of Magog's human head, and his legs and feet were like a cow's as well.

She blinked her eyes, trying to regain normal vision, but she couldn't shake the True Sight. Looking away from Magog's eyes, her gaze fell on the hands resting nonchalantly on his hips. He wore rings on both hands that she could tell were magical artifacts, spells contained in each ring for release at will. Then, her gaze was drawn to Magog's right hip, just in front of where his hand was resting, and attached to the belt was a small leather pouch. The pouch was inscribed with a script that she didn't recognize, but what she found fascinating was a silver thread, no thicker than a strand from a spider's web, exited from the pouch and curled out, through the air, and off into the distance where she could no longer make out the thread.

"Good," Magog crooned, assuming he'd cowed the girl into submission, even if only temporarily. "Now, you are probably wondering who these flowers are and why they're gagged. Well, to answer the second part first, I don't want them spoiling the surprise of the answer to the first part, and to answer the first part second, allow me to make some introductions."

Magog spun Jordana's chair so that she was fully facing the other two girls. Then, he moved the other two chairs side-by-side. Standing behind the blond girl, he placed his hands on her shoulders. The girl twitched in obvious fright and revulsion.

"This fair young maiden is Rachel Brady. She's from California and enjoys long walks on the beach," Magog said. He stroked a finger along Rachel's cheek, making the girl shiver. "As you can guess from her surname, our sweet Rachel is a good Irish lass, like yourself, but her mother is Greek. I do love the Greeks."

Magog slid over behind the other girl. "And this lovely peach is Alannah Hickey, but her friends and family call her 'Sassy,' not because she's particularly sassy, but because her Thai mother insisted that her middle name be Sasithorn. By the way, it's a lovely name with the poetic meaning of 'the moon'." He ran a hand over Sassy's long, dark hair. The girl squeezed her eyes shut, moaning through the ball gag. "I do love this raven hair." He lowered his face and inhaled her scent. Sassy shivered again.

Magog just chuckled and came around behind Jordana's chair. "Last, but not least, Rachel and Sassy, this is Jordana Quinlan. Like the both of you, she has a lovely Irish surname, but her mother is Costa Rican."

"You seem obsessed with our mother's backgrounds and our Irish names," Jordana said.

Magog laughed. "Of course, I am. I'm Irish. Well, part-Irish at any rate. I chose girls who had married men of Irish extraction. You see, Jordy... Can I call you 'Jordy'? Not that you have any choice in the matter. Ha! You see, Jordy, like you, *I*, the great Chemosh Magog, am *their* father, too. Say hello to your sisters, Jordy."

CHAPTER TWENTY-SEVEN

Atlanta, Georgia, USA
Belle Arbor Plantation
Covington, GA
October 28, 2010

Like any practitioner worthy of claiming to be one of The Wise, Gideon kept a laboratory in the basement of Magee House. Unlike most wizards, though, Gideon's lab looked more like a cross between a machine shop, an armory, and a moonshiner's still. Since his magical talent manifested itself in artifice and alchemy, Gideon didn't much need tomes of magical incantations, crystal balls, or bubbling cauldrons. Instead, he brought forth his magic through cleverly crafted devices that were capable of doing things that simple mechanical engineering couldn't explain, as well as a variety of potions, salves, and ointments that recreated a number of traditional spells.

Bruce the Foul-Mouthed Parrot's perch was set up in one corner, but the macaw wasn't there. Gideon found the bird hiding under the work table that was the centerpiece of his lab. Bruce was shivering and singing to himself. The bird let out a squawk of happiness when he saw Gideon. "Giddy!"

"What are you doing under there, Bruce?" Gideon asked.

"Bad guys, Giddy! Bad guys!" Bruce declared. "Motherfuckers! Cock suckers!"

"Did they scare you, Bruce?" Gideon soothed as he brought the bird out of his hiding place.

"Bad guys, Giddy! Hurt Angel Tits!" Bruce declared.

"I know, Bruce. We're gonna go get her back," Gideon told the bird.

Bruce calmed a little, but he was still agitated when Gideon placed him on his perch. Even the apple that Gideon sliced up and put in Bruce's food bowl didn't seem to help the bird's mood.

"Bad, bad guys," Bruce continued to mutter to himself. "I want Angel Tits, Giddy! Pretty Angel Tits!"

"I told you, Bruce: I'm going to go get her," Gideon sighed.

While significantly smarter than an ordinary macaw -- even smarter than a lot of people Gideon had met over his centuries -- Bruce the Foul-Mouthed Parrot was still just a bird. "Pretty bitch. Bad-bad hurt her. Poor pretty bitch," the bird moaned.

"I know," Gideon sighed as he retrieved the sample he'd taken from Princess' teeth. He showed the sample to the bird. "But she got a piece of him for us."

"Bad-bad hurt Cookie," Bruce moaned. "Bruce hide. Bruce shitty bird."

Gideon set the sample in a centrifuge and turned the device on. Then, he held his arm out for Bruce. "No, you dumb bird, you're not shitty. Bruce is a good bird, a smart bird. Hiding was the best thing you could do."

"Bruce shitty bird," the macaw moaned.

"You're *not* shitty, Bruce," Gideon sighed. "C'mon, we should get out of here, let that percolate while we go check on Raven."

"Big Sister is hurt," Bruce moaned.

"She'll be okay," Gideon said. "She's tough. She's a Shaw."

Matt had arrived with a SWAT team from the County Sheriff's Department. The coroner, an ambulance, and a fire engine were also pulling onto the property.

"The coroner's boys are in the know," Matt was saying to Deputy Parker, "but we can't let the fire department guys see them."

They were standing over the body of one of the ogres that Knobs had killed. When Gideon joined them, he reached down and rubbed the "1%" patch on the ogre biker's vest. The creature suddenly looked like a horribly killed human. "There's a glamour built into their colors. Just rub the one-percenter patch to activate," Gideon said. "Your SWAT guys can do it while they're 'securing' the weapons."

"How do you know about things like this?" Matt demanded.

Gideon shrugged. "Cable TV."

Parker snorted. "What's the cover story?"

Gideon rolled his neck. "The usual, home invasion, drug deal gone bad. Backstop it with a rumor that this was a safe house being used by a federal agency to hide some witnesses."

"So, lie, deny, and obfuscate to make the big lie all that more believable," Parker said. "I'm getting so good at this, I should run for public office."

"Your mama would kill you," Matt said.

"Hell, I'd shoot you for her," Gideon added with a wan smile. "Look, I gotta slip outta here and get over to the hospital. Levi teleported Raven out when she was wounded. You'll find Tom Quinlan, Bernadette Cook, and a dog named Princess in the kitchen. Knobs is standing guard over them. I want all three treated with the utmost respect."

"What about... these?" Parker asked, waving a hand at the biker bodies.

Gideon pointed to the still burning corpse of the troll. "Finish what Knobs started for all I care."

"I'll take care of this scene, brother," Matt said. "You go see to Raven and Levi."

"Thanks, Matt," Gideon said. He handed Bruce over. "He's feeling scared and ashamed right now. Just, be nice to him 'til I get back, okay?"

"Long as he stays away from my car," Matt said.

"Bruce, be a good bird for Matt," Gideon said.

"No dive-bomb the dumb ass?" Bruce said.

"No, no dive-bomb the dumb ass," Gideon confirmed.

He nodded to Matt again and went back to his bike. The drive to the hospital was pretty quick, even with the construction going on. Gideon went to the emergency room area first, flashing his credentials to get the information he wanted. He was told that Special Agent Rey MacKeon, Raven's cover identity, was in surgery. The nurse also gave him directions to the lounge where the other FBI agent, the one who'd brought her in, was waiting for the doctor.

Gideon found Levi sitting with his head in his hands. When the younger agent looked up, Gideon saw that Levi's eyes were red from crying. Dried blood decorated his upper lip and trailed from his ears, as well. Levi came to his feet, and Gideon had to catch the younger man when he started to teeter.

"Whoa, boy, sit back down," Gideon commanded. "How's Raven?"

"Don't know, Mr. Shaw. She got shot up pretty bad," Levi said. He ran one of his hands along the side of his head. "She got grazed, here-ish... Doc's think her skull might've cracked."

"She's gonna be fine, Levi," Gideon assured him. "She's tough."

Levi nodded. "I know, but... She's not indestructible."

"I know she ain't," Gideon sighed. "Hey, good call using her cover ID, but it's pretty worthless. One of my bad guys was using it."

Levi snorted. "Figures."

"How're you doing?"

"Not too good," Levi admitted. "I tried to teleport through an EM field. Knocked me and the girls out. Oh, shit! The girls!"

"Calm down," Gideon ordered. "Knobs told me."

"We've gotta figure out where those Dark Word bastards took them, get them back," Levi said, starting to stand up again, but Gideon's hand on his shoulder put him back in his seat.

"We *will*," Gideon said. "But I need my team back up to snuff, Levi."

"Okay," Levi said. He rubbed his head again. "Still hurts."

"Has a doctor looked at you yet?" Gideon asked.

"Uh, no?" Levi said after a few seconds' thought.

Gideon rolled his eyes. "Levi Carmichael, you're no use to me broken." Gideon waved over a nurse. "Is Dr. Navarro available?"

"He's in surgery right now, with the wounded federal agent," the nurse replied.

"How 'bout Dr. Christchurch?" Gideon asked. "My agent needs a specialist."

"I'll give him a call for you," the nurse offered.

"Please do so," Gideon said.

A few minutes later a dark man in scrubs and a gray-haired man in a lab coat arrived in the lounge. The man in scrubs was Dr. Navarro, and the other man was his colleague, Dr. Christchurch. Both men were well aware of the paranormal nature of many of their patients and had, in fact, built their practice around serving that special community.

"Okay, as much as I'm dying to know how Raven is, Levi here really needs seeing to," Gideon said.

"What's the problem?" Dr. Christchurch asked.

"I tried teleporting through an EM field," Levi admitted. "Then, I teleported about twice my usual range with a passenger."

"Gracious!" Christchurch exclaimed as he pulled a small flashlight from his pocket and started shining it in Levi's eyes.

"How is Raven, er, Agent MacKeon?" Gideon demanded of the other doctor.

"Uh, what is the nature of your relationship to the patient, sir?" Navarro asked.

"I'm her father," Gideon growled.

Navarro blinked, taking in Gideon's youthful appearance.

"I'm older than I look, and she's adopted," Gideon snapped.

"Of course, Mr. uh?"

"Shaw."

"Well, Agent MacKeon is lucky that she's... er, well, *what* she is," Navarro said. "The numerous bullet wounds to her torso and limbs would have killed a normal human being. As it is, with the slugs removed and proper antibiotics applied, she is healing at, well, an astonishing rate. I noted several places where... well, bullets must've... *bounced* off her. Amazing, really."

"Prognosis, Doctor?" Gideon growled.

"Well, the one wound to her head, a grazing wound to the temple, shattered her skull, driving some of the pieces *into* the brain. We picked out the worst of it, and the skull itself appears to be regenerating, closing back up to cover the damaged area. I don't know what effect the wound will have on her mind, but physically, she *will* recover. Within a week or two is my guess from her rate of healing so far," Navarro said. "I'm curious... Uh, *what is she?*"

"She's a Shaw," Gideon replied.

Navarro blushed. "Of course, Mr. Shaw."

Gideon turned to the other doctor. "How's that one?"

"He'll live. He may even return to what passes for normal in a few days. In the meantime, young man, you stick to the normal three dimensions, okay? No jumping, porting, slipping, sliding, or whatever else it is you teleporting types do," Christchurch said.

"I'll make sure he stays put," Gideon said.

Christchurch glanced at his colleague. "Put your foot in your mouth again?"

Navarro nodded.

"You'll excuse the curiosity of youth, yes, Dr. Shaw?" Christchurch said.

"I'm not a doctor anymore, Doc," Gideon said with a small smile.

Christchurch shrugged. "Saul and I will take good care of your daughter, Gideon. I'm guessing, from what I've heard about her wounds, that you'll be off to do something... violent to somebody who deserves it?"

Gideon nodded.

"Well, good hunting, and my best to your father when you see him," Christchurch said.

"Thank you, Doc," Gideon said. Once the doctors had left, he got his phone out of his pocket.

"Uh, who're you calling?" Levi asked.

"First, I'm calling my sister. She'll come up here to be with Raven when she wakes up. Then, I'm calling in some backup from the Program," Gideon replied. "We got a war to fight, son."

CHAPTER TWENTY-EIGHT

Miami, Florida, USA
Ochoa Estate
Star Island, Miami Beach, FL
October 28, 2010

"I would encourage you to get to know one another, bond over girl talk, but, as you can plainly see, that conversation would be rather one-sided," Magog said. "Now, the reason that I'm revealing to you that you have... 'siblings' is to remind you, *all of you*, that while you are very important to my plans, each of you is individually expendable."

A door opened and Jordana could hear feet on stairs.

"Ah, our next object lesson arrives!" Magog chortled as he returned the girls' chairs to their original positions facing the cloth-covered table.

For the first time, Jordana could clearly see what was on the table besides the candles. In the center of the table was an ornate clay bowl about the size of a punch bowl. It was flanked by a pair of red crystals, and a sheathed dagger rested on the table in front of the bowl. The black tablecloth was embroidered with mystical symbols stitched in silver thread.

The newcomers stopped on the other side of the table facing the girls tied in the chairs. She recognized Micky, or rather the evil spirit wearing Micky's body, Nahasheron. She also saw that silvery, spider silk-like strand that came from the pouch on Magog's belt was connected to Micky's body, right at the center of her chest. Jordana also recognized one of the other people in the group as Tia Teresa, formerly "Sister" Teresa, her mother's spiritual advisor. The old woman's face was painted like a skull. With a gasp, Jordana realized that Tia Teresa was the necromancer who'd summoned and controlled the revenants that had attacked the family home in Orlando.

Besides Magog's two lieutenants, the rest of the party consisted of six men in black paramilitary fatigues and two people, women, dressed in white shifts with black bags pulled over their heads, their hands bound behind their backs. Each of the female prisoners was held between two of the guards. The remaining two guards, armed with submachine guns, kept their weapons trained on the three girls tied in the office chairs. Jordana took a quick glance at the other two girls. Rachel had her eyes tightly screwed shut and her head turned away. Sassy glared defiantly at Magog, but she was studiously avoiding looking at the prisoners or at Jordana.

"Ah, you see, dear Jordy, Rachel and Sassy know what's coming next. They both came to me at the same time. You, on the other hand, made friends who are quite adept at interfering with my plans," Magog said. "Your boyfriend, or whoever his friends might be, is quite adept with the ritual magics. The cleansing and anti-tracking spells they performed worked just as they'd hoped. Your trail vanished, and you and your little family were hidden from the view of Seers."

Magog waved a hand toward Tia Teresa. "What they didn't count on, though, was the fact that I keep my very own Oracle on staff."

"Wait, what, like the database program?" Jordana snorted.

Magog laughed. "No, like a precognizant, someone who can see future events, a prophet. Teresa here, with the right combination of drugs and mystical herbs, can predict convergences of future probabilities. She predicted that you would be in that park, and she predicted that you'd be at that plantation house. One event led to the other, it would seem. Powerful forces of destiny are at work in your life, Jordy, which is why you're currently my number-one draft choice. Don't get too hopeful, my other lovely daughters. Jordy has proven to be overly spunky, and I have other plans for the two who don't get chosen to be my queen. Remember ladies: important, but expendable."

Magog turned and snatched the bags off the prisoners' heads.

Jordana gasped. "Mom! Kitty!" she shouted.

Kitty had a ball-gag in her mouth, and when she saw Jordana tied in the chair she started struggling. Lucinda, on the other hand, was docile. She wasn't gagged, and her eyes were glazed over.

"I swear to God, if you hurt them," Jordana snarled.

"What god?" Magog spat. "The only god in this room is *me*! *My* will be done!"

The glamour slipped, and everyone could see the horned man behind the attractive facade. Rachel, Sassy, and Kitty all recoiled in fear.

Magog's people stared at him in adulation, adoration. Jordana glared at him in a burning rage. She flexed her muscles against her bonds again. Screws in the chair moaned in protest.

"Stop right now," Magog ordered. He nodded his head toward one of the guards holding Kitty. "Or your little sister gets her pretty little brains splattered on the wall."

The guard had drawn a pistol and pressed the barrel against Kitty's temple.

"Now," Magog continued in a calm voice, "do you understand? Will you cooperate?"

Jordana didn't trust her voice. She just nodded.

"Good," Magog crooned. He snapped his fingers, and the guards holding Lucinda Quinlan brought her up to the table. Magog picked up the dagger. "Do you know what this is, Jordy?"

"A knife," Jordana said quietly.

"Well, functionally, yes, but it's much more. This is an athame, a magical implement, an artifact that allows a practitioner to direct certain energies. However, your original answer stands true, too. It's a knife, a tool for cutting," Magog said.

Without hesitation, he turned, grabbed Lucinda's hair, held her head over the bowl, and slit her throat. Lucinda never cried out, never struggled. She stood docilely, held up by two of Magog's guards, as the lifeblood drained from her body.

Jordana screamed. Rage burned through the anti-transformation serum in her body, strength flooded her limbs, and she flexed again. The chair came apart under her, but the rope still held her fast in place. Hair, claws, and teeth sprouted from her body. The rage was nearly blinding. Then, she was slammed against the wall, knocking the breath out of her.

"Behave or I torture your sister to death," Magog said. His hand was stretched out at her. When he dropped it, Jordana fell to the concrete floor, breathing heavily, the change reverting back to normal.

"Why?" Jordana managed to sob-gasp, tears flowing freely down her cheeks.

"Well, I need the blood of your mother for my ritual, first of all. Second, you know I'm not bluffing about killing the hostage, and, third, Teresa feeds her power on fear, guilt, and shame. Your rage and despair are pretty nummy, too," Magog explained. "Do you understand, my dear, that you can't stop me, and if you cause too much trouble, you'll watch your sister die, and then I'll kill you. I'll dope you up on the serum, and have my men gang-rape you to death. Am I making myself *abundantly* clear, Jordana?"

Jordana nodded. "Yeah. I get it."

"Good," Magog said with a smile. "Now, anything you want to say before I send you to your room, hmm?"

"Yeah," Jordana said. "I won't cause you any trouble, but when my boyfriend finds us, he's gonna kill you."

CHAPTER TWENTY-NINE

Miami, Florida, USA

Ochoa Estate

Star Island, Miami Beach, FL

October 28, 2010

"Your *boyfriend*?" Sassy snorted.

The three girls had been untied and taken, under heavy guard, upstairs to the top floor of the house, which turned out to be a mansion. Jordana was fairly certain that they were in Florida, somewhere along the eastern coast, possibly as far south as Miami, if not farther. The room they'd been locked in was bare of furnishings beyond three mattresses laid out on the floor. They had a bathroom with toilet, sink, and shower, but no cabinets, no windows, just a small shelf with a travel-size bar of soap and an equally tiny bottle of shampoo. Instead of the usual linens, they had toilet paper and rolls of paper towels.

The room had two windows with a view of the ocean and the backyard of the mansion, but nothing else. Bars covered the windows on the outside. They had no curtains, no blankets, no sheets. The mattresses and the pillows were bare. Fortunately for them, the room was quite warm because the guards made them strip off all their clothes before locking the girls in for the night. Jordana looked up at the ceiling and saw a closed-circuit camera in each ceiling corner.

"There's one in the bathroom, too," Sassy said following Jordana's gaze. "It covers the shower *and* the commode. No privacy at all at any time."

"He *really* doesn't want us to escape, does he?" Jordana grumbled.

Rachel had thrown herself down on one of the mattresses as soon as they'd gotten into the room. She rolled over and sat up, crossing her arms over her chest. "Guards on the door, guards under the windows, not that jumping would be an option without the bars," the blond said.

"They have tasers," Sassy added. "They won't kill us, but... Well, have you ever been tased? Trust me on this, it sucks." Sassy pantomimed being hit with a taser, jiggling her whole body like she was having a seizure.

Jordana snorted a laugh. She couldn't help it. "I bet you just gave whoever's watching a thrill."

"Sassy likes to air-dry after a shower and pose for the cameras," Rachel said, blushing at the memory.

"For a California girl, you sure are modest," Sassy teased as she plopped down on the mattress next to Rachel and put an arm around her shoulder.

"I'm from Eureka," Rachel said. She looked up at Jordana. "It's up near Oregon. I'm a preacher's daughter."

"And preacher's daughters fall into two categories," Sassy said. "Either the biggest slut in school or the most goody-two-shoes person ever. Guess which one sweet Rachel here is."

Rachel blushed. "Sassy, stop."

Sassy grinned. "The only good thing to come out of this shitty situation is that my wish for my very own little sister has come true, and now I've got two!"

"Only child?" Jordana asked.

"No, three older brothers," Sassy replied with a heavy sigh. She sniffed. "Uh, they..."

"Magog killed Sassy's father and all of her brothers. They took her little cousin who was visiting," Rachel explained. "Said he only needed one hostage." She sniffed as well. "He, uh, sacrificed our mothers, too."

"In front of us," Sassy snarled.

"Yeah, well, 'daddy' is evil," Jordana growled. She flexed her hands, willing them to become claws, but they'd given her another shot of the serum.

Rachel shivered, despite the warmth of the room. "I can't believe that he's really our father," she said in a soft voice.

"Or that the sick bastard wants to marry one of us," Sassy added.

"It's not us that he wants to marry," Jordana said. At their questioning looks, Jordana continued, "He's going to implant one of us with some demon goddess to be his queen. He tried it once before, about forty years ago, but it didn't take."

"How do you know that?" Sassy demanded.

"My boyfriend told me," Jordana replied. "He'll save us, don't worry about that."

"Yeah, why's that?" Sassy snorted.

"He's highly motivated," Jordana said.

"Because he *loves* you so much," Sassy mocked.

"No, because he *hates* Magog so much," Jordana replied.

CHAPTER THIRTY

Atlanta, Georgia, USA

Magee House, Belle Arbor Plantation

Covington, GA

October 29, 2010

Gideon didn't need a lot of sleep, but he *did* need to sleep, if for no other reason than to dream, to let the subconscious deal with the stresses of life. He'd spent several hours poring over the sample of flesh he'd taken from Princess' teeth, working with it to create a very special enchantment. He'd also spent his time preparing equipment for their mission, readying weapons, loading "special" ammunition, and packing everything. Then, repacking everything. He also kept an eye on a device that was larger than a smartphone, but smaller than most tablets -- the GPS-equipped readout for the tracking devices that he'd given the Quinlans.

The devices had attached to each person's intestinal wall, and would transmit a locating signal on demand. As long as that demand was transmitted from within a ten-mile radius. The devices could be tracked by satellite, but they had to be out in the open for the specially-tasked satellites to "spot" the device's unique radiation signature. Currently, the tracker was registering only one device: the one inside Tom Quinlan. Another nifty feature of the tracking devices was that they could also transmit the vital signs of the person who'd been bugged. Naturally, he wasn't getting any life signs out of Tom, and Gideon felt deeply saddened by that. He'd been actually looking forward to really getting to know Tom and the rest of Jordana's family.

Sleep crept up on Gideon as he sat on a tall stool at his worktable. He set aside the clip he'd been loading with .45 ACP ammunition. He glanced over at Bruce. The bird was snoring on his perch. He'd had a long day, too, reciting formulas for Gideon's enchantments and potions. Gideon stood and stretched his aching back. He kept a cot in the lab for power naps at moments such as this. One of his former mentors, now centuries dead, had explained to him that to be a Wizard, one had to be Wise, and Wise men took sleep whenever they needed it because exhaustion led to mistakes and mistakes caused explosions in labs.

Gideon stretched out on his cot, closed his eyes, and was fast asleep in seconds, more exhausted than he'd realized. In those seconds, though, before sleep claimed him, Gideon prayed. He prayed that Jordana was alive and safe and that she loved him as much as he loved her. Then, he dreamed.

In that dream place he was with Jordana. They stood beside one another on a rocky beach looking out at a storm-tossed ocean. Wind whipped at their clothes and hair. Then, Gideon realized that the wind wasn't whipping Jordana's clothes because she wasn't wearing clothes. Good dream, he chuckled to himself.

"Where is this?" Jordana asked, frowning.

"Scotland," Gideon replied. "This looks like the coast off of Inverness."

"This is weird," Jordana declared. "Why would I be dreaming about Scotland? I mean, I can understand dreaming about *you*. I got a lot of hopes pinned on you, Dyrnwch."

"Well, *you're* not dreaming about Scotland. *I am*. My family comes from the area around Inverness originally. I actually own a little B&B near here. Lovely little farm, kinda like the one I grew up on, but with internal plumbing," Gideon said.

"No, *I'm* dreaming about *you*, dumb ass," Jordana insisted.

Gideon stared at her for a moment, and then, he laughed.

"What's so funny?" Jordana said.

"We're both dreaming, and our dreams have merged," Gideon said. He swept Jordana up in a whirling hug and showered her face and neck with kisses that had her laughing.

"This is surreal," Jordana said when Gideon set her back down on her feet.

"It happens, sometimes," Gideon said. "Especially where *geasa* are involved." He was grinning.

"What, those fae taboo things? Like Knobs' inability to use nicknames or that true... love..." Jordana wound down, staring at Gideon.

"I think we might share a certain *geas*," Gideon said.

Jordana's face broke into a smile. "Really?"

"Yes, really," Gideon said.

"Good because I could really use a rescue about now," Jordana said. "I'm not Magog's only 'house guest' by the way."

"Your mom and Kitty?" Gideon asked.

Jordana frowned and looked down. "He killed Mom in front of me, Gideon. Just cut her throat and drained her blood into a bowl. He's holding Kitty hostage so I won't..."

"Yeah, I get it," Gideon said.

"I've got sisters, too," Jordana said. "Well, half-sisters, I mean."

"Really?" Gideon smiled.

"Yeah, Magog has been running his own one-man breeding program. Rachel, Sassy, and I are his favorites," Jordana said.

"Sassy?" Gideon smirked.

"Focus," Jordana chided.

"Kinda hard with you all naked and stuff," Gideon teased, hugging her to him tighter.

"Ug, yeah, he keeps us locked in a room with, *literally*, nothing in it but some mattresses. We're not even allowed to have clothes while we're in the room, and we're under 24-hour surveillance," Jordana said.

"Show me," Gideon said.

"How?"

"It's a dream. You know it's a dream. Take control of it, and show me," Gideon said.

The Scottish coastline disappeared, replaced by a large room that was as bare as Jordana had said. Gideon looked around, taking in the placement of the cameras, the barred windows, the heavy door.

"I take it these are your new sisters?" Gideon said waving a hand at the other two naked forms sleeping on the mattresses.

Jordana pointed to each girl, naming her, "That's Rachel, and that's Sassy. It's a nickname, don't get started."

"Have you figured out why you three are Magog's favorites?" Gideon asked as he crossed over to one of the windows and looked out.

"Well, neither of them is a thrope, but I think we've all three inherited the immortality gene. Sassy's mom was some kind of witch, and she'd taught Sassy some magic. They give her a shot, some kind of potion that keeps her from casting spells," Jordana said. "They shoot me up with the same serum my mom was using."

"I bet that sucks," Gideon said.

"I almost changed, when he killed Mom," Jordana said.

"Your anger let you burn out the serum more quickly than your metabolism would normally allow it," Gideon said. "Remember something, Jordy: you're more than just a werewolf. You're like me; you're half werewolf. Your other half has power, too. Use it."

"What, like that True Sight thing? The pheromone thing? Like I want him to like me more," Jordana scoffed.

"Jordy, you're half *sidhe*. Magic is woven into the very fabric of your being, and you've accepted one of the *geasa* you were born with. That unlocks a lot of power, sweetheart," Gideon said. He waved a hand at the room. "We're having a conversation in a shared dream. What is this if not magic?"

Jordana smiled. "I guess you're right. So, do you know where we are?"

"Somewhere on the Atlantic coast," Gideon said.

"Yeah, I figure we're somewhere between Orlando and the Keys," Jordana said. "Can't you magic up our location?"

Gideon laughed. "No, not really. My spell to hide you from Magog was too good for that. How did he find you anyway?"

"Tia Teresa is an oracle," Jordana said. "So, how are you gonna find me, us?"

"Remember that pill? It's a tracker, and now that I've got a better idea of where you are, I can track you down quicker," Gideon said. He shrugged. "It's good to know he's got an oracle, though. I can take precautions against something like that."

"Well, you need to hurry," Jordana said. "He's changed the ritual from the one he used on Aggie. Apparently, our virginity *is* an issue."

"You're kidding," Gideon said.

"No, he's already killed one of his daughters because she'd already been with a man," Jordana said. "Sassy overheard the guards talking about it. Said that she wasn't 'pure' enough for the ritual." Jordana swallowed a lump. "Magog had his men rape her to death, Gideon."

Gideon hugged her to his chest. "I'm coming for you, but I've got to wake up now. I don't want to leave..."

"You've got to if you're gonna rescue us," Jordana said.

"Stay alive. Do that for me, okay?" Gideon said.

"I will," Jordana promised.

Gideon sat up on his cot with a start. The tracker was buzzing. He dashed over to it. The satellite had picked up a new signal. He zoomed in on the location. Miami Beach. He grabbed his phone and hit the speed dial. "I've got a location. We're on."

CHAPTER THIRTY-ONE

Atlanta, Georgia, USA
Belle Arbor Plantation
Covington, GA
October 29, 2010

Levi Carmichael was the odd man out, and he knew it. Four of them -- Gideon, Matt, Knobs, and himself -- stood on the edge of a pasture within easy walking distance of Magee House. The pasture was still within the grounds of Belle Arbor plantation. Normally, it was used to exercise Gideon's horses, but Patches and the other animals were safely secured in their barn. Now, the four of them stood just inside the fence, waiting.

Knobs, sensing Levi's discomfort, glanced up at the young agent and cracked a crooked-toothed smile. "Relax, Master Levi. All will work out in the end. We will have justice; we will have victory."

Levi looked down at the goblin. Knobs had tied a black bandana around his head, leaving his long, pointed ears sticking out, and he'd perched a pair of UV-coated, amber shooting glasses on his long, hooked nose. Combined with the black fatigues, combat boots, and tactical vest he was wearing, the green-skinned goblin still looked more like he belonged with the group than Levi felt that he did.

"Just feeling like the odd thing out in one of those 'Sesame Street' songs. You know, one of these things is not like the others," Levi admitted.

Knobs cocked his head to one side. "I'm green. Does that make me Kermit in your little fantasy?"

Levi barked a short, abrupt laugh.

"I call Elmo," Matt declared.

Gideon groaned. "I know I'm gonna regret this. Why, pray tell, do you think you're Elmo?"

"Because I'm the cute one!" Matt declared with a big grin.

"No," Gideon said.

"I don't see it," Levi added.

"Jackass," Knobs sighed.

"Fine," Matt sniffed. "Be that way."

Levi couldn't help but smile and feel a little better. He still felt out of place. Like a little kid playing grown up, and all the grown-ups were bad asses. Gideon and Matt were both dressed in black fatigues, as well, but neither looked like he was wearing a uniform. Both wore customized kits, and Levi was aware that they both carried a number of enchanted items. The one thing they appeared to have in common, though, was the tactical vests they were wearing. Levi was vaguely reminded of the *lorica segmentata* of the Roman legions, but made of

Kevlar instead of metal. It definitely wasn't standard issue. Chain-mail sleeves hung down from the shoulders almost to the elbows, and Levi had noticed that chain mail lined the insides of the vests, too. He was pretty sure the vests were heavy as hell, but neither man seemed to notice the weight. Of course, runes had been stitched into the armor. Levi could only guess what magic was contained in those symbols.

Levi glanced down at his own SWAT-style body armor with its modular load-bearing pouches and pistol holster. One of his pouches held the tracker unit. Gideon had given him charge of the device once they'd narrowed down the coordinates to Miami, Florida, specifically an estate on Star Island. Gideon had also given Levi an old 1911A1 Colt Government model, an enchanted weapon he'd named "Old Reliable." In most respects, it was pretty much an ordinary .45 ACP pistol, but Gideon had said that it was absolutely reliable, and the clip loaded itself. All Levi had to do was rack the slide, and as long as he had ammo on his person, the gun would shoot. Reliable indeed.

"Hey, Gideon, just a thought," Levi said.

"What's that, kid?" Gideon replied.

"How come you only have one self-loading magazine? Seems to me that a never-ending clip of bullets would be a handy thing to have in all your guns," Levi said.

"Yeah, but that one clip is the result of twenty years of enchanting and thousands of dollars of materials. You can't enchant an existing magazine to do that. You have to build it from scratch using special materials. And casting the spells that allow it to search your person for the right caliber ammo, teleport it into the clip, and do it accurately every single time ... well, kid, *that* alone is time-consuming as hell," Gideon replied. "Magic ain't free. Now, don't go losing that clip. It's more valuable than your car *and* your house."

Levi swallowed the lump that suddenly formed in his throat as he checked to make sure that the enchanted pistol and its *extremely* valuable magazine was still in its place in his holster. "Got it, boss."

Gideon chuckled to himself as he watched Levi's nervous twitch to ensure he still retained the valuable magical item that he'd been entrusted with. Gideon wondered if he should let the kid off the hook by letting him know that both Old Reliable and the self-loading clip were enchanted with a spell that would teleport both to Gideon's lab should they become lost. Then, he decided that a little fear would keep the kid sharp. He didn't have the same worries as Levi about his kit, but he'd been carrying a small fortune in enchanted objects for most of his life.

"Incoming!" rawked Bruce the Foul-Mouthed Parrot as he soared down and landed on Gideon's shoulder.

"Why're you bringing the dive-bombing wonder?" Matt asked.

"I'm a pretty birdy!" Bruce declared loudly.

Gideon stifled a chuckle. "He's part of our protection."

"Bruce is a motherfuckin' wall, bitch!" the bird squawked.

Matt raised an eyebrow. "Really?"

"Look, you know how I centered the anti-scrying on Bruce?" Gideon said.

Matt nodded. "Yeah, anybody trying to remote view or listen on us gets an earful of Bruce at his naughty best."

"Right, well, Magog has an oracle working for him. That's how they knew *when* was the best time to hit the estate," Gideon said. "I modified the ward centered on Bruce here with a temporal component.

Should that precognizant bitch try predicting what we're up to, she'll get Bruce's plans to eat an apple and shit in her eye."

"Smelly bird poop!" Bruce said. "Shit in her eye!"

"What about the rest of the team? They're not covered by your ward, are they?" Matt said.

"Nope, but a lot of what's going on, that's a distraction. Get Magog looking one way while you and me cornhole him from the other direction," Gideon said.

"A plan that's a lack of a plan? I *like* it!" Matt snickered.

"My lord," Knobs said, one of his ears twitching. He pointed to the north.

Gideon peered in the indicated direction. "Helo's incoming."

Matt squinted. "I don't see it."

"I got better eyes. Knobs has better ears," Gideon said.

"He's got *bigger* ears," Matt said.

"And you have a bigger arse, Master Matthias," Knobs said with a grin.

Matt grabbed the back of his pants. "Really? Damn. Now, I need to go on a diet or I'll never fit in that prom dress I've been eyeing."

"I make it a general policy *not* to point out to heavily-armed men just how insane they are," Levi said, "but you guys are nuttier than a fruitcake."

"I think you mean fruitier than a nut cake in Matt's case," Gideon said.

"See if I give *you* any of my favors," Matt said, puckering up as if to kiss someone.

"Yeah, I'm spoken for," Gideon said.

"I'm engaged," Levi said when Matt turned toward him.

"I'm an asexual hermaphrodite, and you're still not my type," Knobs said.

"Okay, can I ask a somewhat serious question?" Levi said.

"Sure, piss on the parade of stupid happening here," Matt huffed.

"What's your question, kid?" Gideon replied.

"What's with the old guns you guys are carrying?" Levi asked.

Both men reached unconsciously for the weapons that Levi had mentioned. For Gideon it was a single-action Colt Peacemaker revolver, the Cavalry model with a seven-inch barrel, and Matt caressed the handle of a cut-down Winchester Model 1887 lever-action shotgun.

"Well, same reason Gideon's carrying an old sword, and I have this axe strapped to my back," Matt said. "Enchanted weapons of power."

Matt had a pair of sheaths crossed on his back. The head of a bearded Viking axe peeked out of the top of the left-hand sheath, and the pistol grip of a Benelli M4 semi-auto shotgun stuck up over his right shoulder. He reached up and slid the axe out of its carrier. "This axe, Skull Cleaver, has been in my family for, literally, hundreds of years, most of that time carried by me," Matt said. He returned the axe and drew the Winchester 1887 from its holster on his left thigh. "Not as old, but Blood Beggar here is just as magical. I use her to fire these special enchanted shells that Gideon makes. Kinda like having a 12 gauge bazooka."

"I call 'em 'spell shooters'," Gideon said as he drew out his Colt Peacemaker. "They're enchanted firearms that can be used to fire enchanted ammo and create effects like combat sorcery. This is Avenger. Sam Colt himself taught me how to enchant firearms, and Avenger is the first gun I ever enchanted."

"But you're both still packing modern guns," Levi said.

"Bullets are cheap, kid," Gideon chuckled, "and there's a lot of problems that can be solved just by firepower."

He slid Avenger back into the cross-draw holster on his left hip. He patted the P90 hanging from a tactical sling on his chest. "Sometimes, Levi, just being able to put enough bullets into a monster will kill it." Then, he reached down to the tactical holster on his right thigh and drew out a Para Ordinance P14-45 Tactical. "For things that take more than just a lot of bullets, I have Dyrnwyn here and my dragon-fire rounds."

"Just curious, but do you name all your weapons?" Levi asked.

Gideon shook his head. "No, just the enchanted ones. Matt, though, names *everything*."

"Viking tradition," Matt said. He pointed to the Benelli. "Gore Splasher." Then, he indicated the combat knife on his right thigh. "Tyrfing." He patted the Kel-Tec RFB bullpup battle rifle hanging from a combat sling at his left side. "And this is my new baby, Hole Puncher."

Levi glanced over at Knobs. The goblin was armed with a pair of wicked-looking knives, nothing else. "No guns for you?"

"What need have I of guns, Master Levi?" Knobs replied as he casually drew one of his knives and whipped the blade in the general direction of a tree limb ten yards away. The branch dropped to the ground, cleanly cut through.

"Good point," Levi gulped.

By now the helicopter, a UH-60 Blackhawk, could be clearly seen and heard by everybody. The big helo dropped with deceptive lightness into the pasture, the side doors sliding open just as the wheels touched the ground. Gideon and Matt were already jogging toward the Blackhawk even as a man dressed in commando black was jumping out to meet them. The black helicopter was completely unmarked, except for the tail numbers required by the FAA. Levi and Knobs followed behind Gideon and Matt, Levi gawking the whole way.

Gideon's face split into a big grin when he saw who the man in black was. "Zeus! The Z-man! How's tricks, Lady Killer?"

The other man grinned back and grabbed Gideon's outstretched hand. He pulled Gideon into a back-slapping hug. "You know me. Too little time, too many women to chase," he shouted back over the rumble of the Black Hawk's engines.

"Well, as I live and breathe!" Matt exclaimed. "Little brother!" He grabbed the other man in a bear hug, lifting him from his feet.

"Can't breathe, you big oaf!"

Matt immediately put the smaller man back down on the ground, with an appropriately embarrassed expression on his face. "Sorry. Forgot how delicate you are, Lady Killer."

The commando they'd called "Lady Killer" grinned and slugged Matt in the chest. "That's why the ladies love me, not you. This your team, Highlander?" he added with a nod toward Levi and Knobs.

Gideon nodded. "Kinda scraping the barrel on this one."

"I resemble that remark," Knobs snorted.

"Good to see you, Mister Knobs," the commando said, offering his hand to the goblin.

Knobs shook the hand and said, "And good to see you as well, Master Zeus. How are your lovely mother and sister doing? Is your father still endangering the marlin population in the Keys? Even at his age?"

Zeus laughed. "Yeah, they're all good, Knobs. Thanks for asking."

"Levi Carmichael, this is Zeus Michelakis," Gideon said by way of introduction. "He was in the Teams with Matt and me, most recently. Before that, he's been with The Program for quite a while. Zeus, this is my future son-in-law."

"Raven okay?" Zeus asked.

Gideon nodded. "My sister's watching over her. Raven wanted to come, but she still can't stand up without falling back down. Another few days, and she'll be fine."

"Good to hear. Clock's ticking. Why don't we continue this in the air?" Zeus suggested.

Zeus had five people stuffed into the troop compartment. Normally, the Black Hawk could comfortably transport half again as many troops as were being carried altogether, but between Matt's bulk and that of one of Zeus's people, the compartment felt fairly cramped. Gideon gave each of Zeus's people a good once-over with a quick professional eye.

"This is your team?" Gideon said.

Zeus grinned and nodded. "You're not the only one with a scraped barrel at the moment."

Four of Zeus's five were human or could pass as human, but the fifth member was obviously not human, but a seven-foot-tall primate hominid, a Sasquatch. The hairy humanoid inclined its head to Gideon and made a soft grunting sound.

"You brought a goblin. I should be able to bring a Big Foot," Zeus said.

"I thought you didn't believe in Big Foot or the Loch Ness Monster," Gideon teased.

"Didn't believe in Big Foot til I met one," Zeus acknowledged. "I may be skeptical, but I'm open-minded enough to accept the truth when it's staring me in the face."

"Which I'm told is a very attractive face, by *human* standards," the Sasquatch said in a voice that was both feminine and managed to rumble like a landslide.

Gideon considered Zeus's face for a moment. He really *was* a handsome man, tall, dark haired, good cheek structure, just enough facial hair to make him look rugged... "Yeah, but he's not as pretty as me."

The Sasquatch threw back her head and bellowed a laugh. "I have decided that I like you, even if your face is too smooth and you smell funny."

"This is Cha'a-ka'a, but we just call her 'Chaka' for simplicity's sake," Zeus said.

Gideon made a series of grunting, hooting, and snuffling noises with what sounded like his own name thrown in. Chaka's eyes widened and her jaw dropped open in a very human-like expression of surprise.

"Where did you learn The Speech?" she demanded.

"Spent some time among your people a while back," Gideon replied. "The People of the Great Wood are an ancient and noble species. I learned much wisdom among them."

Chaka nodded her shaggy head. "You are one of the Wise, then?"

"I dabble, know a few... tricks," Gideon said with a wink.

Chaka laughed. "Spoken like my mentor. I, too, count myself as Wise."

"Chaka is my number-two and the team's wizard-slash-medic," Zeus said.

"Thought you didn't believe in magic," Gideon said.

"I don't. However, I do believe in an ancient psionic science attuned to certain inherited mental pathways. It's like Arthur C. Clarke said..."

"'Sufficiently advanced science is indistinguishable from magic'," Gideon quoted.

"So, not magic, ancient esoteric super-science. If you need to think it's magic to make the tech work, whatever," Zeus said.

"I find his mind fascinating," Chaka said. "Open and closed at the same time."

"Yeah, well, I'm afraid I'm about to give the open part of his mind a good stretching," Gideon said.

"Do tell," Chaka said, leaning forward.

"Well, the whole situation boils down to this: we gotta rescue my kidnapped girlfriend from the hybrid elf/godling that kidnapped her before he can implant her with the essence of either a demon or some other godling," Gideon said. "Oh, did I forget to mention that he's got Dark Word cultists, Jaguar Warriors, a powerful demon, and a necromancer-oracle on his side?"

"Deep shit!" Bruce squawked.

Chaka tilted her head slightly, and her gaze became somewhat glassy as she stared at the bird perched on Gideon's shoulder. "Your familiar?"

"I was wondering why you'd bring Bruce the Foul-Mouthed Parrot with you," Zeus added.

"You've affixed a temporally-adjusted anti-scrying ward to the bird," Chaka said. She nodded to herself. "Clever."

"That's part of it," Gideon agreed with a nod. "The other part is the raid I had you arrange through our Miami office."

"DEA agents are gonna be hitting some estate in Miami Beach," Zeus confirmed. "But, they're DEA agents in name only." He turned slightly to face Chaka. "Down there it made more sense to hide Program agents inside the Drug Enforcement Agency."

"The drug trade is lousy with paranormals, which is pretty much the reason why so much of that crap is able to get through," Gideon said.

"The DEA raid is a decoy, isn't it?" Chaka asked.

"Yes and no," Gideon replied. "They have the very real job of taking down a location that we know Dark Word cultists have killed at least three people at as part of some ritual. I'm kinda hoping it'll force Chemosh Magog to move prematurely, and we can track him down, drive a stake through his heart, and ride off into the sunset like the heroes we are."

"There are only ten of us," Chaka pointed out. "Even with the magics at my disposal, will that be enough? Especially since we face a former god. The Old Ones may not have the power they once possessed, but they are still formidable opponents."

"Actually, Chaka, your job will be to keep the lesser threats off my back while my shield brother and I deal with Magog," Gideon said.

"Trust me, Chaka," Zeus said, "they can handle it. We used to call Gideon and Matt 'Chaos and Mayhem' for a good reason."

"Even if you're a powerful mage, do you have the power to defeat an Old One?" Chaka asked.

"I'm not a mage," Gideon replied. "I'm... complicated, and, yes, I believe I have the power to defeat an Old One. I've disrupted his plans before. I lost the woman I loved that time. *This* time? Well, this time, I'm gonna rescue the girl, kick the bad guy's ass into oblivion, and try to find myself a little piece of happily ever after."

"It's like we say in the Teams, Chaka," Zeus said. "The only easy day was yesterday."

CHAPTER THIRTY-TWO

Miami, Florida, USA

Ochoa Estate

Star Island, Miami Beach, FL

October 29, 2010

Magog tapped his foot in time to the music. He was particularly fond of this "Rob Zombie" fellow. There was something both primal and futuristic about the man's music that appealed to the ancient godling. The writhing dancers gyrating before him with looks of worshipful adoration on their faces also appealed to him. Magog sat upon a throne-like chair in the mansion's rather large ballroom. Having a ballroom was old-fashioned these days, but Magog liked it. The room gave his followers a place to worship him. They brought him food and libations and entertainments to please him. All he really needed for this to be perfect would be a roaring fire and his high priests tossing in the squealing bodies of infant boys as sacrifices to his glory. Once he reacquired his full godhood, then, the sacrifices would begin again. No longer would he have to hide from the minions of the White God.

Before his thoughts could stray once again down depressing, angry paths, Magog caught sight of his current high priestess, Tia Teresa. The worn, haggard expression on her face was not that unusual, but the fresh sweat on her brow and the trembling in her hands indicated that she'd had a precognizant vision.

"Speak, beloved," Magog commanded.

"My lord," Teresa said falling at his feet. "We must leave for Isla de Nube Encendida this very night!"

"What have you seen?" Magog demanded even as he motioned for the commander of his guards to join them.

"DEA agents will be carrying out a raid on this compound tonight, my lord," Teresa reported.

"*¿Si, Magnifico?*" the guard commander, Fernando of the Jaguar Warriors, said as he approached. "Your command?"

"From whom did we acquire this residence, Fernando?" Magog asked.

"An allied faction within *Palabra Oscura, Magnifico*," Fernando replied. "The Cult of Quetzalcoatl. We exchanged with them the residence in San Juanito for this one. I was told the previous resident wanted to relocate."

"And who was this previous resident?" Magog pressed.

"Ah, that would be Rolando Ochoa, *Magnifico*," Fernando replied.

Magog frowned. "Some priest or wizard in the employ of our friends in the Quetzalcoatl?"

"No, *Magnifico*, Ochoa is a smuggler, mostly of *la coca*, but also guns, money, women, even jihadis," Fernando replied.

Magog sighed. "In other words, just the type of person the DEA would be interested in." He rubbed his temples and inhaled deeply, coming to a decision. He sent his will into the phylactery on his waist.

Nahasheron appeared in front of him, stepping out of a blurred spot in the air. Her hair was mussed, her makeup smudged, and she had a fiery look in her eye. Obviously, he had interrupted her in some sport or other, not that he really cared.

"By your command, my master," Nahasheron said without the slightest hint of whatever annoyance she might have felt.

"Set up the portal. Now. We're leaving for Isla de Nube Encendida," Magog snapped.

Nahasheron rolled her eyes, but nodded her compliance and stepped toward the door leading out to the lush backyard. She snapped her fingers at some of the dancers to attend her and assist with the preparation of the portal.

"Fernando, beloved, gather my daughter-brides and the hostages. Remind my daughters, especially Jordana, that the lives of the hostages depend on their good behavior," Magog said. "Also, Fernando, unblemished. Do you understand my meaning?"

"A bride with a black eye is not pleasing to her groom," Fernando said with a nod. "I will attend to the daughter-brides myself, *Magnifico*."

"Teresa, beloved, go with him," Magog directed. He stood and with a wave of a finger, the sound system died. He raised his voice slightly. "My beloved ones, the enemy will soon be upon us. Not all of you can make the journey with me to Isla de Nube Encendida. Those who stay will have the honor of doing battle with my enemies, buying the time I need to ascend unto my full power! Then, my beloved ones, then, I will raise you up! Reward you with immortality in *this* world. You will stand beside me, my beloved ones, and you will rule this world!"

"In your name!" screamed one of the dancers. Others quickly took up the cry.

Magog basked in the adulation.

*   *   *   *   *   *

"Something's going on," Jordana mused.

"What?" Sassy asked. She joined Jordana at the window. Then, she frowned. "It's that bitch, Nahasheron."

"Yeah, I know," Jordana said. "What is she up to?"

Sassy shrugged. "Not sure. She's preparing some kind of ritual circle, it looks like." In the short time that they'd had together, the three newfound sisters had discovered a great deal about one another. Sassy's mother had been a sorceress, and she'd trained Sassy in the magical arts. Rachel's father had been a faith healer, and she'd shown an aptitude for the same thing at an early age, far surpassing anything that her father was capable of doing.

"I remember that design," Rachel said a few moments later. "That's how they brought us here. We drove into a circle like that one, and, boom, here we were."

"Ah, it's a portal," Sassy said. "See, Nahasheron can fold space. It's how she teleports. The portal is just a bigger version of the spell she uses to move around."

Somebody knocked at their door before opening it.

"*Señoritas*," greeted the leader of the guards, Fernando. "The time has come for us to relocate to our final destination."

"This isn't it?" Jordana blurted.

Fernando shook his head. "No, *señorita*, it never was. You will be provided with clothing now, nothing fancy, but it will preserve your modesty. I was tasked to remind you all that the lives of your remaining family members are dependent upon your good behavior. *El Magnifico* particularly instructed me to remind *you*, *mi señorita* Jordana. Now, I have been further instructed that my master wishes for you three to remain unblemished. For this to be you must be cooperative. If you do not cooperate, I will torture your family. Nothing in *El Magnifico*'s directions prohibits that. *¿Comprende?*"

Jordana nodded. "We understand."

"We'll cooperate," Sassy added.

Rachel just nodded.

"Excellent! Now, *por favor*, clothe yourselves and come with me," Fernando said.

*　　*　　*　　*　　*　　*

En route to Miami, Florida, USA
October 29, 2010

Aboard the Black Hawk Levi gave a start when the tracker started beeping. Quickly, he fetched it from his pack. "They're in the open!" he yelled. "I'm getting a clear signal from both Jordana and Kitty!"

Gideon grinned, jubilated. "You have a lock?"

Levi nodded with a matching grin. "Yeah!" Then, he face fell. "What the...?"

"What's going on, Levi?" Gideon demanded.

"The signal just... disappeared," Levi said. "I don't understand."

"Let me see," Gideon demanded reaching his hand out.

He felt a weird tug. "Tug" was the only way he could think of to describe it. He'd been feeling a stronger and stronger tug as they'd been flying toward Miami. Now, the tug seemed to be coming from a different direction. He readjusted the screen on the tracker, pulling from the tight view of Miami Beach to a wider view of southern Florida and part of the Caribbean. Two beacons burned brightly in the middle of the ocean.

He handed the tracker back to Levi. "They teleported out of Miami."

"Dammit!" Levi snapped. "This thing must be broken. They're in the middle of the ocean."

"No, they're not," Gideon said. "They're off the coast of Bimini."

"Bimini?" Matt and Zeus echoed in unison.

"What is so special about this place of many bimbos?" Chaka asked.

Gideon cracked a grin. "Funny, Chaka. Bimini is right in the middle of the Bermuda Triangle. Lot of folks believe Atlantis sank out there. Either way, it's an area of mystical importance. I suspect that Magog's gonna make use of it for his ritual, and I have a pretty good idea of where he's gone to ground." He plugged into the helo's intercom. "Pilot? Do we have the fuel to make it to Bimini?"

"No, sir, we do not, nor do we have the diplomatic clearance," the pilot responded.

"Perkins? Is that you?" Gideon exclaimed.

"You don't think I'd let anybody else fly your bird, do you, sir?" Perkins replied.

"Good to have you with us," Gideon said. "Other than fuel, do you have a problem flying into the sovereign territory of another nation?"

"Not particularly, sir, but I believe we were instructed to avoid international incidents," Perkins pointed out.

"Perky has a good point," Zeus said.

"Don't really think that'll be a problem," Gideon said. "Technically speaking, Isla de Nube Encendida doesn't actually exist."

CHAPTER THIRTY-THREE

Bimini District, Commonwealth of the Bahamas

Isla de Nube Encendida

October 29, 2010

The clothing they were given was little more than glorified bathrobes. The white robes covered them all the way down over their feet, which were now shod with white Crocs-style clogs. Teresa insisted that each of the girls wear the hood that was included with the robe. Jordana glared at Teresa, but did as she was instructed.

"You seem to know a lot of the major players," Sassy observed.

"Seems so," Jordana agreed.

"Just means Jordy is more likely to become the, er, 'First Lady' than either of us," Rachel observed. "Not that not being 'chosen' is gonna wind up being a good thing for either of us."

"No, I get the feeling that Daddy Creepiest wants a harem," Sassy said with a shiver.

"Oh, you just *had* to go there," Jordana replied with a corresponding shiver.

"Silence! All of you," Teresa snapped. She pointed to another trio of robed individuals, these dressed in red.

The guards with the red-robed trio drew back the hoods revealing Kitty and two other people. One was a young frightened looking boy. The other was a middle-aged woman.

"Aunt Kathy," Rachel groaned.

"I said to be silent!" Teresa snapped. "Now, unless you want your Aunt Kathy or Sassy's cousin Mike or Jordana's sister Kitty to get hurt, you will be silent and do as you are bidden."

Jordana put a hand on each of the other girls' shoulders and steered them toward the ritual circle that Nahasheron had built. She maintained eye contact with Teresa until she had to turn away. Once eye contact was broken, Teresa shivered. Those eyes had haunted her for years. The same eyes that she saw whenever she dreamed of her own death.

The circle was just ahead. Magog had already stepped into it and disappeared. Nahasheron stood to one side, eyes closed, lips moving silently as she incanted whatever spell was holding open the portal. Jordana forced herself not to shed a tear as she stared at the face of her former friend, stolen by the demon living inside her. Micky looked older now, as if having Nahasheron inside her was accelerating her aging process, and Jordana could smell the dirty, rotten stench that Gideon had described as *undeath*.

Nahasheron opened her eyes to see Jordana looking. She smiled. "You're looking good, Jordy."

"Wish I could say the same," Jordana replied. "When the time comes, I'm gonna kill you, Nahasheron."

"Why me? Teresa's the one who got your mom killed," Nahasheron pointed out.

"She betrayed my mom. You betrayed me," Jordana said. "She'll get hers one way or another, but you... You're mine."

"I seriously doubt that, Jordy. Once this body is used up, I think I'll try little sister Kitty on for size," Nahasheron said.

"Gideon is coming for me," Jordana said with absolute certainty. "Then, I'll kill you."

Nahasheron laughed.

Jordana stepped into the circle. A twisting, tugging sensation took hold. Then, she was somewhere else.

Wherever they were, Jordana could hear ocean waves lapping against the shore. She looked up. The sun was still out, but she couldn't really see it because of the cloud cover. Looking around, she took in a villa-style compound that seemed to have been cut out of the middle of a jungle. A mountain rose up into the air behind the compound.

The guards prodded the three girls forward with Fernando politely adding a belated, *"Por favor, mis señoritas."*

Magog stood waiting for them on the steps of a wide veranda. He'd undone his shirt, sweat glistening on his hairless chest. He spread his arms. "Welcome, my children to Isla de Nube Encendida!"

"My Spanish has gotten rusty since high school," Sassy snarked softly.

"'Fiery Cloud Island'," Jordana translated. "I think the mountain behind him is a volcano."

"You are correct, sweet Jordana," Magog said. "The volcano is... *somewhat* active. It generates both the cloud cover concealing this island *and* the sweltering heat. You may disrobe if the heat makes you uncomfortable."

Jordana decided that she'd rather die of sweat-induced dehydration rather than give the leering demigod what he wanted. A quick glance to the side and she saw that Rachel was clutching her robe even tighter, and Sassy was toying with the belt of her robe as if deciding whether or not to indulge in a little exhibitionism. Then, she tightened the belt with a defiant smirk.

"Ah, so spirited," Magog chuckled. Then, he frowned. "It wasn't a request."

The guards grabbed the girls and forced the robes off. None of the three put up even a token resistance because their family members were coming through the portal now.

Magog clapped his hands. A group of tall, naked, red-haired women came out of the house and knelt at his feet.

"Your command, Great One?" asked one of the women.

"Ah, my handmaids, take the daughter-brides to be bathed and prepare them for the ritual," Magog ordered.

"As you wish, so we are commanded," the leader of the handmaids said.

The red-haired handmaids stood in unison and came toward Jordana and her sisters. Two handmaids flanked each girl and gently led them away. Once away from Magog and his guards, the handmaids began chatting with one another and at the sisters.

"You should be so proud," one was saying. "To be chosen to be His brides, to hold the holy essence of the goddesses... I would be jealous if I weren't so proud of you."

"Your hair is so pretty, my lady Rachel, like spun gold," fawned another.

"Lady Alannah! You should take more care with your nails," scolded a third. "Well, I have just the tools to fix this! And you have such beautiful eyes. You really shouldn't let your hair hang down in your eyes like that."

Sassy glanced over at Jordana. "I wasn't expecting the yenta posse."

The handmaids laughed.

"So droll, my lady," complimented the leader of the band. "Oh, my lady Jordana! Where were they keeping you? In a dungeon?"

"No, a tower," Jordana replied.

The leader rolled her eyes. "So melodramatic. Well, you are in our care now, and you will be treated as the high ladies that you are."

The handmaids took them behind the villa to a second building that appeared to be built right into the side of a cliff. Within the building were all the makings of a five-star spa: hot baths, massage tables, hair and nail-care materials.

"If I weren't about to be sacrificed to be married to my own biological father, I'd be very impressed with this," Sassy said.

Jordana couldn't help but agree. She allowed herself to be led to the pool that was the center of the spa. The water felt fantastic. Her two handmaids began rubbing oils into her skin and shampooing her hair. She couldn't help but relax.

"Relax," she sighed to herself.

"Yes, my lady, please do," one of the handmaids said. "We will take very good care of you."

"I might doze off," Jordana said.

"We will bear you up. You are perfectly safe with us," the other handmaid assured her.

Jordana smiled to herself. She thought about the pheromones she could generate and wondered if the willingness of the handmaids had something to do with that or their devotion to Magog.

She decided to try an experiment. Focusing her will the way that Gideon had described to her, she said, "My sisters and I have been living on oatmeal for the last couple of days. Would you be a dear and go fetch us something... tastier?"

The handmaid bit her lower lip, her eyes glazing slightly. Even her nose wrinkled as if she'd just caught a whiff of something familiar and pleasant. "Fruit and cheese? Would that please you, my lady?"

Jordana nodded. "That would be lovely."

Sassy noticed. She sidled as close as her own attendants would allow and raised an eyebrow.

"Fruit and cheese," Jordana said.

"Uh, sure," Sassy said.

"You know," Jordana said turning to her other attendant. "I'd like a massage now. I could use a little nap while I'm at it. I've got this knot in my back..."

"As you wish, my lady," the handmaid gushed.

"Hope you have a plan," Sassy said.

"No, just winging it," Jordana replied.

*   *   *   *   *

Miami, Florida, USA
Homestead Air Force Base
Homestead, FL
October 29, 2010

The Black Hawk touched down at Homestead AFB south of Miami. Chaka chanted a charm that cloaked her in the illusion of being a large black man with a shaven head.

"No transgender jokes," Chaka grumbled. "This is the only human I've ever met who is roughly my size."

Knobs cackle-chuckled as he established a slightly more robust version of his usual glamour. "Then, good Cha'a-ka'a, I will have to teach you how to craft a more original glamour."

"I would be grateful, Master Goblin," Chaka said with a nod.

"Perkins, get us fueled up as fast as these guys can manage," Gideon said.

"Wilco!" Perkins replied.

An Air Force officer with captain's bars on his collar approached the helo. Gideon and Zeus hopped out to meet with him beyond the rotors' wash.

"Gentlemen, is one of you Agent Shaw?" the captain asked.

Gideon raised his hand.

"I have a message for you from a Director Gold. He says that Agent Durham launched the raid early. Something about a, uh, porthole?" the captain reported.

"Thank you, Captain. I understand the message. We need to refuel as quickly as possible in order to pursue our suspect before he flees into international waters," Gideon said.

"My crews are good, Agent Shaw. You'll be in the air in a few minutes," the captain promised.

"It's appreciated," Gideon said. "Thank you."

Zeus grabbed a vibrating cell phone from his combat harness. "Speak of the devil. It's Ronnie."

Gideon held out his hand. "May I?"

Zeus handed over the phone, and Gideon answered.

"Hey, Ronnie, it's Gideon. Just got Bob's message," Gideon said.

"Where the hell are you?" Agent Ronnie Durham demanded.

"Homestead. Refueling the helo. We already knew Magog was gone," Gideon replied.

"Well, the bastard left a rear guard behind," Ronnie reported. "Mostly mundane cultists, but he had a squad of Jaguar Warriors guarding the backyard where the portal was located."

"How bad?" Gideon asked.

"Miami SWAT was assisting. They made an amphib insertion. We'd told them to expect PCP-popping steroid abusers and had 'em armed for bear, but they reacted like cops when faced with men armed with knives and clubs," Ronnie said with a sigh.

"So, bad," Gideon said with a sympathetic sigh.

"Yeah, I got two dead cops, five badly injured, and some very pissed off, traumatized SWAT guys who're not happy with us," Ronnie said. "I'm not that good of a liar, you know."

"Those *geasa* are a bitch," Gideon chuckled.

"Funny, smart ass. Where's Magog got off to?" Ronnie asked.

"Isla Nube Encendida is what the tracker is indicating," Gideon said.

"You heading there?" Ronnie asked.

"Soon as the helo is refueled," Gideon replied.

"Pick me up. It's on your way," Ronnie said.

"Look, Duchess, I'm about to violate another sovereign nation's territory, technically, and my only justification is the Monroe Doctrine. You don't need to get caught up in my stupid, potentially career-ending, mission," Gideon said.

"Hey, I'm caught up in your stupid, potentially career-ending, mission," Zeus growled.

"Look, Gideon, you can't take the overgrown oaf and the trigger-happy libido with you and leave me behind. I'll tell your daddy on you," Ronnie threatened.

Gideon grinned. "Okay, Duchess, I surrender."

"Good, I thought you'd see it *my* way," Ronnie said. "I owe that sonuvabitch a good one."

"We'll call you when we're close. We'll do a swoop-and-snatch," Gideon said.

"Oh, yippee," Ronnie said with a complete lack of enthusiasm. She disconnected the call at her end.

Gideon handed Zeus his phone back with a grin.

"What did she call me?" Zeus asked with a sigh.

"She called you 'the trigger-happy libido'," Gideon replied.

Zeus nodded. "Fair enough."

Gideon climbed back into the helicopter. "Perkins, we're swinging by the mansion and picking up Agent Durham."

"Wilco," Perkins said with a thumbs-up.

"The duchess is joining the party?" Matt chuckled. "Nice. I'll bet she's pissed. Yeah, she's pissed. Now, we're gonna see some carnage."

"Have you ever known Ronnie to *not* engage in carnage when she's got her Irish up?" Zeus said.

Matt laughed. "This gig just keeps getting better!"

"Are you mentally stable?" Chaka asked with a small frown.

"I have been asking that very question for centuries," Knobs sighed.

Gideon chuckled at the interplay even as the helo lifted into the air. He felt an odd sensation, like he was sleepy, but that really wasn't possible. With the adrenaline flowing like it was, he wouldn't be able to sleep for days. He closed his eyes and stilled his mind, slipping into a trance-like state, a little trick that he'd mastered when he first started studying magic.

*   *   *   *   *

En route to Miami, Florida, USA
October 29, 2010

"Well, this is certainly, er, bucolic," Gideon said.

"Dyrnwch!" Jordana shouted jumping into his arms. "It worked!"

"You decided to take a nap on purpose and make contact," Gideon said with a grin. "Clever girl."

"A regular genius ass," Jordana said with a big grin. "Okay, Magog has moved us."

"I know. We saw it on the tracker," Gideon said. "One of my team tried to get to you before they took you through the portal..."

"That's bad, Gideon. Magog left troops behind," Jordana said. "Look, you need to hurry. We're someplace called, uh, Fiery Cloud Island. It's like freaking Jurassic Park here. I swear, I keep expecting to see dinosaurs."

"Uh, well, actually, you *might*," Gideon said.

"Don't tease me," Jordana said.

"I'm not. Isla Nube Encendida is a piece of Faerie that's kind of... stuck in our world. It spans two universes, which is probably why Magog took you there, not to mention the whole Bermuda Triangle and Atlantis connections," Gideon said.

Jordana frowned. "Okay, still new to the whole magical reality thing here." She shook her head suddenly as if trying to clear it. "It's also irrelevant. Look, Gideon, these handmaiden chicks are getting us ready. I don't think this is a spa day just because Magog wants us pretty. I think it's part of the ritual." Her eyes glistened. "I don't think I have much time left before he..."

Gideon hugged her close to himself. "I'm coming. I will not be too late this time."

"If you are..."

"I *won't* be."

"But *if you are*... don't hesitate..."

"Hey, don't worry, okay? I'm not gonna be late. I've got Perkins at the wheel. If anybody can get us there in time, it'll be him,"

Gideon said. He lifted her chin and kissed her lightly on the lips. "Now, wake up."

CHAPTER THIRTY-FOUR

Bimini District, Commonwealth of the Bahamas
Isla de Nube Encendida
October 29, 2010

Jordana's eyes snapped open. She sat up on the massage table and stretched, feeling refreshed and limber. One thing had to be said for Magog's handmaidens: they were good at their job. The leader of the handmaidens came toward the table bearing a tray with three hypodermic needles on it.

Sassy and Rachel sighed in dismay. The serum used to inhibit the two of them from using their magical abilities was actually harsher on their systems than the anti-transformation potion that Jordana was forced to take.

"My ladies, a final shot before the ceremony begins," the handmaiden leader announced.

"That won't be necessary," Jordana said stepping forward and placing a hand lightly on the other woman's forearm.

"But the Great One has commanded it," the leader stammered as a wave of pheromones swept over her.

"Look, uh, what's your name?" Jordana asked.

"I am called Bronwen, milady Jordana," the handmaiden immediately replied.

Jordana smiled. "That's a pretty name, Bronwen."

Bronwen's smile looked like it was ready to burst. "Thank you, milady!"

"Now, look, Bronwen, my sisters and I are... well, we're, uh, resigned to our fate. I think we're even beginning to look forward to the idea of being goddesses, aren't we?" Jordana said turning toward Sassy and Rachel who were staring at her.

Sassy snapped out of it first. "Oh! Uh, yeah! I've always wanted to be a princess, and a goddess is better, right?" she said with a nudge to Rachel.

"Uh, sure," Rachel agreed brightly, smiling, but still looking somewhat confused.

"So, you see, for us to be our very best for the ceremony, do you think giving us something that will make us grouchy, ill, and just, well, make us uncomfortable? Does that really sound like a good idea, Bronwen?" Jordana said to the handmaiden.

Bronwen frowned in thought. "But the Great One..."

"Isn't here," Jordana said. "*We* are. Your future goddesses. Do you really want to start out our reigns with the three of us, I don't know, maybe a little miffed with you, Bronwen?"

"No!" Bronwen exclaimed.

Jordana patted her hand and gently took the tray away from her. "Thank you, Bronwen. You're very sweet."

"Oh, thank you, milady!" Bronwen gushed.

"Now, do you think you and the other girls could give my sisters and me a little moment alone? So we can organize our thoughts, prepare ourselves spiritually for the coming ceremony," Jordana said.

"As you command, Lady Jordana," Bronwen said, obviously reluctant to leave, but at the same time not willing to disobey her Lady.

When the handmaidens had retreated, Sassy turned to stare at Jordana again. "What the hell?"

Jordana chuckled. "I was kinda force-feeding Bronwen my thrope pheromones. Gideon says that Daddy Creepiest's side enhances my natural gifts." Jordana leaned against the massage table. "Kinda draining, though."

"Yeah, you know, Jordy, I'm not, you know... *that way*," Rachel said lowering her voice almost to a whisper, "but right now... If I didn't know you were my sister, I'd consider, you know, with you."

"She's right," Sassy agreed. "However you did it, you might want to think about bringing it back in before *we* jump you."

Jordana smiled wanly. "I'll do what I can. How do you two feel?"

"Well, give it a couple of hours, and I might be able to toss off a little spell or two," Sassy said. "Too bad Dad wants to eat our souls in half that time."

"Do you think you could run now, if you had the chance?" Jordana said.

"Yeah, I'm not puking my guts up," Sassy said.

Rachel nodded agreement. "But we can't run. We're on an island."

"Just be ready to move. The good guys will be here soon," Jordana said. She flexed her right hand, curling her fingers into wicked, hooked claws. The smile that she favored her sisters with was feral. "I feel like I could do a little damage."

* * * * *

En route to Isla de Nube Encendida
October 29, 2010

"It doesn't look like it's that big," Levi commented when the cloud-shrouded island came into view.

"That's because the island is dimensionally transcendent," Matt said.

"Wait, what? It's bigger on the inside?" Levi said.

Matt sighed. "No, that's dimensionally transcendental. Transcendent means that it lies partly in two or more dimensions. The bit we can see is about a mile or two across, but once we fly into its area of effect, the island becomes about, uh, forty to forty-five miles long, and, maybe, twenty-five to thirty miles across, but that land mass is contained entirely in its own pocket dimension."

"But isn't it supposed to rest partially in Faerie?" Chaka asked.

"Yeah, but the part that's in Faerie is in the middle of the island, a tunnel that runs under the volcano and comes out... Well, I'm not quite sure where, but it looks like an apple orchard. The tree you come out under is about the size of a redwood, but when you get a few yards away, it looks like an apple tree just like all the apple trees around it," Matt said.

"You've been here before?" Levi asked.

"Yeah, the various Faerie courts and councils here and there use the island as neutral ground," Matt replied with a shrug. "Nobody tries to live there, though. It's too... creepy."

Gideon's eyes snapped open.

"Nice nap, partner?" Zeus teased.

"I was in contact with Jordy," Gideon said. "Time is short. We'll have to assault without any kind of plan in place."

"No plan at all?" Matt said with a grin.

"Well, an idea of a plan," Gideon replied with a hint of a smile. "We'll be winging it, gang. Duchess, I want you, Levi, and Knobs to locate Kitty and the other hostages. Zeus, you and Chaka are with me and Matt. We're going after Jordy and the other two 'brides'. The rest of you men will provide security for our LZ. This helo is our only way on and off that island."

"What are our rules of engagement, sir?" asked Agent Smith, one of Zeus' men.

"If it ain't one of us, put a bullet to it," Gideon said. "And don't worry about overkill, either. There's no such thing as overkill, just 'open fire' and 'I'm reloading'."

"Ha! Rule 37," Matt snickered.

"What?" Levi frowned.

"I'll explain the *Seventy Maxims of Maximally Effective Mercenaries* to you later," Matt promised. He turned to Gideon. "What about Rule 4?"

"Perkins?" Gideon said.

"This bird isn't unarmed, sir," Perkins replied. "We have M134s mounted in the doors. 'Close air support covereth a number of sins.'"

"Perky, I always knew there was a reason why I liked you," Matt declared.

"Is it really wise to use a despised nickname with the one in charge of your close air support?" Chaka asked.

"Probably not, but I've never been accused of wisdom," Matt replied.

"We'll be penetrating the island's area of effect in one minute," Perkins reported.

"Lock and load, people," Gideon ordered.

"Drop a fuckin' rock on 'em!" Bruce declared.

"You stay in the helo, Bruce," Gideon told the bird.

"Giddy needs Bruce," the bird said.

"Giddy needs Bruce to stay safe," Gideon replied.

Bruce just whistled.

CHAPTER THIRTY-FIVE

Bimini District, Commonwealth of the Bahamas
Isla de Nube Encendida
October 29, 2010

"We might as well still be naked," Rachel grumbled.

Sassy and Jordana glanced at one another and nodded their agreement. The extent of their ceremonial clothing was a long strip of white muslin fabric that was fashioned into a loincloth cinched at the hips with a belt that appeared to be made of gold coins. They'd been shod with sandals that laced up to the knees with golden cord. The outfit was completed with a golden headband that kept their hair out of their faces.

"I feel like an extra in a bad rip-off of a Conan movie," Sassy sighed.

"I kind of like it," Jordana said.

"You're kidding," Rachel gasped.

"Of course, I'm kidding," Jordana chuckled.

The handmaids had escorted them from the "spa" and brought them into the temple-like structure that had been built into the side of the mountain. Jordana was half-surprised that she recognized elements in the temple's design from her freshman year anthropology classes. The columns spaced along the sides of the room appeared to be Greek in styling, but the altar at the far end of the room seemed more Middle Eastern, possibly Mesopotamian or even Ancient Canaanite. The stone altar was flanked by tall silver stands capped with oil-burning lamps. Bronze implements, bowls, cups, tongs, incense burners, and knives were arranged on a table to the side of the altar along with a variety of organic ingredients. A trio of blinding white lambs were tied to a stake on the other side of the altar.

"Do I want to know what the lambs are for?" Rachel asked.

"You're a preacher's kid," Jordana said. "You should know. Think about the Old Testament."

At the center of the room was a fire pit flanked by two of Magog's Jaguar Warriors. Flames from the pit leapt up higher than either man. The two warriors alternated feeding packets of incense to the flames with bundles of aromatic leaves. The smoke disappeared through a vent in the ceiling, presumably to mix with the smoke filtering out of the volcanic vents that shrouded the island.

"Best behavior. Here comes Daddy Creepiest," Sassy hissed.

Magog was dressed in just a pair of linen trousers. His thick leather belt was cinched around his waist. Jordana noted the phylactery was still attached on one side and the knife he'd used to murder her mother hung on the other side.

"You are all lovely," Magog pronounced. "So lovely, in fact, that I've decided that *all* of you will be my brides, and join me in godhood. Remember, until you're actually bonded with your other half, you're still expendable, as is your hostage. Clear?"

The girls all nodded, not daring to speak and reveal the fact that none of them had been given the shots that would have rendered them helpless.

"Good. Let us begin," Magog said. He turned and made his way toward the staked-out lambs. "Bring them," he tossed over his shoulder.

As soon as he reached the animals, he grabbed one by its hind legs carried it over to the altar. Teresa was waiting with one of the bronze bowls. Magog took out his knife, whispered a few words, and cut the animal's throat. The lamb bleated pitiably as its lifeblood drained out into the bronze bowl. When the blood flow tapered off to a dribble, Magog casually tossed the carcass into the fire pit.

"A burnt offering for myself," he snickered. "Teresa, prepare Sassy first. She's the oldest."

"As you command, my master," Teresa replied as she gathered up the first bowl.

Nahasheron stepped up to the altar next and placed a new bronze bowl upon it. Magog had gathered a second lamb and quickly repeated the ritual bloodletting. Meanwhile, Teresa had approached Sassy. Dipping two of her fingers into the lamb's blood, she began using it to paint symbols and runes on Sassy's stomach, across her breasts, and on her back. The last bit of blood was used to make a mark on Sassy's forehead.

"Jordana next," Magog instructed Nahasheron once the second lamb had been bled.

"Still haven't killed me yet," Nahasheron teased quietly as she began to paint Jordana's body with the symbols.

"Day's still young," Jordana said.

The final lamb was slaughtered, and Bronwen brought the blood to paint on Rachel's body.

"Now, for the long, boring part," Magog said. "Calling out your other halves."

Jordana wanted to tell him to take his time, to make some smart remark, but she restrained herself and cast a glance at Sassy to make sure some snarky remark wasn't coming to her lips. Instead, Sassy was whispering to herself. A small smile spread across her lips. She gave Jordana a wink. Jordana glanced over at Rachel. Their youngest sister had a slight frown on her face. Then, she seemed to brighten ever so slightly. She looked Jordana in the eyes and gave a small nod.

"The cavalry needs to hurry up," Jordana muttered to herself.

*   *   *   *   *

Perkins brought the Black Hawk in at treetop level. The compound cut into the side of the mountain at the middle of the island had been rather obvious from the air. He'd dropped to terrain-following to give them a little bit of surprise when they arrived. The compound they'd spotted from the air was just ahead. The main building looked something like a Parthenon that had been smashed into the side of a mountain. Immediately around it were a couple more pseudo-Greek looking structures also abutting the side of the mountain. Further out, more modern, pre-fabricated buildings dotted the area between the ancient buildings and the low stone wall that marked the boundaries of the compound. The stone wall was ancient, but it had been topped with a chain-link fence and a roll of razor-wire. In the middle of the compound was a wide, circular field that had ritual designs cut into the earth.

The Black Hawk came in above the tree tops, over the fence, and flared into a hover thirty feet above the ritual circle. The doors on the side of the helicopter slid open. Gideon, Matt, Zeus, and Knobs jumped straight out of the helo, falling the thirty feet and landing as lightly as if they'd just jumped from three feet. Knobs pulled a pair of smoke grenades from his harness, pulled the pins with his teeth, and tossed them to either side of the LZ.

Cultists came running from the out buildings. Most were clothed in plain white linen outfits and armed with a variety of melee weapons from kitchen knives to baseball bats. Many of them, though, were armed and armored security men. Gideon, Matt, and Zeus raised their weapons and opened fire. Above and behind them, Perkins positioned the Black Hawk so that his door gunners could open up with the M134 miniguns.

Bodies fell. Blood and bone spattered everywhere.

"Was that it?" Matt asked. The bolt of his rifle had locked back, and he was busy changing the clip.

"Does seem... anti-climactic," Zeus agreed as he slapped a fresh clip into his P90.

Gideon was the first to notice. "Uh-oh."

The bodies closest to them were beginning to twitch.

"They are *not* reanimating!" Zeus exclaimed.

"Would seem that way," Gideon sighed.

A mystic symbol glowed to life in the forehead of one of Magog's cultists. Then, the body rose from the ground like a marionette lifted up by its strings. Already, the eyes were burning with an unholy red light, and the hands were curling into claws as bone spikes burst from the tips of the fingers. The undead cultist opened a mouth that was suddenly filled with pointed, jagged, uneven teeth. The sound it made was halfway between a snarl and a high-pitched keening.

"Wights," Gideon said as he dropped his P90, letting it fall behind him on its sling.

He reached down and drew Dyrnwyn. The .45 was already cocked. He thumbed the safety off, squeezed the trigger, and fired off his first "dragon fire" round. The round that left the barrel looked like an especially bright tracer round. When it connected with the wight's head, though, it exploded in a white-hot burst of energy that consumed the undead creature's head and shoulders.

Gideon tapped the transmit key on his throat mike. "Perkins, you're gonna have to keep the helo in the air for now. Have the rest of the team fast-rope down."

"Roger that, Highlander," Perkins replied.

More of the cultists were reanimating, coming to their feet as if lifted by an unseen puppet master. Matt had shifted to his Benelli, Gore Splasher, firing the gun right-handed, while reaching for Skull Cleaver with the other hand. Zeus was firing precise three-round bursts into the face of any reanimated creature that came into his sights. Gideon blasted four more dragon-fire rounds downrange. He glanced to the side to see Knobs blurring around, lopping the limbs and heads off wights that tried to flank them.

"Hey, Chaka, little torch music?" Zeus shouted to the female Big Foot as she slid off the rope from the helo to join them.

"Of course," Chaka replied.

In her right hand she carried a thick, heavy, symbol-carved stick decorated with feathers and animal bones. Her left hand dipped into a large leather pouch on her belt and came out with a handful of some kind of dust. Chaka flung the dust into the crowd of quickly reanimating cultists. She pointed her stick at them, grunted a syllable or two in her native language, and the wights burst into blue flames that incinerated their bodies completely within three seconds.

"Master, the immediate area is secure for the moment," Knobs reported. "But I sense more of the enemy coming."

Gideon did a quick head count. Two of Zeus' men, Statler and Jones, were still aboard the Black Hawk to man the guns. The other two men, Waldorf and Smith, had roped down with the rest of the team.

"Levi, you have a heading?" Gideon asked.

"Uh, yeah, that-a-way," Levi replied pointing toward one of the ancient structures built into the side of the mountain.

"Knobs, you have your heading," Gideon said. "Get going and kill Levi a path to the hostages."

Knobs grinned. "With pleasure, Master."

"You two," Gideon said to the other two men, "go with Levi and Ronnie. No point in holding the LZ if the helo can't land. We'll just retake it when we get back."

Waldorf and Smith both just nodded.

"Get going!" Gideon ordered. "Time's wasting." He turned back to Zeus, Chaka, and Matt. "Lady Killer, you and Chaka watch our flanks. Matt and I are gonna plow us a road to our goal," Gideon said pointing to the big temple.

"Game face time?" Matt asked with a grin.

Gideon nodded.

Matt laughed. He handed the Benelli to Zeus. "Here, you might need her more than I do." He gripped the axe in his right hand and the RFB in his left. Then, he started growing larger and hairier. Where before had been a heavily-armed and armored man now stood a twelve-foot-tall bipedal armored bear. Matt threw back his ursine head and roared a challenge before lumbering forward.

Gideon rolled his neck and shifted his own shape into a lupine humanoid. He dashed along in Matt's wake as the massive werebear began thrashing through the wights attempting to block their path. Gideon placed precise shots of dragon-fire rounds to put down the wights Matt bowled over. Occasionally, he would lash out with a clawed hand and eviscerate a hapless, still-living cultist. Wherever Gideon slashed a victim with his claws, flames burst forth to consume the body.

The four of them arrived at the entrance to the temple. The massive iron-bound stone doors were shut and barred from the inside. Matt reared back and slammed both of his massive fist-paws into the door. It shuddered, but didn't open. He snorted, mingled disappointment and resentment that the stubborn door wouldn't break open.

"I can get it open, but it will take a minute," Matt growled. He hefted his axe, peered at the door for a second, and began swinging the axe in broad overhand swings, smashing into the door.

"Hey, Matt!" Zeus shouted. "I've got C4!"

The axe paused mid-swing. The giant werebear glared down at his friend. "Well... Okay... In that case, be my guest," Matt replied stepping away from the door.

Zeus tossed a brick of plastique to Gideon. "I'll get this side. You get that one."

Gideon's lupine visage dissolved into his normal human appearance as he caught the explosive charge.

"So," Zeus said, placing his charge on one side of the door, "uh, that fiery claw thing? That new? I've never seen you do that before."

"Yeah, real new. I've never done that before," Gideon admitted. He inserted the blasting cap and activated the remote detonator.

"Really? Any idea why this is happening?" Zeus asked.

"Uh, figure I might've fulfilled a *geas*," Gideon said. "Met my destined true love..."

"Huh," Zeus grunted. He finished setting his charge. "Well, grats, dude."

"Fire in the hole!" Gideon shouted.

The team ducked for cover. Zeus held up a radio detonator switch. "Let's go rescue us some damsels!"

CHAPTER THIRTY-SIX

Bimini District, Commonwealth of the Bahamas
Isla de Nube Encendida
October 29, 2010

Kitty clutched her stomach in pain. All her joints were in agony, her head was on fire, and her jaws ached.

"Can't you see the girl's in pain?" Kathy Brady snarled at the men standing guard over them.

The three hostages had been moved from one of the pre-fab buildings into one of the stone structures, the one with the spa-like area. Kathy, as the only adult, had taken it upon herself to care for young Mike and Kitty. Mike huddled against a wall, his knees drawn up to his chest, his eyes flickering from the armed men guarding them to Kitty and back. Kathy was trying to comfort Kitty.

"Isn't there something you could give her for the pain? Aspirin? Ibuprofen? Something?" Kathy shouted. "Do you even speak English?"

Before either man could reply, a loud engine noise penetrated the stone walls of the spa, followed by something that sounded distantly like a chainsaw. Rapid-fire Spanish issued from the speakers of the guards' radios.

"*Sí, jefe*," one of the guards replied into his radio. He looked at Kathy and shrugged. "Señorita, I *do* speak English, and I have a very effective painkiller right here," he said patting the submachine gun slung across his shoulder. "We will be kind and make this as painless as possible."

Kathy inhaled a breath, preparing to beg for the lives of herself and the children that she'd taken upon herself to protect. Before the first sound came out of her mouth, Kitty snarled and launched herself at the guards. Halfway between where she started and where the man was standing, Kitty's form flowed, bulked up, got furry. Instead of a slender, hundred-fifteen-pound girl, a two-hundred-plus-pound lupine humanoid slammed into the Dark Word guard. Kitty's wolf jaws clamped down on the guard's throat even as her claw-studded hands ripped into his chest. The guard was well and truly dead before the neophyte werewolf had even knocked him all the way over.

His partner cursed in Spanish and quickly swung his gun around to counter the most immediate threat. He managed to get off a three-round burst that slammed into Kitty's flank, knocking the young werewolf off her victim. Kitty tumbled, yelping, a few feet from the guard, but she was already up on all fours snarling at the man who'd shot her. The wounds from the bullets were already closing, healing. Her lupine ears laid down against her skull, and her teeth were bared in a threatening snarl. She sidled slightly to the side, drawing the guard's weapon away from Kathy and Mike.

"Mistress Katherine! How you've changed!"

The guard spun at the sound of the voice. He cocked his head to one side at first sight of the short, green man standing nonchalantly where he most definitely had not been before.

"Hello," the green man said with a nod to the guard. "Can you give me just a moment?"

The guard squeezed the trigger of his weapon, but the green man had... *blurred* and was no longer standing where the bullets were now impacting.

"How rude!" the green man exclaimed.

He seemed to wave a hand at the guard. The man's submachine gun fell apart, cut cleanly in two.

"My master has given me permission to kill every one of you I meet. The choice of whether it's swift and merciful or slightly less fast and incredibly painful is up to you, young man," the green man declared.

"*¡Pendejo!*" the guard snarled.

The green man blurred again, and the guard was on his back, his pants and boots stripped from his body. Then, he was standing again. The green man paused in front of him, one hand cupping his chin, the other tapping a vicious knife against his thigh. He glanced at Mike. "What should I do to him next, young master? Take the rest of his clothes? Rob him of more of his dignity?"

"You sound funny," Mike stammered.

"I'm a funny little green man," the funny little green man said with a wink. He turned back to the guard. "For the boy's sake..."

The knife flashed out. The blade pierced the guard's larynx and came out the back of the skull through the medulla oblongata. The green man lowered the guard to the ground, shielding Mike's eyes from the final breaths of the guard. The green man stood back up.

"Now, Mistress Katherine, if you would be so good as to turn back into your human self. You can do it. You're safe now," the green man cooed.

"Who are you?" Aunt Kathy asked, still shocked by Kitty's sudden transformation and the green man's appearance.

"My name is Philemon Knobs," the green man replied. "I am a friend, here to rescue you."

Kitty's form had flowed back into its human shape. She was naked, her clothing having been shredded by her shapeshifting. "He's the butler," she croaked.

Knobs was instantly beside her, catching her as she half-collapsed into his arms.

"There, there, my dear," Knobs cooed. "The first change takes a lot out of you, I know. Here, eat this." He produced a protein bar from a pocket.

Pounding feet announced the arrival of newcomers.

"Knobs!" a tall red-headed woman shouted. "We mere humans can't keep up with you," she announced, bending over and breathing heavily.

"I felt time was of the essence, Mistress Veronica," Knobs replied. "Our dear Katherine here has had her first change."

"*Mazel tov*," wheezed a tall, dark-haired man. "I really, *really* wish I could port."

"Levi!" Kitty exclaimed. "Is Raven...?"

"She's fine, kiddo," Levi replied. "A week in the hospital, and right as rain. Doctors said so."

"Who are you people?" Kathy demanded.

"I'm Special Agent Ronnie Durham, ma'am," the redhead said. "FBI. This is Agent Carmichael. Those are Agents Waldorf and Smith. You've met Mr. Knobs. Uh, he's a... civilian consultant."

"I am a butler," Knobs said. He winked at Kitty. "Oh, my, we should cover you up, shouldn't we?"

"Oh, crap, I'm naked," Kitty yelped.

Levi shrugged off his backpack. He rummaged inside and tossed a set of hospital-style scrubs to Kitty. "We, uh, were kinda expecting you guys to be... Well, we thought you all might be naked. The robes are..."

"Unflattering," Kathy said.

"Yeah, I was gonna say 'bad'," Levi chuckled.

"Knobs! Where's Jordy?" Kitty demanded as she pulled on the scrubs.

"In the temple, but worry not, my dear Miss Katherine. Master Gideon and his doughty companions sally to her rescue," Knobs said.

"What does, uh, 'doughty' mean?" Mike asked, standing up and walking up to Knobs.

Knobs made a show of glancing around before lowering his voice to a loud stage whisper that everyone would hear. "It means that they're total bad asses, dude."

The boy laughed. "I'm Mike."

"It's short for 'Michael'," Kitty said.

"A pleasure to meet you, young master Michael," Knobs said, offering his hand to the boy.

Mike frowned slightly as he shook Knobs' hand.

"Knobs can't use nicknames," Kitty explained.

Then, Mike smiled. "Okay. So, are you a muppet?"

*   *   *   *   *

Magog frowned. "This is really quite ridiculous. Teresa! Fernando! See to this... disturbance."

"*¡Si, Magnifico!*" Fernando said coming to attention and bowing his head. Then, he was chattering away into his radio.

Teresa merely shook her head and strode toward a painting on one of the walls. The section of wall slid aside, revealing a passageway lined with bodies standing in recessed niches. As Teresa passed each body, a symbol glowed in the cadaver's forehead, and the undead creature stepped out of its niche, trailing behind the necromancer. The wall section slid back into place cutting the procession of undead minions from view.

"Now, where we?" Magog mused to himself with a smile as he took up his chant.

No more than a few syllables had passed his lips before something slammed into the door at the other end of the temple hall. Magog glared.

"Fernando?" he growled.

"I am on it, *Magnifico!*" Fernando assured his master.

The Dark Word soldier opened the entrance to another secret panel. A squad of heavily-armed and armored Jaguar Warriors jogged into the room. Fernando began speaking in rapid-fire Spanish with the squad leader, a surprisingly short, but muscular, man with terrible acne scars on his face and prison tats decorating his chest and arms.

Magog ignored the exchange and resumed his chant.

Fernando approached the door. He'd heard a snatch of conversation. Then, either side of the door exploded into the room. Magog almost casually waved a hand, erecting a shield between himself and the flying shrapnel. Fernando was grazed across the forehead by a piece of hinge.

"*¡Guerreros de jaguar! ¡A mí! ¡Protege El Magnifico!*" Fernando shouted.

The squad formed a wall in front of the door that was still miraculously standing. Something slammed into the door. Something big. The entire door trembled. Then, it tipped over and fell, crashing into the floor with a boom like a giant gong. Standing in the middle of the doorway was a twelve-foot-tall, fur-covered behemoth.

"*¿Bien? ¿Que esperas?*" Fernando shouted at his men. "*¡Dispara!*"

The Jaguar Warriors opened fire.

*   *   *   *   *

"It's still standing, Mr. I've Got C4!" Matt snarled at Zeus.

"But it's off its hinges, dumb ass," Zeus shouted back.

"Huh?" Matt grumbled staring at the door for a second.

"Hey, Matt!" Gideon shouted. "Knock on the door!"

"Oh!" Matt exclaimed.

The werebear charged forward and slammed into the door with his massive shoulder. The door shuddered. Then, Matt reared back and slammed both of his fists into the door, and it fell in with a resounding crash. Matt roared with triumph.

Suddenly, assault rifles opened fire at point-blank range. Dozens of bullets slammed into the massive werebear. None penetrated the armor that Matt was wearing even in his bear form. The impacts made him stumble back a few steps.

"Little bastards!" Matt roared.

The werebear swung Skull Cleaver in a sweeping horizontal arc. Three Jaguar Warriors were torn in half. The fourth crumpled around the blade of the axe, effectively blunting the cutting edge. His next two companions, though, were crushed by his body as all three slammed into the wall at the end of Matt's arc. Matt pulled Skull Cleaver free of the tangle of bodies, swung his RFB around and emptied the clip into the three bodies that he'd squashed together.

All that remained of the Jaguar Warrior squad was Fernando and the squad leader, both of whom had been standing behind the line of warriors. Fernando drew his sidearm, a stainless-steel Desert Eagle .50AE, and began pumping rounds into the werebear's legs. The squad leader threw open his uniform tunic to reveal a vest studded with sheathed throwing knives. Two flew into Matt's face, imbedding in his cheek, barely missing his eye. Two more knives were in his hand and flying toward Matt's face even as the Jaguar Warrior was charging toward the giant werebear.

Matt swung Skull Cleaver in an overhand arc, attempting to bisect the knife thrower, but the Jaguar Warrior nimbly dodged out of the way and flung two more knives into Matt's face and throat. Matt roared in pain and rage. He dropped to one knee. Glancing down, he saw that his left knee was a bloody ruined mess. Matt hadn't even felt the pain as Fernando's heavy rounds had torn through his knee's bones and ligaments. Fernando was dropping the empty clip from his gun and slamming in a fresh one. Matt roared at the Jaguar Warrior.

A furry form flashed across Matt's injured flank, and smashed into Fernando, bowling him over. Fernando's gun skittered across the floor. He was face-to-face with a snarling wolf. The wolf's paws had Fernando's shoulders pinned to the floor. The Jaguar Warrior went for the knives he kept sheathed in his belt, but it was too little, too late. Gideon didn't waste time toying with the leader of the Jaguar Warriors. He ripped the man's throat out with one powerful snap of his jaws. A second snap-bite and the head rolled free of the body.

Zeus came around Matt's other flank, P90 up and looking for a target. The knife thrower quickly assessed the man with the gun as the most immediate threat. One knife left his hand, whirling to strike the submachine gun in the receiver right above the operator's hand. The blade buried to the hilt through the weapon. The other knife slammed point-first into Zeus' exposed throat, and promptly clanked to the floor. The Jaguar squad leader took half a second to stare in shock before his hands were seeking out more knives to throw.

Zeus dropped the ruined SMG. He'd shot out all the rounds in the Benelli before they'd even gotten to the door, but he wasn't unarmed. His right hand dropped to the Heckler & Koch .45 USP holstered on his thigh. His left hand came up and caught the blade of the knife that had just been thrown at him. He deflected the second knife with the first. The USP was up. The target was acquired, just a little bit of lead, an educated guess as to which direction the Jaguar Warrior would try to dodge, and three rounds exited the barrel. Two rounds impacted the squad leader's heart. The third entered his head at the bridge of his nose.

He hit the ground, dead. Zeus pumped three rounds into the man's head to ensure that he stayed dead.

Gideon stood up from Fernando's decapitated body, shaking blood from his muzzle even as he assumed his normal human form. He pointed a finger at the hybrid godling standing at the other end of the room. "Chemosh Magog!" Gideon's voice boomed. "You and me got unfinished business, boy."

CHAPTER THIRTY-SEVEN

Bimini District, Commonwealth of the Bahamas
Isla de Nube Encendida
October 29, 2010

Striding through the tunnel, Teresa felt powerful. Each of the undead creatures following her, she had created from the remains of Dark Word cultist volunteers. Willing subjects made for the best creations. Unlike the revenants and ghouls she normally raised, these creatures were all wights, somewhat smarter and much tougher than the run-of-the-mill zombies. Teresa reveled in the feelings of power as she mentally directed each of her minions. Ahead a panel in the wall slid aside, the hidden entrance to the spa.

As Teresa crossed the threshold she was hit with a vision, the same vision she'd been having for years: the eyes of her own killer. Those eyes were a bright, almost glowing, shade of blue, the eyes of a thrope in the full glory of her shapeshifting power --the eyes, Teresa believed, of Jordana Quinlan. The necromancer almost sighed as the vision faded. She knew that her time on this earth was almost over. Soon, Jordana would become the Great Master's queen, and the queen would punish Teresa for her mortal sins. She was resigned to her fate. However, her future killer was in another part of the complex. Nothing here was going to prove to be too much of a challenge for her.

The intruders' party was small: three men, one woman, and what appeared to be a goblin. Two of Magog's Jaguar Warriors lay dead on the tile floor, both in large pools of blood. Teresa extended her will, seeking the mark she'd placed on all of her Master's servants, the mystic symbol that would allow her to raise their corpses from the dead and continue to make use of their bodies. She couldn't make the connection with one of the men. The mark had been damaged, but the other was still viable.

Necromantic energies flowed into that body. A demon summoned from the darkest regions of the nether realms inhabited the dead flesh, bringing it back to a semblance of life. The terrible wounds to the throat and chest remained but seemed to matter less to the integrity of the body, which began to twitch as the demon attempted to use its new host to get up, to attack the living, and to draw from the sustenance it would need to repair itself and carry on in the service of Teresa and her Great Master.

A silent command went out to the rest of Teresa's minions. The wights swarmed into the room with an unearthly howl. The intruders reacted by bringing their weapons to bear. Teresa maintained a tight leash on her minions, preventing them from attacking directly. She wanted the intruders to die, but before they did, she would mark them, and resurrect them as her slaves. Words of power flowed from Teresa's mouth, the words dark and guttural. Teresa threw out her hands, releasing the spell.

*   *   *   *   *

"Holy crap!" Levi shouted. "Twitcher!"

The body of the guard that Kitty had mauled was trembling. A mystic symbol glowed on his forehead. The guard's eyes snapped open, gleaming red, teeth crooked and sharp, bony claws extending from the fingers. Before the reanimated creature could stand, Knobs smashed his boot heel into the symbol on the forehead. The creature slumped back into death.

"Wight," the goblin spat.

Then, a howling mob of the creatures burst from a previously hidden door. Several of the creatures moved to block the other entrance to the spa. The rest of the creatures split to flank the small party of rescuers and hostages.

Ronnie pointed at the one human in the oncoming party. "Kill the necromancer!" she ordered.

She, Waldorf, and Smith all raised their P90s, aimed at the woman, and squeezed the triggers. Three guns clicked.

"What the hell?" Waldorf cursed.

"A spell of my own devising," the necromancer announced. "It causes the metal in the shell casings of modern firearms to expand while suppressing the fire which exists in the gunpowder from igniting. Quite handy when you consider how ridiculously easy firearms make it for ordinary people to defend themselves against the undead, yes?"

"Mistress Veronica, shall I?" Knobs offered, unsheathing his knives.

"Can you get all of them before they get us?" Ronnie asked.

Knobs shook his head. "Maybe the half on the left, but not the right. I am fast, but even I cannot be in two places at once."

"If you surrender, I will make your deaths quick, and your afterlives... well, maybe not as unpleasant as I could make them," the necromancer announced.

Ronnie shook her head. "You made one very bad mistake, necromancer."

"Oh, really?" the woman said with a sardonic grin. "Do tell. From where I stand, I seem to be the one in total control."

"I am Lady Veronica Durham, Winter Knight of the Seelie Council of North America, and the mistake you made, necromancer, is trapping an *aquamancer* in a room with a giant pool of water."

Ronnie's already blue eyes glowed as she summoned the power of her Fae ancestors. The water in the spa pool exploded in two waves, rushing out and covering the wights, clinging to them like a gelatinous mass. Then, the temperature in the room dropped. The water froze, sealing each of the wights in a pillar of ice that left the head exposed.

The necromancer stared in shock.

"Want to know what your second mistake was?" Ronnie offered. "It was trapping a Winter Knight in a room with a pool and a Wild Hunt goblin. Knobs?"

"Yes, my lady?" the goblin replied with a feral grin.

"Have at it," Ronnie said.

"With pleasure," Knobs cackled. "Cutting and slashing! Chopping and hacking!"

The goblin *blurred* around the room. Each wight's head seemed to explode as the goblin's knives went to work shattering skulls and erasing necromantic markings.

Teresa watched in growing horror as the green and black blur dashed around, making short work of her minions. She was too terrified to even run. The eyes of the woman, this Lady Veronica, were glowing blue with power. Teresa had been wrong. The eyes of her death vision had never been the eyes of a thrope. The eyes of her killer belonged to the Seelie Winter Knight who'd just rendered her army useless with water.

"Levi, may I borrow Old Reliable?" Ronnie said.

Levi handed the old pistol over.

"Your third and final mistake, necromancer? Trapping me in a room with a large pool of water, a pissed-off goblin, and a magically enchanted gun that *never* fails to fire," Ronnie said.

One of Old Reliable's powers was that it created a targeting crosshair in the vision of whoever was using it. Ronnie calmly placed the center of that crosshair on Teresa's forehead. She squeezed the trigger once. The bullet shattered Teresa's forehead and exited the back of her skull with a spray of gore. The next six bullets to impact the body were pretty much out of spite.

Ronnie calmly racked the slide of the magical .45, causing the magazine to reload itself. Then, she flicked on the safety and handed the gun back to Levi. "Thank you, Levi."

"Uh, anytime, ma'am," Levi replied.

"Check your guns, clear the jams. They should work now," Ronnie said. "Knobs, quit playing around. We've got a flight to catch."

CHAPTER THIRTY-EIGHT

Bimini District, Commonwealth of the Bahamas
Isla de Nube Encendida
October 29, 2010

Magog paused in the middle of his ritual and stared at the creatures who'd dared to interrupt him. He couldn't help it, but a chuckle escaped him.

"My, but you do have unusually large balls, even for a werewolf, little wizard," Magog declared. "Yes, I remember you. I thought I'd killed you and your master when you interfered with my plans last time. Oh, yes, I remember you, werewolf. You were all weepy about your wife. As I remember, you jammed a sword through her heart, didn't you?"

"You'd already killed her soul, Magog," Gideon replied. "I just killed the demon you swapped her for."

"And I suppose that you're here to kill me, is that it?" Magog snickered.

"Something like that," Gideon replied.

His right hand came up, and Dyrnwyn spat fire. The dragon-fire rounds impacted against Magog's barrier, creating a glowing spot in the air. Gideon kept squeezing the trigger until the slide locked back. The last round passed through a hole in the barrier and grazed Magog's hand, slamming home into the blade of his ritual athame. The knife spun out of Magog's hand, hitting the floor behind the godling as a half-molten mess.

Magog snarled in pain, grabbing his injured hand with the other. "Bronwen! Do something about that pest!"

"As you command, Lord," the red-headed handmaiden replied.

She waved her sisters forward. The beautiful women began to transform even as they moved. Where before they'd been beautiful maidens, now they changed themselves into hideous creatures. Furry legs ending in cloven hooves replaced previously smooth and shapely appendages. Sharp, curved horns sprouted from their foreheads; fingernails became sharp talons, and their skin became scaled and leathery. Mouths filled with sharp, jagged teeth opened with screams of challenge.

"Kill the interlopers, sisters!" Bronwen cried out.

*   *   *   *   *

"What the hell?" Zeus snapped.

"Glaistig," Gideon replied. "Fae Weapons."

"Not good?" Zeus guessed.

"No, not good at all," Gideon replied.

Matt stood back to his feet, plucking throwing knives from his fur. "They're tough, but not unkillable."

"Let me guess, it just takes a lot to kill them," Zeus sighed.

Gideon tossed his P90 to Zeus. "A whole lot," he said. "You have to destroy the brain *and* the heart. And they're kinda bulletproof."

"Oh, *now* you tell me," Zeus declared as he slammed a fresh clip into the submachine gun. He fired a long burst into the face of the first glaistig to jump at him from the impossible-seeming distance of twenty feet away.

*   *   *   *   *

Before the door had even been knocked down, Jordana had known that Gideon had arrived, that he'd come to her rescue. Seeing him filled her with an odd sense of completeness. She could also *feel* Gideon's presence in her heart and mind. Not quite like the shared dreams they'd achieved so far, but she knew what his intentions were, his priorities. As much as he longed to kill Magog, and she could feel the fiery intensity of that desire, Gideon's primary goal was her safety, her recovery.

With glaistig attacking Gideon and his friends, only Magog and Nahasheron were left to watch over Jordana and her sisters, and Nahasheron was assisting Magog with the ritual. Magog gave Sassy a little shove and gestured for Nahasheron to bring Jordana.

"This will take the fight out of the little wizard," Magog was muttering. The burn on his hand from where Gideon's dragon-fire round had grazed it was almost gone.

Jordana felt a surge of desperation. Then, she knew with certainty that the time to fight had come. She couldn't fully shapeshift, but she'd regained much of her strength and she didn't need to be a full wolf to use her claws and teeth. She brought her elbow up, swung around, and slammed it into Nahasheron's temple. The demon gasped in sudden pain. The gasp became a shriek as Jordana's claws raked her face.

"Run!" Jordana snapped at her sisters.

Sassy didn't hesitate. She grabbed Rachel's hand and broke for the melee near the entrance to the temple.

*   *   *   *   *

Zeus knew from close, personal experience that nearly impenetrable skin wasn't perfect body armor. The weak spots were the eyes, the mouth, and the body's other orifices. He also knew that unbreakable skin didn't mean unbreakable bones. The 5.7mm ammo used by the P90 had been designed to defeat body armor at close range. For a tiny little slug, a single 5.7mm round generated a great deal of kinetic force. The P90 held *fifty* rounds in the clip and had a cyclic rate of fire of 900 rounds per minute. Holding the trigger down for a little over three seconds emptied the clip. Zeus was properly braced, the P90 was excellently balanced, and he managed to place all fifty rounds in a three-inch circle directly over the heart of the glaistig that had jumped him.

A detached part of Zeus' mind observed that even with the leathery, scaly skin, the glaistig's breasts were just about perfect in size and shape. Then, the body impacted with him, knocking him from his feet and into a pillar. The glaistig moaned weakly, raising herself slightly, and baring her teeth. Zeus could see the heart in her chest, torn to shreds by so many penetrating rounds, trying to knit itself back together. He grabbed his USP from its holster, jammed it into the glaistig's mouth.

"This is why they call me 'Lady Killer'," he said and squeezed the trigger.

*　　*　　*　　*　　*

Matt roared. He just swung Skull Cleaver in a series of overhand arcs. Mostly, he missed, but when he connected a glaistig was split in two, halfway down through the torso. He had a number of bleeding wounds on his arms and legs from where the glaistig had dashed in and slashed at him with claws and horns. The wounds, though, were rapidly healing, closing and stitching back together on their own. He didn't even notice, the *berskergang* trance having dulled his awareness of pain and fatigue.

Gideon didn't spare a glance for the raging werebear. Matt was damn near unstoppable in his present form. He was more than a match for the five or six glaistig that had honed in on him. Of greater concern to Gideon was the alpha glaistig who'd decided to charge him. Gideon drew the Bowie knife sheathed on his combat vest. The hilt of the knife was decorated with a snarling wolf, and the blade was likewise decorated with an engraving of a pack of wolves and mystical runes. It was Bright Fang.

Bronwen smiled ferally at him, the claws on her fingers extending out several inches. She licked her lips almost playfully. "Like my nails?"

"Nice trick," Gideon smirked back, "but, uh, mine's better." The Bowie knife glowed and grew into a hand-a-half battle sword.

Bronwen snarled and launched herself at Gideon. He was already moving, shifting into his hybrid form. Bronwen landed right where he'd been standing, her hoof shattering the stone tiles of the floor. She spun on the planted foot, bringing her other foot up in a roundhouse kick aimed at Gideon's head.

Bright Fang's glittering blade swept up, slicing through the leg at the knee. Gideon's free hand reached out and caught Bronwen's hair, keeping her from falling. Then, he rammed Bright Fang through her chest. He twisted and sliced laterally, severing the heart in her chest. He spun again, full strength, and smashed her face into the tile floor. A boot to the back of the head finished the job of crushing the glaistig alpha's brain.

"Run!"

Gideon's head snapped around. Jordana had just slashed Nahasheron's face. Magog was reaching for her. Gideon's will flowed into the sword. Bright Fang glowed, shrinking down into its Bowie knife form. As a knife Bright Fang was incredibly well balanced, and Gideon had spent years perfecting his aim and his skill. The knife left his hand, spinning end over end. The blade buried itself almost to the hilt in Magog's stomach just to the left of his belly button.

*   *   *   *   *

The glaistig had incredibly powerful jaws, and those jaws had reflexively clenched around the barrel and slide of Zeus' USP. He was fairly sure that he'd need a knife and a crowbar to get it back out of the Fae monster's mouth. Not to mention that he was gonna have to replace the slide and the barrel since the glaistig's saliva appeared to be corrosive. He pushed the dead monster off himself. A wince of pain lanced through his side as he tried to take a deep breath. A couple of ribs were bruised, maybe even cracked. He stood with a wobble. Almost immediately his face was smashed into the floor, his nose bloodied by the impact, and intense pain blossomed over his kidney.

Zeus rolled over. Looming above him was another glaistig, this one with her hoof raised, about to bring it smashing down on his head. Then, Chaka loomed behind the glaistig. The Sasquatch woman raised her medicine stick in both hands and brought it smashing down on the top of the glaistig's skull. The Fae monster's eyes rolled up into her sockets. Then, as the glaistig was dropping to the floor, Chaka reached out with her left hand, uttered a guttural syllable in her own language, and released a blast of magical energy through the other monster's spine.

"Bulletproof is not the same as bludgeon-proof," Chaka said, holding out a hand to help Zeus to his feet.

"What was that last bit?" he asked, brushing himself off and assessing what weapons he had remaining.

"Wizard fire," Chaka replied with a smirk.

"Really?" Zeus snorted.

"Actually, it was a concentrated burst of microwaves. Flash cooked the monster's heart," Chaka said. She tapped her skull. "Psionic tech, remember? Wizard fire sounds cooler."

Zeus laughed as he ejected the spent clip from the P90 that he'd managed to hang onto and replaced it with a full one. He also had a tanto-style tactical fighting knife and an ASP collapsible baton. He slung the P90 and grabbed the baton.

"Feel like flash-baking some more hearts after I crack their skulls?" Zeus said.

"Where you lead, I follow," Chaka replied.

Matt's axe clanged on the floor close by. The glaistig who'd just dodged the deadly blade had her attention focused on the raging werebear. She never even saw Zeus and Chaka before they'd dispatched her.

*   *   *   *   *

Jordana reacted instantly. She dashed to Magog's side, grabbed the hilt of the knife, and ripped it down and sideways. Magog screamed in pain as his blood and intestines started to spill from the wound. He backhanded Jordana hard enough to send her flying into the wall. The godling focused his will inward. The blood and gory bits slithered back up into his body, the wound sealing and healing in seconds. Magog never noticed that Jordana had slashed Bright Fang's blade through the phylactery on his belt, cutting it cleanly in half.

The impact with the wall knocked the breath out of her, but Jordana was quick to recover. Her True Sight opened as soon as her eyes fluttered open. She saw the silver thread again. One part was still attached to the damaged phylactery, but that thread was separate from the one that was attached to Micky Dumont's body. Jordana reached out.

She felt the thread. The tiniest little part of it was still connected, but it snapped apart at her touch.

Nahasheron's hand closed around her wrist.

"You know, sweetie," the demon hissed in her ear, "he's gonna *so* punish you for this!"

"Too bad you won't be here to see it," Jordana snarled back.

Bright Fang was still in her other hand. She shoved the knife's tip up under Nahasheron's rib cage and into the heart, willing the blade to be long enough to do the job.

Nahasheron stared into Jordana's eyes. "You know you're just killing Micky, don't you?"

"She's already dead, bitch," Jordana said.

"I'll just get another body and come for you again," Nahasheron said. A cough brought bloody foam to her lips.

"I destroyed your phylactery," Jordana said. She smiled at the look of horror in Nahasheron's eyes. "Oh, and this is the sword that Gideon used to kill Kali."

The demon's scream was pure terror.

CHAPTER THIRTY-NINE

Bimini District, Commonwealth of the Bahamas
Isla de Nube Encendida
October 29, 2010

"Chaka! Zeus! Get the girls," Gideon shouted as he pounded toward Magog.

Matt split the last of the glaistig in half and charged after Gideon. The two thropes leapt over the fire pit, landing between the fleeing girls and Magog. Behind them, Zeus and Chaka were grabbing Sassy and Rachel. Nahasheron was lying dead on the floor. Magog had just stuffed his guts back into his stomach.

"Enough!" Magog shouted.

The Dark Word overlord flung his hands up. Waves of telekinetic force washed over Gideon and his companions, slamming into them like a tidal wave.

Gideon felt his rage burn brighter. He did *not* want to move away from his enemy. Suddenly, he felt himself firmly connected to the earth beneath his feet. The surprise almost shattered his concentration, but he saw Jordana, and the strongest desire in his heart was to hold her, to take her away from this place.

"Impressive," Magog said, possibly more surprised than Gideon that he was still standing. "I suppose you've got some speech prepared?"

"No," Gideon replied.

He grabbed the handle of the old revolver, Avenger. His thumb cocked back the trigger as he drew the weapon. Runes on the cylinder and barrel glowed. Then, he squeezed the trigger as the front sight lined up with Magog. Smoke bellowed from the barrel as the specially crafted spell slug hurled across the distance.

Magog's reflexes were impressive. He was tired of getting shot. So, he stepped to the right and twisted his body. The slug barely grazed his shoulder before smashing into the wall behind him. Gideon's left hand fanned the trigger, and another spell slug was launched. Then, another, and a fourth. Magog continued twisting out of the way, but the shots were too close together. The godling was amazed at the werewolf wizard's speed. The last two rounds left the gun, but Magog was still dodging the third and fourth rounds. The fifth slug tore into his thigh. The sixth shattered his left elbow.

The healing began within milliseconds, of course. The skin closing back up over the wounds. Magog smiled in triumph, not noticing that his healing rate was slower. All he could see was the smirk on Gideon's face as the werewolf wizard holstered the old pistol. Magog was tired of this meddlesome insect interfering in his plans. He raised his hands, and the silver lamp stands floated up into the air. The metal flowed like water, forming into spears.

"I've had enough of you, wizard!" Magog snarled.

The silver spears flashed forward like bullets.

"Gideon!" Jordana screamed.

One of the spears had impaled Gideon through the abdomen, armor and all. He dropped to his knees, hands wrapped around the silver weapon protruding from his gut. Behind him the other spears had barely missed most of the team, but one had caught Matt in the shoulder. He was roaring with pain and had partially shifted back into his human form. The big man was writhing and screaming, the shard of silver firmly embedded in the wall behind him.

Magog went over to Jordana and grabbed a fistful of her hair. Lifting her painfully to her feet, he dragged her over to where she could get a good look at Gideon bleeding out.

"This is what disobeying me brings you, Jordy," Magog hissed. "Now, you will stand here with me and watch your wizard boyfriend bleed to death. Silver inhibits a werewolf's ability to heal." He shook her head, which caused Jordana to cry out in pain. "Then, once this one has died, you'll watch me kill his friends, your sisters, and then, I'll kill you last." Magog sighed heavily. "Now, I have to start all over again."

Gideon laughed and spat a wad of blood on the floor.

"What's so funny?" Magog demanded.

"You're right about the silver and thropes in general, but you're wrong about me," Gideon said. He twisted the spear and pulled an inch or two out of himself. "Oh, god, that *hurts*!"

"Gideon!" Jordana cried out.

"Not as bad as it looks, darlin'," Gideon drawled. "You see, like I told you once before: I'm not really a werewolf." With a shout of pain, Gideon pulled the spear the rest of the way out of himself. He held the spear in front of himself, staring at it. Then, the blood caught on fire. "You see, you over-jumped, self-deluded moron, I am my father's son."

Magog snickered. "And just what is your father that you take after him?"

"A dragon."

*   *   *   *   *

The telekinetic force wave had knocked Matt back into a wall, where he'd fallen on his butt. Then, the silver spear had impaled him. Aside from the pain of being impaled by a spear through the clavicle, the silver made the wound burn like somebody had jammed the sun into it.

"We need to get the spear out," Chaka grunted as she gained her feet.

Matt swung blindly, swearing in several languages and with a variety that would have impressed Bruce. Chaka barely avoided getting a bloody nose.

"We're gonna have to hold him down," Zeus said. "Can one of you gals get that thing out?"

"I'll do it," Sassy volunteered.

"I've got this arm," Chaka said. "You two should get his legs," she added with a nod to Zeus and Rachel.

The Sasquatch caught Matt's flailing arm. With a mighty grunt of effort, she pressed it against the wall. She nodded to Zeus and Rachel. Matt was kicking out with his legs now, trying to twist around and knock

Chaka off his good arm. Zeus caught one of Matt's legs and laid bodily over it to force it down. Rachel piled on top of him for good measure.

"Be quick about it," Chaka snapped at Sassy.

Sassy straddled Matt's chest and attempted to get hold of the spear, but Matt was bucking so hard she almost fell off. Sassy whipped back her right arm and rocketed a fist right into Matt's snout-like nose. "Hey! Trying to help you!"

Matt stared, but he'd also stopped fighting.

Sassy grabbed the spear and pulled.

*　　*　　*　　*　　*

The change was different this time. Gideon felt it. A floodgate of energy opened up in his body, pouring into him from the earth beneath him, the air around him, even the fire behind him, and the water beyond this place. His visage was still lupine, his basic form still a mix of man and wolf, but wings sprouted from his back, and the tail that extended from behind him was saurian, tipped with spikes. He was also bigger than he'd ever been before. Gideon had to lower his head to look Magog in the eye.

"You have my treasure. I want her back," Gideon said in a deep, gravelly voice.

"Do you really think I'm afraid of a neophyte dragon?" Magog snapped. "I've slain your kind before, wyrm, and I have your precious 'treasure' right here!"

Magog pulled Jordana in front of him by her hair, shielding his body with her own. "I could snap her neck in an instant!"

Gideon felt Jordana in his mind. She was shocked at his transformation, but she was still happy to see him. She was also pleased with herself. His eyes narrowed as he noticed the wristband on her right wrist. Bright Fang. He smiled. On his lupine dragon face it looked like a snarl.

"I should tell you something, Magog," Gideon said. "I'm an alchemist."

"I know that, brewer of potions," Magog retorted.

"Potions, serums, poisons... Alchemy is the magic of transformation, combining things that shouldn't be possible to combine," Gideon rumbled. "I created a poison, designed specifically for you."

"Impossible," Magog sneered.

"Think about it, Magog. You killed Jordy's dog because it bit you," Gideon said. "Princess got your flesh and blood caught in her teeth. I used that to create the poison."

"Impossible!" Magog repeated.

"I combined the poison with a binding spell and placed the potion into a metallic matrix of gold and lead," Gideon said. "Molded it into a bullet. Well, *six* bullets. Only needed one, but three have gotten the job done."

"*What* are you blithering about?" Magog screamed.

"One little scratch, one slug in the thigh, and one in the arm. The poison's made its way to your heart, and from there to your brain and all your major organs," Gideon hissed.

"I feel *fine*!" Magog snapped.

"Of course you do!" Gideon rumbled with a laugh. "The poison was for the godling. It bound your power, and it's rendered you mortal.

You could live another fifty or sixty years before old age does you in, but I have the feeling you don't have that long."

Light flashed in Jordana's hand. She spun in Magog's grip, slicing Bright Fang along the arm holding her in place. Magog shouted in pain, releasing her and stumbling away. He stared in shock at the wound on his arm that was gushing blood, *and not healing instantly*.

"What have you *done*?" Magog wailed.

"Justice," Gideon replied.

He summoned the fire burning in his soul and breathed it out.

CHAPTER FORTY

Bimini District, Commonwealth of the Bahamas
Isla de Nube Encendida
October 29, 2010

"You hit me," Matt said, staring at the mostly naked, blood-covered young woman still sitting on his chest holding the silver spear.

"You weren't cooperating," Sassy replied tossing the bloody piece of metal away. "I had to get your attention."

"But you *hit* me," Matt insisted.

Sassy rolled her eyes and glanced over at Chaka. "I think he's in shock."

Chaka let go of Matt's hand and started poking at the wound with a finger. "He well could be, but that might be from the naked female torso staring him in the face."

Sassy glanced down at herself. "Yeah, I'm kinda starting to get used to it."

"Ow!" Matt growled as Chaka poked the wound.

"This isn't healing very quickly," the Sasquatch mused as she ripped open an emergency medical pack. "Turn back into a full human, Matt. I need to clean and stitch the wound."

The hair melted away, and Matt shrank fully down to his normal size. "Hey, you guys mind *not* sitting on me," he groused.

"You know, teddy bear, you're kinda cute," Sassy giggled.

Matt blushed. "Uh, thank-OW! Jeez, Chaka!"

"Flirt on your own time," Chaka said. She glanced up toward the front of the temple, and her jaw dropped open.

Matt glanced where she was looking. "Well," he grunted. "That's not something you see every day."

*　　*　　*　　*　　*

The fire was channeled through Gideon's dragon mouth, coming out in a tight beam no bigger across than a baseball, and blue-white in color. The dragon fire touched Magog just above where the legs joined the torso. Flesh instantly vaporized at the point of contact, the surrounding areas catching fire. The beam worked up along the torso, through the heart, the throat, and face. Magog's head exploded. The two burning halves of his body fell away from one another. Gideon brought his dragon claws down on the burning mass of flesh, slashing and cutting, chopping the remains into ever smaller pieces. Another blast of blue-white fire reduced the remains into even more ashes. Still not satisfied, Gideon pounded the ashes into the floor with massive fists. Then, he blasted the floor again with more fire.

"Gideon!" Jordana shouted. She kicked him in his flank. "Gideon!"

"What?" he snarled.

"He's dead," Jordana said. "And then some."

"Oh," Gideon sighed.

"You and your temper tantrums," Jordana said. "You're not gonna run away again and go pukwudgie hunting are you?"

Gideon shook his head, which turned into a shudder than went down his entire body, like a dog shaking water out of its fur. Then, he deflated into his human form. Gideon dropped to his knees and groaned. "Ow."

Jordana was by his side in a flash, kneeling next to him. "You okay?"

"Not really," Gideon admitted. "Had to channel a lot of elemental energies, kinda been running on piss and vinegar for the last several minutes." He smiled for her. "Was well worth it, though. Help me up?"

Jordana supported Gideon as he stood up. She kept his arm draped over her shoulder as they joined the rest of the group around Matt.

"That was... new," Zeus said.

"First time for everything," Gideon said. "Been blocked from most of my dragon heritage for five hundred years, but I found my treasure at last."

"So, not a werewolf?" Jordana said.

"Half-werewolf, half-dragon, but once the dragon heritage asserts itself, it kinda dominates everything else," Gideon replied. He clutched his stomach and groaned.

"Do you need assistance?" Chaka asked.

"No, just got stabbed through the guts. Be a few hours before it's all healed up," Gideon replied. He glanced at Matt. "Well, brother, if you're through malingering, we've got a helo to catch."

"Malingering!" Matt exclaimed, climbing to his feet with a little help from Chaka. "I got stabbed. With a *silver* spear! And then this mouse punched me in the nose! I've had a bloody bad day!" Matt glanced at Sassy. "Okay, the mouse actually makes it a pretty good day, but still!"

"C'mon, teddy bear, you can tell me all about it on the ride home," Sassy chuckled.

"Don't worry, he will," Gideon sighed.

"At length," Zeus added.

"And in great detail," Chaka said. "I'm just guessing, of course, but I'm thinking that's what will happen."

Gideon and Zeus glanced at one another. "Yeah," they said in unison, nodding.

Gideon produced three sets of hospital scrubs from his backpack along with wet wipes. He insisted that the girls start cleaning the ritual markings off as soon as possible. Then, with Jordana's support, he limped out to where Perkins had finally been able to land the Black Hawk. Matt lumbered along behind them, using Skull Cleaver as a cane. Sassy and Chaka flanked him, both clucking over him like mother hens. Matt, of course, was loving every second of it. Zeus and Rachel brought up the rear.

Ronnie and Knobs were waiting for them. The rescued hostages were already loaded into the helo. Levi jumped out of the Black Hawk to join them.

"What happened to you guys?" Levi gasped.

"Fought Jaguar Warriors, crazy Irish harpy-satyr chicks, and got telekinetically pimp-slapped by a Dark Word pseudo-god," Zeus replied. "What happened to you guys?"

"Uh, Ronnie froze a roomful of zombies, blew up the necromancer's head, and told Knobs to play whack-a-mole with the zombies," Levi replied.

"They were wights, not zombies," Knobs corrected.

"Can we continue this recap in the air?" Gideon said. "Kinda tired, wounded, and beat up here."

"I got punched in the nose by a girl," Matt said.

"You probably deserved it. Jackass," Knobs said. Then, he cackle-giggled, and helped Matt into the helo.

"Gonna be a tight fit," Levi said. "Uh, somebody's gonna wind up sitting in somebody else's lap here and there."

"I think we'll manage, kid," Gideon chuckled as he climbed into the helo.

Jordana and Kitty hugged as soon as they saw one another. Sassy held onto Mike. The two of them shared a seat for the flight, Matt sitting next to them and keeping the boy entertained with his banter with Knobs. Rachel clung to her Aunt Kathy for a few moments.

"How're we set for fuel, Agent Perkins?" Gideon asked.

"Well, we won't have to make a water landing as long as I choose the right direction, sir," Perkins replied.

"Okay, you do that, then," Gideon chuckled. He hugged Jordana and ruffled Kitty's hair. "Take us home, Perky."

EPILOGUE

Atlanta, Georgia, USA
Magee House, Belle Arbor Plantation
Covington, GA
November 10, 2010

"With Thanksgiving coming, I suppose I should find something to be grateful for," Jordana observed.

When she thought about it, she couldn't believe that the entire incident, from meeting Gideon through escaping from Isla de Nube Encendida, had only happened within the space of a week and a half. October was over; the Halloween decorations had gone up and come back down; kids had been trick-or-treating, and now, a couple of weeks later, they were looking forward to Thanksgiving. The world was an entirely new place.

"I don't know about that," Gideon replied. "Matt keeps offering to cook Thanksgiving dinner, and let me tell you, *that* was a disaster the last time he tried."

Jordana shook her head and laughed. The two of them were in the library of Magee House. The big table in the center of the room was now piled with several official-looking folders and documents. Jordana waved at the items on the table. "We might as well get started," she suggested.

"Are you sure?" Gideon asked.

"My heart won't be any more broken than it already is," Jordana said.

Gideon couldn't help himself. He took Jordana into his arms and hugged her. She clung to him like the proverbial drowning victim clinging to a life preserver. For half a second she contemplated putting the business at hand off again, but the wolf in her refused to back down from a fight, even against herself.

She pushed Gideon away from herself as gently as she could. With a deep breath she said, "Let's do this."

Gideon nodded. "Okay, let's start with your parents' wills. Your mom didn't have much of a will. It boils down to you and Kitty divvying up her stuff between you."

Jordana snorted. They'd briefly returned to Orlando on their way back to Covington. The Quinlan family home had been burned to the ground, a vindictive bit of vandalism by the late Tia Teresa. "Remind me to thank Ronnie again for killing that bitch."

"Yeah, Ronnie doesn't need thanks to kill bad guys. She's kind of... motivated," Gideon said. Then, he shrugged. "I guess we all are when you get down to it."

"Was it Aggie for you?" Jordana asked.

Gideon shook his head. "My brothers, Dylan and Llew. They were killed fighting a demon-possessed dragon called Croatoan."

"Wait, like the Lost Colony of Roanoke Island?" Jordana said.

"Now, your dad... Well, old Tom left a good and detailed will," Gideon said.

"Don't change the subject," Jordana ordered.

"He had some pretty good life insurance policies on both himself and your mother," Gideon continued, not making eye contact with Jordana, but consulting one of the folders.

Jordana rolled her eyes and threw hands up. "I give up, you stubborn... dragon-wolf."

Gideon glanced up. "It's a story for another time, darling," he assured her. Then, he cleared his throat. "So, anyway, between the insurance and stocks and bonds, Tom provided roughly seventy thousand dollars each for you and Kitty. Sufficient to get both of you through college, at least."

"What about Kitty's guardianship?" Jordana asked.

Gideon heaved a sigh. "He appointed an aunt of his from Boston as guardian for both of you. He last updated the will about three years ago."

"Aunt Mildred?" Jordana said. "She's a hundred if she's a day."

"Mildred Quinlan is sixty-seven years young, I'll have you know," Gideon sniffed. Then, he cracked a grin. "She's a pretty lively little old lady, though. Told me on the phone that she's more than willing to give up Bingo and Caribbean cruises to look after you girls, but *she* pointed out to me that a retirement community in Miami is not the best place for a teenage girl to grieve her parents and finish school."

"So, do I get to be her guardian?" Jordana asked.

"Well, even though you're of legal age, the courts typically won't put the care of one teenager into the hands of another," Gideon said. "So, my old boss, Bob Gold, applied a little covert government pressure, twisted a couple of arms, and *I* was appointed to be Kitty's guardian. Do you think she'll be okay with that?"

"Hm, well, let me think," Jordana said tapping a finger on her chin. "She'll get to live in a mansion with the ultimate in technological entertainment capabilities, a full-time butler, and her new foster parent is rich... Yeah, call me crazy, but I think she'll go for it."

"I think the word she used was 'yippee', but it was at such a high register I can't be entirely sure," Gideon chuckled. "My sister is helping her redecorate the pink room. They decided to keep it pink, by the way."

"Good," Jordana said.

"You know, you can still live here, too," Gideon said.

Jordana smiled. "I'll move in one day, but it's only been a couple of weeks since my father and Bernadette died in your kitchen trying to protect me. I need a little time and a little space in order to deal with that."

"I understand," Gideon said.

Jordana touched her heart. "Of course you do because you're always right here."

"Alright, moving on," Gideon said. He picked up a different file. "The Program has gotten really good at crafting cover stories over the years, especially with the advent of modern mass-media communications. We've scrubbed all links between the Colombian drug cartel that kidnapped you and your sister, the racist skinheads who killed Sassy's family, and the unknown assailants, possibly Satanists, who desecrated Rachel's father's church and killed him and several of his family members. These are three horrible stories about the truly horrible things that happen in this country. They're bad enough to make national news, but we've provided some scapegoats to bring the issues to a close."

"You set people up to take the fall?" Jordana gasped.

"Sort of. They're all members of Magog's personal cult, they all died while resisting arrest, and they're all just jam-packed full of evidentiary goodness to satisfy any official inquiry," Gideon said. "It's like Tommy Lee Jones said in 'Men in Black.' The public can't handle reality. So, we give them what they're willing to accept and understand. Helps keep paranormals like ourselves safe."

"Okay. So, what happens to Sassy and Rachel?" Jordana asked.

"Sassy is of legal age, and the only close relatives she has left are from her mom's family in Thailand. She's decided that she'd like to transfer colleges to Mercy University. I understand that there's an opening for a roommate in Garden Manor?" Gideon said.

Jordana smiled, happy that she'd get to know her new sister even better. Then, she frowned. "What about Micky?"

"The cartel that took you, kidnapped her by mistake, thinking she was you. When they discovered the mistake, they stabbed her in the heart and left her in a shallow grave next to the one where your mother's body was found," Gideon said.

"Remind me why this cartel wanted me again?" Jordana said.

"Uh, your mom. She was vaguely related, they wanted to use you guys as leverage against your dad, Al Qaeda was involved somehow, but you're not really clear on those details," Gideon supplied. "I've got the file here somewhere."

"No, if my story is supposed to be vague, maybe I should stay vague on the details," Jordana suggested. "What about Rachel?"

"Did you know that Rachel wants to be a doctor?" Gideon asked.

"Yes, Sassy thinks she wants to be famous, and Rachel wants to help people," Jordana said.

"More than wants," Gideon said. "She's an empathic healer by nature, but a degree in medicine will help her realize that ability, and guess what southern university has an excellent pre-med program?"

"Uh, MU?" Jordana guessed.

"No, but Emory does," Gideon said.

"Genius ass," Jordana snickered.

"Her Aunt Kathy was just visiting when Magog's people hit her family. She actually lives and works here in the Atlanta area, right up the road in Lithonia, as a matter of fact," Gideon said. "Rachel's gonna live with her aunt for now. Maybe she'll transfer to Mercy. She hasn't decided yet."

"Speaking of Mercy University, what about your job there?" Jordana asked.

"Well, I thought my cover was well and truly blown, but it seems that Jack and Marcus appreciated me saving their bacon from the fire that day. So, they kinda kept as mum as they could on the whole thing," Gideon said. "Then, within hours of the shooting, my father is on the phone with the university president, giving him the whole nine yards about how the school was founded by his namesake, and that the Shaws have been really good for the school over the years, and that he really thinks that anything involving me and my position should be properly covered up to avoid embarrassing our family and the school, yadda yadda yadda.

"Once he's got the president properly aware of the stick, he starts dropping carrots. As chairman of the Gilchrist Shaw Foundation, he's authorized to endow a scholarship fund, and he's got some alumni lined up with checkbooks in hand to dump some ridiculous sums of money into Mercy University's coffers. Well, that secures the university's official silence on the whole thing. Then, he calls Jack, tells him that he's my boss in the FBI, and that they'd appreciate his cooperation in helping me maintain my cover. Academics can often go places that official government agents can't. Jack came to academia from military intelligence. So, he's pretty gung-ho for God and Country, and he agreed," Gideon said.

"So, you get to keep teaching?" Jordana summed up for him.

Gideon nodded. "Yes, ma'am, I do, and if I need to run off to save the world from evil, I have a much better built-in excuse now." He snapped his fingers. "One good thing about Pa's meddling is that Sassy will get a full ride at Mercy with the Foundation scholarship. So will you, and when Kitty is ready, she'll be able to attend Mercy, too, without worrying about the cost."

Jordana smiled. "That's wonderful."

"Well, I did promise your dad that I'd take care of 'our girls' for him," Gideon said.

"And you keep your promises," Jordana said taking his hand in hers.

Gideon gave her fingers a squeeze. "Yes, ma'am, that I do. Now, I got one more thing to show you, but we gotta go outside first."

Jordana frowned slightly. "Is this a good thing or something that you *think* is a good thing?"

"You'll see," Gideon said cryptically.

He led Jordana out of Magee House over to a part of the estate that she'd never actually visited, the kennel. Each of the pens were now occupied with dogs, big animals that looked like a cross between a German Shepherd, an Irish Wolfhound, and a bear cub. Kitty was playing with some of the dogs, throwing tennis balls in random directions that the dogs would bound off after, even catching them in mid-air.

"My sister is moving back into Magee House, and she brought the dogs with her," Gideon said. They're another layer to our security."

"They're beautiful. What kind of dogs are they again?" Jordana asked.

"Gabriel Ratchets. Uh, think of them like the reverse of a Hellhound," Gideon said.

Jordana chuckled. "Do they breathe fire?"

"Yes, they do," Gideon said.

One of the dogs that Kitty was playing with suddenly *blurred* like Knobs, appeared several yards up in the air, caught a ball that Kitty had thrown straight up, and *blurred* back to the earth. It dropped the ball at Kitty's feet, tail wagging, tongue lolling, ready to keep playing.

"That was cool," Jordana said.

Gideon led her to a pen at the very end of the kennel. Inside a female Gabriel Ratchet was laying down in a huge doggy bed with several pups frolicking around her.

"This little lady is Sally, and she's weaned these pups, and she's quite ready to see them taken off her hands," Gideon said.

The dog whined slightly, but the whine stopped the instant Gideon stroked a finger along the top of her skull. Her tail started thumping against the doggy bed. Gideon smiled as he continued stroking the dog's head. "So, Sally, which of your puppies do you think Jordana should take home?"

"What?" Jordana said.

"Well, you need a dog. Here's a litter. Take your pick," Gideon said. "I know you'll never love another dog the way you loved Princess, but there's still a place in your heart for another dog. Besides, observing a real canine in action is good practice for shapeshifting into a canine. Even magical dogs are still dogs, right, Sally?"

The dog whuffed agreement. Then, she turned and pointed her nose at one of her pups, a little brindled character gnawing on a piece of rawhide for all it was worth. Sally pushed the puppy toward Jordana.

"Weird thing about Gabriel Ratchets, the mother of a litter *always* knows the person that their puppies should be with if that puppy isn't meant to be a part of a pack," Gideon said.

Jordana reached down and cradled the puppy up into her hands.

The pup spit out its rawhide and barked. Then, it promptly released the contents of its bladder.

"I think I've just been marked as this little fella's property," Jordana laughed. Tears glistened in her eyes. "Princess peed on me the first time we met."

"Must be meant to be," Gideon said.

Jordana hugged the puppy despite the wet spot on her shirt. "I think so, too."

"Thought of a name?" Gideon asked.

Jordana smiled. "Yes. I have the *perfect* name."

"Do tell," Gideon said with a smile.

"Pukwudgie."

ABOUT THE AUTHOR

Steven Warnock is from the *real* Covington, GA, a town that he loves a lot, where he constantly prowls Wal-Mart late at night looking for thropes, dhamphir, and glamoured fae. So far his True Sight has failed to work. He is a graduate of Mercer University, where he earned a Liberal Arts degree in Communications and English, which in turn led to a career in Retail Sales, which in turn has left him more than ready to write about heroes fighting overwhelming evil. He's been writing ever since he was a small boy who realized, "Hey, I can write a story as good as this." He's been influenced by many of the greats: Isaac Asimov, Andre Norton, Edgar Rice Burroughs, as well as many current authors.